Praise for Ray Anderson's THE TRAIL

THE TRAIL is an intense psychological cat-and-mouse thriller, written by a bright new talent who is very familiar with military survival strategies and the unique and unforgettable setting that distinguishes this story. Well-written and well-researched, Ray Anderson's debut novel will grab you from the disturbing opening scene and hold you in its grip until the grand payoff at the end of the trail.

—Gary Braver, bestselling author of *Skin Deep* and *Tunnel Vision*

There's a particular darkness in the crimes of a middle-aged man. Murder's thought to be the medium of younger people with poor impulse control, bad nurture and a hormonally-induced taste for the dark side. But when a man at midlife commits murders on the Appalachian Trail, the crimes open a window into something aberrant. **Ray Anderson captures this darkness with extraordinary skill.** He's in total control of his prose, characters and a story that manifests the most disturbing crisis of all— that humans can do these things, and we the readers, are human too.

—Mike Hogan, author of *Burial of the Dead*

This book has more twists and turns than the Appalachian Trail itself . . . **a compelling, atmospheric thriller** . . . Anderson captures the imagery and emotion of the renowned trail like no one else.

—Brett Ellen Block, author of *The Lightning Rule, Destination Known,* and *The Grave of God's Daughter*

AIL perfectly captures the ᵣ ... ᵣtural beauty of the outdoᵣ ... s that unfold. ... e, and ᵣiolent ... *the A.T.*

Baker & Taylor JUL 08 2016

THE TRAIL

THE
TRAIL

RAY ANDERSON

TURNER

Turner Publishing Company
424 Church Street • Suite 2240 • Nashville, Tennessee 37219
445 Park Avenue • 9th Floor • New York, New York 10022

www.turnerpublishing.com

The Trail, A Novel

Copyright © 2015 Ray Anderson.

All rights reserved. This book or any part thereof may not be reproduced or transmitted in any form or by any means, electronic or mechanical, including photocopying, recording, or by any information storage and retrieval system, without permission in writing from the publisher.

This is a work of fiction. All the characters and events portrayed in this book are either products of the author's imagination or are used fictitiously.

Cover design: Nellys Liang
Book design: Kym Whitley

Library of Congress Cataloging-in-Publication Data
Anderson, Ray, 1942-
The trail / by Ray Anderson.
    pages cm
 ISBN 978-1-63026-982-1 (pbk.)
 1. Suspense fiction. I. Title.
PS3601.N54475T75 2015
813'.6--dc23
                              2015009480

Printed in the United States of America
15 16 17 18 19 20 10 9 8 7 6 5 4 3 2 1

DEDICATED TO
THE THRU-HIKER

ACKNOWLEDGMENTS

I WANT TO THANK THOSE readers who gave me helpful criticism. They include Joe and Fran Cucci, Susan Trausch, Virginia Young, Dan Gervais, Gary Goshgarian, Ellie Hawkins, Carol Chubb, Bob Alexander, Brett Ellen Block, who suggested the title, John Lovett, Bill Chase, Dottie Clark, her late husband, Don, my goddaughter, Karen Karlsson, for providing the English to French translations, and others I may have forgotten. Several readers also gave detailed guidance and suggestions. These people are Jennifer Harris, Michelle Ray, Susan Shannon, and my good friend and excellent writer, Alan Kennedy. I owe a special thanks to writer and hiker David Miller, who not only provided me with detailed suggestions, but also allowed me to borrow his trail name "Awol" for my protagonist. Thanks also to my number one hiking partner, Hank Zulauf, who took the back cover photo.

Of course, none of this would have happened without the guidance, teaching, and perseverance of my agent, Sorche Fairbank. She was patient and navigated correctly. Thank you, Sorche. And my thanks to everyone at Turner Publishing. I also want to thank all the A.T. thru-hikers who made the trek with me in 2003. We were an inspired and hardy group.

Finally, my biggest thanks goes to my wife, Nancy, who always keeps a level head and remains the best thing to ever happen to me. To Nancy— all my love.

I'M NOT A GULF WAR vet. I served in a different conflict much earlier. This book is a work of fiction, and the war-time incident I refer to is imagined. Likewise, the astute hiker may note that I took some liberties in a few instances. Most notably, Hell Ridge is different than described because for that scene I simply couldn't pass up that name—Hell Ridge. In writing *The Trail*, I referred to my own journals throughout and used the actual weather (including snow storm) that I encountered. I am responsible for any inconsistencies.

THE TRAIL

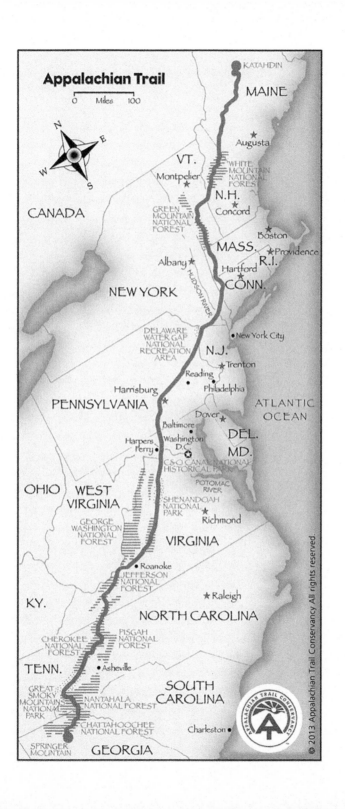

© 2013 Appalachian Trail Conservancy All rights reserved.

THIS ONE WOULD BE EASY; *he knew it the moment he saw her in the lot as he parked his Jeep. She watched him while he clipped up the canvas top and later, when he cozied up to her at the bar, she said, "I've always wanted a Jeep." It was Friday night and there was a sense of relief after a hard work week. Outside of the bar, men and women sucked extra smoke into their lungs and blew it farther with the excitement of the weekend ahead. Inside, eight balls bounced off cue sticks as if shot from cannons. An hour and a few drinks later, avoiding the prominent birthmark across her cheek, he stroked the brunette's face and fingered the pearls around her neck.*

He gave her his best smile. "Would you like to drive my Wrangler up to the lake?"

She didn't blink as she sipped the last of her strawberry margarita through a lipstick-stained straw. "Okay."

But at the lake, as Paul Leroux put a hand on her knee and told her to drive down a dirt road, "It's nice down here—you'll see," *she shrank.*

"Why don't we drive over by the clubhouse?" *she said.*

"Naw, baby, that's no fun." *He patted her thigh and she stiffened.* "Aw, c'mon, sugar—it's okay, I'm not a bad person."

"You never know these days."

"Yeah, you have a point. Tell you what, drive down a little ways, I'll show you how pretty it is, and then we can turn around."

She drove slowly. A rabbit hopped across the dirt road.

"Cigarette?" *he offered.*

"No, thanks. Let's go back. I don't like it down here."

Leroux blew a slow stream of smoke out the window. "Okay. There's a spot up ahead where you can turn around. But you're missing a pretty place." *Smells of spring buds wafted through the windows and she settled into driving. But a half mile later she began to worry.* "So where's this turnaround?" "Baby, relax. Am I making you nervous? It should be up a little ways." *Another quarter of a mile of silence followed. The dirt road tapered and was no longer a road. She had no idea where she was. She looked at him.* "I . . ."

"Right there, see? Pull in over there; I'll drive."

The brunette looked helpless as she drove the Jeep off the shoulder and turned into an opening. She had both hands clamped on the wheel and her lower lip trembled. Leroux crushed his cigarette in the ashtray, reached over, and shut down the engine. He pulled out the keys.

"What are—?"

"Slip over to my side," *Leroux said. He saw the fear in her eyes and just as she was about to shriek, Leroux punched her solar plexus. Her earrings flipped up and flopped back down. She slumped as he pulled her over to the passenger side. Leroux got out, entered the driver's side, and refired the Jeep. He put it in four-wheel drive and drove straight in through the opening, zigzagging around pines, until he could go no farther. He shut off the engine and cocked an ear to the open window as the brunette sucked in oxygen.*

"You'll feel better in a minute."

"Please," *she sobbed, as she held her stomach,* "take me back."

"Oh, baby, you know that's not the way it works." *Leroux leaned over to her and whispered in her ear,* "Let's go find the moon."

PART ONE

Man is nature's sole mistake.

—W. S. Gilbert

I MAY HAVE INTENTIONALLY KILLED *a man.*

Karl Bergman was on top of Springer Mountain in Georgia staring at a rock with a bronze plaque bolted to it. The plaque depicted a map of the Appalachian Trail running through fourteen states, from Georgia to Maine. Bergman's feelings were a mix of excitement and guilt. For the last twelve years, whenever anything positive happened to him, whenever opportunities for joy and happiness presented themselves, festering guilt would tinge the moment, and blacken his soul.

He tried to push back at the guilt and remember the times in his life when he had felt the excitement of new adventure—going away to college, joining the Army, heading out to the Gulf War. This would be different though. He was thirty-six now and needed the challenge of the unknown in a different way; in a way that might cleanse him and rid him of past mistakes.

His morning had started out shaky. He'd called Linda from the motel to say "I miss you already," but she was chilly. Yesterday morning, when she'd driven him to Logan airport, she'd stayed quiet from the moment they left her house.

"I'd sure like your help with mail drops. Makes things easier."

Silence.

Three miles later, "I'll call whenever I hike into a trail town. Know that I'll miss you and will be thinking about you. About us."

Not a word as she casually changed lanes, readjusted the rearview mirror, sucked on a mint.

"Look, I'm sorry about the fight. You want me to drive?"

"I'm just dropping you off. I've got to get to work."

Five more miles of silence. "You know, if you can get a few days off, we can spend it together in a trail town. Take in the local sites and soak in a hot tub together."

Silence.

"You like birding. I wouldn't mind at all if we took a few outings to identify birds."

She shifted in her seat.

"Guess you don't like that idea?" Bergman put his hand on her shoulder and gave it a gentle squeeze.

She turned and looked right at him. "Karl, I'm not in the mood."

Neither said another word until they reached the airport.

"Good luck," she finally offered. He reached over, held her face in both hands and pecked her on each cheek, his usual routine before kissing her on the lips. "I love you, Linda," he'd said, and steadied her face with his hands. She forced a smile and began to tear up, but then pulled away. "Take care, Karl, and go easy on the drinking," was all she could manage to say.

Now, in the dank and overcast late morning, Bergman stared at the trail map bolted on the rock and felt the first drops of rain. He put aside the parting with Linda. *She'll come around.* He inhaled smells of wildflower and oak, watching an eagle dip and soar above the knotted oak and hickory. He relaxed his muscles, and wrapped himself in anticipation, in the acute sense of adventure of hiking more than two thousand miles north over the next six months. Bergman had been a hiker all his life and had always dreamed of tackling the Appalachian Trail. He found it hard to believe that a month ago he'd been about to end his life and now he was here, chasing one of his dreams. He'd finally done something right.

He heard steps from behind, and as he turned, two young men bounded up to the rock beside him, both sporting shiny trekking poles. They shouldered spotless packs, one green and so new it still had a store sticker pasted on it, the other crimson and overstuffed, looked as if it would burst. The taller hiker fumbled with his camera.

"You another thru-hiker?" he asked Bergman.

"I am."

"Can you take a picture of us?"

"Sure." Bergman aimed the camera as they stood by the rock, proudly gripping their new poles. He noted the sorry way their improperly adjusted packs rocked loose about their hips. They'll learn how to snug the straps soon enough, he thought. "Where're you guys from?"

"I'm Blue Sky, from Maryland; this is Vagabond, he's from Michigan."

The boys looked barely old enough to drink. After Bergman snapped the picture they took off their packs and pulled out the hiking register that lay protected in a recess behind the rock. Blue Sky signed in and handed the register to Bergman.

"What's your trail name?"

"Haven't decided yet."

He read their entry: "To Maine or bust—Blue Sky and Vagabond, March 14, 2003." As Bergman considered a trail name, he heard more footsteps, and wheezing. A big boy, stuffed into Gore-Tex pants, waddled toward them followed by two college-aged girls.

"That approach trail is murder," the big kid panted. "If it's gonna be like this the whole way, I might as well quit now." He threw down a five-foot broken branch he'd used for a hiking staff and sat down. Flushed and sweaty, he shook off his pack. "I'm from Louisiana. Hell, I didn't know Georgia even had mountains."

Everyone was silent as they watched him pant. *He won't make it,* Bergman thought, *but who the hell am I to judge?* One of the girls rolled her eyes. These young women seemed determined as they stared at the map on the rock, but Bergman knew their pack-stooped bodies were not conditioned for the physical demands ahead.

"The trick is to pace yourself," Bergman said. He didn't look directly at the boy in Gore-Tex, but said loud enough for all to hear, "Don't do too much, too soon, too fast."

As Blue Sky introduced himself to the girls, Bergman scribbled in the hiking register, "By the time I finish in Maine, I hope, at last, to have found peace." After a moment, Bergman signed "Awol" and dated it. Absent Without Official Leave. *Yeah, that's me,* he thought, *someone gone missing.*

Karl Bergman—Awol—was out of the Army, but the Army wasn't out of him. His five-foot-ten frame was still hard and lean; he could run a mile in under six minutes, and did at least fifty push-ups and two hundred sit-ups every morning. His Buck knife was honed and sheathed and hung from his belt, the tip of the scabbard tied to his thigh. He knew he was better conditioned than any of the kids in front of him.

For several minutes he stood aside and watched the others clucking together—discussing trail names, equipment, where they would camp, and the rain, which had worsened. Those who hadn't already done so pulled out pack covers to protect their supplies. "Big Boy" couldn't find his cover and wondered if he'd remembered to bring it. One of the girls handed him a green trash bag that he pulled over his pack.

Awol zipped his nylon shell, pulled the hood up, and took a last look around the sparse woods of brush and oak. Beyond a sloping patch of ferns, beyond the young-oak woods and old-growth hickories and hemlocks, he could see the blue-gray glimmer of the Cartecay River watershed and, toward the west, the majestic Blue Ridge Mountains. He looked down the trail path, last year's oak leaves pasted in foot-shaped indentations along the way. Somewhere a junco peeped.

Each day during spring, up to thirty aspiring thru-hikers—those who would try to complete the A.T. in one go—begin their quest from this spot. Some, about 10 percent, attempt to hike south from Maine, but most choose to start here and follow seasonal weather north. In an average year, only 20 percent finish. The trail passed through unforgiving terrain in the lower Appalachians, Smokies, and Whites. Hikers fell sick or got injured almost always in the wild, away from food and supplies.

It was nearly eleven a.m. when Awol glanced at his watch. He shouldered his pack, picked up his poles, and with a friendly nod to the group, took his first step north.

CHAPTER TWO

THAT SAME NIGHT, LINDA FOUND a letter from Karl tucked under her pillow. She sat on the bed in her nightgown with her cat Muffin beside her and read the page again.

Dear Linda,

The last time I tried to do this it backfired on me, and I gave up. I'll try again.

First, I am sorry for waiting so long to try to explain my behavior. I don't understand myself sometimes, so I can only imagine what it must be like for you to deal with me. Please understand that I do love you, always have, and always will. But before I can commit to the life you deserve, I've got to clear my head, and face some things I simply have not been able to talk about—things I've struggled with every day since Desert Storm.

Linda, my drinking and isolation have nothing to do with you. When I see it coming, I can't stand myself, and hate myself even more when I push you away. Counseling would be of no help, at least not right now. My goal is to work the mess out of me during this hike—I see no other way.

If all this seems sudden, it is, yet it isn't. I don't think you realize how close I came to taking myself out a month ago. But I didn't want to miss out on a life with you, which is why this trip is so important. I want to fix myself, so that we can work on us.

I've turned the remodeling business over to your brother for now. It's the busy season, but we hired good help. God willing, I'll be back in six months.

Please wait for me, Linda. I love you more than you know.

Karl

Five years together, and she still didn't feel that she knew Karl. His moods, his silence whenever she tried to reach him, his drinking; it seemed he was always trying to keep her at arm's length. Once after they made love, she'd caressed his leg scars. He pushed her hand away and remained distant for two days. He wouldn't talk about the Gulf War. He was attentive and caring, but didn't want to discuss marriage. She loved him, but doubted a hike would make the difference. And he refused to get help. It was time to move on.

Linda set the letter on the bed and watched Muffin stretch out beside her and purr. She'd been able to sense his dark moments coming. The moments lurked in corners and they'd both been more anxious lately when he lost control. She massaged the tabby's ear, then picked up the letter again and walked over to her desk. After another read, Linda folded the letter, dropped it into the wastebasket, and turned out the light. In the bathroom, she reached into the medicine cabinet for her . . . *What?! He didn't pack his meds?*

CHAPTER THREE

TEN DAYS AFTER SHELLEY SYVERSON of Bryson City, North Carolina, was reported missing, her body was discovered several miles west of Fontana Lake. Sergeant Vickers of the Bryson City Police Department was in his chief's office, recounting what had happened.

"Some boys, teenagers with their dogs, discovered the body while walking in the woods. They messed with the pit she was buried in."

Chief of Police Roland Stevens bit his lip. It had been a frustrating night. First there was a phone call from the father of the thirty-one-year-old victim demanding to know why, in the ten days since his daughter was reported missing, nobody had searched that parkland. She had last been seen at a bar four miles away. The chief had to tell him that the medical examiner said she'd been deceased for that long. It wouldn't have made any difference. But the father kept lashing out in his grief, "You should have found her!" To add to the chief's frustration, he had just received a call from the press wanting to know if this murder was related to the ones in Sylva and Rainbow Springs. They would be coming in for a statement. He needed to go over everything again with his sergeant to make sure they hadn't missed anything.

"Messed with the pit how?"

"Well, Chief, the dogs found the grave and the dogs and kids dug her up partway. She was naked and bruised about the face. While I waited for you and the medical examiner, I looked all around, but didn't find anything worth noting." Vickers took off his hat and tapped it against his palm. Sweat stains blotched the inside rim. Before removing the hat, he looked his fifty years. The bald head made him look sixty. "I'm thinking that this is similar to what happened in Sylva."

The chief considered the comment and took a sip of coffee. Two carved duck decoys stared at him from a table by the window. He removed glasses from his round, heavy face and rubbing his eyes asserted, "You and I are going back out there now, and we're not coming back until we find something."

THAT SAME HOUR, AT A convenience store twenty miles to the south, a six-four, heavyset man in his mid-thirties picked up a copy of the *Smoky Mountain Times*. The man, Paul Leroux, poured himself a large coffee, grabbed a couple of jelly donuts, and asked for two packs of Marlboros. He retreated to his Wrangler, expertly entered traffic while lighting a cigarette, and several minutes later, pulled into the parking lot of a tractor distributor. He parked at the end of the lot in the shadow of a huge John Deere and locked his doors. He wolfed down the donuts between slurps of coffee, tilted the seat back, and closed his eyes. It was Friday and he had called in sick two hours ago.

He gripped the folded newspaper in his lap. The front page showed a picture of a woman in a blouse and pants standing by a picnic table, beaming. He noticed she'd turned her head so as to not show the camera her birthmark. Below, the headline read "Staple's Employee Strangled". He had seen it on the news last night. "A brutal killing in Bryson City," the reporter said, "the third area murder in fourteen months."

Paul Leroux noted the sweat on his palms as he unfolded the newspaper, but his hands didn't shake; not even a little. He'd been through this before.

SERGEANT VICKERS AND HIS CHIEF stared at a two-foot-deep rectangular pit beneath a pine. "What do you think happened here?" Chief Stevens asked. He poked around with his foot before getting down on his hands and knees.

"No signs of struggle," Vickers said. "I figure he killed her somewhere else, then brought her out here. He must have had a shovel."

"Let's think about that, Sergeant. You realize how far away our car is? Half mile? How'd he get her all the way here while carrying a shovel? There are no signs of dragging."

"Somebody helped him?"

"He may have walked back to his car and come back with a shovel," Stevens said. "Let's have another look around."

Stevens headed deeper into thickets on the theory the killer wouldn't have disposed of anything back toward the dirt road where the squad car was parked. Soon they encountered too much undergrowth, and had to bushwhack. "Okay," Stevens said, "you circle back west to the car; I'll circle back east. Blow your whistle if you find anything."

Twenty minutes later, Stevens heard three whistle blasts. He responded with one blast and headed toward the sound. He was pleased his sergeant remembered the routine. A minute later he heard three more short blasts and responded in turn. They did this two more times, until the chief was able to holler to Vickers. The chief arced around a windblown ash and spotted Vickers as he stood near a clearing, arms akimbo.

"Whatcha got, Vickers?"

Startled, Vickers jumped, then pointed to tire tracks on a patch of dirt. "These look fresh. Only a small four-wheeler could get this far in. We're less than a hundred yards from the grave, I figure. I sight-measured it from that ash to the pines near the pit." He puffed out his chest.

"Yep, these are fresh all right," Stevens said. He pulled the camera from his knapsack and took several close-ups of the indentations treaded into the dirt. "Must have parked right here. Let's go see, Andy."

Andy, the proprietor of Andy's Collision, considered himself a sleuth and assisted the local police from time to time. His specialty was tracking. Footprints, animal tracks, tread marks; if it made any kind of track, Andy had a good chance of identifying it. The men collected in his small office as Andy studied the pictures with a magnifier, toothpick tucked in his small mouth. He cross-referenced the book he'd pulled and moved back to the downloaded photos.

"Could be from a Jeep," he said. "I see these treads on 4x4s." The toothpick rolled to the other side of his mouth. "But I'll need to get out there and take measurements. Are there tracks from both sides of the vehicle?"

"Yes," Vickers replied.

"That helps, getting the front or rear wheel-to-wheel side-width. But to really narrow it down, I need to get the distance from front to rear axle. The vehicle was parked, right?"

"Right," Stevens said. "We suspect this guy left the vehicle for at least twenty minutes, given the distance to the grave."

"Not very long, but maybe long enough. When a vehicle is parked, if it's on damp soil like this, the weight of the vehicle will impress all the tires into the ground, which gives me my wheelbase."

"We'll bring you out there right now," Stevens said.

THE JEEP EASED OUT OF the tractor lot. After reading the morning paper, Paul Gaston Leroux convinced himself they had no evidence, but he felt vulnerable, and knew that after them finding three bodies in such short succession, his days here in North Carolina would be ending soon. He turned on the radio—Garth Brooks. He didn't want to move. He worked at the furniture factory as a stainer. The pay was acceptable. He had managed to keep to himself in Franklin for three years and, despite the murders, felt settled for one of the few times in his life.

Leroux massaged his temple at a stoplight. He had not slept well last night. He couldn't believe the body was discovered this soon. A twinge of dread returned. *Christ, they never found a thing in Kentucky and that was nine years ago. Those goddamn dogs.*

He tried to make up his mind on how to spend the day, and thought about going to a matinée. As the news came on the radio, he was startled to see a police car hidden in a turnoff. He didn't reduce speed at all— just drove straight ahead. He obeyed speed limits and, as a habit, drove in the right lane. Too often he had read of the criminal brought down by the broken taillight, the expired inspection sticker, the out-of-date plate. Leroux knew that would never happen to him, and he smiled as he watched the trooper's car shrink in his rearview mirror. He decided to go to the matinée and headed for the mall.

For all his smugness, Leroux was not aware that his passenger side mirror had been loosened by a pine branch he had banged into when he drove his latest victim into the forest. Nor had he noticed the small dent below the mirror.

CHAPTER FOUR

Leroux devoured the last of his taco and wiped his mouth with the remaining tatters of his napkin. He looked around the food court as he sipped a jumbo Pepsi through an oversized straw. He had an hour to kill before the movie started.

He found himself ambling in and out of the shops and noticed an unfamiliar sign that read REI. Wandering into the store, he was surrounded by an array of backpacks, mountain climbing equipment, sleeping bags, tents; all kinds of outdoor paraphernalia. To his right was a rock climbing wall, and a cute blonde in red shorts was in a harness, climbing straight up. As she grabbed at rocks and crevices with her hands and fingers, she hugged the wall with the entire length of her body, oblivious to the hoots from a redneck below. "Eeeeeyah! WAY . . . TO . . . GO . . . GIRL!"

Leroux was transfixed, and had to steady himself as he watched the woman slither up the rocks. After she reached the top, he wandered to the book section where two young men talked. The taller one, all elbows and angles, was an overly enthusiastic salesclerk.

"See, this is what I mean," the clerk said, as he grabbed a map. "You plan the trail in sections. This map shows the section for southern Virginia; this other one here is for Pennsylvania. A thru-hiker carries only the section he needs."

"I see," the customer said, a slight guy dressed in maroon corduroys and beat-up Converse sneakers. "So . . . I have to stop and get maps after I do each section?" His mouth stayed open as he stared at the clerk.

"Tell you what," the clerk put the maps back and reached for a book, "if you're serious about a thru-hike of the A.T., you should read this book first. It helps you plan out the whole thing, state-by-state. It explains how mail drops work, lists the key towns for food and supplies, what to bring."

Leroux picked up a different map titled "Appalachian Trail, National Park Service." On the cover was a picture of a hiker carrying a large backpack and walking alone on a narrow path in a forest. It looked isolated. He unfolded the map and stared at a red-marked trail which he was amazed to find worked its way north from Georgia, all the way to Maine. The trail ended at Mount Katahdin, and he remembered his father telling him about this forbidding mountain. As young men, his father and several friends had come down from Quebec City to climb it but bad weather had made their ascent treacherous, and he remembered his father saying how lucky they had been to get back down alive. He put the map back.

On his way to the exit he neared the salesclerk, now at the register, who handed a bag to the customer. "This Appalachian Trail," Leroux interrupted, "how do you get to it?"

"From here?"

"Yeah."

"Take 64 west to Winding Stair Gap. Pick it up right there."

Leroux thought for a minute. He'd had no idea of the existence of this trail the entire time he'd lived in North Carolina. He remembered seeing hikers thumbing rides, but never paid them any attention. He assumed they were local campers.

"How long does it take to go all the way?"

"Six months—give or take."

———————

FIFTEEN MINUTES LATER, LEROUX ENTERED the theater with a large popcorn, "buttered-in-layers," he'd told the concessionaire, and a new cola. He picked a back row on the far side of the entrance, and an aisle seat so he could extend his legs. Putting the popcorn on the floor and placing the soda in the cup holder to his left, he leaned back, closed his eyes, and waited for the theater to darken. By habit he would remain in this posture, unmoving, until the feature attraction began. Above his closed eyes stretched thick, brown eyebrows. Nostrils flared from a prominent Roman nose. Large hands crossed in his lap. Many of his most relaxed moments had been in the isolation of a blacked-out theater. As he sat there in comfort, gently breathing, the germ of a preposterous idea began to form.

CHAPTER FIVE

AFTER THE MOVIE AND ON a whim, Leroux took Route 64 west. Ten miles later at Winding Stair Gap, he saw three hikers together on the eastbound lane, looking for a hitch. One of them was a good-looking blonde. He drove a mile farther and turned around. The two young men wagged their thumbs, and Leroux slowed and braked on the graveled side.

"Can you take us to Franklin?" one of the boys asked.

"Yeah, I can do that. Where in Franklin?"

The boys helped the girl into the front passenger side.

"The Franklin Motel?" the girl said.

"Okay."

The boys squeezed in with their gear into the back. The girl smiled at Leroux.

"Thanks, really appreciate it," she said.

"So," Leroux asked her, "Camping?"

"We're hiking the Trail," she said. "But I wish we hadn't started so early. I slipped on ice yesterday and twisted my ankle."

"Uh-oh. Y'all mind if I smoke?" Leroux said, not waiting for an answer as he lit up and pulled onto the road. He shot her a glance. "In town for a while?" She kept smiling, even as she spoke.

"I might rest my ankle a couple of days."

"Uh-huh." Leroux took a drag and wanted to touch her, but tapped his cigarette in the ashtray. "I'm Paul, by the way. Nice to meet you."

"Hi, I'm Phoebe."

"There a Laundromat in town?" one of the boys asked.

"I think there's one on Main, near the motel," Leroux said.

"Good. I'll pig out while my clothes get done; after that I'm leaving," he said to his buddy.

"Me too, soon as I resupply," the other boy said. "Don't have enough cash for motels—hostel maybe."

Leroux dragged on his cigarette.

WHILE THE BOYS UNLOADED PACKS and poles from the back, Leroux reached in the glove box for a piece of paper. He scribbled on it and handed it to Phoebe as she started to climb out of the vehicle.

"After you rest that ankle, Phoebe, give me a call, and I'll take you back to the trail."

"Wow, what a trail angel. Thanks," she said, still smiling as she closed the door.

CHAPTER SIX

RAIN BEAT DOWN ON AWOL as he tramped by brambles reaching out over the mossy path. Under a hemlock he took a minute to pull off his hood and put on his hiker's sombrero. The full brim drained off water better, and a hat instead of a hood gave better ventilation. He'd been walking briskly as the terrain was easy. The trail wound slightly uphill and was marked with white blazes (two-inch by six-inch painted vertical rectangles) on the bare trees every hundred yards or so. Awol had planned his first camp at Hawk Mountain Shelter and had already hiked four miles, halfway. *So far, so good.* His green pack seemed like a natural extension of his back; the harness was adjusted to prevent the pack from swaying and to keep the center of gravity down near his hips. After a swig from his water bottle, he poled north past trout lilies and bright chickweed. The reddish, blotched leaves of the lily contrasted with the white weed, and Awol remembered how loose chickens on his uncle's farm pecked at the small petals that grew everywhere. The two-foot-wide path snaked on through oak, hemlock, and flowering dogwood, which arced over the trail making frequent tunnels, forcing Awol to duck and crouch.

Throughout his life, Awol had tried to do the right thing. One of his great grandfathers had been a preacher who wrote books extolling temperance and caution. But he also had an uncle who was a convicted embezzler and a cousin who'd been acquitted of murder, the charge reduced to manslaughter. Awol often wondered if his genes contained a mixture of these personalities, and he often speculated about what measure of good and bad he had received. Awol unpocketed the ziplock bag of gorp Linda had given him in the car. "Here," was all she'd said. He placed his trekking poles against a pine and looked at the bag of nuts, raisins, dates, and dried fruit. He removed his pack and pulled out the small lightweight rubber mat he had taken from his kayak before he left. Awol placed the mat on a wet rock and sat down, peeking between tree limbs at the gray-brown fields in the valley below.

Linda. He'd known her since high school back in Rhode Island, when he and her brother Tom started hanging out together. Back then he was shy and she was a popular cheerleader a year ahead of him. She was out of his league, but that didn't stop him from admiring her. It still surprised him how quickly they hit it off when he moved back to the old neighborhood after his divorce. He and Tom started the kitchen-and-bath remodeling business that summer. At first, she would come by and help while they were getting the office set up; then they started grabbing lunch together. They fell in love. But that was five years ago.

He scooped out another handful of gorp. Linda hadn't agreed to send mail drops, so he had mailed the first box himself before leaving and given her a list of addresses, hoping she might change her mind. Ideally, a drop box would contain food and supplies such as fuel tabs, alcohol swabs for keeping clean, tiny tubes of toothpaste, and other lightweight, useful items. They would be sent every week or so under his name to a designated post office. "Please hold for Appalachian Trail thru-hiker." *So what if she dumps me. I'll hitch or leg it to food stores on my own.* He felt a blip of optimism. The rain had even let up. Awol sealed the bag of trail mix and rolled up the mat.

THAT AFTERNOON, AWOL MADE HIS first camp at Hawk Mountain. At more than three thousand feet, he could see a section of the logging road he had crossed two miles away. In a stand of pines ahead of him, he could hear the spring. Behind him stood a dilapidated, three-sided wooden shelter with an open front and pitched roof. It had adequate room for six, but already eight people had squeezed in. Confusion reigned. Awol noticed a hiker trying to blow up his air mattress, but the air kept hissing out.

"Damn! Why won't this valve work?"

"Cause you're not twisting the cap on right," Awol hollered, pointing to the cap and doing a twisting motion with his hand as he walked by. The young man jerked his head up at him. *Okay, settle down. This is what happens when I decide not to pack my meds.*

On one side of the hut, under the overhanging corrugated tin roof, another hiker bent down over his shiny stove. He had directions in front of him and his head kept bobbing back and forth from the directions to the stove as he fiddled with a control. Inside the hut under the front overhang, socks, polypro undershirts, and briefs hung from a makeshift clothesline.

Awol had planned to tent and unpacked his gear in an open, flat spot near the fire pit. The rain was back to a drizzle as he assembled his solo tent. The flexed rods jumped out of their folds like magician's wands as he unhooked them. In less than ten minutes the green oblong tent, screened in front, was framed with the rain fly over the top. Although this was the first night on the trail for everyone here, it was not a new experience for Awol. He had camped and hiked in mountains since boyhood, and in the Army he had always felt at home in bivouac.

He spotted the sign for water and followed the blue blazes to the narrow stream he had heard earlier. Two older hikers, a man and a woman, were coming back, each holding a transparent one-gallon bag of water.

"Hello," called out the woman.

Her partner, a tall balding gentleman, extended his hand to Awol. "I'm Seeker and this is my wife, Wisdom." He was also carrying a small meshed bag that said PUR filter on it. Part of a hose stuck straight up. *American Gothic for the A.T.,* Awol thought, holding back a smile.

"Are you thru-hikers?" Awol asked.

"Well, sort of; we've been doing the trail for one month over each of the last six years and we'll finish in Hot Springs in three weeks," Seeker said proudly.

Awol looked at the bags of water, about to say something.

"I know," Seeker said, holding up his bag, "you think we must drink a lot." His smile widened, "We're trying to help the kids" —he gestured toward the shelter. "It's their first night and they need all the help they can get."

Later in his tent, after a meal of noodles and cocoa, and aided by a headlamp, Awol wrote in his journal. His last sentence read: "Today I met a Seeker of Wisdom."

———————————

EARLIER THAT SAME AFTERNOON, CHIEF Roland Stevens of Bryson City stood in front of his station next to a U.S. flag and faced a camera. "Wait! Don't roll it yet," he hollered. Stevens stepped aside, pulled out his handkerchief, and blew his nose. He took extra time wiping his lips and patting puffy cheeks trying to think again how he would phrase a statement. *Brief,* he thought. *Brief but confident.* He reset his glasses and stepped up again. The cameras rolled.

"We will work day and night to catch this killer. We will leave no stone unturned until he is caught." He felt stronger. "My fellow citizens, we need to be prudent and cautious, but we cannot live in fear. If anyone has any information please contact us." He gathered up his notes, hoping to be finished.

"Do you have any leads?" asked a reporter.

"How come there wasn't a search of that area to begin with?" asked another.

Chief Stevens wanted to avoid one question so he answered the other, "We do." He stepped away with Sergeant Vickers and the microphones and cameras followed them toward the station.

"Chief," the second reporter persisted, "if you had to do it over again, would you have searched the parklands?"

A microphone was thrust into Stevens's face. "We have been searching."

"But wouldn't a full-blown search of that area have turned up evidence? It doesn't seem like you have very strong leads."

Stevens's face reddened.

"We know what he's driving," Vickers blurted. At once Vickers knew he'd made a huge mistake and his legs went wobbly as Stevens grabbed his shoulder and guided him through the door.

"No more questions," Stevens shouted.

Inside he called Vickers into his office and slammed the door.

"You idiot!"

"I know, I blew it," Vickers said.

Chief Stevens sat by his desk flapping his notepad on top of his knee. "Jesus, Mary, and Joseph."

"If we knew exactly what he was driving," Vickers said, "I never would have said a word. Because . . ." Vickers threw up his hands, "Andy said he was not certain—"

"But almost sure it was some type of small Wrangler," the chief cut in. "—and with all the microphones and cameras, I just forgot," Vickers concluded.

Stevens eyed his sergeant, "We've gotta find that Jeep fast, and track him to it."

———————

A LOUD RAP AT THE door startled Leroux. He peeked under a blind and saw the Domino's car at the curb. He opened the door and handed the acne-laden kid fifteen bucks.

At nine o'clock he switched the TV from basketball to the local news. He grabbed another Molson from the fridge and sat in a large upholstered chair in his den. Cranking the chair halfway back so the footstool extended, he kicked off his slippers and massaged one foot with the other.

The newest development in the murder investigation was the lead story. Leroux blinked once when the chief said he had leads. At the end, when Vickers made his blunder, Leroux shivered, as his brain jumped into overdrive. He listened to the final comments from the reporter and turned off the TV. He toggled off the floor lamp beside him and, for several minutes, stared at the dead TV in the dark.

Leroux figured they must have found his tire tracks. He tried to calculate how many Jeeps he'd seen on the road and how many Jeep owners lived in a radius of twenty-five miles. *Not too many*, he reasoned. The good news was he had bought the Jeep from a small used car dealership in Pennsylvania. But the law had ways of finding out who owned a Jeep. He pictured some wonk at the North Carolina DMV firing up his computer and searching the registration database. Leroux decided he'd hit the road as soon as possible, but without his Jeep.

Leroux's rented bungalow had a small detached garage. He'd stopped garaging his vehicle once he realized he'd never encounter a significant snowstorm down here. In the last two years his garage had become cluttered. But that evening he cleared the floor, moving trash barrels to the side, pushing cardboard boxes of old magazines and newspapers to the other side, and moving a tool bench left behind by the previous tenant. He stared at the bicycle a friend in Kentucky had given him.

He shut off the light and reopened the garage door. Hank, his neighbor across the street, had his lights on. Through the picture window Leroux could see the TV screen flickering and the back of Hank's head as he watched it. Neighbors on both sides of him were also up and about. It was 10:12 p.m. Leroux looked around one more time, before carrying the bike into the house.

At midnight, surrounded by darkness and a silent street, Leroux emerged from his house and pushed his Jeep into the open, unlit garage. He eased the garage door down and locked it.

CHAPTER SEVEN

IN THE MURKY DAWN, AWOL pressed a button on the side of his watch—6:00 a.m. He unzipped the sleeping bag to the steady patter of rain on his tent.

He pulled off his nylon T-shirt and briefs and returned them to a color-coded ziplock bag he put into the bottom of his pack. He drew out the clothes he'd wear today from the bottom of his sleeping bag, where he had stashed them the night before. They were warm and dry. Yesterday's clothes had been laid out at the end of his tent and Awol fingered their dampness. He'd repack them for tomorrow. He felt the morning's dankness and added a long-sleeve polypro to the day's clothes. By rolling and shifting his body in the small tent, he got the clothes on including shorts, a hooded shell, and Gore-Tex pants. He tugged wool socks over liner socks and double knotted his boots at the tie.

Breakfast was a packet of oatmeal with cold water poured into it, stirred to paste with a plastic spoon. Awol sprinkled in gorp and ate sitting up in his tent. He heard rustles and grumbles from the tent next to him as he finished breakfast with a PowerBar and an extra swig of water. The grumbler wasn't happy about the weather. After rolling up his sleeping bag and fitting it into a trash bag to keep it dry, Awol hooded up and crawled out into rain.

His waterproof food bag waited for him up on a tree limb where he had slung it by rope, high enough to be out of a bear's reach. Today's lunch was already ziplocked and packed at the top. Awol watched a neophyte wander near him looking out of peepholes cut into his makeshift trash bag rain gear; he was searching for where he'd hung his food bag. Awol had learned many hikes ago to put his initials on the bottom of his sack.

The campsite came alive. Everyone was hyped; it was the second day for thru-hikers and, for most, the first full day on the trail. At the shelter, thirteen hikers unwrapped themselves from their bags. Two had slept in the very front, at the foot of all the others, and two had rigged up body tents—bivy sacks—on each end of the shelter under the overhangs. Underneath one bivouac was a rectangular spread of Tyvek water-resistant insulation paper used by contractors. Awol witnessed the ingenuity and the chaos.

"I can't find my other boot. Has anyone seen a boot like this?" A hiker held up his leg.

Awol watched as Vagabond, the first thru-hiker he'd met on the trail, spotted a boot underneath the shelter where it had been kicked during the night. "Is this it?" he asked, holding up a boot and dumping water out of it.

"Shit."

Two girls grabbed their clothes draped over the makeshift clothesline at the same time, shaking the line, and two T-shirts near the other end fell off, missed the planked floor, and plopped down into slop.

"Oh, I'm so sorry; I didn't mean to."

Awol turned back to his own matters. He had his tent down, bagged, and tied to his pack in eight minutes. He filled two water bottles and gave the remaining water from his bag to a tenter next to him. After placing the water bottles in nets on each side of his pack, Awol rechecked his food for the day and transferred a Snickers to his shell pocket. Now that he didn't have to manipulate his cold fingers, he pulled on a light pair of insulated gloves. He looked up at the cloud-darkened sky and after tightening the rain cover on his backpack, positioned the pack upside down on the ground, harness side up. Like a scuba diver, he inserted both arms into the shoulder straps and in one motion lifted the pack straight up and over his head, letting it slip down onto his shoulders. He clicked the wide belly strap, picked up his poles, and made a final check at his campsite.

This daily ordeal of packing and unpacking was the way it would be for every thru-hiker living on the trail in the months ahead. Everything needed was hauled on one's back; it was why in the days to come, every hiker discarded or mailed home extraneous items. Unconditioned legs ached and new hikers would forever be rearranging their gear, readjusting their straps and ties, looking for ways to ease the burden.

Walking past the shelter, Awol witnessed close to eighteen hikers huddling under overhangs by their stoves or by their packs, stuffing bags into the packs, taking them back out, reopening the same bags and stuffing them back in again. He watched hikers bump into each other as they carried water bags, toilet paper, and stoves.

He saw a butterscotch-skinned man, older than the others, cross the trail and disappear behind a thick oak. *He walks like . . .* There were a few hikers waiting for the privy and he needed to pee, Awol thought. He watched him return back across the trail. Again he was reminded of . . .

Poor fucking Harrison. What did I go and do?

In this instance, Awol's shoulders dipped and he bent his head down. Often, when he thought about it, he'd put his hands on his hips. This time, he closed his eyes a moment as he leaned on his poles. Awol straightened up and pulled up the sleeve of his shell. He squinted at his watch as he fixed to head north in the rain. It was Saturday, 6:51 a.m.

LEROUX SLEPT FITFULLY. HE'D SET the alarm for 6:00 a.m., but now it was 6:19. He rubbed his eyes and got out of bed, overwhelmed with all he had to do. He lit a Marlboro on the way to the bathroom after grabbing his notepad from the end table. *Thank God it's Saturday; banks and stores will be open, and the DMV is closed.* He glanced behind the shade of the bathroom window—overcast, misting.

Munching peanut-buttered toast and sipping black coffee, Leroux fired up his computer and examined his bank accounts. Then he finished a letter to his Canadian cousin, begun last night before falling asleep at the table.

Cousin Ray,

J'espere que tu vas bien. Because your English is better than my French, allow me to continue in English.

You have always been my true friend and you've told me in the

*past you would help me as payback for that time in Presque Isle. I
need your help. Enclosed is a money order made out in your name
for $1,800. Please cash it and establish a separate account for me
at your bank. I can't go into detail (you will understand when I see
you), but I'll be coming to Canada sometime before the end of this
year and will be asking you to send me money from time to time.*

*For reasons you will understand later, I can't be reached at this
mail address or by phone. An opportunity has come up and I must
take it now. I have always trusted you and ask that you please keep
this confidential, even from Jacques and all the rest.*

*I enjoyed reading your Christmas letter, as usual. Merci, je
t'embrasse et donne mes meilleurs voeux a la famille.*

Cousin Paul

Leroux put the letter in the prestamped, addressed envelope but
didn't seal it. He picked up the notepad and with a black marker blotted
out the task completed, but added "Post Office" as he scanned the next
listed item: Car Rental. Back at his computer, he found information on
Avis. Leroux smoked and thought. He couldn't take a chance with the
Jeep. He pictured the cruiser he'd seen sitting by the highway yesterday
morning. Glancing through a list of numbers behind his ashtray, he
grabbed the phone.

"Hello, Billy there yet?" Billy worked at the convenience store and
had once given Leroux a lift home when the Jeep had to be serviced.

"Hold on," a girl's yawning voice said, "he just came in the door."

"Yo!"

"Hey, it's Paul. I come in most mornings. I got ten bucks if someone
can drive me downtown."

"You the guy with the Jeep?"

Leroux shut his eyes. "No. But sometimes. I use my neighbor's wheels
to come up and get the paper for him and smokes for me, but he's gone.
Your brother, Kevin, knows me."

At 8:15 a Dodge Ram pickup with overhead ladder racks and tool
boxes on the sides pulled into Leroux's driveway. The lettering on the
door read, "No Job Too Small, call Kevin." Leroux saw a wheelbarrow,

stepladder, and sawhorses in the bed of the truck as he climbed in the passenger side.

An hour later, Leroux had rented a car and bought a paper. He pulled the rented Subaru up to his bank, and read the latest on the Bryson City killing. Nothing new. He asked the teller for a money order for eighteen hundred dollars, eleven hundred dollars in twenties and fifties, and three hundred dollars in traveler's checks. After going to the post office, he drove straight to the mall and parked next to the entrance for REI.

CHAPTER EIGHT

ON TOP OF A FOLDER on Chief Stevens's desk was a thirteen-page fax from the state Registry of Motor Vehicles listing Jeep owners in North Carolina. It detailed each owner's name, address, vehicle ID, year, and plate.

"Look, I'll do what I can," the duty sergeant in Raleigh had said, "but I ain't gonna be able to pull all this together today. We're short-staffed this weekend 'cause of the funeral."

Stevens leaned back in his chair while holding the phone. He knew about this. A trooper from Raleigh had been shot on duty, and the funeral, with police procession, was to be today.

"Might have it for you tomorrow."

"I appreciate your situation, Sergeant—my condolences. I will need it by Sunday for sure," Stevens had said.

Chief Stevens was surprised to have received the fax that afternoon; he counted over seventy names in the tri-city area, but was disheartened when he figured that in the time it would take to check them all, the killer could be long gone. Then he realized the list had all kinds of Jeeps—Grand Cherokees, Rubicon Unlimiteds, Wranglers. He concentrated on standard Wranglers, which Andy had suggested, and felt better. Additional names could be eliminated for the time being, like the name of a woman he recognized, knowing that her husband was deceased. A few Wranglers were assigned to the government, and he crossed those off as well.

After making notations for Bryson City, he gave the list to Sergeant Vickers and told him to show the names for greater Franklin, and Sylva, and fax them to the police chiefs there. They could do some scouting too.

Vickers shuffled to his office, took a yellow hi-liter from the mug on his desk and marked the nearby locations. He peeled off a Post-it note and placed it on the top right of the front sheet, adding "Gary and Frank, check these out and give me anything you've got. Need ASAP, Vickers."

Thirty minutes later, the phone rang—Sergeant Ralston from the Franklin police. "You know that fax ya sent? None of the names are in this jurisdiction. Is there a page missing?"

Vickers couldn't believe what he heard. He'd never liked Ralston. "What do you mean not in your jurisdiction?" Vickers picked up the stapled document, "I see a guy right here—Leroux—lives in Franklin."

"There's no one here on my list from Franklin unless it's one of the ones crossed out. Didn't see anybody in Frank's area either."

"What? I didn't cross out anything I hi-lited—"

"Then, that's your problem," Ralston said. "You done crossed them all out for our areas. You shouldn't hi-lite something and fax it; it comes through as a blot."

"Ralston, we're trying to catch a serial killer up here, and I don't think I need instruction from the likes of you." Vickers slammed down the phone.

A minute later, after fidgeting in his chair while looking at the fax, he gave it to a rookie cop with instructions to retype the hi-lited listings, and fax it again.

Leroux, sporting a tweed jacket, reading glasses, and a scally cap, walked into REI and scanned for a different sales clerk from the one he questioned yesterday. A folded newspaper under his arm and shoes polished to a high shine completed his altered look. He patted the lumpy wad of cash in his pocket and walked to the book and map section where he picked up *The Thru-hikers Handbook* and the A.T. trail map for North Carolina. Leroux fingered a field guide for the trail and glanced back as a clerk came toward him.

"Can I help you?" The name tag read *Mike.*

"Mike, my brother sent me down here. He's going to hike the A.T., and I'm supposed to get him what he needs. He sleeps days and works nights, so I'm the gopher."

"For a thru-hike, a lot of equipment is needed. What does he have now?"

"Nothing. That's what I'm here for. Just get me what he needs to hike all the way. He's about my size."

"Oookaaaay. Let's start with a tent—gotta have a place to live."

Soon, Leroux had a growing pile of gear by the register. He had to keep saying, "Whatever you think, Mike." "I'm sure he'll like it." "I don't know. What would you do?"

Mike, the store's gear freak, had a field day. Leroux felt better. The kid was so intent on the gear, he barely even looked at Leroux. "Now, many like the WhisperLite stove and it's good, don't get me wrong—heats up fast—the new model simmers, but it's cumbersome and you gotta always get fuel. Here, check this out." He held up a small rectangular half-inch high box of metal that folded up on the sides, "This is what the NATO troops use. You put a fuel tab down here and light it—get some tin or aluminum flashing and make a windscreen to put around it. Takes longer to fire up, but it's compact as you can see—cheap and it will never fail you."

"Sounds good, Mike," Leroux said, as he glanced out windows and through the doorway. *C'mon, kid, let's get done.*

And so it went—boots, sleeping bags, mattress pads, "See, some guys dig the Ridge Rest pad and I'll be the first to admit it folds up easy and you don't have to blow it up each night, but—and here's the thing—it's uncomfortable. The Therm-a-Rest here is comfortable—you want the long or short one?"

"Whatever you think, Mike." *Christ, kid, hurry the fuck up!*

Poles. "See these?" Mike picked up a set of Leki hiking poles. The poles were collapsed for easy handling and Mike adroitly extended them. "Five or six years ago you started seeing hikers with poles; eight years ago they were nonexistent. These things help prevent knee problems—'course if you over-hike, anyone'll get hiker-hobble—but these poles have springs inside, and the poles plunge down when you plant them. Down hills is where they really help; the springs work like miniature shock absorbers to reduce the thud, thud, thud and save your knees . . . expensive, but—"

"Look, I know you'll treat us right; let's finish this. I have to get back to my office."

Mike selected men's XXL polypro undershirts, shorts, and Gore-Tex gloves. "And this," Mike held up a Marmot hooded shell, "the one thing that'll save your brother's ass in cold, wet weather. Don't leave home without it," he chuckled.

Leroux looked back over all his equipment as Mike handed him two bandannas, SmartWool socks, and liners. Mike headed back to a rack when he remembered to get matching leggings for the shell.

Leroux wondered if it was all necessary and his head became heavy. He wandered over to his pile and realized that what he saw was his sole means of getting to Canada, or at least to Maine. The law was closing in. He'd never before been a person of interest. *Jeep's pegged, can't drive it. Get new wheels, they still come and ask about my Jeep. I stay, they come right to me. I strangled that cunt not six miles from here.* Leroux was perspiring and wanted a cigarette.

I could take the rental north. He thought again about this as he had last night. *But I'm still fucked. I'm traced and found with the rental. Airports, car rentals, all will be checked.* Leroux flexed his fingers and wanted to light up. He thought about phoning cousin Ray, but the more he considered it, the more rash and desperate it seemed; it would tip off Jacques and the entire Ouilette family. Leroux glanced at the store exit. *Right now the situation's hot for a Jeep owner in North Carolina. Okay, take a bus to, say, Massachusetts. But what if they show my picture on TV?* —"You got fleece? What about fleece?"

"Huh? No. I mean, yeah. Skip the fleece." *I gotta stay out of sight. So what I gave ID to Avis. By the time they trace me, I'll be on the trail. They won't have a clue.*

Leroux looked again at the pile of gear. *I've got the best plan right here. I'm the person least suspected to try something like this and I beat everyone to the punch. It's clean. It's simple.*

He saw Mike coming to him, palms up, consternation spread across his face. "Hey, you know what? I totally forgot about a backpack!"

CHAPTER NINE

CHIEF STEVENS AND VICKERS EXAMINED their crime scene photos. It was midafternoon and the day had not gone smoothly for the chief. Their rookie cop had left to assist in a three-vehicle collision on Route 441 north of Whittier. Stevens, with twenty-three years on the force, couldn't remember the last time three vehicles had collided anywhere in his district.

At about the same time, he got a call from the governor for an update on the murder. That, and the following drop-in visit from the mayor, distracted him. After the mayor left, a hysterical woman walked in claiming her purse was stolen—"in broad daylight!"—at the Burger King parking lot. This was when Vickers told him the rookie had not finished retyping the list of Wrangler owners. While the chief dealt with the woman, Vickers grabbed a piece of paper, wrote down the information in longhand, and refaxed it to the Franklin and Sylva Police. That had been an hour ago.

Vickers and Stevens now focused on a photo of a torn limb and branches Stevens had taken close to the spot where they found Jeep tracks.

"The Jeep banged into this pine branch and broke it," Stevens said. "This I'm sure of. It's about the height of a side mirror and I'm certain we can find some type of scrape, dent, or busted mirror on the Jeep. The four Wrangler owners around Bryson have no rap sheet, nothing, at least according to our files. You know this guy, Hickey," Stevens held up the file to Vickers, "and you say he'd never be a suspect. That leaves these three guys to look at first: Sark, Bradley, and Curtis. We need to see their Jeeps."

"How? We can't show up and search without probable cause."

"If the Jeep's parked outside, we find a reason to stop and look at it. If garaged, we still gotta look at it, or follow them. We stop them on the road for whatever reason—make one up—and check out the Jeep. It's only Saturday," Chief Stevens read his sergeant's notations on the fax again, "Gary's got three guys in Franklin and Frank's got one in Sylva. We can crack the case this weekend."

THAT NIGHT, LEROUX SAT AT his kitchen table studying the A.T. map of North Carolina. His blinds were drawn; his notepad was next to him; the TV in the den was on mute. All around him lay gear, pamphlets, wrappers and tags, water bottles, mess kit, stove, fuel tabs. He'd lugged it all in from the Subaru and dumped it in the kitchen. He put down the map and picked up the pack again, played with the straps, unzipped a pocket, and pulled out more stuffing jammed inside to bulk it up and make it appear full-sized. He unfastened the acetate-covered ID tag and threw it into the overflowing trash can.

Leroux stubbed out his cigarette and hauled himself to the kitchen sink. He turned on the cold-water faucet, bent down over the sink and scooped water onto his face, rubbing it onto his eyes. He did this several times before drying his face with a clean towel. He picked up the to-do list: hide rental car, clean out Jeep, pack. Leroux inserted above "pack," "Buy food!"

Leroux got up to brew more coffee, and grabbed another Marlboro. From what Phoebe had said, and from what he gathered from his handbook, shelters bordered the trail. The map showed accessible towns in which to procure food and supplies, but the distances bothered him. Franklin, for example, was ten miles from the trail and his heart sank as he realized he would never be able to pedal his bike all the way from here to the trail, certainly not with a fully loaded backpack. He couldn't take the rental to the trailhead. Even if he hid the car near it, the car would be discovered in the vicinity of the A.T. He studied the map again, this time spotting a U.S. Forest Service road intersecting the trail, eight miles north of the gap. It occurred to him that the factory was four miles in the same direction. He could park the Subaru at the factory, where they'd expect to find the Jeep Monday morning. No matter if the police found his rental there, he worked there, and no link would likely be made to the Appalachian Trail.

Leroux figured that even though he had cut the distance in half, the problem of a full backpack and a cheap, undersized bike remained. He tried to picture the road. The first half of the distance, where he'd drive to the plant, was gradually uphill. But the rest of the way, where he had to pedal, was flat, as he remembered it. He looked at his ashtray and the peanut M&M wrappers beside him, and convinced himself he was fit enough to handle four miles on bike. *Yes, I can do this. I just need a couple of breaks here.* He felt details coming together and inked out "hide rental car" with the marker. With a fresh cup of coffee he headed to the garage.

CHIEF STEVENS WAS HOME WATCHING the news and going over the day. He'd found Bradley's Wrangler parked in the driveway next to his house. With apologies that he was checking out a bulletin for a "hit-and-run" he was able to examine the maroon Jeep. Nothing. Same at the Sark residence; everything checked out. Vickers called him soon after he returned home; both Wranglers assigned to him were clean. Frank and Gary left messages saying they would complete their checks tomorrow.

At 10:30 Stevens kissed his wife goodnight and hauled himself upstairs to bed.

LEROUX CLEANED OUT HIS JEEP. He pulled out papers with his signature or handwriting stuck under the seats, retrieved his registration and sunglasses from the glove box, and pocketed the Sudafed he found, along with a small address book.

As he closed the passenger door, he noticed scratches and a dent below the mirror. The mirror mount was loose, and also scratched. He looked closer and saw a tiny leaf and twig wedged in behind the mount. Now he remembered hitting branches as he drove into the woods.

He pulled out the leaf and twig in the loosened mirror mount, letting them drop to the floor. Then he thought better of it, picked them up, and put them into his pants pocket. At the last minute, he remembered to reach in for the short entrenching shovel he'd bought some time ago at an Army Navy Store.

Back in the house, Leroux convinced himself that he had taken a last look around his garage, had turned out the garage light, and that no one had seen him as he closed and bolted his garage door. At eleven o'clock he picked up his maps and A.T. handbook again. He tried to read up on the trail from the handbook while referring to the main map, but kept nodding off. After another cup of coffee and two more Marlboros, Leroux realized he had forgotten all about the late evening news. He turned the muted TV off and thought of doing a last to-do list. Instead, he plodded to his bed, exhausted, at 11:50.

CHAPTER TEN

LEROUX WOKE UP SEVERAL TIMES during the night, jumping at every creak and rattle, and at 7:25 a.m., sat up exhausted. He brewed the last of his coffee, cooked eggs with ham, and made toast. He was almost out of cigarettes.

After eating, he turned on CNN loud enough to hear from the kitchen, where he studied the setup instructions for his tent. He thought back to his boyhood in Maine when he and cousin Ray slept overnight in a pup tent in Père Ouilette's backyard. He hadn't been in a tent since, and the diagram looked involved. Wanting to give it a test run, he set it up in the den. CNN covered the upcoming invasion of Iraq and other top stories, and when the local weather came on, he paused and paid attention. A cold front was moving in. "Lots of rain over the next few days and possible snow in higher elevations," the weatherman said. Leroux went to the kitchen and wrote "wear rain gear" on his notepad.

A few minutes later, he returned to the den to watch a report about three serial murders in North Carolina and how they might be linked to other murders in Ohio, West Virginia, and Tennessee. "The recent killing in Bryson City indicates a modus operandi similar to the other strangulations and burials," the commentator said. They showed footage of the grieving father in Bryson City that Leroux had seen before. "Residents of this rustic hill country worry about a ruthless local killer who may strike again." Leroux watched familiar footage of the police station in Bryson City and Chief of Police Roland Stevens next to the flag. After listening to Stevens's comments again, Leroux noted the time on his watch and backed into the kitchen. He managed to calm himself by deciding that if they came for him today, he'd know what to do. If he was granted another day, then fate meant for him to escape. Meanwhile, he'd focus on the here and now.

At half past nine, while taking down his tent and struggling to ram it back in its sack, the phone rang. He was not expecting anyone and listened for a message on his answering machine. The caller ID read "unavailable." He listened to silence and then a click. Leroux was frightened, anxious, and felt he should step up his pace. He headed out to get his trail food, and more cigarettes.

Fifteen minutes later, as Leroux grabbed a shopping cart at Feeley's Supermarket, Patrolman Wallace of the Franklin Police drove up to Leroux's house and parked his squad car. After ringing the bell several times, he peeked into the garage door window and saw a Wrangler. This was the first of three addresses Wallace had been assigned to check. He decided to go to the other locations and come back later, when someone was home.

LEROUX SWUNG A CART DOWN the breakfast aisle and spotted oatmeal. His father used to make it all the time for him and his brother on weekends when they lived in Maine. Leroux dropped the cylinder of Quaker Oats into his cart. He followed this with a box of granola. He wheeled down another aisle and grabbed a loaf of white bread, then exchanged it for a loaf of rye which was firmer and more compact. *There's cocoa. That'll work.* He grabbed two boxes.

He hustled down aisles dumping boxes and bags into his cart. He'd go back, put everything into his pack, and escape this afternoon. He would drive straight to the plant and sit in the parking lot until dark. He didn't want to be seen on the road with his backpack.

He proceeded to check-out and paid in cash. He exited the supermarket and looked for his Jeep. Puzzled at not seeing it, he realized he forgot to buy cigarettes and tramped back, bags and all, into the store. He twisted around after remembering the Subaru and reminded himself to get smokes at the convenience store on the way home.

As he bought a carton of Marlboros at the 7-Eleven, a squad car pulled up and a young officer emerged. Kevin, standing behind the counter, handed him the cigarettes.

"No Jeep?" Kevin asked.

Leroux looked at him and handed him some bills. "Keep the change, Kevin."

Though Leroux passed close enough by the officer to see his name tag, he was pretty sure officer Wallace didn't hear the exchange; nevertheless, Leroux drove down the next street over, behind his house, and circled into his street from the other end, all the while checking in his mirrors. Leroux backed into his driveway. Inside the house he felt sweat trickle from his armpits, and glancing in the bathroom mirror, he saw a flushed face and nervous eyes. *I've got to get out of here.*

PATROLMAN WALLACE, AFTER LEAVING THE Leroux address, had been dispatched to a break-in two miles away. The chief needed an investigation and report. Wallace finished and had stopped for a soda at the convenience store. His watch read half past ten and he was off at noon. He thought of going back to the Leroux address but figured it would look better to his chief to at least stop once at all the Jeep addresses. If there was time, he could swing back on his way to the station.

Leroux returned to the kitchen and noticed all the papers and tags on his table. They would search the house. Leroux got a heavy duty trash bag from his tiny pantry and combed through all possible evidence, ditching it into the bag. He took up the magic marker, blotted through the rest of his list and trashed it. He tore off the top sheet of scribbling from his notepad and noticed indentations from his pen on the next page, so he trashed the entire pad. He put gear wrappings, cellophane remnants, bindings, equipment tags, pamphlets, brochures, warranties, anything he found that might indicate REI or a trail hiker, into the trash bag. He collected instruction sheets he might need and placed them on top of his maps and trail books. He went to each room, trashing more notes from his bedroom night table, emptying baskets, satisfying himself that no one would be able to figure out that he'd jumped onto the Appalachian Trail.

Lastly, he unplugged his PC and dumped it into the bag along with all attachments, including floppies, CDs, and anything that could be traced, especially any porn.

As Leroux closed his blinds, he saw Hank standing and looking right at him from his window across the street.

Leroux started jamming items into his pack but couldn't squeeze everything in. He glanced to the kitchen floor at bags of food, boots, a large sleeping bag, the rest of the clothes. Even when he unzipped side pockets and stuffed things in there, he became frustrated as he realized he had it all screwed up, that he'd never get everything in. Then it dawned on him; he needed to wear these hiking clothes.

He settled down and dressed as a hiker. With a clearer head he returned to the kitchen and saw the A.T. map with the picture of a hiker on the front of it. He studied the image and noted some items were tied on top of and underneath the pack—like Phoebe's. He sneaked to his garage for rope. He didn't want to leave it as potential evidence, anyway. He unlocked the garage and found the rope on the shelf under his bench, right where he had left it. As he looked at it, he became aroused thinking about the brunette's face in Bryson City, her eyes pleading as he pulled on the rope he now had in his hands. Leroux felt a surge within his penis and the erection; he let the urges multiply and pulled out several sets of latex gloves from the bench drawer. He understood this quick and not unwelcome burst of desire had much to do with his overall state of affairs. It was always like this—dealing with any tense situation rattled him, and he would have to stifle his urges. He closed the garage door, but forgot to lock it.

CHAPTER ELEVEN

PATROLMAN WALLACE DROVE TO THE second address, but had found an empty garage and no one home. While proceeding to the third address, he saw a Jeep coming toward him. As it drew near, Wallace lit his roof gumball and gave a couple bursts of siren. The Wrangler slowed and stopped as Wallace wheeled across the road and pulled behind. As Wallace got out of his cruiser and walked over, he noted the driver kept both hands on top of the steering wheel.

He looked in on a skinny, startled young man, all of eighteen.

"Your license and registration please."

The driver handed over the documents. Wallace recognized the name, Parker, as the owner of the empty house he had just come from. "This your Jeep?" He noticed a few scratches on the hood and a ding by the door handle, but they were starting to rust.

"No, it's my mom's, I just dropped her off at her sister's in Green Creek. I wasn't speeding was I?" Wallace ignored the question and seeing the driver side looked good, with mirror intact, walked around to look at the other side. He didn't see any dents or dings on the passenger side and the mirror was solid.

"How'd you get the dent in the rear bumper?"

"Backed into a guard rail."

"Your dad like Jeeps?"

"My dad died. My mom let me pick this out used at Dodd's last year, when I graduated high school. I'm helping her pay for it, but she owns it."

Wallace handed him back the papers. "You're fine, Son, sorry for the trouble."

_____

LEROUX, BACK IN HIS KITCHEN, was fussing with tangles of rope, stuff sacks, and assorted gear bags. It was a quarter past eleven, and he needed to hurry. He put the TV on mute so he could concentrate. Just as he pressed the mute button, the shrill ring of the phone made him jump. For a second he almost believed he'd caused the phone to ring by pressing the button. He froze, waiting for the answering machine.

"Hi, Paul? This is Phoebe."

_____

AFTER LETTING THE KID GO, Patrolman Wallace turned around and continued to the third address. The smart looking Wrangler sat in the driveway and, it turned out, the man answering the door was the proud owner of the new Jeep. Wallace couldn't find a nick on it.

At eleven-thirty, Wallace thought of taking a shortcut back to the station so he could finish his reports by noon. At the last minute, before turning, he continued straight; he'd check the Leroux address one more time.

_____

LEROUX TOOK A LAST LOOK around. He put the TV volume back on and patted himself again to be sure he felt his cash and traveler's checks in the ziplock bag. He had placed two trash bags over his pack, which was squished onto the car floor behind the seats. Earlier he had carried to the car another bag of remaining clothes and stuff sacks, along with the original bag of trash and receipts to be thrown away. He grabbed his poles and locked up. He hid the poles under his shell and threw them into the trunk. The trunk lid was halfway down when Leroux stuck his hand under it to stop it, and caught a finger on the latch. He yanked his finger free, stuck it in his mouth, and sucked on blood—he'd forgotten the bike.

At half past eleven that morning, Leroux drove out of his driveway for the last time. Seven minutes later, Patrolman Wallace stared at the drawn blinds of Leroux's house. He parked the squad car in the driveway and glanced again through the garage window on his way to the house. He rapped sharply on the back door.

CHAPTER TWELVE

AWOL APPROACHED WOOD'S HOLE SHELTER in the afternoon. He had just hiked twelve of the twenty-seven miles since his first step north from Springer Mountain. It'd been raining all day and he was glad to see the wooden sign on the oak directing him to the shelter. He turned onto a path lined with bluets and stopped to enjoy the beauty of the moment. On his way again, he crossed a creek where he filled his water bottles and bag. The creek was running fast from all the rain, and the water felt ice-cold as it splattered on his hand and wrist.

Four people were in the lean-to and two of them had already squirmed into their sleeping bags. Those two announced themselves as Baby Steps and Turtle, petite girls with tired faces. The other hikers were Dreamwalker and Beetle, two young men he'd already met. He had gotten used to the constant use of trail names; no thru-hiker on the Appalachian Trail used his or her given name.

"Want to sign in, Awol?" Beetle handed him the hiker register.

"Yeah." Awol opened to the entries for Sunday, March 16, and learned that a dozen people had come by. Awol looked over the comments. Most complained about rain; many complained about blisters. Some scribbles were hopeful. Awol wrote, "Piece of cake."

With space in the lean-to and rain-soaked duff covering the forest floor wherever he looked, he opted to bed inside. He untied his mattress sack from the bottom of his pack, took out the air mattress, and blew it up. Pulling out the trash bag that held his sleeping bag, Awol dumped it out and rolled the bag down the length of the mattress. He draped the trash bag over the bottom of his sleeping bag. All this he'd accomplished while standing outside under the front overhang. He hopped up onto the shelter floor and sat on the trash bag, took off his boots and squeezed the water out of his socks and hung them over an inside clothesline. His hooded shell he hung on a nail. After getting out his dry nightwear, he moved to the inside back corner of the lean-to and discretely peeled off the rest of his clothes, replacing them with dry underwear and shorts. After wringing out the clothes and hanging them over the line, Awol unpacked a paper-thin camp shell and put it on.

Awol felt more comfortable and put on dry socks and sandals to give his feet a break. Later he would put on the ski hat stuffed in his pocket. Plugger and Amble, whom he'd met before, arrived and everybody adjusted their bed rolls to make room.

"You all like this rain?" Plugger yelled to the group, as he doffed his pack. Several days removed from his last shave, Plugger looked scruffy, a black beard beginning to take hold on his broad, happy face. The other hiker, Amble, was quiet. He pulled out a bag of gorp and offered some to the girls. Each of them took a handful.

"Just don't let it snow." Baby Steps said. "How can you see where to step if the trail is covered with snow?"

"Might have to get snowshoes," Plugger laughed.

Awol listened to the banter as he wrote in his journal. Later he cooked a meal of freeze-dried chicken stew. Still later, after six more hikers tramped to the hut and set up in front of and around the group, he pulled out gingersnaps and bit off pieces while hikers traded tales, asked questions about upcoming terrain, requested or gave help regarding equipment, offered water, discussed blisters, aches, and injuries, struck up friendships and quiet alliances, yearned for sunshine and warmer nights, and restudied maps of tomorrow's plans. By 7:30 that evening everyone was hooded up in their bags and only the girls whispered to each other in the dark. Awol snored.

LATE SUNDAY AFTERNOON ON MARCH 16, Chief Stevens was in his Bryson City office studying a state police report he had received that cross-referenced the files of Wrangler owners in North Carolina. He had already heard from Frank, who'd looked at the Jeep in his area and had found no suspicious damage. Stevens found no Jeep owner in North Carolina had served time and no one listed had been indicted. He was studying the list again for possible clues, when he took a call from Chief Gary Odle, his counterpart in Franklin.

"Got a person of interest on the edge of town—a Paul Leroux," Gary said. "My patrolman didn't find the guy at home, but saw the Wrangler in his garage through the window."

"Yeah?"

"I told him if he could raise the garage door, to take a look at it. He did, and there's a dent on the passenger side by the mirror, and the mirror is shaky."

"Got anything on him?"

"Clean."

"Is someone watching his house?"

"Don't have the man power, Roland."

"Gary, if this guy Leroux doesn't come back, can one of your guys roll the Jeep out of the garage? So I can take a close look at it?"

"Risky. Leroux could contest in court that we went into his closed garage without a warrant."

"Not a problem if the Jeep somehow got outside."

"Let me call you back."

CHAPTER THIRTEEN

Phoebe was still smiling as she emerged from the motel office. Her pack and poles lay on a plastic chair next to a beat-up planter that offered cigarette butts and dirty, colorful bits of chewed gum. Leroux pressed a button releasing the passenger door lock. Before he stepped out, she had grabbed her pack and walked to the rear of the vehicle.

"Let me help you with that." The trunk was not fully closed because of the bike handlebars; Leroux had tied a piece of rope from the trunk latch to the bumper. Leroux eased the pack onto the back seat while she turned to get her poles. He eyed her sleek legs—she sported tan hiking shorts and boots with gaiters.

"Sure do appreciate the ride," she said. "Sorry about the Jeep."

"Yeah, it's in the shop. No problem, glad to do it."

He eased the Subaru onto the highway and shut off the radio—the local news had come on.

"Did you hear about the killer?" she said.

"Sure did. Terrible. You need to be careful, Phoebe."

"Shouldn't have to worry about him where I'm going."

Leroux reached for a cigarette. "No, I wouldn't think so. Where are you from?"

"Rhode Island. I go to Brown University in Providence."

"I see. Long ways away. What's your major?"

"Biology. I'm taking a semester off."

"Uh-huh. You have family in Rhode Island?" Her legs glowed beside him. Leroux adjusted his rearview mirror.

"My mother and sister live there. My father passed away last year."

"That's too bad. Rough on the family?"

"It was a long illness—cancer—so we knew it was coming. But . . ."

Leroux kept tapping the steering wheel with his fingers. "Let me know if the draft is too much," he said, lowering the window. "Don't you have someone to hike with?"

"I did, but she left. We started early, on March 1. The cold weather bothered her, I think."

"Most hikers start later?"

"Yeah, end of March, beginning of April. My sister gets married in August and I'm in the wedding, so I wanted to have plenty of time."

"I see." Leroux smoked. "Well, you need to stay alert, Phoebe. You're all alone—wait a minute, what about your friends that came with you?"

"They're gone. I only met them after I twisted my ankle; they just came in for supplies that day."

"So how is the ankle?"

"Much better, thanks."

"You won't hike far on it today, probably."

"No, it's just four miles to the next shelter. I took a late checkout so I could soak it this morning."

The shelter info squared with what Leroux had learned this morning from the thru-hiker handbook. And he'd found a gravel road, denoted on the map, which brought him to the A.T. a mile and change up from where he would drop her off.

"Looks like rain," she said. "Yuk."

Leroux pulled into the trailhead. Not a soul. He stepped around and opened the back door.

"Where is everybody?" he asked, as he pulled out her pack and poles. It was noon.

"Most hikers are still behind me."

"Well, you take care," he said, as he stuck out his hand. "You'll need to watch yourself so you don't slip again if it gets wet out."

"Thank you so much," she said, shaking his hand. Her grip was warm and sure. Still smiling, she turned and headed for the stream and footbridge.

A FEW MINUTES LATER, LEROUX parked his car off to the side, near the end of the up-trail graveled road. According to the map, the trail lay dead ahead about fifty yards. Working around the bike, he was able to stick his hand into the trunk and pull out his compact shovel. He folded up the head, stuck the shovel under his jacket, and pushed the handle under his belt. Angling further north around some brambles, he soon came to the trail. Leroux looked around the foot-and-a-half-wide path and hid in some ferns and scrub behind several pines. He was glad to see he was below a small ridge; perfect cover from hikers walking north or south. Everything was blooming or budding—bushes, trees, flowers. He imagined himself on the trail. He sniffed the air, sniffed again and listened. He was alone.

By the time Leroux spotted her, a hundred yards down-trail, he had already picked his spot. He didn't think anyone would be walking where he had in mind. She approached and paced by; the muscles in her calves and thighs twitched. Her hips rocked. She was still smiling.

Leroux drew behind her. He got within three yards, two—she was a yard in front of him. She hesitated and when she turned and looked up into his grin—just before he knew she'd scream—he short-jabbed her midriff.

"Phoebe! Where's that smile?"

CHAPTER FOURTEEN

THAT EVENING, LEROUX DROVE DOWN an alley and pulled up to the dumpster behind a hardware store. He saw no one. He slid out with the tied trash bags, raised the lid of the bin, and threw in the bags. He dropped his spare keys into an open cardboard-screw-box in the bin and closed the box. A black-and-white cat poked its head from under the loading dock and snaked over to Leroux. He reached down and frisked it around the ears, then hopped into the rental and drove away.

He parked in front of a food mart and shuffled in. Picking up a plastic basket near the door, he grabbed a box of ziplock bags, two Cokes, a large Italian sub—"The Works"—and a bag of Fritos. He walked up and down each aisle, stopping in front of stationery. He grabbed a notepad, a twin pack of Bic pens, and a bag of rubber bands. At the last minute, he selected a mini-flashlight and a box of Band-Aids. Clicking the light on and off, he proceeded to the counter.

Back in the car, the thrill of Phoebe worn off, Leroux again began to doubt his plan. *Shit, the freaking rain.* A mile later at a stoplight, *Why not pay cash for a room at Budget and leave tomorrow night? No. They've found me out from the Wrangler and are checking everywhere. Got to go; this is the perfect time to escape—a rainy Sunday night. I'm up for this.* Halfway to the plant, *I could drive north to some other town, let the rain ease up. But it means restudying maps, trying to find a different trailhead, and dealing with the car. No, stay on plan.* Driving the road up to the plant, *I ditch the bike in the area and tent near the trail tonight. Yeah, baby, this is going down.* He pulled into the lot.

He sat in the Subaru, fished in the bag for the sub, and opened a Coke. He looked out at the large warehouse where they assembled sets for furniture dealers in the area. He worked at the far end as a stainer and intercepted assemblies as they came off the line, an isolated job, which is why he took it. He wore a mask while handling the power sprayer and everyone pretty much left him alone. He didn't expect anyone to come by until six in the morning, when his supervisor arrived to open shop.

With a surge of resentment at having to flee again, Leroux thought about how he had gotten himself into this situation. Everything, he felt, could be traced back to one thing; his life changed when his mother started sleeping around and his father kicked her out. They'd been living in northern Maine, the next town over from his Canadian cousins, the Ouilettes. Leroux's father wanted to take Paul and his younger brother, George, back to Canada. But within twenty-four hours their mother had pulled them out of bed, packed them into their aging Toyota, and driven them to Florida to live with her sister. The same sick feeling of being taken away consumed Leroux now as he sat in the parking lot. He was twelve, and he cried all the way to Key West. They'd left behind his dog, his model cars, all their things. He never got to say good-bye to his friends or his cousins, and what bothered him most was that he never saw his father again.

Leroux tore into the sub. He'd hated Key West. The heat, the bugs, the constant parade of people and traffic, and watching his mother become the mirror image of her bed-hopping, bar-happy sister. Despite his pleas, his mother never agreed to go back to Maine, not even for a visit. Four years after their arrival, his mother and brother were in an accident. Crushed to death under a semi. She'd been on a three-day bender, and never knew what had hit her. George had taken a few hours to die.

Three days after the funeral, his drunken aunt tried to molest him under a knife, saying that at sixteen he was old enough now to take care of her. He resisted and she managed to pierce his shoulder with the knife before he wrestled her away and fled. After that, he grabbed the savings he'd been socking away to take him back to Maine, and left Key West for good with his friend Rick, who was seventeen.

The boys hitched from Key West to Rick's uncle in Memphis, where

Rick spent his summers. The uncle put them to work on his farm where they cultivated tomatoes, peppers, squash, asparagus, all day long under a hot sun for room and board and twelve dollars a week. On weekends, they were allowed to go into town, and that's where things took another turn for the worse. Rick had planned to introduce sixteen-year-old Paul to sex, and took him to the back-alley massage parlor where Rick had been initiated the summer before. It had been a tough time for Leroux; he wasn't stable. His brother and mother had been crushed to death. His aunt, a molester, had knifed him. He had no idea where his father was, but suspected he was in Canada. His aunt had no legal claim on him and he never wanted to see her again. Uprooted from all he knew for the second time in his life, Rick was his one friend.

He was excited to be in Memphis with Rick, but going to the cathouse didn't seem like a good idea. At the parlor, Leroux was scared. Rick had disappeared with a busty redheaded woman in a halter top who pretended to know him, and Leroux ended up in an upstairs room, struggling to unzip while an auburn-haired woman old enough to be his mother was counting the bills and coins he had handed her. The brunette sighed at the pocket change and shook her head as she turned around to Paul, who, Rick had told her with a big wink minutes ago, knew all about sex. "At least this will be quick," she sighed. She walked over to him and yanked on his zipper, which had caught on some threads of his tucked-in shirt. "Jesus Christ," she said to him, "can't you undress yourself? Hold still!" She tried yanking, then stepped back. He was humiliated, and panicked. With one great tug he ripped the pants around the zipper and pulled them down as he hobbled around on one leg. "Now look at what you done," she laughed.

Leroux saw the cruel smirk as she pulled off her shirt. She jiggled her tits as she drew closer to him, just as Leroux started to ask something. This was all happening too fast and he wasn't ready. She held up a finger, "Save it, Sonny. So you know all about sex, huh? Let's see whatcha got," she said, as she grabbed and yanked down his briefs.

Reliving this, Leroux seethed in the car. He still fantasized about finding that bitch and making her suffer. Six years later he'd gone back to Memphis to find her, but the parlor was closed and no one knew anything about her. He remembered her staring at his flaccid dick when

she pulled down his briefs. *All I needed was a touch, a little understanding.*
"I'm not good enough for you, Sonny? Are you gay or something?"

"No, no, it's just . . . ," he tried to tell her.

"Don't expect your money back. If you can't do your job, I can't do
mine. Get out of here. You're wasting my time." She opened the door and
pushed him out, as he shuffled and tripped over his ruined pants, and a
few minutes later, after Rick finished, the brunette grabbed Rick in front
of Leroux to whisper something in his ear. Rick looked at Leroux's ripped
pants, then at his face, and howled.

Leroux smacked the roof in the car. *I got something that'd straighten
that cunt out now.*

Leroux raged in his vehicle and remembered a time two years after
that summer. A town in West Virginia. On a feverish summer night he
had a sweet gal in the truck down by the lake, a cutie he had met in a
diner earlier in the evening. They necked and Leroux was aroused. He
asked her to unzip him and she hesitated. He realized that he wanted to
smack her for that hesitation. He did. The shocked, fearful look in her
eyes became her downfall. Leroux fisted a tuft of hair from the back of
her head and smacked her again, harder. His cock became enormous as
she covered her face with her hands, and wept. "Put your hands down,"
Leroux commanded in a steady, even tone. He was in charge now. She
complied. "Now, you gonna do what I tell you, sweetheart?" She squeaked
out, "Yes." He told her again to unzip him. She pulled down the zipper.
"Now take it out." She peeked out the window and Leroux belted her a
good one on the side of her head. Her brown hair flopped across her face
and a rose colored barrette fell out. He held up his still closed fist under
her nose, "You're not paying me close attention, sweetie." He spoke with
authority; his prick felt ready to burst. "Now I'm gonna ask you again,
nicely, Take . . . It . . . Out." Sweetie moved quicker and when she had
all of it in her trembling hands, she looked up at him, terrified. Her
head was tilted up and angled to the side as she sniffled, "Please." Leroux
absorbed the exhilaration, the power of dominating a woman. He lifted
her chin with his little finger, the rest of his fist still closed, "Much better,
sweetie. Now you know what you're gonna do for me, and it'd better be
good." When he was satisfied, feeling like a king, he dumped her off at
the corner. Leroux blew town right afterward.

LEROUX FINISHED THE LAST OF his sub and took out the bag of Fritos. With oily hands he wrestled with the Fritos bag, trying to open it. *The strongest man in the world, if he has greasy hands*—POP—the bag spilled open and corn chips flipped around the seat, into his lap, onto the floor. He started picking up Fritos close to him, popping them into his mouth. He opened the other Coke, guzzled the fizzing liquid and munched. *If they find Phoebe, I'm fucked.* He began to fret again. *Why did I have to do her on the trail?*

He glanced at his rearview and side mirrors. After two smokes, Leroux got to work. From his rearview mirror he'd counted twenty vehicles that had driven by. After rearranging his pack, which had taken an hour as he tried to find more space, thought what to put in each of the pockets, and figured ways to protect his food and cigs, he realized he had not filled his water bottles. *Jesus!* Luckily, he still had the key to a side door of the shop at the far end of the warehouse, given to him as the third backup person to open shop if no one else could.

He walked over with his new flashlight and let himself in. In the tiny restroom he tried to position his water bottle under the faucet. The bottle was too tall. He shined the light around the office and spied a coffee cup holding pens and pencils. After cleaning the cup under gushing water, he used it to pour cold water into his bottles. As he was about to leave, he beamed the flashlight around. He figured there was nothing he needed, but couldn't resist grabbing a short hammer/ax combo amongst the tools lying in the tool crib. At 8:55 p.m., he returned to the car. He locked himself inside and after running the heat on high, full blast, for fifteen minutes, he turned off the engine, tilted the seat back, and slept.

CHAPTER FIFTEEN

AROUND MIDNIGHT THAT SAME SUNDAY, patrolman Cooper of the Franklin Police, in civilian clothes, drove up in front of Leroux's house in an unmarked car with his lights off. In the passenger seat sat an informer well-known to the department. The street was dark, quiet. The passenger stepped out and went to Leroux's garage, eased the door up, and disappeared inside. A minute later, Leroux's Wrangler rolled out into his driveway, the only noise the faint sound of rubber moving over wet asphalt. The man gently closed the garage door and stepped back into Cooper's car as Cooper pulled away.

AT THE SAME TIME THE informer was complicating Leroux's life, Leroux pulled his bicycle from the Subaru's trunk and locked the car. A dim security light glowed over the entrance to the offices of the plant. The night was silent and black; rain still fell, but not as hard. Leroux set his pack on the hood of the auto and swung himself into it. It took several minutes to adjust the straps; still, the pack felt heavy, unwieldy. He got on his mountain bike, took three or four full pedals and abruptly circled back to the car. He unlocked the car and retrieved his poles. He collapsed them and worked them into place under the rope of the tent sack. After taking a final look around, he locked the car, shifted into the pack again, and remounted the bike.

For the first mile or so, Leroux had no problem. The grade was flat.

Then he started uphill and had to crank hard; halfway up he got off his bike and walked it. When he got to the top he coasted down, but in less than a minute, he headed into another rise. He didn't remember these ups and downs. At two miles he came to a flat section but heard an approaching vehicle. He hurried off the bike, walked it to the side of the road and lay down in the muddy ditch with it until the car passed.

Leroux knew he couldn't continue much longer on the bike. The pack was too heavy, his butt was sore, his knees were burning, and he was huffing and puffing. The small rises had taken out his legs even though the overall grade had been relatively flat. Leroux flicked sweat from his cheeks and guzzled water. He walked a while with the bike. If he remained on the road, he would come to the Forest Service Road leading to the trail.

He tried the bike again, but it was no use. He didn't have the legs to tackle even a slight change in grade. Seeing a silo up ahead on the left, Leroux neared a gravel driveway leading to a rambling farm house. He crossed the road and left the bike leaning against the mailbox. He headed the bike in the opposite direction; let some kid have it, he thought. He recrossed the road and walked again, figuring he'd gone three miles. Again, he heard a vehicle from behind and stepped off into the weeds and mud, lying down until he heard the pickup roar into the night.

A hundred yards farther, near a lone street light, Leroux spotted a definitive path angling to the right. He'd get off the road. This path angled, in Leroux's estimation, as a hypotenuse, and would save the time of walking another mile to Forest Service Road and then taking a right and hiking a good mile on that to finally reach the A.T. Leroux slid onto the path.

Without the occasional street light, he ran into his first problem: blackout. He took out his flashlight and walked for a while until he ran into his second problem: a pond. He banked to the left and started counting steps; in the event that he couldn't see the path, he figured he'd circle the pond once, then count out half the steps again before heading in approximately the same direction. But in the dark, Leroux lost the path and added steps. When he'd circled the pond and started counting again, he overshot and threw off his angle. Now, he couldn't find any path at all. He looked around, hoping to find a way through the undergrowth in front of him. With the pond in back of him, he beamed the light to find some type of clearing. He took what appeared to be the easiest way and tramped forward, but couldn't see worth a damn and kept stumbling. And swearing. And stumbling. He needed his poles and took off the pack. Holding the flashlight in his mouth, he untied his poles. He wanted his headlamp but couldn't remember where he had buried it, and with the rain he didn't want to open up his pack and get everything wet.

Leroux held the light in his mouth and wheezed for oxygen as he kept driving the poles to push himself through brambles and thickets. He was powerful enough to muscle through, but he had no endurance, and had completely exhausted himself. After swigging water, he busted his way through to a clearing and sat down. He took the light out of his mouth and several minutes later caught his breath. Lost. He'd have to camp here for the night.

Holding the light again in his mouth, Leroux untied his tent bag. *Thank God I learned how to do this before I left.* He spilled out the tent poles and anchor stakes from the sack. The ground was level and after kicking away a few rocks and branches, he set up. The tent took time to erect in the rain, which was falling harder, and the light kept jiggling as he sought to find the proper grommets and clips for attaching the support poles. Eventually he finished; the tent fit well and was anchored in its chosen spot. Leroux fastened the rainfly and crawled inside. Crouching over his pack, he untied the sack containing his mattress. After angling the flashlight from a side tent pocket, he found the black rubber valve stem at the end and started blowing into it, huffing and blowing under the dull glow of indirect light, as the mattress unfolded like a giant streamer. After several more blows he twisted the cap and angled the mattress so he could fit in the tent without his legs sticking out. He felt his soaked pack. The inside was moist, but the sleeping bag was dry.

Minutes later, after a smoke, after removing the wet leggings and shell, his boots and socks, Leroux, with effort, worked his way into the bag. He switched off the flashlight and listened to the steady patter of rain on the tent. He zipped up the bag to his chin and pulled the hood of the bag around his head, feeling warm and dry. *Not too shabby. And I've escaped.* Staring at the pitch-dark canvas roof and listening to the rain, he felt ballsy about pulling off his plan. Just as he started to get drowsy and warm, Leroux began to feel the Fritos, the sub, and untold number of snacks pushing down through his intestines. He tried squeezing his legs, but that just made it worse.

CHAPTER SIXTEEN

MORNING. LEROUX WAS SORE AND chilled as he emerged from his tent. Drizzle had soaked the forest floor, and fog obscured his view. He had no idea where he was and couldn't see much more than he could last night, so he squirmed back into his tent to make coffee. Leroux found his stove and set it up like the clerk at the store had shown him. He unfolded the pan, filled it with water, and set it on the stove. He couldn't find the fuel tabs and as he ransacked through his pack, he knocked the pan of water off his stove into the hood of his open sleeping bag. *Shit!* He grabbed his sock, lying there from last night, and wiped up water inside the hood. Some of the water ran down the side of the bag and into Leroux's briefs. As he jerked his butt up, the last of the water flowed underneath him so when he planted his butt down again he felt the icy water soak his scrotum.

Fussing around, Leroux found the plastic bag of tabs and refilled the pan with water. He lit the fuel tab positioned under the pan and put the lid on. Leroux watched the stove, smoked, waited. After several minutes he heard the water boil, which he added to the coffee grounds. A few moments later, he took his first sip, and smiled. He extracted packets of cheese and crackers from the food bag. He was surprised he wanted liquids more than food; he sipped water while finishing a packet of crackers and made another cup of coffee.

Leroux managed to put on dry clothes, repack his stove and mess kit, and get somewhat organized without any more mishaps. He looked at the map, and located the pond he had encountered last night. Although he couldn't see the sun itself, he could discern a low glow behind the fog and clouds. Knowing that to be east, he positioned himself toward what he reasoned was north. If he continued northwest, eventually he'd cross either the Forest Service Road, or the trail. With renewed confidence, Leroux disassembled the tent and packed up. He hoisted the pack onto his shoulders and began bushwhacking with his ax.

Thirty minutes and a half-mile later, Leroux realized he'd forgotten his trekking poles. *"Fuck!"* He started again. Then he remembered what Mike had told him at the store. The last thing he needed out here was a knee problem, and if anyone needed poles and the advantages they offered, it was he. Leroux fingered a Marlboro and headed back to the campsite.

———————

MEANWHILE, CHIEF STEVENS WAS IN Franklin examining the passenger side of Leroux's Wrangler. He pulled back the loosened side mirror, and with tweezers, picked out a twig caught behind it. The end was torn off. He placed it in a plastic bag, examined the door at the bottom and discovered pine needles. He put them in the bag. Stevens moved to the hood and picked out two pieces of pinecone buried in the seam where the hood closed to the frame. He felt around by the front bumper and found a pinecone squished between the bumper and the front of the vehicle. That went in the bag as well.

"Gary, let's get a warrant."

———————

IN LESS THAN TWO HOURS they had their warrant and were prying open the side door of Leroux's house. They entered Leroux's kitchen at 11:15 a.m., and in no time, they had Leroux's bathroom comb, with several hairs attached, and Leroux's toothbrush sealed in an evidence bag. They retrieved fingerprints from the phone. Stevens was rifling through Leroux's pants, which he had pulled from the bedroom hamper, and from a pocket he pulled out a twig and leaf. As Stevens put them into his bag, he noticed the end of the twig he found in the pant pocket had a small paint chip attached, the same green of the Jeep. Upon leaving the house and proceeding to Drexel Furniture, hoping to make an arrest, Chief

Stevens was figuring out how he could steal the spotlight from Gary and make an announcement to the press first.

LEROUX SLAPPED AT A BRANCH that snapped in his face and stumbled over roots in the sylvan land. He wanted to crush something. It had been an hour since he had turned back toward the campsite. Somehow he'd veered off his bushwhacked trail and found himself back at the pond. He tried going back again the way he thought he had last night from the pond, to look for the campsite. He was still looking as he thrashed about, stumbling and muttering. At last Leroux stopped and sat on a log in the light rain to try to regain his senses. *So what if the poles are found and who would find them anyway if I can't? I'll find some in a day or two. Gotta get on this damn trail.* Settled, he hauled himself up, looked for the glow to his right where the sun should be, and took a course north by northwest. Five minutes later, Leroux came upon the tent site and picked up his hiking poles, right where he'd left them.

AT 11:15 THE GLOW FROM the sun, still behind clouds in the drizzle, had moved so high in the sky Leroux was not sure which way was true east. He looked at the map but couldn't figure out where he was.

Just don't panic. He worried that he might not have gone far enough west and saw that if he went too far to the north, he'd miss intersecting the trail. *I'll have to wait it out and watch the sun sink west. Then I'll keep a little north of west and go as far as I can. I don't like it, but there it is.*

He sat against a rock. Pine and oak trees offered cover from the rain, and he had room to set up his tent if he had to. Leroux pulled out his stove and opened a packet of noodles. He poured water into the cook pot and his stomach took a turn—*water.* He was almost out. He had enough to cook with but no more to drink. He felt helpless as he tracked his water usage; two bottles to start, but a bottle used last night while biking and this morning for the coffee-making ordeal. Today a new bottle, but he'd needed it to hike and didn't realize—*Christ!* He stopped pouring and stared at the pot. With a sigh, lips pursed, he trembled while emptying the water from the pot back into the bottle. He couldn't believe his stupidity and felt once again this entire escape plan was, for him, preposterous. He made a lunch of two chewy bars and packed up. He considered going back to the pond for water, but realized it would be a total defeat; he needed to find a stream, not a dirty pond. He did have a half bottle of water left. He studied the map again and noted streams due west. *Should I go now, or wait until the sun falls?* Leroux tensed. *Got to do something. I'll walk left of the glow in the sky. As the sun sinks I can follow it true west.* This time he remembered to look around before leaving, and collected his poles.

CHAPTER SEVENTEEN

MIDAFTERNOON, LEROUX'S EARS PICKED UP a faint sound. His left heel bothered him; his throat was parched. He had a mouthful of water left. He sat down for a moment and tried to hear the sound again. He untied his left boot and lifted off the sock, fingered the blister, and rebooted. He picked himself up and continued to bushwhack while trying to keep the sun at two o'clock. He heard the sound again. He worried it might be rain creeping toward him and then had an epiphany. He cocked his head and cupped an ear to the sound. He tramped several more yards, stopped and closed his eyes. With conviction he headed left and soon the sound became unmistakable—running water. Leroux bounded through a thicket down to a ravine with a stream, no longer feeling the blister on his heel. He threw off his pack and dropped the poles. He stepped to the edge, stooped down, and splashed water on his face and the back of his neck. Then, still dripping, he uncapped his water bottle and gulped what was left.

After Leroux filled his bottles, treated the water, and ate, he got out his field guide about the trail, and read up on the southern Appalachian forest. *Got to keep my ass in gear out here.* Trees of basswood, birch, and ash surrounded him. The odor he'd been smelling turned out to be skunk cabbage. *Need to pay attention to everything; this is my home now. I need to study the thru-hiker handbook and learn all this hiking stuff. Dad would have liked that.* He looked at the sun, half-covered with clouds and falling into the west. With renewed energy, he picked up his poles and checked to make sure he had everything. He headed straight for the sun.

Thirty minutes later Leroux was moving at a snail's pace. He'd encountered a rock ledge that extended to his right and left and appeared impossible to get around. Stopping to check his map again, he saw concentric spirals drawn west of the ravine and stream now behind him. He was convinced by the map that he was headed dead on for the A.T., save for this mountain in front of him. What he hadn't realized was how far north of west he'd gone. *I will never again do something like this without a compass.* He realized he wouldn't even get close to the A.T. tonight; a reasonable goal would be to climb this ledge and camp on top of the bald—elevation 2,927 feet—the map showed. But only if he could make it before sundown.

An hour later Leroux understood that he wouldn't make it to the summit. His blister had become more than a bother, and if he wasn't prudent he would run out of water again. The grade steepened and the sun had disappeared behind the mountain. Leroux retreated to the top of the ledge and set up his tent under a louring sky. He heard thunder and it started to rain again. At six o'clock, lightning flashed as he crawled, exhausted, into his tent.

A thunderstorm washed over the area. As rain beat on the tent, and as he watched lightning through the flaps and listened to the accompanying thunder, he remembered a documentary about some famous general who said, "A step backward is sometimes necessary for a victorious step forward."

After the storm passed, after popping and tending to the blister, after noodles and cocoa, he sat bone-weary in dry clothes in his tent and said a prayer to the Almighty, or to whomever it was that might forgive, and help. *I'm a wretched soul. A twisted, damaged brute. Bring me out of this— deliver me—and I will begin a new life, one of atonement.*

Settled and hopeful, he slept soundly through the night.

CHAPTER EIGHTEEN

THE FOLLOWING MORNING, TUESDAY, MARCH 18, Chief Stevens of Bryson City, took a phone call from Chief Frank Porter, his counterpart in Sylva.

"They got a match for our case. The DNA from this guy Leroux, in Franklin, matches DNA we got from our victim's fingernails."

"Okay! That's what I needed to hear."

Chief Stevens recalled the Sylva case, a female beaten and strangled and found in a shallow grave at an abandoned factory site fourteen months ago. If he remembered right, the victim was a thirty-three-year-old secretary. "Anything on Gary's vic?"

"Also a match. Just talked to him. Has to be the same guy for your woman."

Gary's victim had been a new mother, only twenty-seven, also raped, beaten, and strangled eight months ago near Rainbow Springs. Chief Stevens felt a surge of optimism. Nothing back yet on a DNA match with his victim, but he was certain it was coming. This was a huge development; he reminded himself that he'd taken the lead in finding the murderer, and would surely be recognized.

After talking with Gary and again with Frank, Chief Stevens reviewed the plan with Vickers. "He's blown town; he didn't show up at work, and he hasn't been home." He pushed paper to Vickers, "We divvy up the work; here are the places we contact: bus stations, car rentals, trains . . ." "What about an APB?" Vickers asked.

"State's got it handled." The chief handed Vickers a blow-up of Leroux's picture, taken from his driver's license, "This will be on the news tonight and it's being sent everywhere."

"We can feel good about this, Chief."

Stevens was silent for a moment. "Vickers, I want us to be the ones who capture this guy."

LEROUX WOKE EARLY. HE NUDGED a new blister on his toe, winced, retrieved a pack of soggy Marlboros and threw it down in disgust. Rain thumped on the tent. Determined to have a smoke, he reached into his backpack and pulled out the squished, damp carton. He was ornery and wondered where the hope was that he'd had upon falling asleep mere hours ago.

At eight that morning, Leroux started up again from the ledge. It didn't take long for him to begin to slip and slide. The combination of mud and ruts, Leroux's aches and poor physical condition, and a pack that added sixty pounds, contributed to his agony. No trail to follow, he had to bushwhack.

TWO HOURS LATER, LEROUX COLLAPSED next to a stump. His hands trembled as he twisted off the cap to his water bottle. He couldn't drink much or he'd run out. He looked up, trying to imagine the summit. The rain had eased and the mud had lessened, but he was only halfway.

Leroux loosened his boots; the bandage had worked its way off the heel blister and his wet sock had rubbed it raw. The toe of his other blistered foot throbbed; he felt the sock pinching it. Leroux pulled up both socks and retied his boots. After another swallow of water he capped the bottle and reflected that this and whatever happened over the next months was the price he had to pay for his crimes. He convinced himself if he bore up, he might, at least in his own eyes, become deserving of a better life. He told himself this was his way of "doing time." He climbed again.

AT NOON, LEROUX REACHED THE summit. It was windy and bare of trees. The rain had turned to a mist and between clouds, he saw sun. He took out his map, which was folded to show the area and sealed in a zip-lock bag, as the guidebook had suggested. Leroux looked through the plastic at the map and back to the horizon. On top of this bald, despite patches of fog, he had a view. He confirmed terrain, mountains, and ponds matching his map and ran his finger down where the trail should be: *over* here *and straight across to* there—*not far, once I get down.*

With renewed hope, Leroux dug out food. He ate nuts, two oatmeal chewy bars, three slices of bread with peanut butter, crackers and cheese, and took sips of water. He knew he'd be able to get more water because he could see it; the issue was how long it might take to get there. Beyond the tableland below him, he could make out a snakelike shimmer of river where, according to his map, the A.T. crossed. He secured the water bottle—a third was left—and packed up.

Two hours later, Leroux stepped on a rock that chose to wobble, and down he went, his head scraping the rock he had stepped on. Untwisting his leg and sitting up, he wiped the smear of blood off the side of his head and looked at a grotesquely bent hiking pole. He jammed the point of the pole into the dirt and pulled on the crooked stick attempting to bend it straight. It snapped. Leroux's quads burned as he stabbed the remaining pole into the ground and bumbled his way down.

He reached the bottom in the late afternoon, looking like a monster out of a comic book: ripped leggings, torn sleeve, blood caked on the side of his head, a clean pole in one hand, and a tree branch for a crutch in the other. He threw down the branch and without stopping, eyes fixed to a spot, stumbled on. At least the rain had stopped.

IN BRYSON CITY, CHIEF STEVENS was in a conference call with Gary in Franklin, Frank in Sylva, the FBI in Raleigh, and the governor of North Carolina. Stevens spooned more sugar into his coffee mug and stirred while sitting at his desk in front of the speakerphone. Vickers sat in a chair facing the chief.

"Chief Stevens, what can you report?" the governor asked.

"I'm afraid, Governor, I have nothing positive to report yet about the suspect's whereabouts. We've checked everything."

"You're saying we have no trace, no leads, nothing?"

"We did find his rental car parked at his place of employment, Governor. That's all we've got this far."

Silence. "So," the governor replied in a mocking tone, "am I given to understand this man, Leroux, has simply disappeared off the face of the Earth?"

STOOPED AND FAVORING HIS RIGHT leg, a hiker emerged from a copse of pines. With a lone hiking pole he pushed himself up a small rise. The battered man slowed down and stopped at the top. He turned his head to the right and dropped to his knees.

Leroux stared at the narrow path not fifteen yards in front of him. Again he turned his head to the right where he saw, painted on a tree, as shown on the front of his A.T. map, a crisp blaze of white, one of many thousands marking the Appalachian Trail from Georgia to Maine. Miraculously, a lowering sun emerged from behind the clouds in front of him. The rays of sunlight made the white blaze shine like a beacon, and Leroux perceived it as a sign giving him his wish for a new beginning, right here, right now. Still on his knees, he looked at the path beyond the blaze. Paul Gaston Leroux pushed himself up with his pole and trudged north.

PART TWO

---

*A desperate disease requires a
dangerous remedy.*

—Guy Fawkes

"**D**AMNIT, LINDA. WHY CAN'T YOU accept that I *am* doing this for us? It's not selfish." Awol sat on the motel bed. "Wait a minute . . . just listen to me . . . I don't want to lose you, but I need this . . . uh-huh . . . I don't know, and I won't make up any excuses—I should have shared some of my shit with you; I was wrong not to . . . but I step into North Carolina tomorrow, and I'm committed to seeing this through . . . I know that's the way you feel, but what am I supposed to do here. . . ? Right, I see . . . Well, Linda, if this is the end for us, are you going to say something sweet for me to remember you by?"

Awol looked into the receiver end of the phone before slamming it in the cradle. "Evidently not." He listened to several semis roll by and peeked behind the drawn shade. Rain, rain, nothing but rain, and he was craving a drink for one of the first times since he'd started the hike. It was the afternoon of March 22, his first day off—a zero day hikers called it—after seven consecutive days of hiking. He was in Hiawassee, Georgia, and it had felt good to get the mail drop he'd sent to the PO, to take a hot shower and soak, to do laundry, eat, and prepare the next mail drop for Fontana Dam, ninety-six miles ahead. But the argument with Linda upset him. She was sticking to her word that it was over, and he felt miserable about it. He'd hoped she would change her mind.

He agonized again about stepping out for a drink, just one, but fought to push it out of his mind. That's the way it was for him; when he was active, moving, accomplishing, he didn't think about the booze, which had derailed him. The last time had been five weeks ago, when the pressure and guilt inside became too much. He'd barely survived that one. Now, using every ounce of willpower in him, he forced himself to take another hot shower, and went to bed early.

The next morning he felt more settled, as if he had passed some sort of a beginner's test. He was ready for the miles ahead, and the day brought sunshine as he headed toward Dick's Creek Gap. Yesterday in Hiawassee he had met several hikers, and three of them were with him now. They had hitched a ride from the motel to the trail in the back of a blue Chevy pickup driven by a heavyset lady and her pooch. The day was alive with hope and good cheer, hopes for sun, hopes for good health and no injury in the months and miles ahead. In other words, the hope of making it.

One of the young hikers stepping down from the tailgate was Nightwind, and although she was hopeful like the others, she was also upset because her hiking partner had taken a bus back to Maryland early that morning. Her partner had wanted to quit after the third day and Nightwind had talked her out of it. "Sue," Nightwind had begged, no longer bothering with her friend's trail name, "please don't make any decisions until we take our zero in Hiawassee. You'll feel better then, I promise." At the motel, in tears, Sue had complained of blisters, the "goddamned rain, the fog, what's the point? You can't even see anything. One day off isn't going to change that." Nightwind understood, but told her to sleep on it, knowing full well Sue was going to go back to Maryland. Sue had managed a laugh at the bus stop, "Maybe next year we do Everest." Nightwind waved good-bye as the bus pulled away. She met and confided in Awol as she walked back to the motel to get her pack.

"What you need to do, Nightwind, is let it go." He moved to the curb and gave her the inside as vehicles drove past. "Perhaps it was meant to be, so put her out of your mind for now. You'll meet new friends on the trail, and if you're going to make it, you need to stay positive."

"Oh I know. It's just . . ." She looked up at a flag waving from a pole on a school lawn. "Here we are at war, with soldiers dying in Iraq, and I'm upset because my friend doesn't want to hike with me anymore. Guess I'm being stupid."

"No." Awol gazed at the flag, "You're human and feel alone. But you'll get through it." He looked up at the flag again, "We all do, one way or another."

NIGHTWIND HIKED WITH AWOL INTO the gap. Mountains on the west side of the pass peaked into morning sun; mountains on the right were backlit. High Octane and Krazy K were ahead of them and when the path narrowed into a tunnel of silky-white rhododendrons and they had to go single file, Nightwind slowed to take the rear. Over the next months, they all would hike over this great mountain system of eastern North America. Some states used regional names for their section of the trail: Vermont's Green Mountains; New Hampshire's White Mountains; the Allegheny Mountains, the Catskills, the Great Smoky Mountains, which they would tackle soon; all these mountains, and others, constituted the Appalachian chain, which ran from the province of Quebec, Canada to northern Alabama.

Awol thought he heard a sniffle behind him, but it might have been his imagination.

"Nightwind, I don't mind if you hike with me until you feel better."

"Thanks, appreciate it. I'll try not to slow you down."

"You won't. Don't be offended if I don't say much."

THEY STOPPED TO REST AND eat at noon next to a stream bordered by flat rocks facing up to the sun. Awol filled a water bottle, and took off his boots and socks. He watched Nightwind as she took out bread, peanut butter, and jam from her pack. She had an attractive, narrow face with hazel eyes set close together. She kept her dark wavy hair up, wrapped in a bandanna, while she hiked. She had an athletic body; Awol estimated she was no more than twenty-five.

"Your feet sore, Awol?"

"No. Learned a long time ago, the best way to avoid blisters is to air out feet and socks when you break."

"Want some gorp?" She offered her bag and he took a handful.

Several minutes passed as they watched the stream ripple over rocks and meander toward the basin. Through the linden and tulip trees, they distinguished white starbursts of bloodroot along the ridge.

"Those white blossoms are pretty," she said.

"Pretty but potent. That's bloodroot; the roots exude a poisonous sap that can burn your skin."

"Oh."

He watched her think about that and turn her head to other spots. "Soon we'll be in North Carolina. You ever been there?" Awol said.

"I passed through it by car, when my folks took my sister and me to Disney World. We were little so I don't remember. You've been there?"

"Visited the Marine training facility at Camp Lejeune once. My uncle trained there during Vietnam."

"Were you in the military?"

"Army." Awol made a cheese sandwich with the pumpernickel he had bought in town.

"Did you go overseas?"

"Gulf War. First one."

"Was it as crazy over there as it is now?"

Awol took his time answering. "Yes."

They watched the water gurgle over rocks. He turned his socks over and angled the boots to sunlight. After his sandwich and a puddin' stick, Awol lay on his back and closed his eyes, letting the sun beam down on him. He squinted open his eyes to see Nightwind do the same.

Awol heard that she had a boyfriend and arrested any thoughts of a fling, common as it was out here in the wilderness. He yearned for Linda. She was the one who kept him stable. When he did go off on the occasional binge, although she disapproved, she didn't nag him and seemed to understand it was his way of coping. Why did he keep pushing her away? He thought of the Persian Gulf, Desert Storm, and then Linda again. She was the human resources manager at a bank in Boston, and he understood why. She was an expert in dealing with people and never held a grudge. Awol chuckled to himself as he remembered how exasperated she became when arguing with him, shaking her head, throwing up her hands. But she would be the first to laugh at the situation, and make up. Except for this time.

He resolved to enjoy these precious minutes of sun; the weather often turned in the mountains, and he recalled from his map the upcoming climb to Sassafras Gap, before reaching Muskrat Creek Shelter. He squinted toward Nightwind again. She was relaxed, on her back with her knees up, absorbing the sun. *God, she's pretty.*

As they packed up a short while later, they heard voices. Three hikers broke into the clearing: Blue Sky, Vagabond, and Songbird, who was glad to see Nightwind.

"Hey, Nightwind. Where's your partner?" Songbird asked.

"Well . . ."

Touching Nightwind's boot with his stick, Awol said, "I'll save a spot for you at Muskrat. See you all in North Carolina."

Later at camp—he hadn't been successful in saving her space inside the shelter—seeing she was exhausted from the climb, Awol walked over to Nightwind's tent with hot noodles. She accepted them and joined him outside at the fire pit, where the pungent smell of hickory smoke filled the air. She ate quietly as the fire crackled, and Awol sensed she would tough it out.

Later, back in his tent, Awol completed his journal, pulled in the day's clothes he had aired under the sun's waning rays and, with his headlamp, read from *Life of Pi,* given to him in Hiawassee by a hiker, in exchange for *A Rumor of War.* He'd been interested in the parallels of Vietnam to his experience in the Gulf, but now he was in the mood for something lighter, something that might take his mind far away from war and grief. He was sound asleep by eight o'clock.

Next morning Awol broke camp early and, before leaving, walked over to Nightwind's tent, where she sat on a log, putting on her boots.

"Be good, Nightwind; see you on the trail."

"Okay, Awol. Hey, Awol?" She gave him a relaxed smile and tilted her head. "Thanks."

CHAPTER TWENTY

THROUGH FORESTED AND OPEN FERN-COVERED woods, hikers tramped a well-worn path some eighteen inches wide. If a squirrel, chipmunk, or any such animal cared, he could watch a lone hiker, or sometimes groups of three or more in single file. The hikers might be talking; probably they were quiet and lost in thought, especially if they were climbing. If climbing, the animal found it strange that these creatures followed blazed switchbacks up and down hills and mountains. Up they go and suddenly a blaze ramps them up to the left, to avoid going straight up; they follow that blaze for a while, but soon they are ramped up to the right, again to avoid a straight-up. The critter avoids these silly switchbacks and scurries straight up and over the elevation.

Awol, hiking alone, was one of the first to make it to North Carolina's Carter Gap Shelter, twelve miles north of Muskrat Creek Shelter. There he met Recycled, a fit, cheerful older guy, with bowed legs and a shock of wavy white hair.

"Why do you go by Recycled?" Awol asked.

"My trail name used to be Mustang. Last year I'd hiked as far as Pennsylvania before snapping my ankle. Wait till you see all the rocks up there."

"I've heard. Is it as bad as they say?"

"Worse."

"My hat is off to you for starting all over again."

"Decided I wanted to do an honest thru-hike. Wife says I'm stubborn."

They shared dinner, and conversation on the military, war, and adjusting to civilian life. Recycled was a plumber whose first career had been in the Navy. His wife was the daughter of a Navy officer, and he showed Awol pictures of his family. Awol mentioned his two sons, his ex, and Linda, but showed no pictures. Before retiring to their tents, Recycled asked Awol what time he planned to hit the trail in the morning and Awol let him down gently.

"I'm on the trail by seven and you are welcome to leave with me, but I have to warn you, I don't like much company or conversation while hiking. Out here for the solitude, and to clear my head."

"I understand. I met someone like you last year. A former Marine. Did his bit of socializing at camp, moved alone during the day."

"War will do that to you. Being out here is the best thing for it."

NEXT MORNING IT LOOKED TO be another good day to hike, cool and clear. Awol had slept long enough but turbulently, dreaming of the Army. Last night's dream had Awol reliving his qualification with the M-16 rifle at Fort Jackson, SC. Basic Combat Training had been rigorous, including the weapons and tactics portions, but he had kept his focus and became one of three in his company to shoot "Expert," before moving on to Advanced Infantry Training. In the dream, as in the past, he rushed from target to target. At this one he was to kneel and shoot when a target of a silhouetted man popped up somewhere in front of him at 200 yards. One shot—Bingo! Then, run in a crouch—"Head down, soldier!"—to the next, and instructed to lie prone and scan to shoot another pop-up at 250 yards. Up again.

The imposing Puerto Rican drill sergeant had come out of nowhere and yelled in his face, "I hope your mother dies today you sick fuck. Shoot you fool bastard, SHOOT!" Awol felt the dream and the actual experience in him as he crossed a creek and shifted his pack in the North Carolina woodland. "You crazy asshole, you keep settin' up, the oily A-Rab cockroaches'll over-run you. SHOOT, YA MOTHERFUCKER, SHOOT!" Bergman had refused to be intimidated. He aimed and remembered what they had told him in class, "Do not, don't ever, snap a trigger—squeeeeeeze. Always squeeeeeeeeze." And squeeze he did, knocking down every target but one while the sergeant ran with him and yelled. After he finished the course the sergeant drew up to him and looked with satisfaction into his eyes, "Well done, Bergman, extremely well done." Two months later Bergman was an officer candidate at the Infantry school in Fort Benning, GA.

Awol noticed he was perspiring, more from the memories than any exertion. He stopped and drank water. The dream had agitated him but Awol figured it had occurred because he was out in the wild, sleeping in a tent, eating from a mess kit, hauling a pack again all day long. It could be a reminder to stay alert, to keep his head about him. He wondered how often he'd dream about the war on the hike, and if it would help him remember enough of that day to face the truth of it.

AWOL ATE HIS MIDDAY MEAL at a waterfall, off the trail enough to ensure he'd be alone. If Recycled was near, he would see him tonight. Awol laid out his socks and boots in the sun. He massaged his feet and toes and embraced the moment. The meal of puddin' sticks, peanut butter, crackers, and cheese tasted as good as anything he'd ever had, and the water was sweet and pure. All felt good and right, and Awol understood that this particular spot at this particular juncture was, for him, a magic moment, a glimpse into the peace he hoped to attain. He watched a deer pick about the snakeroot by a fallen oak forty yards away, on the other side of the stream. Snakeroot, or Black Cohosh, he remembered from his reading, could be used as a remedy for snakebite. Awol wondered if it tasted good to the deer, or if she was eating it for medicinal purposes. Occasionally the deer stopped to look at him. He took out the Canon Elph from the small case belt-strapped to his shorts, and focused on the deer, then angled to get the waterfall. Through the viewfinder he saw sunlight beaming down on the rocks in the stream.

As he released the shutter button, he caught a shadow and looked up from the camera. *Funny . . . could have sworn.* He looked around, trying to remember if he'd heard anything when he took the picture. The sky had darkened; it was clouding up. Awol packed up and moved to the trail.

AWOL CAME UPON BIG SPRING Shelter by midafternoon. Recycled had already arrived and had taken an inside wall. Not wanting to look as if he might be avoiding Recycled, Awol said hello and placed his pack at the opposite side. A spot next to a shelter wall gave some privacy and made it convenient to hang things on pegs and nails.

Recycled was glad to see him. "How did I get ahead of you? Do you bushwhack your own trail?"

Awol lifted off his pack. "Found me a nice spot near a stream and took a nap."

"Should've done the same. Beautiful day wasn't it?"

"It was. Anything beats rain."

Recycled handed Awol the shelter register and after reviewing comments and signatures of recent hikers, Awol signed in. He noted Recycled's comment, "It's déjà vu. Stayed here last year. Going to make it this time, God willing."

———————

HE AND RECYCLED FINISHED EATING in the gloaming, by the fire. Ten other hikers were camping for the night, four of them in tents. Hikers had begun to fine-tune their routines. They unpacked with precision, found what they were looking for, attended to water needs. Most had been on the trail for two weeks, and Awol was getting to know them all. Age, gender, physical ability, made no difference when bonding with a fellow thru-hiker; when it counted, everyone looked out for each other.

Later in the shelter Awol finished writing in his journal and after reading a couple of pages in his book, turned off his headlamp. From the stuff sack he used for a pillow, he pulled out his ski cap. He pulled it down over his ears and zipped up the sleeping bag while two hikers still wrote in their journals, and another two talked in whispers.

From where he lay, Awol stared out at a three-quarter moon, and watched a wisp of cloud wash over it. A great horned owl hooted and he wondered what animals were sleeping and which were awake. He'd already heard a mouse scurrying around the shelter looking for food. The food bags looked like punching bags in the moonlight, hung from nails on ceiling rafters. Even though mice couldn't get at these bags, they'd find the slivers of rice dropped while preparing a meal, cracker crumbs, and the occasional stray M&M. Awol thought of taking a whack at the critter if it came near him, but resigned himself to live and let live.

CHAPTER TWENTY-ONE

LEROUX'S FIRST NIGHT ON THE Appalachian Trail had passed without incident; he couldn't even remember it. He had been enervated and so sore that he'd barely been able to set up his tent.

Within minutes after first heading north on the trail, he had come to the river he'd seen from the bald. After crossing the rustic foot bridge, he replenished his water. He felt too tired to move, but had to find an isolated place to camp. Hearing shouts in the woodland behind, he gathered up his gear and trudged ahead. Leroux tramped for a half mile and encountered a brook. He moved off to the right and after pushing through some branches, found a place to set up. But first he sat and drank. He didn't eat, he didn't smoke; he drank. After tenting up, he drank again. He squirmed into his bag as the sun disappeared behind distant hills, and slept through to midmorning, like a bear in hibernation.

LEROUX AWOKE FAMISHED. AND SORE. Every muscle, every ligament, was stretched and stiff. He thought he might stay put and rest for the day. After coffee, oatmeal, cocoa, and several cigarettes, he felt better. By then it was noon, and the day was sunny; he should go a few miles. The farther away he'd get, the safer he'd be. But he didn't feel like packing up the tent just to set it up again two or three hours later. And he didn't want to run into people. Instead, he hung out his wet clothes and took a nap.

He woke at quarter after three in the afternoon; the sun had topped over trees, dropping lower in the west. He pulled out some candy and looked around. He knew he should move on, but it was too late, getting dark. At five he cooked another meal, smoked, and brought his clothes back into the tent. He got into his bag at seven and fell into a fitful sleep.

HE DREAMED HE WAS CLIMBING, escaping. He kept looking behind him in the dream as he lunged for the next handhold. But something was holding him, restricting his movements. He tried to fight it off. The desperation in the dream became unbearable; a frantic Leroux yelled out in his sleep and burst through the zipper in his bag. In a sweat he sat up. Panting, and still confused, he looked out through the screen at a nearly full moon staring down at him. He distinguished trees and surrounding growth; it seemed no darker than the storm-clouded day he'd hiked in. He heard water rushing in the brook with a singular clarity. At once Leroux wanted to pack up and move north under this moonlight. With purpose, with energy, with conviction, he dismantled the tent and packed.

While putting on dry hiking clothes, he checked the campsite. He grabbed the one pole and put it by the pack as he pulled out water bottles. He moved to the stream and filled both to the brim. Returning to his pack, he adjusted his headlamp, hoisted the pack and pushed to the stream. He reached into his side pocket to make sure he remembered his bag of Trail Mix and felt something else with his fingers. He pulled out his other set of keys and threw them into the brook as he cut to the trail. He beamed the headlamp to his watch, 11:10 p.m.

Leroux moved; action felt right. He was sore, but he was alert, refreshed. He could see well enough under the moon and with his headlamp. What's more, the terrain was easy compared to yesterday, as it should be; after all, he was now on a marked trail. He was careful of roots and lifted his feet as he plodded along. The trail was quiet, and it felt like just him and the world. The moon seemed to follow him and with his eyes now used to the low light, the silhouettes of pines and oaks sharpened. He welcomed the night breeze on his back.

He crossed the occasional stream and came upon clearings where moonbeams enfolded him. He felt invigorated even though he again began to feel the blister on his heel. He thought he might do more hiking at night and sleep during the day off-trail. It certainly would minimize his contact with others.

He heard and watched a small plane fly across the moon and wondered where the pilot was going and if it was important. The trail, which at first had seemed quiet and still, came alive as his senses fine-tuned. He smelled traces of skunk; owls hooted intermittently. Sometimes he heard a rustle he suspected was a field mouse or a chipmunk, and made a note to look up nocturnal animals in his book. Once, a flying squirrel flattened his tail and glided across the path. *Beautiful. Won't always be like this though. Got to stay alert; be careful; not make any mistakes.* Leroux pulled up his hood as night got deeper and the chill tightened around him.

At three in the morning Leroux smelled wood smoke and made out a shape ahead. As he drew nearer it looked to be a tiny house. Leroux tiptoed closer and heard snores. He had just passed a marker so he knew he was on the trail. Leroux leaned over to a sign nailed to a tree: he was at Cold Spring Shelter. After a moment he recentered his pack and walked past the hut. The moonlight cast its glow into the wide-open front of the shelter, and Leroux spied bed rolls, packed like sardines, on the floor inside. Sacks hung from inside rafters, backpacks from pegs, clothes from a line in front. He was fascinated by what he saw and slowed his step, when someone inside sat up in his sleeping bag and looked right at him. The person stared and Leroux froze; he could have touched the person with his hiking pole.

"Wow. You coming or going, man?"

Leroux remained frozen. He pointed his stick down the trail.

"Who are you? What's your trail name?" Another person sat up, still hooded in a bag. Another's snore was truncated. "Do we know you?" the first one asked.

Leroux turned and ambled down the trail.

"He's Moonwalker," the second one said. "If it's not his trail name, it should be," the first agreed.

Leroux was nonplussed and nearly stumbled into the first of several tents he hadn't noticed. He had veered off the trail and discovered the backs of more tents set up under the moonlight. He backtracked, noting from the sign beside him that he was on his way to the privy. He angled around and saw the trail lead to the front of the tents. He glanced back to the hut and noted one person watching him. Something else by the fire pit began to move. The bundle near the smoldering embers coughed and he realized it was someone in a sleeping bag, cowboy-camped under the stars. As he passed another tent, he was startled by a young man who came from behind a tree, putting his dick back into his briefs. The boy looked at Leroux and up to the moon.

"Yeah, hiking in moonlight is great, I bet. Did I hear someone say you're Moonwalker?"

Leroux grunted and shuffled on with a nod.

I'm staying away from these lean-tos. Not sure what they mean by a trail name; but any name that replaces my real name is fine by me.

LEROUX HAD BEEN HIKING FOR five hours. The terrain was becoming difficult, his foot more painful, and he was getting tired. He felt the heel blister rubbing the back of his boot at every step and knew it would be a problem. His pack was still not adjusted right and he winced as he felt the strap rub against raw shoulder through his shirt. Four o'clock in the morning by his watch; in a couple of hours it would be daylight. He hoped to find a stream, but the terrain steepened and he didn't feel like pushing any farther. He sat on a rock and pulled out his map and cigarettes. He learned he was ascending Copper Ridge Bald, summit 5,200 feet. The nearest spring was a mile and a half after the summit. *Too far.* He checked his water—one full bottle. It would do, but he couldn't use much when he camped because he had a taxing climb in front of him.

It took him longer this time to find a level campsite. He pulled out the ax and chopped away at roots and branches in an isolated spot east of the trail. The headlamp afforded him enough light to set up his tent and get settled. He hauled out his food bag and grabbed more snacks, ripping open a bag of nuts and two packages of cheese and crackers. After, he smoked amid ferns in the morning light and wondered if he could give up cigarettes. That would be huge, he thought. Still hungry, he slathered two slices of bread with jam and peanut butter, and felt energized once again. The sun was rising as Leroux picked up the trail data guide to study the terrain ahead. Later that day, he sat by a stump, pulled out his dog-eared field guide and learned about the land around him.

CHAPTER TWENTY-TWO

Awol ABSORBED THE PREDAWN HUSH outside. Inside the shelter he heard snores and the occasional stirring. He was cold and as his eyes adjusted to the early light, he made out the contorted shapes of hikers huddled in their bags, the hoods covering everything but noses and mouths. He sat up. Forty-five minutes later, Awol put on gloves and started off by frost-covered ferns and mountain laurel that overhung the path. The tramp, tramp, tramp in boots felt good as his feet warmed up and came alive. He worked up a sweat quickly, lifted the ski cap to the tops of his ears, and unzipped his shell at the neck. It was a good day to be alive.

He slowed down as he gained on a porcupine ten yards in front of him. He could see bristles as the fat creature waddled its hind end back and forth. Awol followed at the critter's pace and chuckled at how it seemed to work so hard to move up the path. A short distance later, the porcupine turned left and wiggled out of sight.

The terrain leveled. This was unusual, and welcome; North Carolina so far had been one hill after another. The ups, like the downs, hadn't been long, but they had been continual. A cow pasture that stretched before him loomed like an island and was a pleasant surprise. Awol stepped up the A-framed stile and over the wire fence, as several Holsteins eyed him while munching tufts of grass. The A.T. crossed many farmlands, and this property owner had sunk stakes with painted white blazes to mark the trail. To his right, a football field away, a hatted farmer in a dull red tractor gave him a wave. Awol raised his right pole and, with a flourish, saluted him.

Stepping over another stile near round bales of hay, at the opposite side of the pasture, Awol thought back to a morning thirteen years ago. Reveille, when the entire company of over nearly 100 men and women stood at attention in front of the barracks. It was OCS graduation. As the sun inched onto the horizon, the colonel of the Infantry Student Brigade, in full uniform, was escorted to the speaking tower to give "orders." Bergman had wondered how the colonel was going to do this at one time, with so many new officers. His own request was to Germany, and all the others were waiting to hear if their requests would be granted. Would the colonel call each by name? Finally, "Paraaaaaade REST!" After the one-foot shuffle, hands clasped behind backs, dead silence lingered as the colonel took his time looking them over from his perch before issuing what must have been one of the shorter order commands on record.

"Ladies and Gentlemen, I hope you all like camels and deserts." It was 1990, and Operation Desert Shield was in full swing.

———————

AT NOON, AWOL APPROACHED WINDING Stair Gap and found another hiker thumbing for a ride on Route 64. Awol had already hiked over nine miles and was hungry. The notion occurred to him that he could get a hot meal, buy more food, then come back out on the trail.

"Yo, Awol," Jersey hollered, "you coming into town?"

"Wasn't planning on it. Where's town?"

"Franklin. Ten miles this way."

Awol put down his pack and pulled out a map; Franklin was a decent sized town offering full services. As he folded the map, a pickup swung onto the shoulder and the driver pointed to the back. Without a second thought Awol hauled himself over the tailgate right behind Jersey.

In town at the red light, the driver hollered through the cab's rear window, "Y'all headin' to Budget? That's where most hikers go."

"Sounds good to me," Jersey said.

An hour later, Awol felt guilty as he drew a hot bath and emptied a box of Epsom salts into the tub. He'd shared a large pepperoni pizza with Jersey, in addition to a heaping salad. *Jumping into town wasn't part of the plan,* he thought, *but with Linda out of the picture, I've got to resupply on my own and it's always good to do laundry.* Awol got into the tub and basked. The motel was a flophouse; the ceiling tiles were water stained, ants crawled along the edges of the floor, but the water was hot and his gut was full. He planned to get a good sleep and hitch back to the pass early tomorrow. Awol enjoyed the soak, but knew rough days were coming; snow was predicted in the Smokies.

BEFORE RETIRING, WHILE REPACKING HIS laundry and food, Awol turned on the news. He'd been anxious to learn about events in Iraq. After the national news, while waiting for the local weather, he listened to an update on the hunt for a serial killer in the Franklin area. He remembered seeing a newspaper headline about this at the food mart; he hadn't realized the hunt was in this part of the state. "The search continues for the suspect, Paul Leroux, last seen at this store a week ago." Awol watched a convenience store flash on the screen. "If you have any idea of the suspect's whereabouts or if you spot this individual, please call the number on your screen." A blowup of the suspect replaced the convenience store image, while the number to call flashed at the bottom. Awol turned the TV off, pulled the string hanging from the ceiling bulb, and crawled into the dingy bed. He was asleep within minutes.

THE NEXT DAY, BACK ON the trail, Awol hiked deeper into North Carolina. He heard the whispers of a brook and stopped for a meal fifty yards east of the trail. He unpacked his baggie of rationed food as he sat on an overturned stump overlooking the brook, where he took off his boots and socks, and let them air out. Awol noticed several broken branches and twigs to his right and suspected someone else may have been by. Curious, he moved further to his right while chewing cheese-crackers. He came upon a small clearing and noticed from impressions in the ground that someone had recently used it for a tent site. On his way back he walked barefoot on some of the flat rocks in the refreshing stream. While watching his footing, he caught a glint of something. He reached down and picked up a key ring with two keys and a piece of two-inch scrimshawed ivory on it. Awol thumbed the etched seacoast scene, turned the ring over a couple of times and put it in his pocket.

––––––––––––––––––––

AN AFTERNOON OF ISOLATION, THE way Awol preferred it. He hadn't seen a soul since he'd overtaken a couple of hikers back on the bridge. He had to keep his head focused on the ground, anyway, as what the terrain lacked in elevation, it made up with gnarled roots, rocks, and constant hills and twists and turns. It was like climbing up and down a lopsided and shaky stepladder—all day long. Awol passed through a cove of flowering magnolia and once again thought about the Gulf War tragedy that haunted him. He couldn't recall all the specifics of the night. If he tried to think about it directly, it would change colors and put on a disguise. Awol had to wait for atmosphere and details to surface. He hoped that by pushing his body and getting rid of everyday distractions, and booze, and the frigging meds, he might clear his mind. He looked up to clouds scudding across the sun. He zigged and zagged with the trail. He waited.

CHAPTER TWENTY-THREE

TWO DAYS LATER LEROUX WAS nearly out of food. His watch had stopped, and he had developed a serious limp from the now festering blister on his heel. He had only been able to cover eleven miles since he had camped east of the trail on the back side of Copper Ridge Bald. He'd used up the Band-Aids, which never lasted and became squished in his sock, aggravating other areas of his foot, and he suspected the dirty, bloody sock had infected the blister. He checked his handbook and learned he would soon come upon US-19 at Wesser, NC, which was a mere thirteen miles out of Bryson City. He wondered if he should have entered the trail further north. The last thing he wanted was to go anywhere near Bryson City.

As he approached a pass, he hobbled to the side of the trail and looked down to Route 19. He remembered coworkers at the plant who had once invited him to go kayaking out at Nantahala Outdoor Center in Wesser, which should be nearby. Pulling out his guidebook he spotted it right on the Appalachian Trail. There was no way around it. One way or another he had to cross over the road and go through this outdoor center. He had missed this when he was planning. A short while later, he was able to stop and study the wide, slow-moving river, and observed kayaks wending around the turn to Nantahala. He put on sunglasses.

Fifteen minutes later Leroux walked into the outfitter store at the Nantahala Outdoor Center.

"Moonwalker! That you? What's with the hood and shades?" Leroux recognized the hiker who had stared at him from a sleeping bag at the shelter.

"One stick in the moonlight, yeah I remember you," grinned another.

"Gentlemen," Leroux said, nodding.

"I'm Spiderman," said the first, "this here's Jailbird." He pointed to the second.

"Last time I saw you," Leroux said to Jailbird, trying to appear casual, "you were taking care of business by a tree."

Jailbird grinned again as Spiderman pointed, "And this here's Mighty Mouse." A girl in ponytails and shorts smiled at Leroux.

Leroux tapped his pole on the floor a couple of times and moved to the side. He felt funny under the hood, conspicuous. All three were trying to see through his shades.

"Should we call you Moonwalker or what?" Spiderman asked.

"Fine with me. Surprised y'all aren't ahead of me."

"It's awesome here. Stayed here last night," Jailbird said. "Rented a kayak this morning," Spiderman added.

"Yeah? Bet that was fun. Hey, what do people do for blisters around here?"

"Moleskin, man, moleskin," said Spiderman. "They sell it at the counter."

Leroux tapped his pole again on the floor, "Well, that's what I need."

"What happened to your other pole?" asked Jailbird.

"'Fraid I didn't watch my step and tripped on a root."

"Tell them at the counter and I bet they give you a used stick," Spiderman said. "They did it for Tiger Paws back at Neels Gap."

Leroux began shuffling toward the counter, "Okay, thanks for the tip. You guys take care."

"Right on, Moonwalker," Spiderman said, pumping a fist.

At the counter Leroux bought a mini first-aid kit which included moleskin, gauze, tape, a tube of unguent. "This kit has a needle; sterilize it under a flame when you pop a blister," said the clerk.

"Uh-huh. Got any Vaseline for abraded shoulders?"

"Yep, but this is better." The clerk pulled a tube of Icy Hot from the shelf.

"I'll take 'em both."

"Got painkiller?" the clerk asked. Leroux looked at him. "You know, Ibuprofen? Motrin?"

"No."

"You need that. Hikers call it Vitamin-I."

Leroux looked over the plastic bottle of Motrin he'd been handed, "Okay. Also, I broke my other pole when I fell. Got something I can use?"

"Too bad you didn't keep the broken one, could've given you a brand new one. Let me look out back."

While he disappeared behind a curtain, Leroux happened to look down behind the counter and spied a newspaper with the print backward to him. The front-page picture, although twisted backward, looked eerily familiar. He made out the headline by reading from right to left, "STRANGLER SUSPECT STILL LOOSE." He made out three letters in smaller caps, DNA. Leroux reached over and flipped the paper upside down just before he spotted a hiking pole bisect the curtain.

Leroux put the traveler's check back into his wallet and paid cash. The watch and compass would have to wait. Outside again, he scanned the shops looking for a newspaper box and hobbled over to the news vending machine next to the Laundromat. Empty. He walked into the Laundromat and looked down at a newspaper scattered in sections on a table. Two hikers sat at the table eating meatball subs dripping with tomato sauce. The aroma made Leroux's nose twitch. He thought how easy it would be to grab this girl's sub, which was practically in front of him, and wolf it down. He despised the girl for having it, and something about the way she chewed while holding the steaming sandwich inches from her nostrils enraged Leroux. He watched her turn the end of the sauced up sub to her mouth and slide in the last bite.

She finished chewing and looked up, "You can get one in the restaurant around the corner." The young man next to her got up to check his dryer of clothes which had stopped, and left his sub on the wrappings it came in.

"You reading the newspaper?" Leroux asked the girl.

"Take it."

Leroux gathered up the sections and folded them.

He needed to buy food and wanted to fix his blister. He looked around and realized he also needed to do laundry. Two more hikers came into the Laundromat with bags of food. He exited and headed for the restaurant, figuring he'd read the newspaper article in the restroom.

The restroom was crowded and the stalls were occupied. Leroux thought of the possibility of his own private room, but gave up the idea.

He was a marked man; motels were being checked everywhere, and a motel would use up too much cash. He had to get back on the trail. Newspapers were sold out; what saved him now were his shades and a hood, even though it made him stand out. He would tent up as soon as possible, and attend to his foot.

Leroux spied a grocery on the opposite side of the street. He entered the mart and was told by the bony old woman at the counter, "Please leave your pack outside; you missed the sign on our door." Leroux dropped the pack and poles by the steps. He picked up a basket and grabbed noodles, hard cheese, peanut butter—

"You know," said the woman, picking up the newspaper, to a young girl stocking shelves, "the police are on this big search for the strangler in the towns and cities, but have they checked the river? This guy could have brought a kayak or canoe down here and is escaping down river." Her shrill voice ripped right through Leroux.

"That's a thought," the girl said.

"Seems to me, the police are looking only in the obvious places."

Around cans, between shelves, Leroux eyed the woman sitting rigidly on her stool. She looked like a troublemaker, mouth open, peering at the paper, glasses hung by a string around her neck. He felt the blister throb within his boot.

He made his transaction as quick as possible, looking to the door the whole time, as if someone were impatiently waiting for him. For all the woman's bluster, she never even took a good look at him or any other customer in the store. Ten minutes later, Leroux was on the trail hobbling north, climbing the sharp, unrelenting ascent out of Nantahala. He winced at every step as his heel back-slid into the boot. To compensate he kept jamming his big toe into the front of the boot. He jerked his poles and his body shook as he sweated up the trail. After what seemed like hours of struggle with little gain, Leroux slipped and fell. He rolled to his back, out of breath, tasting the salt from sweat-stained lips, only to look up at fast-moving rain clouds. The rain began, lightly at first, but with the promise of increasing fury. Leroux, still supine, looked next to him and watched tiny rivulets of water build. He watched as one rivulet joined another and then another, and as a mini stream, they swirled by a tiny bump of dirt. The tiny stream gathered more strength from other rivulets and climbed a tiny ridge of mud; the stream inched by his arm, around his hand.

Thunder rumbled close-by, and the rain came full on. Big drops, heavy drops, mean drops. Leroux sat up. *Okay—this is the price I pay.* Leroux looked up to the sky and let the rain snap onto his face—*I deserve this, and I'll take it all.* "Okay!" he hollered to the purpled sky. "Okay!" He felt tears mixed with rain. *I'll pay the price. Throw it at me.* Leroux reached for his poles, turned himself over and, after a brief moment hunched over his sticks, trudged upward again.

CHAPTER TWENTY-FOUR

Awol reached the Nantahala Outdoor Center three days later, arriving at noon. Two red kayaks cruising down the river reminded him of the time he and Linda had vacationed in the Adirondacks and brought their kayaks. Looking around, he imagined that Linda would love Nantahala. The whole place had an air of camaraderie and was set up for outdoor enjoyment. But as tempting as it looked to him, Awol didn't want to get distracted. If he rented a kayak for the afternoon, he'd have to spend the night. He had already taken an unplanned night in Franklin.

He refilled his water bottles in a restaurant bathroom and climbed the outside stairs to a veranda, which offered a view of the main street. He sat down in a plastic chair and took out a diminished bag of gorp. Munching on what he'd come to think of as birdseed, he recognized several newly arrived hikers below. He imagined their conversations as they looked at the bright red and yellow kayaks tied by the river, the sun sparkling off the water. They pointed to the Laundromat and bunkhouse and glanced at the restaurant. Awol watched them talk amongst themselves, then head to the bunkhouse, and knew they were done for the day. *A dozen years ago I might have done the same*, he thought. *But I've got the rest of my life to jump into kayaks.*

Awol allowed himself to linger on his perch for several more minutes. He could easily pick out the thru-hikers, ragged with their beards, their muddy packs with tent-sacks and mattress-rolls attached, and watched several more come up the street. One young hiker held his thumbs under shoulder straps and Awol thought, *That could be my son in a few years.* His sons. Awol felt twinges of regret, twinges he had felt several times since starting the A.T.

His ex had taken his two sons, Kenny and Gregory, clean across the country ten years ago. It had been an ugly divorce. Within two years she'd married a Silicon Valley engineer and lived in a wealthy subdevelopment. Not long after, she'd sent a picture of the two boys standing with fancy bikes by a landscaped lawn, an enormous new-looking house behind them. When she'd left him, the boys were three and one. He had hardly been able to see them, never mind get to know them, while in the Army, and resented how she pushed for the divorce and hightailed it from Massachusetts to California.

Awol wondered how his sons lives had passed him by. He remembered seeing them for an afternoon when they were eight and six. He'd saved money to fly to California and bought them plastic rifles that shot plastic balls. He took them to a park and showed them how to hold their rifles and how to aim. He sent them identical Christmas gifts and every year got a printed thank you card, but when they started attending private schools, what affection they'd had for him faded away. He didn't send boxed gifts this year and hadn't written them letters in over two years. He still sent the annual Christmas card, his sons' names on the envelope, care of his ex's address, with two twenty-dollar bills inside, one for each. It had been a lost cause, lost as soon as his ex had left him. Here on the veranda, he felt an entrenched malaise crawl around inside him. Something else he had to face head on and accept: his drinking had gotten out of hand and had played a big part in the divorce. But at the end of this hike, Awol intended to have his head on straight, and reach out to his sons. Enough was enough.

Awol rummaged through his food bag, and stuffed all his collected garbage from the last few days into a trash receptacle. On top of the receptacle a section of the *Smoky Mountain Times* headlined the killer from Franklin. Awol took a moment to scan the article, which detailed how Paul Leroux was wanted for three local murders, but had disappeared. Awol gazed across the river to the mountains where he was headed and stuck the paper into the bin. For the rest of the bright afternoon he ascended the Appalachian Trail out of Nantahala, and only then did he realize that he'd never even thought about having a drink while in town.

IT'S THE MIDDLE OF NIGHT—*noise, shelling, confusion. His squad has just been disgorged from the rear exit ramp of the Bradley M2 Infantry Fighting Vehicle. They've been dispatched to assault an airstrip, held by the Iraqi Republican Guard. Resistance is fierce; the pungent odor of flamed oil permeates the air. He feels what he imagines is a branding poker scorch his thigh. He's knocked around and becomes separated from his men. He sees flashes of light at nine o'clock. Iraqi Republican Guard? Command told us to expect them from all directions. But on my flank? Harrison's over there.*

More blasts and he again sees flashes—same location. He shoots back, dead on another Bradley. He doesn't remember squeezing the trigger, he simply shoots. Confusion reigns, radios squawk, and he realizes too late that the rocket propelled grenades are coming from his right flank, not his left. He hobbles and drags himself toward the Bradley as he shits his pants and dry-heaves.

Awol bolted up screaming, and covered his eyes. He swayed and shook. He kept his face covered, but when he began to realize where he was, peeked through his fingers. Slowly, he placed his hands in front of him. The inside of his tent was black in the midnight. *It'll pass.* But as Awol closed his eyes, he felt the writhing, groaning body in front of him. A flare arcs overhead and Bergman sees the face and the eyes, staring into him.

AT DAWN AWOL WAS OUT of sorts. He couldn't bring himself to grunt anything to hikers he met at Grassy Gap. He hiked alone all morning, and when he broke for a meal, he moved well off the trail, unpacking his rations atop a boulder he'd climbed. The day was foggy and damp, as if the sun was off duty, which matched his mood.

IN THE AFTERNOON, ON AN arête before Brown Fork Shelter, the gloom cleared. Awol picked a secluded spot on the rock-strewn ledge, banging his sticks to skitter any rattlers who might linger there, and watched sunlight brighten through the haze. He looked at spruce and balsams across the ledge while he swigged from his water bottle. He leaned back against rock and let the sun warm his face as he closed his eyes. Birds chirped; a breeze whispered.

For what seemed like the millionth time, Awol tried to reason it through. *How did Harrison get so far on my flank? Did I know he'd be there? Yes. We exited from the left. But the flashes . . . no, the flashes were the result of enemy rocket propelled grenades hitting American tanks and Bradleys. Harrison was in direct line of that Bradley M2 when I heard blasts and saw flashes. I shot Harrison. I shot and killed my own non-com.*

Awol had done something back then that he had never done before—panicked. *But was it panic? Or did I know Harrison would be to my left? Fourteen hours earlier at drop-off, Harrison had refused a direct order.* "Let Perez take point, Sir. I'm short, I muster out in three weeks."

"Sergeant Harrison, I gave you an order."

"Fuck! I oughta frag ya!" Harrison yelled.

It was Corporal Jones, Harrison's friend, who stepped up. "I'll go, Sir." *And it was Jones who stepped on a mine and had his legs blown off. After the mine tragedy, Harrison was uncontrollable. He stirred up the men against me and—Private Perez admitted as much—conspired. Fourteen hours later, he was in position and I shot him. That's where he should have been. But . . . In firefights, this dreaded scenario could happen.* Killed by friendly fire was a rarely-mentioned, but all-too-common statistic. *If God sat in front of me right now, could I say I didn't know Harrison would be there? I didn't see anything but flashes. And later, I did something shameful.*

———————

AWOL BECAME RIGID AGAINST THE ledge, reliving it all. *I am disgusting.*

THE PRESIDENT OF THE UNITED STATES OF AMERICA, AUTHORIZED BY EXECUTIVE ORDER . . . , TAKES PLEASURE IN PRESENTING THE BRONZE STAR MEDAL WITH COMBAT "V" to Lieutenant Karl J. Bergman, United States Army, for EXCEPTIONAL HEROISM DURING OPERATION DESERT STORM . . . WITHOUT REGARD FOR HIS PERSONAL SAFETY . . . UNDER FIRE BY ENEMY FORCES IN THE REPUBLIC OF KUWAIT . . .

Awol rubbed his eyes as he remembered how he stood in front of the colonel to receive his Bronze Star, with combat "V." How the major and captains congratulated him. He had told them when he was put in for it, he was not deserving and preferred not—

"Lieutenant?" the colonel had said, looking up from his metal desk. "You were wounded and lost your top man, but led your men on to secure that airstrip. Captain Ruffini reports you took over and kicked ass until reinforcements backed you. You are a hero in the grand tradition of the Army. I would have approved a Silver."

Awol never mentioned what had happened in his report. How he had looked down into the open eyes of his dying noncommissioned officer. Knowing eyes of a soon-to-be dead man, eyes that looked straight into Bergman's soul.

"Harrison?"

"You." Harrison reached up and tried to grab Bergman's throat, "You shot . . . I saw . . ." Furious, knowing eyes looked up at Bergman. "You," he rasped. Damning eyes that had haunted Bergman every day since.

Bergman had never revealed the truth. No one had voiced suspicions; but his men were sullen and jittery. He'd told himself he'd own up and check out of sickbay to see the colonel—to tell him it may have been friendly fire. But one day had led to another, a full week had gone by; then Desert Storm was over. Awol held his head. *I wasn't afraid of punishment. I was confused. I was so goddamned horrified and ashamed. I, a trained infantry officer, had shot and killed my best non-com. I couldn't bring myself to admit it was me. Of course I fired the shot that killed him. I had my eyes glued to the spot where I had aimed; then I crawled there. But . . . did I know it would be Harrison? And how was I to explain this to the brass now? I should have. I didn't.*

After Desert Storm, a fellow captain had said that he appeared despondent, and might want to talk with someone about Post-Traumatic Stress Disorder. He cringed at the thought. *Christ, I killed my own man. How could I talk about that?*

The sun sank below the horizon. Awol looked skyward. He was stuck here for the night, but the evening would be clear. He put on his shell and took out the water bottle. He sat and watched the alpenglow color the crags.

CHAPTER TWENTY-FIVE

LEROUX HEARD APPROACHING FOOTSTEPS. "HELLO in there. That you Skylark?"

Leroux grabbed his sunglasses and pulled up his hood. "No, this is Moonwalker."

"Oh, I'm sorry, this is Malibu. Have you seen Skylark? I'm supposed to meet her here."

Leroux wanted to peek out at this woman, and tried to divine her features by closing his eyes, "No, I don't know her, but I'll tell her you're here if I run into her."

"Okay, thanks. I need to camel-up, how's the water at this place?"

"Fine. Down to your left a hundred yards." He heard her move and shuffle off her pack.

"Okay if I set up next to you? It's a full house tonight."

"Sure."

For two days Leroux had nursed himself in his tent at this campsite near Trye Top. Hikers had come and gone; Leroux had stayed hidden in his tent studying the handbook, field guide, and his maps. His heel had become so sore and the rains so bad upon hiking out of Nantahala, that when he stumbled on the campsite, he went to the secluded far end and set up. He managed to get his water without being seen and ate in his tent. He didn't cook hot meals, but made coffee and hot chocolate.

Leroux had planned to cook a hot meal tonight, outside. Now he wasn't sure he should. He heard Malibu finish clicking the tent snaps and rustle into the tent. A minute later he heard the "bop" of empty water bottles and listened to her hoof it to the spring. He opened his flap and sneaked a look. Her tent was ten feet away. He had no working watch, but guessed it to be around five o'clock. He would chance it. *Better to eat a quick meal now before everyone does later. And I can wear sunglasses while it's still light out.*

He heard her again a few minutes later. "Hi, Moonwalker, I'm Malibu." She swung her bottles down next to her pack. "Guess Skylark's not coming."

"Nice to meet you." Leroux sat Indian style, keeping his eyes on the pot in front of him.

Several minutes elapsed. "Have you heard a weather forecast?" Moonwalker asked.

"More rain, and snow is coming in a couple of days. That was the forecast in Nantahala. What happened to your foot?"

Leroux glanced at his bandaged heel. "Got a bad blister."

"Using moleskin?"

"Yes. With ointments."

"Try to keep your socks dry. Change them when they get soaked and stuff cotton into the boot where it rubs. Worked for me."

Moonwalker perked up at this. "Yeah?"

"Want some cotton?"

Moonwalker glanced at her. She was pretty, healthy, blonde. She smiled at him and disappeared into her tent.

"Here, try this."

Moonwalker took the ball of cotton from her. "Thank you, Malibu."

Two hikers came over; one young man had a bag of gorp, the other a Frisbee. "Malibu," the first one said, "Skylark told me to tell you she's staying another night in Nantahala."

"Why am I not surprised? Meet Moonwalker. Moonwalker, this is Skittles and Hawk."

Moonwalker gave a smile under his hood. He dumped the macaroni into his pot, shook in the cheese, and stirred.

"How do you like the Esbit?" Hawk asked.

Moonwalker had to think. "I like it fine."

"Nice and light," Skittles said, "but takes a while to heat up, doesn't it?"

"Well, yeah. But, as you say, the stove is light and convenient."

Hawk smiled at Malibu, "How 'bout some Frisbee?"

"Let's do it." She got up and stuck her hand into Skittles' bag of gorp.

Leroux was glad to see the guys go, but wished Malibu had stayed. He felt the warmth in his crotch as he watched her stretch to throw the Frisbee right over someone's tent and then heard laughs from inside it. *Was she coming on to me? No. Just the typical sweetie.* He appreciated the cotton though. He watched her bend over, thirty yards away, to retrieve the Frisbee from some undergrowth where it had rolled. He felt the bulge in his pants. Leroux found it incredible that he would be sleeping the night ten feet away from her. He looked at the other tents. *Nobody else here, just me and Malibu. She would trust me and look to me for protection. She would get scared being all alone in her tent and I'd offer to come over, so she could feel safe. Oh, man. Would I do her? Or save her for another night? But she was kind to me. I might threaten her and she would be my slave each night; I'd fuck her brains out and save her for a night under a full moon. Sooner or later she'd turn against me, like all the others. Then I'd do her.* Leroux scanned to his left and picked the perfect spot.

LEROUX LAID ON HIS SIDE on top of his sleeping bag, facing her tent in the inky blackness of his own. He viewed the glow from her tent. He listened to her scribble into what he suspected was her journal. He heard another rustle of paper and wondered if she might be writing a letter. He sniffed long and deep and smelled a trace of perfume. *No, not strong enough for perfume. Deodorant.* He fantasized about her putting on roll-on deodorant under her armpits, down into her navel, over the hair around her crotch. He watched her vulva pulse as she glided the roll-on over her vagina. He felt her eyes looking at him and understood she had been looking at him all the while. She smiled at him and halted the roll-on stick, then pushed it into herself; with her other hand she reached to him.

Leroux opened his flap and crawled outside for a smoke. He sat in front of his tent and lit up. The night was clear with an almost full moon above him; a fire languished in the pit ten yards away. Everyone was in their tents. A few minutes later, Malibu opened her tent flap and came outside. He listened to her walk over.

"Could I have one of those?"

She had done up her hair in a new yellow bandanna. She wore red shorts and a white cotton sweatshirt under a sleeveless vest. She had on flip-flops.

"Sure." Leroux reached the pack of Marlboros up to her and pulled out his lighter. She sat down not quite next to him and leaned into the flame. She made to guide his hand, but didn't touch him.

"Thanks. Not what hikers are supposed to do, right?"

Leroux chuckled. "We'll keep it our little secret." She drew and blew a stream of smoke up into the moon. Leroux lighted another for himself.

"You thru-hiking Moonwalker?"

"That's the plan."

"Thought I might drop out with all the rain, but now I'm planning on going all the way."

Moonwalker said nothing. He felt the urge creep into his soul. He fought the possibilities swarming his mind. He watched as she curled her lips around the cigarette and drew again; she'd inhaled slightly and he spied wisps of smoke from her nose as she blew up to the moon. She looked away to the fire ring where a few embers cooked, and Leroux thought this was deliberate, so that he might better note her ample breasts. Her face was firm and confident with a smile of pure white, even teeth. Her arms weren't big but they looked strong. She turned to him. She was messing with him. He was certain.

Moonwalker turned straight ahead. He was glad his hood was on.

Minutes later, back in his tent, Leroux was all jacked up. *Got to keep away from this bitch. Got to take care of business and work my plan.* He tried to put her out of his mind. As sure as he knew anything, he would either have to keep away from her or do her.

CHAPTER TWENTY-SIX

THE NEXT DAY, APRIL 2, Awol climbed Shuckstack Fire Tower to spectacular vistas. The afternoon was clear and, alone on the summit of Shuckstack Mountain, 4,020 feet, Awol had a good view of the peaks and valleys in the Smoky Mountains. With rough weather predicted later in the week, this was an ideal time to shoot panoramas, something he wanted to get developed, and send to Linda. The fire tower was a short distance from the trail. He removed the compact binoculars from his pack and scanned high humped timbered-hills to the west. He panned to his right and noted a crest-line trail to the north. As a breeze blew in from the east, he heard the stanchions creak and felt the tower shift. With the binoculars Awol spotted a lone hiker descending to the pass. He was a good mile ahead of Awol and looked to be a thru-hiker. He watched the hiker stop and disappear off the trail.

The following day, at Mollies Ridge Shelter, Awol stopped for a meal. He used the privy, filled his empty water bottle from the spring, and set his food out on a battered picnic table. He concluded from table crumbs that someone had been by, and went to get the shelter register. He sat down again, spooned peanut butter and read the recent entries. Two minutes later another hiker showed up.

"Hello," Awol said.

The man stopped. He was wearing sunglasses and had strips of cotton gauze under his pack shoulder straps.

"Howdy."

Awol watched him as he looked around and tamped one of his poles.

"Someone switch a pole on you?" Awol noticed the poles didn't match.

"Huh?" The man seemed puzzled or annoyed about something. He looked to be in his thirties, big guy. The man looked down at his pole. "Oh, that. Yeah, guess that's what it was."

Awol took out his pen and began to write in the ledger. He was aware of the hiker rescanning the shelter, the fire pit, him. He was still standing.

Awol put down the pen, looked up at him, "I'm Awol," and offered his hand.

The man shook it and sat down backward to the table. "Moonwalker," he said.

The man's grip was powerful. Awol picked up the pen, signed his name into the register, and handed the register to Moonwalker.

Awol saw the man was perplexed. "Guess you don't stay in shelters. Most thru-hikers sign in and make some comment. You thru-hiking?"

"Kind of."

Moonwalker looked over the entries and Awol offered him the pen. Moonwalker hesitated, but took it. Awol watched him scribble something with his left hand.

Awol ate. Moonwalker sat and smoked. After a few moments, Moonwalker pulled out his water bottle, drank the last third of it and ambled to the spring. Awol watched the back of him as he hunched down. He looked over at Moonwalker's pack leaning against the seat of the picnic table. The blue Kelty looked muddy, but new. He spied the hammer/ax strapped on the left side and found this strange. He shifted closer to the pack and twisted it to him. The tool looked to weigh a couple of pounds, but hikers were compulsive about trimming all weight possible. They'd cut excess strapping, buy expensive but light titanium cookware, use a mini toothbrush. Unless he bushwhacked, Awol thought, why carry an ax? He slanted the register to him and read the last entry, "Moonwalker, 4/3."

"Something puzzling you?" Moonwalker said.

Awol turned obliquely to the voice, "Just wondering what the ax is for." He turned fully and faced Moonwalker, who stood ten feet behind him.

They stared at each other.

Moonwalker yanked up his pack and slipped the bottle into a side sleeve. He hoisted on the pack and picked up his poles.

"Hey, man. I was just wondering, okay?"

"Nice meeting ya," Moonwalker said.

"Same here. Adios."

Twenty minutes later, Awol was back on the trail. He expected to catch up to Moonwalker, but didn't see him in the afternoon or later at the campsite.

AFTER LEAVING AWOL, MOONWALKER HIKED off-trail forty yards east into woodland. He wanted this man, Awol, to go by him and remain ahead of him. He selected a place behind a giant boulder and took off his pack. Moonwalker looked at the top of the boulder and noted it would afford a view of the trail. He found a way up the boulder and was surprised at his strength and agility as he climbed to the top. He knew he couldn't have managed this three weeks ago. He crouched down and waited, hidden behind bosky terrain. Soon, Awol poled by. Moonwalker observed the compact, sturdy profile. The man appeared efficient and purposeful as he worked his poles around rocks and roots. He watched him scan to his right and left twice, before he poled out of sight.

CHAPTER TWENTY-SEVEN

IN HIS TENT, MOONWALKER CHANGED the dressing on his blisters as he had done every night since getting moleskin. He applied unguent over and around the blisters and dabbed petroleum jelly to the inside of his boot before placing cotton over the dabs. He kept the cleanest sock on the blistered heel during the day and aired out his feet at night. During those two days after Nantahala, when he had nursed himself, he'd rinsed his clothes in the rain as best he could, but it had taken those two days for them to dry. He wanted to launder his clothes and get a watch and compass; he also needed food. He examined the map and noted Gatlinburg just over the North Carolina line in Tennessee. His heart leapt. *This is worth a shot. Gatlinburg's big enough, I won't stand out, I can get food, supplies.* He figured he could make it to Indian Gap in three days—Gatlinburg was fifteen miles northwest.

MOONWALKER LEFT CAMP AT SEVEN the next morning. He had slept well, his clothes had aired out, and he was dry. He'd had his oatmeal, coffee, and two Marlboros. After an hour of tramping, he spotted a hiker far up ahead. He gained on the hiker and distinguished the curly hair of a woman. Moonwalker followed and watched her butt shift to and fro. She had on black shorts of a light material and as she stepped, the shorts flung back, exposing strong, defined thighs. Her legs were slender and rich; her backpack hid her upper body. She planted the sticks with determination, and in her high-top boots, which accentuated her calf muscles, she looked sexy.

Moonwalker stalked her for a good twenty minutes and worked himself up to a frantic state. He couldn't believe the irony; he used to fantasize this. In Kentucky, West Virginia, Ohio, North Carolina, he had labored, not always successfully, to get women out into the wild. He remembered the time in West Virginia when he could have strangled the blonde in the motel, but too risky, and how when she refused to take a moonlight drive up by the lake, he had to knock her out, tie her and bring her up there at two in the morning. He lured women into forests just like this. *Why risk leaving evidence in town when you can get a woman isolated?—and don't the bitches come alive in romantic settings! The best part is seeing their naked bodies, shimmering, glistening in the moonlight.*

Moonwalker wobbled a rock with his stick and it rolled. She looked around and stopped. Moonwalker paused as well.

"Hi. Didn't mean to startle you." He gave her a smile.

"No problem, I was thinking of taking a break anyway." She rested her sticks against a tree and pulled out her canteen. "I'm Nightwind."

"A pleasure, I'm Moonwalker."

He held out his hand and she gripped it. Her grip was modest. He noted the hazel eyes and long brows. Moonwalker thought about how a drug pusher will *chip*. The pusher doesn't get addicted, but takes advantage of the situation in a marginal way, and will *chip* marijuana, say, taking just a bit at a time. He saw an analogy here; he wouldn't do anything stupid, but he could chip.

"Care for a cigarette?"

"I don't smoke."

"I'm sorry," Moonwalker said, "shouldn't have even asked. You're an experienced hiker and practice good habits." He sat down and lit up.

"Well, I'm not what you would call an experienced hiker, but I am trying to practice good habits." She was sitting on the opposite side of the trail near her poles. She pulled a bag of gorp from the pack and took a handful. "Want some?"

"Love some." He reached over for the baggie and took a handful. He palmed up the baggie back to her and touched the bottom of her fingers when she lifted it off. "Very tasty. Thank you."

"I hike with Songbird; she's close behind me," she said.

"I don't think I've met Songbird yet. You start the trail with her?"

"No. My partner left me back in Hiawassee, so I've teamed up with Songbird, Vagabond, and Blue Sky. Do you know those guys?"

"I may have met them. Can't say I remember."

Moonwalker observed the pleasant but frank look on her face, and absorbed her body as she stared into his sunglasses. Every inch of her skin was spotless. Perfection. And she was poised. He wished he could smell her better. Male hikers, sweating for days in the wilderness, were putrid. Female hikers, he had noticed, were not, but each had a distinct body odor, which intrigued Moonwalker. This one, he mused, had tried to mask her odor with something. He stared at her curly black hair. His sunglasses were dirty, but he resisted the urge to wipe them.

"They'll be here soon," she said.

Moonwalker smiled and stared. He didn't move a molecule, didn't breathe.

"It's going to be nice out today," she said, tapping her heel up and down.

It was as quiet as the silence before Bach.

She looked southward on the trail and took another handful of gorp. He saw her eyes flit to brambles on her left, pines on her right, then eye an open space. He could see her fear multiply and this positively thrilled him; he felt as powerful as Osama bin Laden but realized anything further could become a costly mistake. After another long moment he stubbed out the cigarette and got up.

"Think I'll push on. Have a pleasant day, Nightwind."

"Thanks."

———————

MOONWALKER SET UP CAMP OFF the trail again. He pondered the idea of trying to engage another woman at a campsite, but the risks were too great. He couldn't afford to get any kind of reputation. He figured he'd let this band of hikers slip away, but he couldn't delay much longer, as he needed to get resupplied soon. That night, in his darkened tent, he touched himself and fantasized about Malibu and Nightwind. He decided not to release himself but to save it. For whom, he did not know. He did know he would be out of North Carolina soon.

CHAPTER TWENTY-EIGHT

TENNESSEE! THE A.T. BORDERED STATES in several places, and when Moonwalker realized that he'd have a chance to get supplies in a neighboring state, where he might be able to hide a bit easier, he took that chance in Gatlinburg, Tennessee. He knew it was still a risk, but he was out of food, and if he didn't get his clothes laundered and get scrubbed himself, he felt he would become diseased. Rain had fallen the last two days and everything was soggy, including his cigarettes. His clothes were so worn and loose, they barely stayed on him.

He hiked into Indian Gap and became hopeful when he saw several cars in a parking lot. Moonwalker shivered in the cold rain as he watched the cars from a stand of pines. He noted viewing scopes, the kind you pop a quarter into and swing around to see panoramas. Information sideboards were staked up to give visitors explanations. He tightened up his hood and put on shades. He felt his three-week beard, which seemed a badge among the male hikers. A Dodge Caravan swung into the gravel lot and Moonwalker walked over to it. The rain was steady as the driver slid down the window.

"Any chance you can swing me in to Gatlinburg?"

The driver, a young man with textbooks beside him, hesitated. "Wasn't planning to go to Gatlinburg."

"I see." Moonwalker looked despondent. "Got ten bucks if you can help me out."

Thirty minutes later Moonwalker stood at the counter of a small motel off the main street. He was still hooded up and made sure the proprietor had seen him place his sticks outside next to the backpack and had watched him wipe his feet several times on the mat.

"Tell me you got a small room where I can neaten up and get some sleep." The clock behind the desk read half past one.

"Why the sunglasses?"

"Lost my regular glasses in the mountains. These are prescription and I need to wear something."

"Got a room for forty dollars on the upstairs corner."

"I'll take it. Cash up front okay?" Moonwalker held up two wilted twenty-dollar bills.

"Cash is fine, but you need to sign in and give us your address."

Moonwalker handed him the money and penned: Richard Brown, 541 West Main Street, Boise, Idaho. He left off the zip and ignored the phone portion. "Chief, can you do some laundry for me?"

"Don't do laundry here, but for an extra six bucks I can get it done for you."

"All right. I'll bring it down, but I need it back in a couple of hours."

———

MOONWALKER WAS IN HIS SHABBY room, as grand to him as the Taj Mahal. He spent twenty minutes in the shower lathering with all the tiny soaps he could find. He wanted to binge on food, rest, and resupply all at once. After his shower, he stared at himself in the above-sink mirror. *So . . . this is Moonwalker.* He patted his less puffy cheeks, rubbed his beard, and fingered a more pronounced chin. Satisfied, and knowing the laundry would take a while, he pulled the shade and sank into the chair in front of the TV.

In the evening, clean and dressed in dry, laundered clothes, including snug new hiking pants that he'd found on sale in a sports store, he read a newspaper in a pizza shop off Main. He felt refreshed and confident. The U.S. invasion into Iraq was keeping other news off the front page and into the background. An overhead TV was on and all he saw or heard was Iraq. He'd combed the Asheville paper and had learned nothing new about the strangler other than the search continued. He nibbled on the remaining pizza crusts, and pulled out his field guide, opening to a section describing flora and fauna on the Appalachian Trail. He was pleased to note how many of the woodland plants and flowers he now recognized.

As he prepared to leave, he glanced up the street and spotted Nightwind go by. He beat it out the door and walked up to the corner as she followed a friend into an ice-cream shop. He watched them stand in line and order enormous cones. He wanted Nightwind. After what seemed like an eternity, he turned and walked the opposite way, back to his room.

After repacking his supplies and setting his new watch to the correct time, he counted his cash and was relieved to learn he should be able to make it at least to Virginia without a problem. He focused on his plan to keep himself on track, and set himself up with a local, recommended by the proprietor, who would drive him back to the trail at eight o'clock tomorrow morning.

But try as he might, Moonwalker couldn't sleep. Under bed covers, staring at a black ceiling, he fantasized about Nightwind. He knew where his thoughts were taking him and understood what was going to happen next, even though it could ruin everything. He let it happen and the obsession took root. This obsession to find her, stalk her, dominate her, took hold of Moonwalker and permeated thought and reason. He let the compulsion to do her seep into every pore.

Two hours later he was still awake, but calm spread across his face. He had a plan. It involved risk, but he would make it work. Moonwalker sank into the deepest sleep he'd had in weeks.

CHAPTER TWENTY-NINE

Moonwalker had been stalking Nightwind since getting back to the trailhead at Indian Gap. He'd called the driver taking him back to the pass and asked him to come earlier, at 7:00 a.m. This way he felt sure he'd be back before her. He hiked a half-mile into the Gap and noted a new quickness to his step. *I'm getting stronger.* He hid fifty yards east of the trail.

He divined she most often hiked alone. A good hour went by when, through his binoculars, he watched her approach with her girlfriend. Songbird, he supposed. This didn't surprise him; he figured they would start out together. He followed well behind, losing them around turns and hills, seeing them again when the terrain leveled. Two hours later they took a break. He spied with his field glasses while atop a small ledge hidden from the trail. Several minutes passed, and Nightwind moved on alone. He took his time and caught up to Songbird a half hour later.

"Coming from behind, don't want to startle you," he shouted.

"Oh, thank you. Beautiful day isn't it?" She was a petite blonde.

"Yes, it is. I like when it's bright enough to wear sunglasses."

"I'm Songbird."

"Moonwalker. Feeling good today—hoping to do about seventeen. How about you?"

"I'm gonna struggle to do twelve."

Just what Moonwalker was looking for. "Take your time. Worst thing you can do out here is rush into an injury. Anyway, nice meeting you." He moved by her.

THAT NIGHT, MOONWALKER CAMPED NEAR Pecks Corner Shelter where he knew they'd be. He hiked a wide arc around them, and tented to the north of the shelter. He was close enough to hear shouts from the shelter and later, before sundown, he stowed his headlamp and ventured in the direction of voices and the smell of campfire, recognizing deer tracks and scat, as he bent low to the ground.

He hid sixty yards on a diagonal to the shelter and a pale-gray spiral of smoke. With his field glasses, he spotted Nightwind by the blazing fire with Songbird and another hiker. She had changed her bandanna and shorts from red to green. Moonwalker sat with unblinking eyes and watched her eat. She poured a crimson liquid from her water bottle, which he suspected was Gatorade. Moonwalker lay down on his stomach and steadied the glasses on a rock. He spied on her for twenty minutes, after which he followed her with his binoculars as she moved to the shelter. She disappeared inside and emerged holding a jacket. He watched her put it on and zip it while talking to hikers at the shelter. He held her in sight as she returned to the fire, gathered up her mess kit and bottles, and disappeared down the path toward the stream. Moonwalker waited. She returned up the path—*getting dark, hard to see her face*—and for the last time ducked into the shelter.

Moonwalker sat up and let the binoculars hang, but still gazed on the shelter. She should tent, he thought. It bothered him she was being shared by others.

Back in his tent he reexamined his maps and guidebook. He located what looked to be a perfect spot about a half-day's hike ahead. Hell Ridge, a cliff at six thousand feet. To the west was wilderness; to the east the cliff. Moonwalker fantasized into the night.

AT SIX O'CLOCK MOONWALKER WAS on the trail, the earliest yet. He wanted to reconnoiter the cliff, and arrived at Hell Ridge at noon, noting with a thrill the sheer drop-off. Wind gusted from the west, perfect. Moonwalker pictured a sun setting in the west, then a huge moon, rising. Walking west across the trail into scrub and down a small grade behind boulders to isolation, Moonwalker unpacked and reviewed his plan. He figured it'd be two to three hours before Nightwind approached. Moonwalker couldn't see the trail from where he was which meant no one could see him. Twice he'd heard voices.

After lunch Moonwalker was supercharged. He repacked his food and trash, organized his gear so that he could bolt afterwards, and went over to a chosen spot. He lay down and thought everything through. Moonwalker was not surprised his compulsion had taken over; he couldn't stop himself and didn't want to.

At quarter of one, Moonwalker pulled out his field glasses and walked parallel to the trail until he could see the approach. *The best thing about Hell Ridge is the height. At six thousand feet, I watch hikers plod to me.*

Twenty minutes passed before Moonwalker spotted a hiker. He timed his approach and fifteen minutes later watched him put down his poles and stare from the cliff. The hiker dropped his pack and pulled out his camera; the gorgeous afternoon offered terrific views. It was still windy though. Moonwalker huddled by rocks and wished the hiker would leave. He spotted three more hikers cresting; one of them was a woman. He was relieved to find he didn't recognize any of them, but became anxious when they stopped and joined the first hiker on the arête. Moonwalker steamed as the three joining hikers unpacked and took out cameras. It was two o'clock.

At quarter past two, Moonwalker espied a hiker with a red bandanna—Nightwind. She traveled alone. Frustrated, he turned his glasses to the group and just as he willed it, the group began packing up. With huge satisfaction Moonwalker observed them putting on their packs and picking up their sticks. Within five minutes they were gone. Moonwalker was fired up as he watched Nightwind pick her way—*wait. What's this?* Another hiker crested about five minutes behind her. *No!* Moonwalker grimaced while peering through the binoculars. Within the next few minutes he had wanted to position himself on the ridge with his binoculars and offer Nightwind a look. Moonwalker had figured they'd have the place to themselves; too early in the season for southbound thru-hikers, plus it was midweek.

That miserable cocksucker. Moonwalker watched him gain on her and wanted to crush him like a beetle. During the few minutes he had left to decide, he thought about OJ, or whoever the killer of Nicole Brown Simpson was, and how he ran into Ron Goldman and had to kill twice. *I could throw this bastard off the ridge in a heartbeat and drag Nightwind off the trail. Oh, the fear in her eyes then.*

He observed the two of them coming—*the prick will intercept her just as she gets to the ridge.* Moonwalker heaved a sigh. *No. Can't risk it.* He huddled, watched, and listened as the wind blew bits of conversation his way.

"Nightwind, hey, wait up."

"Hamlet! Where'd you come from?"

"I've been stalking you." He took one of his poles and aimed at her butt. "Wow, check out the views."

"Fabulous. Get a picture of me standing on the ridge." She stepped up and faced west with the vista behind her.

Hamlet took her camera. He waited for her to smooth her hair and snapped the picture. "Wait, I want a shot with my camera." He knelt down, and smiled at her, "Turn me on Nightwind, gimme your best sexy profile."

Nightwind turned her face to him with a sensuous smile, she put her tongue up at her lip, threw out her chest, and angled her leg. "Now we're cruising . . . yeah, we are cruising." He pressed the button. "I'm going to send a blowup to your boyfriend."

"Ha! Okay, Hamlet."

They laughed and took off their packs. Hamlet unwrapped a PowerBar and Nightwind picked from her bag of gorp. They both sat on the ridge and watched hawks ride the wind currents in front of them. A range of hills and mountains across the valley appeared stately and bright under the afternoon sun. A lake to the far left sparkled.

Fifteen minutes later they packed up. Before leaving they stood on the ledge, their poles planted in front of them, and took a last look. Then without a word they moved to the trail and poled north.

CHAPTER THIRTY

MOONWALKER OPTED TO CAMP WHERE he was. His mind was frantic, his insides unspent. He had rubbed himself when he watched Nightwind on the ledge, but saved it. He closed his eyes. *Later.*

He took out his cigarettes and, not in the mood to do anything at the moment, walked up to the ledge for a smoke. About the time he'd accepted that Nightwind would have to wait another day, he heard the telltale clank of hiking poles and then footsteps. He didn't turn to look.

"What a beautiful view."

A woman's voice. He turned.

"I know you—I'm Songbird. You passed me yesterday."

Moonwalker fixed his eyes on her. "How ya doing?"

She laid down her sticks on the other side of her and smiled as she took off her pack. "Great. How are you? Moonwalker, right?" She placed her pack by her sticks.

"Good! Yep, I'm Moonwalker. Mind if I smoke?" He felt inner turbulence settle; new sensations came alive.

"Not at all. I gave it up."

Moonwalker nodded to the view, "This is what it's all about, isn't it?"

"Yes. Look at those mountains. Hard to believe we hiked over them."

They took in the view in silence for several minutes while he smoked. The sun behind them lent a sharpened glow to the conifers below. The cuts between the mountains were defined by gaps, ridges, and the distant lake.

Moonwalker scanned the trail and drew his knees up. "Yep, this is what it's all about."

Songbird pulled out her camera.

"Want me to take your picture?" he said. She handed the digital to him. "Step up there." Moonwalker squished his cigarette and cropped the shot as she broke into a wide grin. He smiled as he handed her back the camera. *She's a cute one, and just as rotten inside as all the rest.*

"Now let me get a picture of you."

"No. I prefer you don't. Thank you anyway."

"Oh, come on. I'm trying to get pictures of hikers I meet."

"No, please—"

"But I insist." She snapped the picture of the standing, sun-glassed Moonwalker looking right at her. "I should have made you take off your sunglasses," she said, as he watched her return the camera to the left side pocket of her pack.

Moonwalker feasted his eyes upon her. *You sorry bitch. I said no and you ignored me.* "Want to share a quick lunch with me? You're waiting for your friends, right?"

"No. They're up ahead. I'm always last, so I'd better keep on going."

"Oh, but I insist," he gave her a wide grin, "you've got plenty of time and the view is spectacular." She looked a couple inches shorter than Nightwind. Compact and spunky, she had straight blonde hair and a sweet round face with playful blue eyes.

When Moonwalker stood up to take her picture on the ledge he had checked the trail. *No one.* With the advantage of sunglasses, she couldn't see his eyes as he scanned again, to make sure. *Not a soul.*

"You want ramen or macaroni?"

"Where's your pack, Moonwalker?"

Moonwalker feigned surprise at the question. "Right over there," he pointed across the trail, "I'm camping here tonight so I can watch the moonrise later, right from the ridge. Come on; let's have something to eat."

They stepped off the rocks and she hesitated. "But, where's your stuff? Wouldn't you eat here on the ledge?"

"Songbird," he put a tender touch on her shoulder and inhaled her scent as he drew closer and pointed, "I'm right over here." But as she said, "No, I think I—," he dealt a short, practiced blow to her solar plexus. She went limp and her mouth opened, sucking for air. This was all the time he needed to carry her across the trail into scrub.

"You'll feel better in a minute, sweetie. Don't try to scream; it won't do you any good because we are all alone, and I don't want to have to punch you again." He said this while carrying her like a baby to his camp. While she rasped as she pulled in air, Moonwalker gagged her. He pulled out the bandanna he had tucked in his shell pocket and after stuffing it into her mouth, picked up a length of rope he had laid under his pack and tied her hands behind her back. "Now you be nice, little bird." He rolled her over on to her back, grabbed the other piece of rope and tied her legs together. He watched her gagging with the bandanna.

"I can fix it for you, but I'm not up for any screaming. If you want to speak to me properly, sweetie, I'll remove it." She pleaded with her eyes.

"Well, if you promise to be good." He reached over and yanked out the bandanna. She coughed, spit up, and wailed. "You're not being good, sweetie." Moonwalker socked her in the nose and this time brought the bandanna around from behind her head and tied it so the knot was fixed in her mouth. Moonwalker bent over her, his face inches from beseeching eyes; her tanned legs trembling as he placed a hand over her crotch and whispered, "Well, aren't you a pretty sight. Now you be a good little songbird, or I'll have to teach you some manners." He got jacked as she tensed and held her breath. He absorbed the fear in her eyes while he playfully walked his fingers over her abdomen and then made a fist as if he was going to punch her there again. She twisted, shut her eyes, and gargled from her throat.

Moonwalker walked back up to the ridge and pulled the camera from her backpack. He looked at the last image, pleased to see new definition in his face, more hair crowding his ears, the fuller beard. He deleted the shot, drew out the digital memory card, and twisted and crumpled it. He edged to the cliff and to the left noticed it dropped straight down. The drop was so sheer the bottom seemed to tuck in underneath him. He crouched down and looking over the edge saw crevasses between boulders. As if aiming a clothespin in the neck of the milk bottle, Moonwalker dropped the destroyed memory card and it disappeared into a black hole. He dropped the camera next, and watched as it banged around several rocks, and disappeared. He hid her pack and sticks behind rocks off to the side and returned to his prey.

It was late afternoon and, except for the occasional gust of wind out of the west, quiet. Moonwalker heard a few late hikers straggle on by, not even bothering to stop for the view. Silence. Not even the occasional airplane. Nothing. Already the sun was sinking. Moonwalker sat backed to a boulder eating macaroni and cheese; Songbird, tied and gagged, stared at the sky. She started to shiver and Moonwalker unrolled his mattress. He didn't inflate it, but rolled her over, put the mattress down, and rolled her back on top of it. He went back to eating his macaroni and cheese. She shivered again and Moonwalker pulled the fleece from his pack and placed it over her. He tucked it under her chin.

"Have some macaroni." She stared at him. "Now you know you gotta be good." She stared. "I'll let you go when this is all over, but only if you're nice and respectful. You understand me?" She nodded. "Well, let's give it a try then."

Moonwalker bent over and slid the bandanna down so the knot was under her chin. He shifted her with the mattress so she leaned against other rocks across from him. She breathed through her mouth and stared at him. "Why are you doing this?"

Moonwalker held her head up and spooned over some macaroni. "Open wide, sweetie."

She took it in and chewed. "I've got to go to the bathroom."

"Last I knew there weren't any bathrooms out here." He pulled her up higher with the mattress still behind. He spooned over more macaroni. "Please, listen," she said. She closed her mouth to the macaroni. He waited with the spoon. "I need—" Moonwalker slid in the macaroni and she spit it out. Moonwalker smacked her across the face and shook his head. He wiped the spoon off by rubbing it against her breasts and brought a fist next to her face as she started to whimper and shake. He leaned into her. "You're starting to get me upset, sweetie. You wanna see the sunrise tomorrow? You wanna see your friends again?"

"Yes," she sobbed. She looked up at darkening sky. "Can I go pee . . . please?"

"No, you can't. You . . . haven't . . . been . . . good. And if you leak in front of me I'll slice you six ways to Sunday." Moonwalker felt as powerful as the president as he watched her shake with sobs. He held another spoonful of macaroni in front of her. "Now you take this and you better eat it right."

UNDER LENGTHENING SHADOWS, MOONWALKER PACKED up. He looked at her. Her eyes were closed, but he could tell she was squinting at him. *What a little bitch!* Her blonde hair was messed as she sat askew against the rock. All at once, he smelled urine. He turned her around so her back was to him, whisked her up by her armpits, carried her fifteen feet further in, and leaned her against another rock. She cried and jerked in spasms. He pulled down her shorts and panties and walked away.

Moonwalker walked up to the trail and crossed over to the ridge. He looked at the gibbous moon still rising in front of him. *One more hour. Yes, one more hour.* He stepped forward and looked down over the edge. He felt the wind on his back. *Okay, she was taking a picture, a gust of wind, a scramble for footing, a "terrible, tragic accident." But, it also could have been suicide. The leap to end it all.*

He watched stars surround him from the ridge. The sky was clear. *I could do her right here. No. They'll search here.* He shuffled back to his victim and heard noises. He discovered her ten yards away from where he'd left her, pants still down, cringing behind a big stone. She was disheveled and had been rubbing rope against rock. A film of sweat matted her hair to her face; her muscles were tensed. If he untied her, she'd spring like a bobcat.

"Now why are you trying to leave me? You know you're not being good. Do I have to teach you manners?"

"You bastard! Why—" Her head snapped as Moonwalker backhanded her. "Please," she squealed. Blood trickled from her nose again.

He grabbed her by the hair and dragged her to a spot by his gear. He wanted to do her. He looked up, but the moon wasn't high enough yet to see her as clearly as he wanted. He leaned her back up against the rock and sat across from her, drawing his knees up. He lit up and offered her a drag but she turned her face away. He watched her as he smoked.

"Where are you from?" he asked.

"Florida."

"What part of Florida?"

"Clearwater."

He was careful not to blow smoke in her face. Moonwalker took the fleece and tucked it around her. He took out his water bottle and uncapped it. "Here, take a sip." Holding it to her lips he tipped it. She swallowed; he waited and tipped it again.

"Thanks."

Moonwalker tightened the cap and put the bottle in his backpack. He looked backward toward the moon where he discerned a faint glow waking up the gloom.

"Moonwalker? Is there some way I can help you?"

He noted the plea in her eyes, but also a frankness and clarity, which unnerved him. He smoked and watched her.

"Why me, Moonwalker? What have I done to you?"

"Nothing and everything." He was surprised he'd said this. He wanted her fear, not conversation. He extinguished his cigarette and looked into her eyes.

He reached over, untied the bandanna which had twisted from her mouth and put it into his shell pocket. "You want me to let you go, Songbird?" He saw a flicker of hope in her eyes. "How do I know you'll keep our secret?" Her eyes were wide open.

"I will, I promise. I've got nothing against you, Moonwalker."

He reached over with his knife and cut the rope binding her legs. He put on his best shameful face and looked away from her, down to the ground; he poked the knife into and out of the dirt. "You say you promise. How do I know you'll keep your promise?"

"Moonwalker," she said, in a whisper, "I won't hold this against you. I promise I won't tell. I will help you. What do you need? Please trust me. I won't breathe a word to anyone."

Moonwalker meekly played with the knife, still poking it in and out of the dirt. He looked up into her eyes, reached over—"come here"— pulled her tenderly to him and with the knife cut the bonds to her hands. He held her as she wept and shook. As he one-handed the knife to his pocket, and reached to his pack for gloves, he rasped into her ear, "I wish I could believe you, but sweetie, you haven't been good." She stilled instantly. Moonwalker yanked her face into his and smiled. He examined her eyes. Just as she tried to bolt, he was upon her like an animal.

TWENTY-FIVE MINUTES LATER, MOONWALKER still wore latex gloves as he carried the clothed, limp body to the trail. He had his pack on and his two poles were lengthwise underneath the body. He listened and looked before crossing the A.T. to Hell Ridge. He placed her on the ground and got her backpack and poles. He took her poles and held them vertical over the ledge before releasing them. He pulled her backpack over and wiggled her into the straps. He thought about taking her food and money—*no, it must look like an accident.* Moonwalker made sure to fasten the sternum strap and pulled it up a notch, bringing it closer to her neck. Under a bright moon Moonwalker shuffled the body with backpack up to the edge. He moved her more to the left and, hesitating only a moment, heaved her over.

CHAPTER THIRTY-ONE

AWOL GOT AN EARLY START from Groundhog Shelter, twenty-three miles north of Hell Ridge. He immediately ran into dropping temperatures and snow, a dank, heavy snow mixed with rain by a cold and bitter wind. He stopped to put on gloves, pulled the hood of his shell over his ski cap and zipped up. He drank from his water bottle and remembered hiking as a boy with his father. "Drink often, Karl, and always in cold, rainy weather."

"But why?" he had asked. "You sweat less in the cold and it seems weird to drink in the rain."

"That's the problem," his father had said, "hypothermia sneaks up on you, you don't realize what's happening as your body becomes dehydrated. In cold, rainy weather, you forget to drink—big mistake."

By late morning it had gotten worse. Awol had slipped twice and gone down once, bruising his arm. He was climbing Max Patch, a bald of 4,600 feet, "Stunning views at the summit," the guidebook said. He crested the top and squinted for cairns showing the way. With the swirling snow and sleet, Awol couldn't see ten yards in front of him. He headed in the wrong direction until, as the swirl momentarily cleared, he discerned a cairn to his right. He found the way down and advanced one measured step at a time. At one in the afternoon he found the sign for Roaring Fork Shelter. He tramped the hundred yards and discovered three hikers inside.

"You guys are beddin' down early," Awol said to two hikers in sleeping bags.

"Hell, we never left," one said as the other laughed. The third grinned as he stirred Ramen in a larger than normal cook pot. They introduced themselves as "The Three Wise Men."

"But how do you know who's who?" Awol asked.

"Makes no difference," the cook said. "We're all in cahoots." The other guffawed again.

Awol looked outside and watched the snow swirl. The next shelter, Walnut Mountain, was only two miles away and he had intended to hike there after a quick snack. It would set him up for thirteen miles into Hot Springs tomorrow for resupply.

The smell of noodles enticed Awol to get out his stove and cook a hot meal. God knows his body needed it. He stirred his pot and noticed a lump on his forearm from his fall. After a meal of steaming noodles, Awol made himself cocoa. Two more hikers burst in through the snow and fog.

"Jesus Christ!" the red-faced one said, "what's with all this freaking snow? I can't see anything out here."

Awol witnessed the other hiker half collapse to the floor, and pulled out the hiker's water bottle. "Here, you need water and dry clothes. Drink up."

Later, after attending to both men, Awol figured he'd spend the night. It would be a longer day tomorrow, but he could rest up now and handle the extra time it'd take to get to Hot Springs. Despite the hot meal, he was beat.

By nightfall, thirteen hikers had crammed into Roaring Fork Shelter in various states of fatigue and agony. No one wanted to tent; ten inches of snow was on the ground. To retard the icy, swirling wind and snow from coming into the shelter, two hikers tied their ground tarps together and hung it from the rafter in front. It helped. Awol laid out his air mattress and part of it bumped into Rambo's, right next to him.

"Let's see if I can angle mine this way," he said to Rambo.

"Appreciate the gesture, but here comes another friendly hiker."

Awol heard the clink of hiking poles getting louder and a hiker blew in through the tarps. He was bundled up and covered in white. "Two more guys are right behind me," he said. He looked around as his pack dripped onto the floor, evaluating options for where he might set up. Hiking poles lay stacked in all corners. Several makeshift clothes lines zigzagged from rafters above. Stoves and cook pots were attended to by hikers who hunched over their food as if their life hinged on these last morsels. Every nail in the hut had something hanging from it and now hikers began to double up and triple up on the same nail. "Jesus, looks like a bomb hit this place," he said.

"Fireball!" hollered Rambo. "Is that you? You look like a polar bear, what's happening, man?"

Fireball pulled off his pack and held it out behind the tarp to wipe off the snow. Next he disappeared outside the tarps to slap himself free of the flakes. He came back in and said to Rambo, "I'll tell ya what's happening; I'm gonna hit Hot Springs tomorrow, and I'm gonna soak in a tub with a large pizza and a six-pack beside me. That's what's happening."

Later, in the black of night, as snow, sleet, and wind beat about the roof, everyone heard Fireball say, "Jersey, I'll take a burger with extra cheese, and gimme an order of onion rings while you're at it."

"Comin' right up," Jersey said. "And who had the chocolate shake?"

"I had the chocolate shake," someone sounded out. "With extra fries. Remember?"

"Oh. That's right, and Rambo gets the Banana Split."

"Hey," someone else hollered out, "whatever happened to my chili dogs and beer?"

"Oh, shit," said Jersey, "I gave them to Moonwalker and he done left." Chuckles all around.

"Moonwalker!" someone said, "now there's a strange dude."

"Yeah," another said, "Nightwind said Moonwalker's creepy, and that he stalked her. She turned around and there he was staring at her through his sunglasses."

"What's with the shades anyway?"

"Hell if I know."

"Someone said he showed up at a shelter under a full moon around three in the morning, but kept on going."

"He's the Moonwalker."

"Is he the dude with the ax hanging off his pack?"

"Yeah, that's him."

"I remember him. I was having a snack and all of a sudden this guy comes out of the woods behind me, off-trail. I joked about a privy he must have found, figuring he took a dump. He looks at me through his shades and doesn't say anything. Then he says, 'I don't think there is a privy out here.'" Laughter. "Then just like that, he leaves."

Awol listened to the banter and thought about Moonwalker. The son-of-a-bitch was odd, no doubt about it. He pursed his lips and wondered where the hell Moonwalker was in this weather.

Next morning at half past five, Awol was the first to awaken and he peeked outside. The snow was light, but another foot had fallen during the night. He reckoned the temperature was twenty-five to thirty degrees. He needed to do fifteen miles today to reach Hot Springs where food and lodging awaited him. He regretted he hadn't pushed himself another two miles yesterday.

Awol reached for his boots and encountered his first problem. Frozen. Not only the laces; he couldn't even bend the boots—they were like bricks. He stepped into them and tramped in place while he cooked oatmeal.

"Whoa," said one of the Wise Men, squinting through the tarps, "we may have to hang for another day."

"Jersey, I'll have extra onions in my omelets," Rambo hollered. "And don't forget the grits."

"Screw the jokes, man; we got some serious shit to handle today." Jersey stared around the tarp. "You guys mind if I piss in here, it's too cold out there."

"Hey, how'd we end up with just guys here last night?" Rambo said.

"Women aren't as batty as they look. Being here like this is stupid, they probably stopped way back." Jersey said.

Awol continued to tramp in place more to keep his feet warm than to loosen the boots. The oatmeal felt good; the hot chocolate even better. He had arranged his gear the night before, and at 6:10 he was ready, but looking out from the shelter he noted a second problem: The morning light showed two-foot drifts along the trail.

"Okay, men, who's ready to saddle up?" Awol barked. "We need the biggest stud here who can high-step drifts. Where you step, we'll step."

"I'll be ready in a few," said Radio Shack.

"Good man, Radio Shack. Let's show these wimps how to hike in snow."

"Shit, Awol, now you know why they call us the Three Wise Men. Got to take it easy out here."

Awol smiled. "Yeah, yeah. Meander from town to town like you guys and I might reach Pennsylvania before I die."

Outside, his boots beginning to flex, Awol noticed yet another problem. So did Radio Shack.

"Awol, can you see any blazes on the trees?"

"Nope. Wind's been blowing north—snow's covered all the blazes. You've got to sense the trail route and then look behind you to check for south bound blazes on the other side of the trees."

"Beautiful. If we were heading south, no problem, right?"

"Just think, we can always turn around and hike backwards."

Radio Shack blazed a decent trail. But Awol had trouble stepping into his tracks. He hadn't realized how tall the guy was. *He must be six-four.* Awol continued to kick out the extra stride length, but it was tiring. He felt like a ballerina doing continual splits.

Radio Shack turned around to check for a blaze and saw Awol lagging. "Am I going too fast?"

"Nah, you're too tall for me. You go ahead."

"Want me to take shorter steps?"

"I'll leg it out myself. Go on, Radio, I'll catch up later."

For two miles Awol made his own tracks in the drifts and followed where the guy walked. He turned backward every so often to confirm a blaze. Awol noted the tracks took a right turn to the next shelter. *He never did get a proper breakfast and wants to take a break.* Awol tramped on alone.

Before he began the ascent of Bluff Mountain, Awol took in water and gorp. As he tipped the bottle to his mouth, he spotted two crows flutter from the pine beside him. Snow fell from the branch they alit from and shook off snow from a lower branch. This repeated on ever lower branches until a thump splattered beside him. He thought of Jack London's "To Build a Fire," how the same occurrence extinguished a newly lit fire, which had been a man's only hope for survival. Awol capped the bottle and pushed on. It was a whiteout and he had to keep constant vigilance for indications of a trail. At times, when he could see further ahead, the way suggested itself. When the snow swirled and his view was limited, he had to guess. Twice he had gone off the trail and the extra work of tracking back to start anew exhausted him. He began to wonder if he could make it to Hot Springs. At least if he had to tent overnight, he was carrying what he needed, but he forced himself to put the thought of tenting out of his mind.

Poling up Bluff Mountain took all the energy he could muster. The drifts frustrated him; he likened it to hiking laps in a swimming pool filled with two feet of paste, except he was going uphill. He hadn't seen a soul on the trail and became unsettled which, in the wild, was unusual for Awol. The weather invited hypothermia, and he stopped often to drink, but his clothes were soaked, and he couldn't stop for long, or risk deadly chills.

The snow got heavier halfway up the mountain and Awol regretted he hadn't taken a break at the last shelter. But he had to summit and get to this point on the other side before he'd have a chance of making it. He drove on. He felt his toes cramping in wet socks. He couldn't remember ever hiking in conditions this bad. Awol's eyes darted in all directions as he looked for a way to make things easier; he squeezed his poles unnecessarily tight. The physical struggle of ascending Bluff Mountain in ever worsening drifts had taken him to his limits. He scanned again to see where he could tent if his body fell apart, but encountered nothing but steepness. He stopped for gorp and drank again.

An hour and fifteen minutes later Awol reached the top. He could barely see and realized this was the critical point; he had to find the right way down. He found a blaze, confirming north, and laid both poles down pointing the tips in that direction. *So far so good.* He took off his pack, pulled out a set of dry socks, and leaned against scrub. He removed his gloves and his fingers worked lazily in the cold to untie his boots. Awol smacked one boot against the other, shaking out snow as best he could and massaged each foot to reduce the cramping before putting on a dry sock. His feet felt better; he drank and pushed on. It was half past one.

As he poled down the other side of Bluff Mountain he discovered countless blow-downs jackstrawed across the trail. Deadfall lay in front of him as far as he could see. *Shit!* Awol kicked a lump of snow. He stopped and wondered if he should tent the night back on top. He plodded around, over, and under limbs, figuring it would end soon. The farther he got, the more he knew he wasn't going back uphill to the summit. He slipped and slid and ducked and crawled under the blowdowns and trudged on.

Halfway down, a good-sized oak was pitched across the trail. He had to climb over it. He straddled the trunk, and in bringing his right leg over, he slipped and his left foot caught on a limb. He fought to retard the slippage so he wouldn't tear a ligament, but he kept sliding down the angled oak and couldn't undo his foot. His right foot touched a knob on the trunk and he stopped the slide but his left leg and foot were over-stretched and tangled. Holding the precarious foothold at the knob, he managed to take off his pack and throw it over. This helped and he had the strength to pull himself back up and untangle the twisted foot. He swung off the trunk and stood up. Awol felt the leg throb, but had no choice but to tough it out.

He reached the bottom of Bluff Mountain favoring the pulled leg and using his two poles together as a crutch. The last rainy miles into Hot Springs were brutal on his bad leg and foot, but Awol knew he'd been lucky. A measly two inches of snow clotted the path, and by the time he got to Hot Springs, it was gone.

CHAPTER THIRTY-TWO

For THREE DAYS AWOL NURSED his leg and foot in Hot Springs, North Carolina. Today it felt much better; tomorrow morning he planned to leave. Awol stood by the post office, overlooking Bridge Street in Hot Springs. This was one of the few times the A.T. ran down a street through town. It was a sunny morning. The snow storm had been a freak one and much of the snow had melted in the mountains.

He talked with Nightwind and Hamlet who had come into town yesterday. "No," Awol said, "to the best of my knowledge, Songbird hasn't been by."

"What happened to her?" Nightwind asked. "I haven't seen her in three days."

"She'll probably show up today," Hamlet said.

"I want to leave tomorrow," Nightwind said, "I'm not waiting anymore."

"She could have gotten hurt," Awol said.

"We didn't get the snow you did; storm was ahead of us." Hamlet said.

"What about all the blowdowns?" Awol said.

"Trail maintainers were working the area by the time we got there and had made reroutes," Hamlet said. "I don't think she'd have had any trouble."

"She would have wanted to get into town and chill out here," Nightwind said. "This isn't like her."

In the unseasonably warm afternoon, Awol walked to a bench outside Bluff Mountain Outfitters with his book, *Undaunted Courage,* a five-hundred-page account of the Lewis and Clark expedition. He didn't want to carry something this heavy on the trail, so he kept it in his "bounce" box, which he kept mailing to himself up the A.T. to a post office. The box included toiletries, town clothes, trail maps, supplies.

He looked up as he began reading a new page and saw Moonwalker hiking into town. He recognized his loping gait and the sunglasses. He watched him go into a convenience mart at the corner and later emerge with a bag. He saw Moonwalker look at him and meander across the street and into a restaurant. Awol continued to read, but crossed to the bench on the opposite side of the street and read there.

A half hour later, Awol put down the book and got up to stretch as Moonwalker came out of the restaurant.

"Moonwalker, right?"

"Right. And you're . . . ?"

"Awol. We met a ways back."

"Yeah. I remember."

"So how's it going?"

"Not bad. They cook a nice meal in there."

"You got that right." Awol put his foot up on the bench. Moonwalker looked to the mountains.

"Staying in town?" Awol asked.

"Thinking about it. Where are you staying?"

"Andersons' motel; you walked by it coming in."

"There's a thought. Well, good seeing you. Gotta get to the post office."

"By the way, have you seen Songbird?"

"Who?"

"Songbird. Small blonde."

"Don't know a Songbird. Maybe I've seen her, but I don't remember meeting someone by that name."

Awol eyed Moonwalker's frame. He'd dropped some weight, especially around the middle.

"Why do you ask?"

"We've been expecting her for a couple of days."

"Quite a storm. Maybe she waited it out."

"Maybe." Awol crossed his arms and stared at the ax hanging off Moonwalker's pack, "But I don't think so."

"So." Moonwalker tapped his sticks on the pavement. "Post office up on the left?"

"At the flag. You in a hurry?"

"Nice meeting you again."

"Adios."

AT A DIFFERENT POST OFFICE, 110 trail miles south, near Fontana Dam, North Carolina, postman Riley looked at a box addressed to Gloria "Phoebe" Strekalovsky. At the bottom it said: Please Hold for A.T. Thruhiker. The carton had sat in the same spot for weeks, and Riley was getting twenty new cartons a day addressed to hikers. Experience told him this was probably a no-show; he pushed the carton to the back under a table.

That night, against his better judgment, Awol walked into the nearest bar and ordered one Bud Light. He clanked his bottle with a few hikers and a local. After several minutes, his bottle not quite empty, he accidentally on purpose knocked the bottle over and watched the rest drain out. He was agitated and felt his fingers wanting to shake. He said goodnight and walked out while he was still in control.

TWO WEEKS LATER, GRIZZLY AND Gambler, who'd begun their thru-hike on April 1, were snacking at Hell Ridge. A gusty afternoon buffeted them as Grizzly plucked from a bag of gorp.

"Gambler, we need to haul ass if we want to make Hot Springs by Saturday. I'm running low."

"We'll make it."

"But it's got to be Saturday morning before the PO—shit! There goes my hat." Grizzly, seeing it fly off, got on his belly anyway and peered over the escarpment. He continued to look.

"Dude! What are you doing, man? That hat is gone."

"Somebody's down there. No shit, Gambler, take a look."

Gambler crawled to the edge and peeked over. "Christ, this ain't good, man. HEY! CAN YOU HEAR ME?"

SIXTEEN DAYS OUT OF HOT SPRINGS, Nightwind was unpacking her bedroll at a shelter when Hamlet came in off the trail.

"Nightwind, did you hear about Songbird?"

Her eyebrows shot up in alarm. "No. What?"

"They found her in the rocks below Hell Ridge back in the Smokies. Remember where we stopped and took pictures? She fell right off the ledge."

"What? Are you serious? Who told you this?"

"They found her the day before yesterday; it's in the papers."

Two other hikers came over. "Yeah," one said, "someone else mentioned it. Did you know her?"

Nightwind sank down on her bedroll, stunned. She wiped her eyes with her bandanna. "Jesus. That's terrible. What the hell is happening out here?"

Hamlet sat down beside her. "She was right behind us; I passed her. Remember the wind on the ridge?"

"But she was a careful hiker," Nightwind said. "She never took chances and always kept to her own pace."

"Is it possible she jumped?" asked the other hiker.

"No way, not Songbird," said Nightwind. "Jesus, first my partner leaves me, and now this."

NEWS TRAVELED FAST ON THE A.T. because of comments in shelter registers, but it generally traveled one way—behind you. Awol was in a Laundromat in Damascus, Virginia, a trail town 189 trail miles north of Hot Springs, when he first came upon the account of a dead hiker who had been discovered off Hell Ridge. Awol remembered the ridge and located it on his maps.

"Recycled, did you see this?" Awol passed the paper to him. Recycled was at the opposite end of a clothes-folding table, writing a letter.

Recycled looked at the article. "No. Did you know her? Says she was thru-hiking."

"Met her once or twice. Seemed like a nice kid."

Recycled read, "Ellen 'Songbird' Sorensen, 22, Clearwater, Florida, discovered by two hikers, pack still on her back." He looked up to Awol. "What a tragedy. Do you think the wind blew her off?"

"Nah, I don't think so. Besides, if it's windy, you'd be even more careful, right?"

"Maybe she committed suicide."

Awol took the paper back from Recycled and read the article again. "Possible, but why jump with your pack on? No mention of a suicide note. And from what I've read, women don't jump."

"So, what do you think?"

Awol hesitated. "It was windy . . . maybe she stumbled. But it doesn't add up for me. Might be foul play. She could have been pushed."

IN RALEIGH, NORTH CAROLINA, DETECTIVE Peck was taking a phone call from Mrs. Strekalovsky, Phoebe's mother, in Rhode Island.

"Detective, I didn't keep the number, but I'm sure Gloria told me she was at a motel in Franklin. I haven't heard from her since. That's not like her, especially since she's got her sister's wedding coming up."

"I see," Peck said, "what did you say her trail name was?"

"Phoebe. I put both names on the box."

"Good."

"She said she would call at every mail drop—I did mail her next box to Fontana Dam, which was on the list she gave me. I'm wondering if I should mail the box after that—Hot Springs, it says."

"Okay, we'll check and see if she's been by at Fontana Dam. You say she sprained her ankle."

"Yes, but she said she was going back to hike in a couple of days."

"Okay, I'm writing this down. Mrs. Strekalovsky, we often get calls about late hikers this time of year, and what we usually find is that it's injury related. She may have given up the hike and is on her way home as we speak."

Detective Peck sent a Missing Person report on Gloria "Phoebe" Strekalovsky to the Franklin Police Department, advising them to contact the Fontana Village PO and to check records of area motels. He also penned a note advising them to contact U.S. Forest Service Park Rangers. Then he went back to work on the cop-killer case which occurred out of his own headquarters.

WHEN MOONWALKER ENTERED HIS ROOM in Damascus, Virginia, he was startled when he looked into the mirror—he didn't recognize himself. *Well, hello Moonwalker.* He'd known for a while that he'd been dropping weight—the end of his belt hung, but a seven- week beard, the long hair covering his ears, and the new and peculiar angles to his face gave him an entirely new look. His face might even be called handsome, in a rugged way. Moonwalker was relieved; this was not at all what he looked like in the newspaper. He was creating a perfect, permanent disguise. In another month he'd be entirely unrecognizable and could discard the sunglasses.

Moonwalker had used the last of his money to secure the room and called his cousin who agreed to express mail cash, in U.S. dollars, to the motel in care of "Moonwalker." He alerted the proprietor a packet would arrive tomorrow.

THE NEXT DAY, MOONWALKER WAS jubilant. He had just received his mailed envelope of cash and had finished a wonderful meal of meatloaf, potatoes, gravy, corn. He was having a piece of rhubarb pie and a second glass of whole milk. He had heard a thru-hiker burned about six thousand calories a day and craved fats. Hiking had steeled Moonwalker. He was becoming fit and felt stronger than he'd ever been. It would only get better, as he lost the fight for extra fats and kept dropping weight on the Appalachian Trail. *Disguise? I couldn't ask for a better makeover.*

Relaxing on the restaurant veranda he drank Molson, smoked, and watched a full moon rising. Then he saw her pass on the other side of the street right in front of him. Her hair was down and she was walking alone—Nightwind.

CHAPTER THIRTY-THREE

WHAT IS IT THAT DRIVES a thru-hiker? For some it is simply the accumulation of miles—and movement. To tread ever forward, mile by mile, is to accomplish. For many it is an escape to adventure. For some it's the desire to be alone and enjoy hard-earned scenic wonders; for others still, the desire to meet new friends, and soul mates. But whatever the reason, many become disillusioned and give up along the way. By the time one reaches Virginia, only the hard core remain, and simple things are huge—water, fruit, vegetables, a good night's sleep.

For most thru-hikers, the night before entering a trail town is anticipation, filled with excitement. They try to arrive in town early—before noon—so they can attend to needs and then eat, rest, eat more salads and ice cream, chill out. Some hikers can't sleep the night before entering town; they crawl from tents and look longingly from hilltops to distant lights of a trail town below, imagining themselves in the flux of humanity once again.

Considered the friendliest hiker-town on the entire Appalachian Trail, Damascus, Virginia shared a distinction that few trail towns did—the A.T. passed right through it. Thru-hikers experienced quickness in their legs as they began a nine-mile descent from mountains, hills, and streams into a town overrun with hikers. Sitting on the edge of the Mount Rogers National Recreation Area, Damascus offered mountain biking, rafting, and tubing as well, but the town belonged to hikers, especially thru-hikers.

Awol laid out his hiking gear on a cot in Dave's Hostel, run by Mount Rogers Outfitters. He planned to go out tonight; it was his last night here and he was up for a good time. He might even permit himself one drink. But first, he'd be back on the trail tomorrow and wanted to rid himself of excess weight. On the PO scale his pack had weighed forty-two pounds and he was shooting to get it under forty. He cut extra strapping off the pack. He threw woolen gloves into a cardboard box; weather was warmer and his Gore-Tex gloves would do. He threw in a jersey, an extra water bottle, the heavy fleece. Awol came to the keys found in the stream and fingered the scrimshawed ivory. He guessed the hiker who had camped by the stream lost them. He looped them through a clip on the back of his pack, figuring Damascus was the one place an owner might spot them. Finished, Awol opened the screen door and stepped into town.

THE FISH AND GAME DEPARTMENT of the Great Smoky Mountains National Park had recorded the death of Ellen Sorenson as an accident. An autopsy had not been requested by her parents nor performed by federal authorities. The game warden's report noted "neck abrasions from pack strapping" which was consistent with the position of the dead hiker. When they had found her, her backpack harness was twisted under her neck. The body was dispatched to Florida and a private funeral service took place two days later.

The tragedy had been in the news, but buried in the back pages of the North Carolina papers. Iraq continued to be the top story. If anyone from the North Carolina police departments had noticed the newspaper account, nothing had been mentioned.

Moonwalker picked up his Molson and snuck to the corner of the second floor veranda. He observed Nightwind cut into a hiker's Bed & Breakfast, off the main street, where she idled with two other hikers, one of them Awol. He had planned to stay in town another day. Moonwalker was vigilant, but was losing his fear of the law. The demise of Songbird was a non-issue. He had read the news account and was relieved—"a terrible accident."

He watched Nightwind as she leaned on one leg and angled her ass in the evening light. She crossed her arms in front of her and arched her shoulders as he suspected she felt a chill. She flung her hair, flicked it again, and leaned on the other leg. *Does she know I'm watching? Is she taunting me?* Resolve took hold and swelled. Moonwalker sipped his Molson in the moonlight, all the while focusing on her. *Yes, you will be the next one. Got away before, but you won't this time.* He wanted to swoop down off the veranda, pick her up, and fly off. *Just me and Nightwind. Back up to the mountains.* He cupped his ear as she stepped away from the other hikers and hollered back, "Yeah, I'm leaving right after breakfast."

The fact that Nightwind might hike with another didn't enter into Moonwalker's immediate calculations. His mind was made up; he'd find a way. *I'll stalk and chip. I'll be patient and wait my chance. It's a long way to Canada. The irony . . . don't even want to leave the trail now if I could. Got it all right here. Every day.*

Moonwalker had spotted Awol in town earlier and avoided him. *Fucker might be on to me.* But he contemplated more, and dismissed him. He watched Awol, cigar in hand, wobble from the Inn to the hostel. He ground out the cigar before he entered.

THE NEXT MORNING AWOL WAS nursing a hangover and angry with himself. Nightwind, Hamlet, and Recycled were having their breakfast on a restaurant porch and watching a rainstorm get stronger by the minute.

"Here we go again," Hamlet said. "This rain looks like it's going to settle in and stay."

"I hate the rain," Nightwind said. "I'm forever slipping in the mud."

Awol moved to the wall where his pack leaned and unzipped it. He pulled out his shell as Moonwalker came onto the porch.

"Moonwalker, give us some sunshine," Recycled said.

"I'll do my best," Moonwalker said, as he looked at the rain. He spied Awol and the packs lined against the wall. He walked to a table, slid off his pack and placed it next to him. Then wondering what to do with his poles, he picked up everything and headed to the wall. As Awol left his pack and walked back to the table, Moonwalker placed his gear at the wall next to Awol's. Right away he noticed his keys, scrimshaw and all, dangling from Awol's pack. His legs went weak. He was slow to lean his poles next to his pack as he stared at his keys. He turned around to see Awol looking right at him.

"You got a cabin or a car up here?" Moonwalker said.

"Why do you ask?"

"What's with the keys?"

"Oh that. Found them on the trail. Figure someone might have lost them, and this way, they're easy to spot."

"I see."

"Pull over a chair, Moonwalker," said Recycled. "You know everybody, right?"

"Yes, I believe so." Moonwalker smiled at Nightwind. "How we all doing?"

Everyone shuffled to make room at the round table and the waitress accommodated as she provided an extra place setting and handed Moonwalker a menu.

Nightwind didn't return a smile to Moonwalker. "Well, we're not too happy about this rain," she offered.

They looked out as rain bounced off the street and made a racket on the porch roof.

"What can I get you?" the waitress asked Moonwalker.

"Pancakes. Lots of them. And coffee." Moonwalker caught Nightwind rolling her eyes and his gut hardened.

"Moonwalker," said Hamlet, "can I ask why you always wear sunglasses?"

Not taking his eyes off of Nightwind, he saw her smirk. When she read his face, she put her hand over her mouth as if to stifle a yawn.

"I have sensitive eyes. I take medication for it and the glasses help."

"What kind of medication?" asked Awol.

Moonwalker played with the whiskers on his chin and studied Awol. *I'm going to have to kill this motherfucker.* "Eye drops."

"I see."

As they ate, Moonwalker noticed that Nightwind would not look at him and talked as if he wasn't at the table. *You think you can laugh at me and ignore me? You fucking bitch. You've dug your own grave.*

They finished pancakes and omelets and French toast drenched in syrup, ordered another round of coffee. Already 8:10, they hoped the rain would ease. Awol and Nightwind went to the restrooms, which was what Moonwalker had been waiting for. At an opportune moment, while Recycled and Hamlet were absorbed in discussion, he reached over and picked up Awol's dirty fork by pinching the edges halfway up the curve of the handle. As Recycled and Hamlet talked, he ambled over to his pack with the fork and placed it into a ziplock bag. He fixed his eyes on his keys hanging from Awol's pack while stashing the bag in his own and returned to the table.

All but Awol drank coffee; he sipped orange juice. Hamlet was discussing Songbird with Recycled. "She was right behind us," Hamlet said. "Each day she'd start out with Nightwind, but she would always arrive later at camp. We don't know how it could have happened."

Recycled looked over to Awol and said, "Awol thinks she could have been pushed."

"Now, why would someone do that?" Moonwalker said, looking straight at Awol. "You push her, Awol?"

They all looked at Awol.

"Moonwalker, take off your glasses a minute," Awol said.

Everyone's movements went into slow motion.

Moonwalker put both arms on the table and leaned in. "Mr. Awol, you want my glasses off, why don't you try taking them off."

"Hey," Recycled said, "the rain's got us all down, let's . . ."

Nightwind got up abruptly to leave, followed by Hamlet. Moonwalker and Awol sat and stared at each other.

Recycled put his hand on Awol's shoulder, "C'mon, Awol, let's make some miles."

After breakfast a gaggle of hikers brooded about Main Street wondering whether to wait for the rain to ease or move on. Awol had already made up his mind. Fueled with anger, he poled off. Two others followed. Moonwalker smoked under an awning, waiting for Nightwind to make a move. The stakes had changed; the keys had been a shock, and now he knew Awol was watching him. But he could chip, and when Nightwind headed out in front of Recycled, Moonwalker sucked a last mighty puff and threw up his hood. The rain was incessant.

TEN MILES LATER AWOL WAS taking a break in Saunders Shelter, a quarter mile off the trail. The morning hike had cleared his head, but he wasn't happy about the night before, nor breakfast today. He kept telling himself that he drank last night to see if he could do it within reason. But he hadn't been able to stop when he'd told himself to. He tried to convince himself that after 460 miles he owed himself a fun night out, but knew that was a bunch of crap. He reminded himself that he wasn't out here to drink, screw around, or get involved in Moonwalker's shit. He needed to deal with some serious shit of his own. Plus he still had a business back in Boston and, of course, there was Linda. He wasn't going to give up on her. Nevertheless, Moonwalker had gotten him steamed.

———————

AT LOST MOUNTAIN SHELTER, AWOL chose to tent next to a rill, hidden by lilies. The rain had stopped and it had turned sunny in the late afternoon. Nightwind, Recycled, Hamlet, and four others piled into the shelter. No sign of Moonwalker.

Moonwalker lay prone ninety yards to the northwest and had his binoculars trained on Awol. He watched Awol eat with Recycled by the campfire. *He's gotta go.* Moonwalker spied Hamlet and Nightwind talking at the corner of the hut. *Hamlet likes Nightwind; she tolerates him. Hamlet won't be a problem; Awol's the problem.*

That night Moonwalker evaluated every possible scenario. He concluded it was too risky to do Nightwind while Awol was around. And killing Awol to get to Nightwind was plain stupid. *There are other women I can have, others who will come my way. My goal is Canada. But I can chip. And Nightwind will be on the trail for a long time.*

———————

IN THE MIDDLE OF THE night Moonwalker woke up thinking about Awol. He put on his headlamp and drew out his maps and handbook.

CHAPTER THIRTY-FOUR

IF AN EAGLE WERE TO eye the Appalachian Trail from high above the earth and if his eye could penetrate trees and flora on this May day, he would see sprinkles of northbound thru-hikers in the Mid-Atlantic States, perhaps one or two entering southern New England. He'd see clumps of northbound hikers in Georgia and North Carolina, and a band of southbound hikers starting from Maine. But most of all, in May, he would see large clumps of hikers pushing north through Virginia. More than five hundred miles, about one-fourth of the A.T., lies in Virginia and tackling all those miles in the damp spring brings what hikers call the Virginia blues.

OVER THE NEXT WEEK MOONWALKER stalked Awol. At times, he could barely keep up. Got plenty of trail left, he thought, as he took a break at a shelter and examined the register. Awol had written the last entry: *May 3. Here for lunch. Will take a zero in Pearisburg. Awol.*

Moonwalker was alone in the shelter and after putting on gloves, he tore out Awol's handwritten comments from the journal. His watch read 3:10 p.m. *Awol was here a couple of hours ago.* He studied the handwriting and noted the ink matched all the previous entries. He picked up the very end of the pen clipped to the register and placed both pen and torn register page in a baggie where there was another page and pen, fingered by Awol.

MOONWALKER NEARED MILL SHELTER WHERE he was sure Awol camped. He was too tired to hike north of the shelter, which would have isolated him more. He felt other hikers wouldn't be coming this late—six o'clock—and when he viewed the sign leading a quarter mile east to the shelter, he made camp south of it.

He bushwhacked and listened for voices; he smelled their fire. The sky darkened, but he took time to scout around and find a spot where he could see the camp. He focused his field glasses and spotted several hikers, some familiar, but didn't see Awol.

———————

MOONWALKER WAS IN HIS TENT staring at the dark. *Something's not right.*

Awol was also awake in his tent in front of Mill Shelter, a hundred yards north of Moonwalker, also staring at the dark. He wondered why when he hid to the west of the trail sign for the shelter, waiting on the hunch someone was following him, Moonwalker, on seeing the sign, had chosen to bushwhack to the southeast. *Yes, he wanted to spy on the shelter. But why? Is he a Peeping Tom?*

———————

AWOL BROKE CAMP ON A raw morning, and only Amble stirred as Awol stepped off at 6:35. When Awol reached the trail he moved across it to the west and hid by the boulder as he had the day before. At 6:55 he heard a rustle to the east and Moonwalker emerged from brambles onto the trail. Moonwalker scanned the trail and headed right back into rough. Awol stayed hidden by the rock. At 7:30 Amble, Spiderman, and Stilts spilled onto the trail.

"Why did Awol leave so early after getting in late?" Amble asked.

Spiderman checked his map, "What? I don't know." Their voices were shrill, and cut the morning air.

Minutes later Moonwalker emerged again and stepped north. Awol wanted to confront him. *No. I'll track this bear.*

Ten miles later Awol came upon Jenny Knob Shelter. He glanced at the register and read the last entry:

Howdy, A. Why are you following me? I'm behind the privy. M.

Awol removed his pack. He unclipped his scabbard, peeked through cracks in the siding of the shelter and looked at the path to the privy. He would wait until another hiker showed. Moonwalker might not be there, but he suspected Moonwalker would spy on the privy. Awol soaked in every sound.

Fifteen minutes later another hiker came. The woman looked to be late thirties or early forties, and sported a light daypack with a bed roll. Her hiking poles looked new; she was a touch heavy, but attractive.

"Hi. You a thru-hiker?" she asked.

"I am. And you?"

"I'm out for a couple of days. My sister's meeting me in Pearisburg." She gave the impression that she was athletic, had been fit at one time, but had let herself go, and was out to regain her fitness. "Any water here?"

"Follow those blue markers. It should be down a ways."

"Thanks."

Awol watched her take off her pack and head to the spring. He stood up and marched to the privy, at the last second grabbing his sticks. Up and around the bend, forty yards later, he swung open the door. Empty. He walked inside anyway so he could peer through the slats to the rear. No one was there, as he expected. He looked to the right and left and behind him. He exited the privy and walked behind it, half expecting to find something placed there by Moonwalker. He looked on the ground—nothing. As he turned to go back he saw knife-scrawled on the backside of the privy: "Howdy."

Awol stared at the scrawl. He'd put himself on a collision course with a man who was a complete mystery. Awol was suspicious of him, but lacked anything concrete. *What if this guy's just a strange dude? Deviant, but not a threat to people, and I've got him riled. He may not even be a peeper and I'm creating a problem.* Awol figured he was being watched, but leaned on his poles to think. *Okay, I'll back off. I'll give him the benefit of the doubt.* Halfway back Awol stopped for a moment, turned around and walked back to the privy. He slid out his knife and scrawled below: "OK, you win."

Marching back, he pondered his decision to disengage. *I'm sure he watched me scrawl the message and he'll think I'm a wimp. Exactly the leverage I want if I need the element of surprise later.* Awol yanked up his pack, slipped it on, and pushed off. He didn't look back.

SEVERAL MINUTES LATER MOONWALKER CAME out of hiding from across the trail. He had managed to spy on the privy as well as the shelter. The woman's pack was still there and he met her coming back from the stream carrying two water bottles. She had stuck a stem of mountain laurel into her hair, and was smiling.

"Hello," Moonwalker said.

"Well, hello yourself. Another thru-hiker?"

Moonwalker smiled as he unloaded his pack. "Yes. I'm Moonwalker." He extended his hand.

"I'm Margie. Only out for a couple of days."

"So nice to meet you." Her hand was warm. "Be right back."

He walked to the privy.

"WELL, MARGIE," MOONWALKER SAID, AS he rounded the shelter, "looks like you picked some pretty good weather. It was a bit nippy this morning, but it feels good now."

"Yes it does." She smiled and took out her food bag.

Moonwalker did the same. "Let's see what goodies I've got here today." He rummaged through his bag. "Let's see—"

"Want some cheese? I brought too much, I think."

"I'd love a piece."

She handed him the piece and brushed his hand.

"Tastes good, doesn't it?" she said.

"Um," Moonwalker grunted. He chewed, took another bite, and looked up to a sunny sky. "Smell the honeysuckle? I'm thinking I might camp somewhere around here tonight."

Margie let an opportunity slide, but looked as if she was thinking about camping there as she drew up her knees and wrapped her arms around them. "It's so nice out here."

Moonwalker thought his plan through and went over the map in his mind again. He took out his guidebook and confirmed his thoughts; I'm close, just six miles away, to Route 606 which is a short walk to Route 42, where I can hitch out. Good sense told him what he should do right now—get out of here and hitch north a couple hundred miles. Start anew, different trail name, no shades. Get women up there on the way to Canada.

Just one problem. He'd gotten that uncontrollable urge. Again. And it needed attention. A victory over Awol, the increasing sense of power and fitness, an immediate escape plan in place, and this attractive, receptive woman beside him had contributed to a burst of anticipation and sexual hunger. Moonwalker let the desire build. He sat rigid and had to close his eyes. If his life depended on it, he could stand up and leave. *But am I in danger here? Is there a gun to my head?*

"Want more cheese?"

"Huh? Oh. Thank you."

"Sorry, didn't realize you were dozing."

Moonwalker almost wanted another hiker to show. But he knew, and he didn't know how he knew, that nobody was near.

"So what do you do, Margie?"

"I work in a camera shop."

"Take a lot of pictures?"

"No. I'm not into photography. It's just close to where I live, plus, the owner is a friend and the customers are nice."

They sat side by side, looking out of the shelter, their legs hanging over the floor edge. They watched a chipmunk scurry around the fire ring.

"What do you do, Moonwalker?"

"I paint houses, but quit to do this. I'm self-employed and can make my own schedule. Want some gorp?"

"Okay."

Moonwalker handed her a baggie, "Take as much as you want."

"Thank you."

Moonwalker felt too warm all over and rocked back and forth. He rubbed a thigh. He needed to leave, this instant.

"Margie? Would you like to camp with me tonight?"

She remained calm and didn't move. "Do you mean here?"

"No." Moonwalker gave her a pleading look. "Somewhere private, where we might be alone. Together."

"Oh. Sounds like I'm being propositioned." She looked into his shades and smiled.

"You are."

Margie looked to the front and her profile transfixed Moonwalker. She was lovely and the stem of pink mountain laurel in her hair built a strange excitement in him. "Well I just met you, Moonwalker," she said in profile.

He thought she was teasing him and Moonwalker did not like this. He was not up for games. He looked at her neck. *I could twist it like a chicken's.*

"Well, kind of hard to do a normal courtship here. And you'll be gone in a couple of days. I'm hoping we can go with the spirit of the moment." He gave her his best smile.

Margie fingered the mountain laurel in her hair and put her hand on top of his. She pointed to a clearing thirty yards out. "Do you like blueberries? There are some just starting to ripen, and they're delicious. See over there? Some bushes are ripe down by the stream. Let's go pick blueberries, and we can talk more . . ."

It's never easy. I'm in a jam, half in, half out. Work with me, bitch, just say yes. Or no.

"Margie. Would you like to come and camp with me tonight?"

Margie drew her hand away. She looked favorably upon him and said without the slightest trace of superiority and with a soft, polite frankness, "No, I don't think so, Moonwalker. But I do appreciate your asking."

Moonwalker found himself getting up; it was as if each leg informed the other—follow. He readied his pack and hoped she wouldn't say or do anything else and he might be able to extricate himself, to hitch on out of here, to regroup, to—

"Moonwalker?"

He hesitated and turned.

"I'll let you kiss me goodbye."

It was the word "let"— that one syllable, those three letters. "Did you say 'let'?" Moonwalker stepped over to her and leaned down as she turned her face up to him. He caught her scent as he kissed her sweetly on her lips and rammed his fist into her midriff.

Moonwalker was calm as he scanned the trail with the woman on his shoulder. He unhitched the rope hanging from his pack and hustled away from the spring to the west, the least likely direction. As he swung by some pines she began to gasp and he pulled his bandanna from his pocket and stuffed it into her mouth. She was not heavy for Moonwalker, as he carried her down a small grade. He tramped into woods and came to a depression. The north side was exposed, but only to forest. He laid her down and struggled to tie her. *God, she's a strong bitch.* He made sure she couldn't cough up the bandanna and then tied her to roots, forcing her to remain on her back. He snuck back to the shelter.

Good. No one has come. He donned his pack, picked up all the sticks and her day pack. As he returned to Margie, he sighted a way through a saddle to the northeast which would enable him to leave the scene and drop back on the trail north of the shelter.

BLOOD COVERED HIS LATEX GLOVES. Margie had put up such a fight he'd had to bash her head with a rock. Moonwalker was broken, all for naught he thought. Just before the peak moment, after he entered her and had looped rope around her neck, she managed to poke one of her fingers into his eye. He'd lost his grip on the rope for an instant, enabling her to stick her hand into the loop. He grabbed around for a rock. His eye hurt and he couldn't properly strangle her as he pumped inside her. He was distraught as he pulled out. No fear in her eyes, no joy for him, just her dead stare. This doesn't count, he told himself. This doesn't count.

CHAPTER THIRTY-FIVE

TEN WEEKS AND 944 MILES later, Awol was approaching U.S. Route 20, five miles east of Lee, Massachusetts. This afternoon Awol intended to cross over the road and hike seven more miles to October Mountain Shelter where he planned to camp.

As he hiked down into the sylvan gap where Route 20 crossed the Appalachian Trail, he observed two police cars parked off the side of the road. Nearing the junction it appeared three policemen had detained Strider and Trudge with whom he had camped, off and on, the last several days. As he drew nearer, however, an officer mumbled something to them and they moved away.

Awol stood still as all three policemen walked to him. "Are you Karl Bergman?" the lead officer asked.

"Yes." He glanced at Strider and Trudge.

"You are under arrest for the murder of Marjorie Santoro in Virginia." The second policeman pulled the knife from his scabbard while the third took his hiking poles and removed his pack. The lead policeman turned him around and brought out the cuffs, "You have the right to remain—"

"Whoa. Hold on a minute. I don't know this Marjorie person; I'm sure you have me mixed up with some—"

"If I were you, I'd say nothing more. We're taking you in."

Part Three

The conscience is a thousand witnesses.

—Hobbes, *Leviathan*

CHAPTER THIRTY-SIX

MOONWALKER HAD HAD THIS DREAM before. He was running. People chased after him; he couldn't see them, but he could hear them. He ran faster down a hill and sprang off to the right. Down again he angled toward thicker woodland, over rocks, side stepping scree. He'd lost his pursuers, but as he gasped behind a balsam, he heard voices and then heard them renew the chase. His fears multiplied until, with a dedicated convulsion, he woke himself.

He lay in bed, soaked, the sheets tangled and extended to the floor. A moment passed. He loved this moment of resurrection as calm enfolded him.

His bruised eye hidden by sunglasses, Moonwalker, with patience, had been able to string three hitches, which got him from Virginia to Allentown, Pennsylvania. Despite this new escape and the planting of evidence from Awol near the grave, Moonwalker had shown his hand. He hadn't stayed on plan and the murder of Margie had been a wasted effort. Moonwalker cursed himself as he lay in bed. *Once again, some bitch fucked me over.*

Although trucking companies don't allow their drivers to pick up hitchhikers, drivers do anyway to help them stay awake, and for the camaraderie. On the last hitch, a trucker had taken a liking to him and the driver called a contact at the Allentown depot asking if he could find a room for Moonwalker. Through a friend, the contact came up with a cheap room in Coopersburg, south of Allentown.

Moonwalker had stayed in his room for the first three days. His eye began to heal and he rested. He had a small fridge for the milk he used on his morning Corn Flakes or Grape-Nuts. Across the street was a trucker's diner where he ate lunch and dinner. His cousin mailed him money, and, for a while, Moonwalker had been content to stay out of sight. But then Moonwalker began to miss the trail. At night he would fantasize and empty himself over Nightwind, or Malibu, or someone else he'd met on the trail. In his darkened room, with the lights of semis pinching through the busted shade and dancing on the ceiling, Moonwalker would imagine chicks in front of him as they hiked and planted their sticks. He watched their calves and thighs twitch and tighten, their butts become defined as they bent forward to climb. He wondered where Nightwind and Malibu might be at this moment and pictured them on their sides, their legs drawn up, sleeping alone in their tents. Isolated tents, separate, hidden, where only Moonwalker had access. One tent called to him. He burned with desire as he watched Nightwind pull open her sleeping bag exposing full, milky breasts. She was warm, she was dreaming under a full moon. He felt her draw his hand to her breast and she beckoned him to lean down to kiss her ripe nipples. Moonwalker did. He felt her on his fingers and brought the taste to his lips. Nightwind.

IT TURNED OUT THE DINER needed a part-time dishwasher. On a whim, Moonwalker offered to dish-wash for free meals, no money, therefore no paperwork, and no questions. At the end of his lunch, the proprietor agreed. He could start tonight and work weeknights from eight to ten. Over the next weeks, Moonwalker showed up at eight Monday through Friday and received a free take-out lunch and dinner each day, including Saturday. The restaurant was closed on Sunday. One waitress was obese, the other was old; neither turned him on, and Moonwalker thanked the Almighty for this favor. Each Friday he left five bucks for the waitress who prepared his takeouts.

He did this for two weeks. He'd been holed up for almost a month. He considered his circumstances. Margie's body was most likely found already. He hadn't the wherewithal or the time to make and hide a grave, so he had turned it into an opportunity to set up Awol. Although he'd taken a risk, he was in no rush to get to Canada. Moonwalker knew once he reached Canada, he would have to try to change his life, resist his compulsion. He now realized that he didn't want to change.

He reckoned the law would conclude that a killer was loose on the A.T. when they uncovered the newest body. He had left Virginia a month ago and the bulk of hikers, the most opportunities for more women, were in that band. He needed to figure out how far those women he left would have advanced in this last month, and enter the trail behind them. *I'll be able to read the doings of everybody in front of me in the trail registers. Perfect.*

Moonwalker rechecked his maps and guidebook, and calculated it would be another two weeks before the likes of Nightwind, Hamlet, and all the others he'd met, reached the greater Allentown area. He listened to the news and read the newspapers every day and appeared to be in the clear. He figured that when the body was discovered, the authorities would make hiking estimations from the approximate date of death, and place the killer further ahead from where he planned to reenter the trail.

Moonwalker kept to himself for another two weeks. He stayed in his room during the day, studying his guidebooks and reading from newspapers and news magazines; and he watched the news on TV. He walked outside at night, after work at the restaurant but became moody and nervous. Sometimes he felt he should have hit the trail a month ago and stayed with his original plan to get to Canada as soon as possible. But it would be a gift to fall in behind this band of women and they should all be about to finish hiking through Pennsylvania.

Every few hours Moonwalker would get so antsy he'd resort to pushups and deep-knee-bends in his room. After twenty-five pushups he kept on pumping, exhaling ever louder gusts of air through rounded lips, sounding like the pneumatic air hose in a service station. His face blotched red as he set himself to do a total of forty without stop. His back remained as straight as an ironing board. Next, with his heels on a telephone book, he charged into deep-knee bends. He was a caged animal and four or five times a day he pushed through this routine. He found he hadn't wanted to spend money on junk food and had forced himself to stay with proteins and vegetables which his body, after weeks of hiking, craved anyway. He had told the waitresses, "The daily special, extra veggies, no gravies, no rolls, no butter and no desserts." He'd tried giving up cigarettes; he had cut back, but couldn't give them up completely.

After his fitness routine, Moonwalker calmed down, and felt clarity. Before bed one night after fifty pushups, forty-three without stop, and a hundred deep-knee-bends, Moonwalker came to an understanding. He remembered the story about the scorpion. The scorpion promised the frog he would not sting him if he swam him across the pond—gave the frog his word—then later the scorpion stung him. "You gave me your word," said the frog. "But I am a scorpion, and what I do is sting."

Moonwalker accepted the facts. He stared at the ceiling and realized nothing was going to change when he got to Canada. When he had killed Phoebe just before he escaped, and then killed Songbird so easily on the trail, he'd lost his fear. And sense of urgency to hike north. *It's easy to find women out here. It will be harder in Canada with the Ouilettes around. I'm going to Canada—Ray says he can sneak me over—but on my own schedule. If I get caught, it will be my own fault. But no matter what, I won't let them toss me in prison.*

———————————

A WEEK LATER, JULY 20, after forty-eight days off-trail, a physically charged Moonwalker reentered the Appalachian Trail at Blue Mountain Summit on Pennsylvania 309.

CHAPTER THIRTY-SEVEN

Awol WAS BOOKED AND HELD without bail. He maintained his innocence and insisted on a lie detector test. He voiced suspicions about the earlier demise of Songbird and was questioned about that death, which had been written off as an accident. Awol agreed a killer was loose on the trail, but it wasn't him. Awol told the investigators he knew who the killer was and that he'd been set up. During the interrogation he remembered meeting Marjorie Santoro at Jenny Knob Shelter; the same place where Moonwalker left a message in the register and wrote on the back of the privy. He was certain Moonwalker had hidden there and had watched him hike away.

In a surprising change of heart, Linda drove out to lend her support, and wrote a personal statement which she handed to authorities. It gave a summary which corroborated Awol's answers to wheres and whens before his hike, and ended with comments about his military background and a plea for circumspection, for she felt a big mistake was being made. Awol pointed them to two entries in his private journal, which had been confiscated, that noted his suspicions about Moonwalker. The investigators interviewed Strider and Trudge who had been asked by the police to remain in town. They made supporting statements and Trudge was able to locate Hamlet who, though he couldn't state with certainty that Awol wasn't in the areas at the estimated times of death, was adamant in his support of Awol. "Absolutely no way," he repeated to the investigators. A thorough examination of Awol's journal, an interview with yet another witness, Nightwind, and finally a lack of evidence

cleared Awol of any involvement with Ellen "Songbird" Sorenson. They
had taken his boots, and Awol assumed that they compared imprints
with photos of tracks near Santoro's body. He knew they wouldn't find
his DNA on the victim, nor his fingerprints on her body. Awol passed a
lie detector test and was released on July 25, four days after being booked.
"We'll find you if we need to," the investigators said.

Awol was shaken. He withdrew and wouldn't speak, not even to
Linda. During the ride to Boston, she drove and Awol didn't say a word.
That night in her home, Awol reached over to her as he lay on his back
in the dark. He squeezed her wrist, "Thanks." But that's all he said and
all he did.

For the next few days Linda let him be. She saw him brood and knew
he was unsure of his next step. And she knew he was trying hard not to
drink. On the third night he snapped out of his funk. He came behind
her as she readied for bed, lifted her up off her feet and carried her from
the bath to the bed. He laid her down and raw passion overtook him.
He was rough and as he emptied himself into her she asked him to take
it easy.

"I'm sorry, Linda. I didn't mean to—"

"It's all right. You've been through a lot." They nestled beside each
other, and held hands in the dark. "But, it's over for you now, Karl."

Her statement had the opposite effect of what she had intended.

"No. No, it's not over. It's not over at all. I know who the killer is,
and I'm going after him."

Awol was shouting as he bounded out of the bed and turned on the
light. He looked at her with anguished eyes as he came to her side of the
bed. "I left him alone, even though I knew something wasn't right with
him, and he raped and killed her. Linda, I could have stopped it."

Linda sat up and pulled the bedsheet around her. She saw the chaos
in his eyes. "Don't say that. How could you have known?" She reached
out to him, but he avoided her. "Karl, you may have had suspicions about
this guy, but you couldn't have known he was going to kill that woman."

Awol wrapped a towel around his waist and paced the bedroom. He
came back and sat on her end of the bed. "I should have known how
dangerous this guy was. I should have trusted my instincts. Ever since
Kuwait, I've been second guessing myself. But no more."

Linda caught the panic in his voice. "You couldn't have known. Why are you blaming yourself? What were you supposed to do? If he is the killer, he could have killed you too." She reached out to him again.

Awol stood up. "You don't understand. I should have stayed and confronted him. We would have had it out and I could have stopped him—I could have saved that woman's life." He'd been looking away from her as terrible memories from another time and place climbed into his brain. The bedroom was hot and oppressive; he smelled the heat of night as he loosened the towel. "I'm sorry, but I need to be alone right now. Please don't come near me for a while, okay?"

"You need your meds."

Awol burnt her a look and went to the medicine cabinet. He uncapped two bottles and dumped the contents into the toilet, then flushed it. Still not satisfied, he took the bottles and caps with him to the bedroom window by Linda, shoved up the screen and threw them out. Linda turned away from him and jammed her face down into her pillow.

Several days went by and Awol remained agitated. During the day he examined newspapers at the library hoping to find new information, and twice he called the Lee Massachusetts Police department to see if they had made progress. "Is there any way I can help? Do you want me—"

"No, stay put. We'll contact you if we need to," they had said.

He worked through his pack item by item. He put aside what he didn't need, threw the keys with scrimshaw away, cleaned all his equipment. He managed to reduce his pack weight to thirty-five pounds. This included four-and-a half days of food and two liters of water. Instead of taking a roll of duct tape, he wound some around his water bottles. He removed the cardboard tube from his roll of toilet paper. He cut half the handle off his toothbrush, discarded his spoon and fork and bought a titanium spork, used his knife to again shorten straps on his pack. He trimmed his shoe laces. When he was done he put his pack, poles, and boots next to the doorway in the family room.

"What the hell is this?" Linda glared at the pack.

"If he's out there, I'm going to get him."

She started to say something but turned around and stormed to the kitchen.

AFTER THEY FINISHED DINNER, LINDA took a different approach.

"So, Karl," she said, after a sip of espresso, "what did you learn from Hamlet? He called this morning, right?"

"He did." Awol reached for more wine colored grapes. "Said no one's seen or heard from Moonwalker. No mention of him in any of the registers."

"He's left the trail. He's gone for good, right?"

Awol didn't respond. He breathed a sigh and popped a grape into his mouth. "You told the police everything you could. They'll be on the lookout."

"What do they know? First of all, to them he's only a suspect because I say so. Second, I don't know his real name, where he's from, where he's going. Third, I don't know anything about him other than he's left-handed, big, and wears sunglasses supposedly because of some eye problem, which I'm sure is a crock." He fingered a slice of cheddar and some more grapes and drew them to his plate. "My gut says he's the killer. We didn't like each other. I told you what happened at the shelter. He knew I was on to him, and he must have planted his shoddy evidence from me where he ditched the body. I did not touch that woman."

"I believe you. The police believe you. He set you up. Let it go, 'cause there's nothing you can do."

"I hate to admit it, but you may be right. I missed my chance—"

"So put it behind you. And I think we should try to make a go of it." He didn't reply. "It's what you want, right?"

"Yeah. But you know, of course, I aim to finish this hike, one way or another." He looked at her.

"That's the worst possible thing you could say to me, Karl Bergman. You bastard. I came back to you; I brought you home for Christ's sake. For what? So you can dump me again?" Standing now, after bumping the table hard enough to knock the grapes off Awol's plate, she gained fury. "Go ahead on your fucking hike!" she yelled. "If that's all you care about," she threw the placemat at him, "go ahead. Get the hell out of here! But don't come back. I am done."

THE NEXT AFTERNOON, THREE WEEKS after his release from jail, his business partner, Tom, dropped Awol off at the A.T. trailhead in Lee, Massachusetts. Awol had thought about buying a gun, but understood there would be a waiting period and more background checks and that gun laws varied by state. He'd been searched by the Massachusetts police, and felt packing a gun would need a lot of explaining on a hiking trail if he was apprehended again. Not to mention the excess weight, ammo, and security issues while hiking the trail. He crossed Route 20 and didn't stop as he poled by the spot of his arrest. He glanced at the spot while passing, but pushed the memory of it out of his mind.

THE SAME MORNING, AUGUST 15, Moonwalker had also crossed Massachusetts U.S. Route 20, and was on his way to Kay Wood Lean-to.

CHAPTER THIRTY-EIGHT

THE ARREST AND SUBSEQUENT INVESTIGATION of Karl Bergman led to a discussion with rangers of The Great Smokey Mountains National Park, where the body of Ellen Sorensen, trail name "Songbird," had been found. The rangers, who were called by the police in Massachusetts, considered the suspicions of Bergman as told to them by the investigating officer. This led to an exhumation and autopsy. Despite the deterioration of the body, the doctor performing the autopsy was able to distinguish rope abrasions from the strap abrasions around the young women's neck. Further investigation revealed she had been violated. In his report, the doctor concluded the cause of death was strangulation. The modus operandi matched that found in the recent investigation of the corpse of Marjorie Santoro, discovered in Virginia. A killer was loose on the Appalachian Trail.

In Virginia, bulletins were sent out to police departments of towns along the trail. Subsequent bulletins were sent to the capital offices of all states north and south of Virginia where the Appalachian Trail crossed. The bulletin sent to Raleigh, North Carolina, sat there for several days before transmission to several police departments, one of them Franklin. By the time it got there, Chief Gary Odle, who always read such bulletins, was on a hunting trip, and Sergeant Ralston plopped it into his chief's overflowing in-box.

The police in Massachusetts presumed the killer had left the trail. No other foul play had been reported during the ten weeks since the Santoro body was found and that body was not far from the other corpse discovered four weeks earlier in the Smokies. Although Bergman had educated them about the goals of a thru-hiker, the investigating officers in Massachusetts saw no reason why a so-called thru-hiker would kill twice in the south and keep trudging north to Maine. They thought the more likely scenario was a section-hiker, one who selects a section of the trail to hike and then leaves. Further south however, questions lingered: Did the killer come back to the trail? If so, when, and where? In Virginia, two officers were put on the case. But in Massachusetts, the case was filed.

ON AUGUST 16, MOONWALKER WAS at a shelter seventeen miles north of Kay Wood Lean-to. Earlier he had walked through the town of Dalton, Massachusetts, another of the few towns that sat right on the trail, but didn't linger after his double cheeseburger, fries, strawberry ice cream, and two large cokes. He was ram-rod fit from a month of hiking since he had left Allentown, but that hadn't helped in his endless battle with the mosquito. Despite "Off" and other bug juice squirted on exposed skin, he still sweated when he hiked and drew mosquitoes in swarms and the swarms, no matter what he did, moved with him, covering him with bites. He flapped his bandana about him, swearing and fussing, but was unable to threaten anyone.

As he tramped by birches and buttercups, he realized fewer hikers were on the trail. He'd encountered only four thru-hikers in two days and one of them was a south bound hiker, a *sobo*. He'd heard many hikers had left the trail; most remaining hikers were ahead of him. Any north bound hiker would have to summit Mount Katahdin, the northern terminus of the Appalachian Trail, by October 15 when Baxter State Park in Maine officially closed. Hikers tried to finish the trail in September to avoid the cold and harsh weather of northern Maine in October. Moonwalker was not concerned about this; he had no reason to climb Katahdin and planned to call his cousin when he got into Maine and arrange for pick up. He was in no hurry and looked forward to cool weather—anything would be better than this humid caldron of summer heat.

After another mile, he came upon a vacant shelter and had lunch. Moonwalker was in a muddle. He had arrived at the conclusion he wouldn't be able to do Nightwind, and was still upset that he'd botched Margie. He hungered for the next woman. *Someone ripe.* It had been weeks of near solitude. Looking out from inside the shelter he caught a deer running by the empty fire pit and watched it disappear into the afternoon. A welcome breeze came up and kept most of the mosquitoes at bay.

While munching, Moonwalker read entries from the shelter ledger and recognized several trail names of hikers who had passed through. Nothing interesting. He back-paged to entries of hikers from last year and read some of those. He read one in French which told of two hikers coming from Canada into Vermont. He wondered about that as he flipped through some of the other pages. He picked up his handbook and maps. Moonwalker made an interesting discovery. The Appalachian Trail intersected Vermont's Long Trail, which continued straight up right through the top end of Vermont into Canada. He backtracked with his finger and noted that one third of the way up into Vermont, the A.T. separated and swung east toward New Hampshire and Maine. The A.T. and the Long Trail were contiguous for ninety miles in southern Vermont. Moonwalker once more picked up the register to absorb the details in French, before packing up and heading north.

CHAPTER THIRTY-NINE

Awol BROKE FROM HIS SULLEN mood soon after entering the forests of southern Massachusetts. He stepped by wood sorrel, and when he noticed the green, shamrock-shaped leaves, he felt ready for a change in luck.

In the afternoon, when he was hot and sweaty, when the mosquitoes buzzed like dragonflies, when he was near out of water, he encountered his first change in luck. Some trail angel posted a piece of cardboard on a pine trunk: *Ice Cold Gatorade straight ahead on left—20 Yards. Enjoy!*

Trail angels: The term chosen by the hiking community that referred to those compassionate souls, some of them former thru-hikers, some empathetic retirees, some young people learning to do a good turn, who brought unexpected joy along the A.T. This was Awol's third experience with a trail angel, the last being after a tough climb up Mount Rogers in Virginia. A young boy handed out fruit and bottles of water with his father on the summit; both had come in on horseback. Awol spotted the blue cooler between two poplars. Six bottles of Gatorade were left in a melting slush of ice. He felt so buoyant picking out his drink that he wanted to leave a tip. Trail angels by nature didn't accept money, but he noticed someone had thrown some quarters into the cooler.

Walking a few yards off-trail gave him a better view of the town of Cheshire in the valley below. A white steeple looked like it grew out of orange maples. He observed a yellow bus pull near a brick building and could make out students heading to the bus. Vehicles inched along winding roads, and he spied the U.S. flag high on its pole waving to him. The Gatorade felt as good to him as any beer he'd ever had, and he realized that no matter what happened to him in the days and weeks ahead, life, humanity would still go on.

IN HIS TENT AT KAY WOOD, Awol connected events leading to his arrest. Agitated, he crawled out into the dark and stood in the stifling summer stillness. The humidity was oppressive. Two hikers were in the shelter; he could hear them snore. He scanned the sky hoping to see a shooting star, but midges and gnats soon found him and after several minutes, he crept back into his tent and sat Indian style on his bedroll. He thought about the interrogation, how he was told he may as well own up, for his fingerprints were found at the scene; "Yes, I met her at the shelter"; "No, we're talkin' the murder scene," the interrogators had said. "The victim's pack was with her. Utensils and pens had your prints." He remembered Moonwalker being at the breakfast in Damascus, which could explain utensils, and thought about how he at first had been incriminated by his own fingerprints, which had been on file since his divorce and the custody fight. He had threatened his ex that he could take his boys away and would. She had taken out a restraining order on the advice of her lawyer. In a costly moment of drunken rage he had argued with the police officer issuing the restraining order, threw it on the floor, and was arrested. When they ran his prints near Marjorie's body, it must have first seemed that they had an easy resolution to the case.

AWOL PUSHED FORWARD OVER THE next two days and took his time regaining rhythm. Terrain was moderate, not unforgiving, as it would be in the White Mountains. He hiked by bell-like pink blossoms of mountain cranberry in an understory of pine striplings. Oxeye daisy grew along hedgerows in white-and-yellow sunbursts. Such colorful splendor should have brought a surge of joy; instead, he considered his plight and the rough trail ahead. The White Mountain range started in New Hampshire and continued into southern Maine. New Hampshire alone had forty-eight peaks rising over four thousand feet. Awol had reviewed his maps and prepared himself for a cold and taxing autumn. He'd lost almost a month. On the positive side, he was only ten trail miles from the Vermont border and his juices were flowing again. Although he felt he'd blown his last chance with Linda, the outdoors calmed him. He resolved to not beat himself up anymore. *Moonwalker may or may not be out here.* The other matter he resolved was to finish this thru-hike. Even though he lagged behind, he would stay on the move and finish up at the summit of Maine's Mount Katahdin by October 15. *Twelve years has been long enough.*

CHAPTER FORTY

Gary Odle, Chief of Police in Franklin, North Carolina, returned from his duck hunting vacation on Monday morning, August 18. He met with his officers and then held a staff meeting which ended at ten. After too many calls and interruptions, he disappeared to grab a bagel at the deli downstairs. When he returned he tackled his overflowing in-box. He thumbed through documents, printouts, bulletins, and attempted to prioritize the assortment on his desk. At 1:10 p.m., he took a closer look at the bulletin describing the findings on the Appalachian Trail in the Smokies and Virginia. After rereading the bulletin a second time, he called Chief Roland Stevens in Bryson City.

"Did you see the bulletin from State about those hikers who were raped and strangled?"

"No. What's it all about?"

"Hold on. Jeannie, fax this over to Roland and Frank." He handed his secretary the bulletin before turning back to the phone. "Some killer is loose on the Appalachian Trail who likes to rape and strangle women, in an awfully familiar way."

"You don't say. Doesn't that trail go all the way up into New England?" Stevens said.

"Yep."

"Hmmm. Are you thinking what I'm thinking?" Stevens said.

"The sicko gave us the slip by jumping on the trail."

"Yep."

While reviewing the file of Paul Leroux for the umpteenth time,

Chief Stevens had an idea. He got on the phone with the personnel manager at Drexel Furniture. After reading through their faxed pages, Stevens called a friend's hiking buddy. At four o'clock Chief Stevens called Gary back and conferenced-in Frank from Sylva.

"Guess what I found out about our Mr. Leroux?" Stevens was practically crowing. "Seems like our guy has family in Canada. And, check this out, according to my hiking friends, you can switch off to another trail in Vermont, called the Long Trail, and it will take you right up into Canada."

"How'd you find out about family in Canada?" asked Frank.

"Drexel Furniture. Human Resources had a copy of his life insurance forms, listing beneficiaries living in Canada."

AFTER CHIEF STEVENS HUNG UP the phone he remembered the Missing Person Report Vickers had been working on. He was about to summon his sergeant when Vickers walked in the door with the file. The look on Vicker's face let him know what his sergeant was about to say.

"I'd checked with the PO at Fontana Village as soon as I got this from Raleigh, just like you asked," explained Vickers. "The person I spoke to didn't see any hiker package. See, I noted it right here."

Stevens looked at the file.

"I called them back. A different person says he's found it, stuffed under a table."

"She was last seen at The Franklin Motel?"

"Right. And I told Mrs. Strekalovsky the package in Fontana she had sent to her daughter was probably picked up. No one saw her in Fontana. My guess is she's somewhere on the Appalachian Trail between here and the Dam."

"Bring out the dogs," Stevens said.

CHAPTER FORTY-ONE

ON AUGUST 18, MOONWALKER CROSSED from Massachusetts into Vermont. The next day, needing food and supplies, he headed out to hitch into Bennington. The town was five miles west according to his handbook, and as he walked out of thickets onto Route 9, a muddied pickup was about to swing out of the trailhead parking area. Moonwalker waved him down.

"Need a ride?"

"Super!" Moonwalker stepped around to the passenger side as the driver cleared paintbrushes and a caulking gun off the seat.

"You thru-hiking?"

"No, I try to get out here every summer; headin' north as far as New Hampshire."

"You hear about the killer on the trail?"

"What's this now?" Moonwalker didn't flinch.

The man looked over and pointed a thumb behind him. "Two women were found raped and strangled, one in the Smokies, other in Virginia, both on the A.T." The man was reckless as he leaned the truck around a curve.

"I met some hikers who were talking about someone who fell off a cliff, but no murders."

"That's what everyone thought—that she fell. Turns out she was raped and strangled."

"Yikes!"

"Just dropped off my sister's boyfriend and his buddy. They told me the guy could be hiking from town to town and headin' north."

"Why go to all the trouble when he can hide in the forest down there? Who would find him?"

"That's what I think too. But still, can't trust anybody anymore. You're always gonna have sickos in the cities, but out here?" said the driver, swinging his arm across the wind shield to the mountains in front of them. Moonwalker offered the driver a Marlboro. "No thanks."

MOONWALKER, LOADING HIS BASKET AT the Grand Union Supermarket, had intended to do his shopping and hitch back to the trail, as it was still morning. But this new understanding of his circumstances worried him and he had trouble calming himself. Whenever this happened, he invariably had an immediate and pressing urge to find a woman. *Stifle it. Think!*

"That the library?" he asked the cashier, pointing to a brick building with an ornate cupola.

"Town Hall; library's next to the police station, around the corner."

"Uh-huh." Moonwalker grabbed the local paper, a New York daily, and the Boston Globe from the rack.

"Heading north?"

"South."

"What's your trail name?"

"Don't have any—only out for a short time. Any rooms in town?"

"Most hikers stay at The Bertram, up the street on the left. You can get single rooms and they're hiker-friendly."

Moonwalker avoided the library and later in his room scanned the papers. He was glad to see the police were concentrating their efforts in the south. *But gotta make some changes.* After studying his maps and an Atlas the desk clerk was able to rustle up, Moonwalker, writing some last minute scribbles in his pad, made a trip to the Mart across the street. Two hours later, after rinsing his razor and sneaking to the dumpster out back of the motel, Moonwalker was in bed, watching news about the Iraq war on TV, satisfied with his new plan.

CHAPTER FORTY-TWO

AFTER THE WRITE UP IN Virginia papers—a front page story—the killings became the topic of conversation for every hiker. South bounders walked right into the news. Comments were made in every shelter register about the murders. Females bonded and hiked in packs; men were on the alert. The questions of the day were always the same: Was he still on the trail? Where? Was he heading north or was he hanging in the south?

When the news reported Paul Leroux, the suspected rapist-strangler wanted in the North Carolina killings, was also suspected in the Smokies and Virginia trail murders, most felt the killer hung in the South, stalked his next trail victim, killed her, and hid in a nearby town. Nothing had been reported north of Virginia, and most northbound women breathed easier, but they still were all too aware the killer could be in their midst.

WHEN MOONWALKER HITCHED BACK TO the trail after his night in Bennington, Vermont, he hadn't hiked one mile when he came upon a shelter. Once there, he reached for the register to see if he knew anyone who had been behind him when he went into town. And there it was: *Heard Awol is on the trail again, right in front of me—welcome back! Recycled, 8/21.*

Moonwalker sat on the shelter step and stared at the entry. Although he felt fortunate to make this discovery, he wished he didn't have this complication right now.

Moonwalker sparked up a Marlboro and stared at the entry again. He estimated Awol was a full day ahead of him. Not much—so he wouldn't hurry. He headed toward the next shelter, eight miles north, and tented south of the shelter for the night.

In his tent, Moonwalker lay on his bag. A rustle of leaves blew; he heard a limb creak and angled his head to see out the tent flap. Wisps of cloud crawled over a hazy half-moon until it was completely covered. Moonwalker was addled; so much swirling around in his mind. He closed his eyes and tried to distract the inchoate urges assembling inside him. As he swelled, he recognized one of the feelings adding to his confusion. He was lonely, and had been for a long time. He began to entertain the notion that he might find a woman, a hiking partner, someone he could talk with, someone who would accept him, one who'd love him and would never mock him. He brought his hands up and covered his eyes trying to control his emotions, but for several minutes, he sobbed into his palms, his head jerking, his body contracting as if he had chills. He sobbed out of loneliness, he sobbed because he could almost feel what it might be like to have a relationship with a woman who loved him, and he sobbed because he knew he would never let a woman get that close to him; he'd rape and strangle her first.

His despair turned to anger. *Women are a different species . . .* the prostitute in Memphis, his mother, his aunt, other women who'd scorned him, flitted in and out of his mind. He wiped his face. *Can't trust the bitches. Not a one.* His head cleared and once again, with singular clarity, he obsessed about one woman in particular. Nightwind.

CHAPTER FORTY-THREE

MOONWALKER KEPT TO HIMSELF THE next two days. At the end of the second day he approached Stratton Pond Shelter and heard voices and shouts from the pond. He maneuvered himself into the thicket and drew up his field glasses. His heart leaped and his groin charged as he witnessed three women in T-shirts and shorts splashing about. He dropped his pack and crept closer and closer on his knees. Fifty yards away he focused his binoculars on the full breasted one bursting through a clinging T-shirt. *"Well I'll be—Malibu! Oh you delightful, wholesome little trick. No, no sweetie, don't turn on me . . . come back. That's it, you come back to me."* Moonwalker remembered her from back in North Carolina when she bummed a cigarette at his tent and blew smoke at a full moon. His hands shook as he saw her nipples through her thin shirt. Two young men came down to join them and Malibu flipped water at them. She turned and leaned over to cup water in her hands and Moonwalker observed her buttocks tighten. His throat was dry and he felt sweat moisten his armpits.

He flattened down in a patch of bunchberry with the glasses propped up in front of him and watched. He didn't try to restrain himself and as he watched he rocked himself forward and backward while remaining on his stomach. Faster and faster he heaved himself among the shaking stems of white petals while he watched Malibu cavort with friends. One of the guys walked toward her. He was young, fit, and tanned. He started flipping water back at her. Malibu turned right into Moonwalker's lens as she scrunched away from the boy, folding her arms across her chest. As the boy drew behind her still flipping water, Malibu arched her back, dropped her arms and thrust her breasts out. Up and out her tits expanded as she looked to heaven with a wide grin. As Moonwalker erupted he had to lay the binoculars beside him and stifle grunts. Spent, he picked them up and refocused. She had let the boy wrap himself around her, but seconds later pushed him off. Moonwalker decided she'd be the next one. Nightwind he could save a while longer. He concentrated on Malibu. *Did I forget you, sweetie? No, of course not. I have your scent.* He tensed when the boy tried to put his arm around her again, but she sprang away and swam with strong, sure strokes over to the others. The boy followed with quick, sloppy chops. Moonwalker felt better; the boy was just a diversion. She stepped out of the pond, and the boy was left talking with others.

Moonwalker edged back to his pack, picked a level spot, and set up his tent.

CHAPTER FORTY-FOUR

Eᴀʀʟɪᴇʀ ᴛʜᴀᴛ sᴀᴍᴇ ᴅᴀʏ, ᴀᴡᴏʟ approached Vermont Route 11. He hobbled down to a small parking area hoping he could hitch the six miles to Manchester right from the lot. He was eleven miles north of Stratton Pond and anxious to get medicine and find a room. He had rolled an ankle while fording a stream; a mid-sized rainbow trout had distracted him, and he'd foolishly tried to stab it with his pole. He didn't attribute the consequence to bad luck, but to fate, which had punished him, even though his pole swung wide and the fish wiggled on. It wasn't a bad sprain, but enough of one that he needed to apply ointments, to ice it, and to elevate it.

Aᴡᴏʟ ᴘᴜᴛ ʜɪs ᴘᴀᴄᴋ ᴀɴᴅ sticks behind the seat of a newer model Yukon, and climbed in next to the driver.

"What's going on; I miss anything this past week?" Awol asked after thanking him for stopping.

The driver sipped bottled water and offered Awol a fresh bottle. "Just Iraq, lots of problems over there, doesn't look like we're getting out any time soon."

Awol nodded and pursed his lips.

"Any news about the Trail?"

The driver glanced at him, looked back at the road, and turned to Awol again. "There's a serial killer on the trail. It's been on the news."

"I'd heard a little about that. But I've been out of circulation. What's the latest?"

"He's murdered five women. The last two were found near the trail."

Awol ruminated on this. "Can you drop me at a post office in town? I'll walk from there."

He'd been wanting to mail Linda a couple of prints, one a peregrine falcon he had photographed for her, as well as a picture of kayakers winding down a stream. At the post office, he attached a note: *I can't get you out of my mind. Miss you dearly. Karl.*

AFTER HE READ THE NEWSPAPERS for himself . . . *investigators are certain all five strangulations were committed by the same person* . . . Awol, on impulse, called Linda from the motel.

"Guess you've heard the news," he said.

After a moment of silence. "I must tell you, Karl, I was expecting another call. Which is why I picked up."

"Okay. Understood. But did you hear?"

"I did, actually. Hold on a minute."

Karl looked at his watch. She'd been gone over two minutes.

"So. I guess you're relieved," she said.

"Did you ever doubt me, Linda?"

"Well, no. But . . ."

"But what?"

"I never doubted you, but I've heard of women like me who later found out their husband or boyfriend is a monster." Awol stayed silent. "I mean, you were arrested. Right?"

"Right. So, are you relieved?"

"Relieved about what? I'm glad it's over for you, if that's what you mean."

He ignored her distance. "It's not over, Linda. He's still out here."

"So let it go. He's somewhere in Virginia, right?"

"I'm not so sure. It's what the killer wants everyone to believe. The more I think about it, the more I think he's heading north like I am."

"Let the police do their job. It's out of your hands. And if you think he's heading north, you are crazy to stay out there. Let it play out and then you can go back and finish your important hike." She tried too hard to sound nonchalant, he thought.

"Do I detect a note of sarcasm?"

"There's no further reason to talk is there?"

"I know . . . I blew it for us."

"Yes, Karl, you did. And now I need to go."

"Look, can't we—"

"It's too late for 'can't we,' Karl. You're all bottled up about your manhood with this crazed killer, in addition to something else from over a decade ago. You're a zombie unless you're drinking. You need counseling, but I'm done with asking you to get help. I never was a priority in your life. No, Karl, I'm done."

"Linda, I promise—"

"I'm not going to sit around while you play Army and try to catch a lunatic. Forget it. Good-bye."

AWOL RUBBED BENGAY ON HIS ankle and elevated it. He tried to distract himself by watching baseball on TV. He hated to admit it, but he was beginning to feel vulnerable. This was his second trail injury. Ordinarily he would have shaken off this nuisance in a matter of hours, but it wasn't going to be so easy this time. He could tape the ankle, but chose to take an extra day in town.

As restless as he was, he would keep the promise he'd made earlier to himself, and not go out for that *one* drink. He loved Linda and understood that part of his dismay was that he was missing her. He missed her quiet humor, and he missed her touch and physical warmth. Most of all, he missed her acceptance. She had never nagged, only tried to help and reason with him. What a fool he'd been. He realized he'd gradually broken the union with his drinking and by refusing help, by refusing to share any of his pain. He'd selfishly kept the relationship on his own terms. Awol denied he'd lost her for good though. Maybe he could solve the problem by buying a ring here in Manchester and going home with it tomorrow. He visualized how they'd wake up in each other's arms. The more he considered it, the more he wanted to do it. *I go home and marry her, take her on a well-deserved honeymoon, and pick up the trail next year. It makes sense. Moonwalker will have been caught and next year I come to terms with Desert Storm like I'd planned.*

But no. I made a promise to myself, and going home tomorrow doesn't solve the Linda problem if I can't solve my own issues first.

CHAPTER FORTY-FIVE

MOONWALKER PUSHED OFF EARLY NEXT morning and hiked north of Stratton Pond Shelter before he expected to meet anyone on the trail. A mile north of the shelter he stopped and selected a spot from which to observe, a spot where he could see hikers take a bend in the trail to the west. He waited. An hour later he saw Malibu. She looked gorgeous in a black short-sleeved poly pullover and red shorts. Months of hiking the trail made her legs taut and strong. She had headphones, and he could see her mouthing words to what he assumed was music. He let her go by and waited several seconds; all good things took time. As he was about to emerge from his hiding place, he saw more hikers. He recognized two young men he saw yesterday and a minute later the other two girls he had seen at the pond followed. He let them pass and waited several minutes before entering the trail.

He followed at a safe distance all morning and stopped for a snack at midday. He didn't show himself until he came to Route 11 where the five of them had congregated in a parking lot. The blond boy of yesterday was talking to Malibu; the other guy was checking his guidebook. The two other girls were sitting on their packs.

"Howdy," Moonwalker said, walking over to them with confidence in his man-of-the-outdoors look. He felt relaxed in his new body, snug hiking shorts and new Nike T-shirt. He touched the much shorter belt he'd also bought in Bennington—he'd lost eight inches around the waist.

They all looked up and said hi.

"Heading to town?"

"That's the plan," the blond boy said. Malibu said nothing as she retied her boot. "Been hiking long?" the blond continued.

"I just come out and do a stretch in the fall."

"Oh. Do you have a car?" asked one of the girls sitting on her pack. "I'm Turtle and this is Bluebell," she said, pointing to the gal sitting on the pack next to her.

"No, only out for a few weeks. I'll call my wife when I get ready to quit—she's in Massachusetts." He glanced at Malibu who looked at him without any recognition. He took off his pack and rummaged through it trying to look as if he had something else on his mind.

"So," the other boy said, turning back to the others, "I'm thinking we stay over tonight and hike out tomorrow."

"I'm in," the blond boy said, smiling at Malibu.

"Okay, but I'm running out of money," Bluebell said.

"At this rate we'll be broke before we even get to Maine," Turtle said with a sigh. "We'll hitch first," she said to the group. "See ya in town."

Moonwalker pulled out his cigs and offered a Marlboro to the young man and Malibu. The boy declined; Malibu took one, as Moonwalker expected. She said thank you and smoked quietly. Moonwalker suspected she was trying to dump the boy and this thrilled him.

"Do you guys have trail names?" Moonwalker asked them. He looked to Malibu and she smiled, "Yes, I'm Malibu." She leaned further back on her pack and drew up a knee.

"I'm Jersey," the boy said.

"Uh-huh. Randy. The pleasure's mine." Moonwalker squinted while he took a drag. He was sitting next to his pack and flicked an ant off the harness. "Someone on the trail told me . . . day before yesterday . . . ," he jammed the cigarette in his mouth, twisted his pack, and batted the harness to shake off more ants, "some type of killer could be out here. You hear about that?"

"Yep," Jersey said, "the cops pulled a guy off the trail in Massachusetts."

"Massachusetts! Where I'm from—you get the name?"

"His trail name was Awol," said Malibu. "He was a pretty quiet guy. We were surprised to hear he was arrested."

Jersey butted in, "They said he wasn't the killer. He was released, and he's back on the trail."

Moonwalker stared open mouthed at Jersey and glanced at Malibu, "They let him back out on the Trail?"

Malibu stubbed out her cigarette, "Our turn, Yogi's got a hitch," she said to Jersey.

"You coming?" Jersey asked.

"No. Think I'll push on," Moonwalker said. "You all have a grand time."

Malibu smiled as she walked by Moonwalker. "Thanks."

Moonwalker watched them walk to the road. They didn't look back.

CHAPTER FORTY-SIX

AWOL HAD WOKEN IN THE middle of night. The Gulf War again. He couldn't fall back asleep. *Of course Harrison hated me.* "*Why me, sir? Have one of the new guys lead.*"

"*I want someone with experience, sergeant.*"

"*I'm short—got only three weeks left.*"

"*Harrison, I gave you an order.*"

"*FUCK! I oughta . . .*" and Corporal Jones, Harrison's buddy from Detroit, now a paraplegic. When the motel clock radio read 7:25 a.m., he reached for the phone—he wanted to catch Linda before she left for work. Although he wouldn't be buying any ring today, nor go home to her any time soon, he wanted to tell her that he cherished her. The phone rang. Four rings, eight rings, ten rings. The answering machine wasn't on; he'd try again later.

His ankle was somewhat better. The extra day of rest had made a difference, but he felt twinges of discomfort as he moved it from side to side. He put on a last application of Bengay and wrapped it.

Awol was back on the trail at 9:35, an atrocious start time for him. The day was sunny, but he was in turmoil. He'd had a rough night and sixteen hundred miles into his hike, he had to admit that nothing had been resolved. He tramped by mushrooms—orange, white, little domes, big domes—out of sorts, but relieved to be alone. He tried to settle down, take it step-by-step; think. He kept to a slower pace.

Two miles later, Awol approached Bromley Mountain Shelter, which sat next to the trail. He halted as he saw a man and girl, in profile, sitting

on the shelter floor. They appeared to be studying a map. Fifty yards
in front of him, the man talked and pointed with his finger. Awol later
wondered what made him stop on the trail at this spot. Was it that he
didn't feel like meeting anyone yet? Was it that the shelter popped up out
of nowhere, so soon, so close to the trailhead and he wasn't ready for the
distraction of registers, etc.? Why didn't he give them a nod and just go
on by? He'd concluded he simply wanted to avoid human contact, so he
sat down, to think, out of sight, and waited for them to move on.

Awol leaned against a maple just off the trail and munched gorp. He
looked down in front of him and noticed a stubbed cigarette. He peered
through the leaves at the shelter and noted the man was bald enough to
pass for Mr. Clean. His bare scalp reflected sunlight coming in through
the forest. He had a black eye patch. Awol stared at the man. His lack
of facial hair indicated a day hiker. Awol tried to ignore them and focus
on his own thoughts, but something about the way the guy sat, leaning
back against the corner post, was familiar, and it unnerved Awol. The girl
looked tiny next to him. Every so often the man glanced out to the trail,
then back at the girl.

Awol decided that he didn't want to wait any longer but right when
he reached for his poles, he saw the big man pull out a pack of cigarettes.
The pack was red and white. He offered one to the girl and fingered
another for himself. Awol froze in the halfway up position. The man
struck a match and lit both cigarettes with his left hand. *Moonwalker?*

Awol felt a pull in his stomach. Moonwalker. He recognized the long
legs and the way he angled his head when he talked. He had lost a good
forty or fifty pounds and looked fit. Solid. The girl was in trouble. Awol
wanted to wait for a few more minutes, hoping other hikers would come
by, and then he'd confront Moonwalker and expose him. But he knew
that no matter what, he had to get the girl away from him.

After ten long minutes, Awol watched in dread as Moonwalker and
the girl began to pack up. Awol made his move. He smacked his poles
against rock and watched Moonwalker jerk his head to the sound. Awol
slapped rock again with his poles three measured times before emerging
from the side, back onto the trail right in front of them. Awol looked at
Moonwalker's eyes the entire time he walked up to him.

"Howdy!" Awol said.

"Do I know you?" Moonwalker said.

"Moonwalker, you looked better when you wore those sunglasses, sported a beard, and needed a haircut."

The girl stared at Moonwalker.

"And who might you be?" Moonwalker said.

Awol felt foolish; the bastard hadn't flinched. "The question is, Moonwalker, who in the hell are you?"

Moonwalker bounded off the shelter floor and threw his hand up. "Look friend, most people have trail names out here. Now, I'm gonna ask you nicely—what is your name?"

The girl looked startled. *Must be cool. I want to ram my pole into his throat. Think of the girl.* Awol leaned on his poles and in a regulated voice said, "Okay, Moonwalker. My trail name is Awol and—"

"Awol!" Moonwalker took a backward step toward the girl, mouth open. "Did you say Awol? Malibu, isn't this the guy the cops pulled off the trail?"

Malibu looked at Awol and back to Moonwalker. "Well, I only heard —listen, didn't you—"

Moonwalker addressed Awol with a raised voice and both index fingers pointed right at him, "Mister Awol, I don't know who the hell you are, but let's get one thing straight—"

"Yo, what's going on?" Yogi and Jersey hiked up and Jersey edged over near Malibu. Malibu stepped down from the shelter floor and stood beside him.

Moonwalker's face reddened, "Ladies and gentlemen, this is Awol. Yes, the very one arrested for murdering women. Mister Awol, this young lady and the two other ladies coming up behind you are to be left alone. Do I make myself clear?"

Awol was stunned at the turn of events. All his life, whenever backed into a corner, he'd been at a loss for words. Words failed him now. He must speak; he had important things to say, but the words caught in his throat.

"You're the one the cops pulled off the trail. And here you are, again, sniffing around these ladies. They should have locked you up and melted the key."

"Moonwalker—"

"Let me explain something to you, Mister Awol, I'm not Moonwalker. I don't know who he is and I don't care, but I do care that you're getting too close to this young lady. I'm warning you, you keep your filthy hands off her and any other lady. Do I make myself clear?"

Malibu grabbed her pack and spoke to Moonwalker, "It's all right. I don't think he came up to harm me. C'mon, Jersey, we're out of here."

She was about to step off when Awol walked around Moonwalker and reached in the shelter for her poles, which she had forgotten. "Here, you'll need these." Awol looked into her eyes and said for all to hear, "Please be careful and don't go anywhere near this man. His name is Moonwalker. He may look different now, but he's been on the trail, stalking women." Awol turned to Moonwalker. "He's—"

Before he even turned completely around he felt the fist explode in his face. Awol was out cold.

CHAPTER FORTY-SEVEN

WATER SPLASHED IN HIS FACE and Awol thought it odd because it hadn't been raining. He heard voices, but everything was murky with the throbbing head pain.

"Is he going to come around?" Bluebell said.

"Yeah," Jersey said, "throw more water on him." Jersey tapped his cell phone and walked to a new spot. "Can't get a signal."

Awol opened his eyes and saw them gathered. He tasted blood in his mouth and coughed as he tried to sit up.

"You okay? He really walloped you," Yogi said.

"Where is he?" As Awol made words his face hurt; it felt as if his nose was pinched over the side of his face.

"He hightailed it out of here," Jersey said "He's been gone for several minutes while you were knocked out."

Awol looked up at Malibu, whose eyes were red, "Thank God you didn't go off with him." He tried to get up and Yogi and Jersey lifted and half carried him over to the shelter steps where he plunked down.

"Your nose is broken," Turtle said. She soaked a camp rag with her water bottle and, after wringing it out, draped it over his nose which continued to bleed. "Keep this over it. You need to go back in town and get fixed up."

Awol held the wet rag in place, "Before anything, we have to tell the police that the serial killer is up here on the trail. We need to make a statement at police headquarters."

Jersey broke a dead silence, "How do you know he's the killer?"

"I'd always had my suspicions about him. He's a dangerous guy. Trust me, I've met him; first time was in North Carolina before the first murder on the Trail. Until now, he'd always hiked with sunglasses, even at night. Back then he had a full head of hair and a beard."

"Okay, stop! He's right," Malibu said. She sat down on her pack. "I met a big guy called Moonwalker near Tennessee and I remember he wore sunglasses. I bummed a cigarette by his tent. It was weird because he was hooded up with sunglasses on a warm night. Jesus."

"Listen to me," Awol said. He moved his head forward, "Man's a killer. Crafty. He tried to set me up for the murder in Virginia, which is why I was questioned in Massachusetts. And, yes, I was cleared.

"He's probably watching us; you see the binoculars he carries? We need to stay together and get to the police."

They hiked back to the trailhead. Awol coughed up blood part of the way, but his nose stopped bleeding, and no teeth were broken. Awol, Turtle, and Malibu got the first hitch and Awol pressed the driver to take them straight to the Manchester Police. Fifteen minutes later, Bluebell, Yogi, and Jersey showed up to support Awol's statement.

UNDER THREATENING CLOUDS IN A moody sky, Moonwalker was a couple miles north of the shelter where he had tattooed Awol. He had thought about sneaking west and flanking the shelter to see what they'd do, figuring the boys wouldn't come looking for him, but he had been so goddamned worked up he had to get himself away before he did something extra stupid.

Moonwalker slowed and stopped. He checked his guidebook and noted he had just ascended and descended Bromley Mountain. He hadn't even realized it. He sat by the edge of the trail and chugged from his bottle. He clenched his left fist and felt a sore knuckle. *Wish I had wasted him. I had her. She was coming with me and the cocksucker ruined it.* He flung a handful of stones and dirt across the trail.

Moonwalker grabbed his sticks, but closed his eyes and leaned back against birch. He heard a light wind rustle up leaves; the breeze felt satisfying. He let the sticks fall and kept his eyes closed. He visualized his father in high leather boots climbing a hill in front of him. He watched him slow down and turn to him. "C'mon Paul, you go in front of me so you can see. Over there—see the mountains? Canada loves her mountains and her mountains love Canada." *Why did my mother have to screw it up? Why did she have to drag me and George to Key West? If only I could have stayed with Pere, or even Grandpere Ouilette.*

Bivouacked a hundred yards south of Peru Peak Shelter, rain thumping on his tent, Moonwalker checked the map. He estimated he was forty-two miles from the junction where the A.T. branched off to Maine and where Vermont's Long Trail headed due north to Canada. He needed to hurry.

So, there it is. Awol's going to the cops; they will expect me to stay on the A.T. I'll get off the A.T. and take the Long Trail straight up to Canada.

CHAPTER FORTY-EIGHT

THE MANCHESTER, VERMONT POLICE WERE aware of a killer somewhere on the A.T. They had received bulletins and a picture of Paul Gaston Leroux who did not look anything like the individual Awol and his fellow hikers described. With the impassioned statement by Awol, made all the more arresting by his smashed nose, and supporting statements from the other five hikers, they called Vermont State Police who contacted North Carolina State Police, where the bulletins had originated. Seeing the opportunity to make a sensational arrest, the Manchester police chief called in a doctor to attend to Awol's nose and after Awol insisted that no one else at hand knew Moonwalker or the Trail as well as he, Chief Carlson agreed to let him assist in developing a plan to capture the suspect. The hikers stayed in town for the night with free rooms obtained by Manchester's finest.

ON A SUNNY AFTERNOON IN Bryson City, Chief of Police Stevens sat at his desk trying to complete evaluation forms for his two new officers, but he kept looking out the window. It was Thursday and this weekend he planned to go duck hunting with friends from the Bryson City Rod & Gun Club. He had asked not to be disturbed so he could finish the forms. Tomorrow morning he would conduct the appraisals of his rookies. That he didn't mind; he knew what he was going to say. He did mind completing the involved paperwork, which drove him nuts. Copies of the forms went to State and they had to be filled out perfectly. He'd already been criticized several months ago for inattention and insensitivities in completing appraisal forms. So he was frustrated and jumpy when he heard Sergeant Vickers shout his name and knock on his closed door.

"What!" He watched Vickers open the door partway and stick his head in. "What is it?"

"You want to be in on this, Chief. Vermont police are on the horn; they believe our killer is on the Appalachian Trail in Vermont."

"No kidding. Was I right or what? Put the call in to me and stay on the line.

"Chief Stevens here, and my sergeant, Vickers." He listened. "Uh-huh . . . Sergeant Vickers, pull me the file . . . Yes Sir. Well, if he's hiked all that way, I'm not surprised he looks different."

Vickers handed him the notes about the Long Trail and Canada.

"I'm looking at my file. He has family in Canada, in the province of Quebec. Based on discussions with hiking friends, the quickest way to Canada is . . . right . . . that's what they told me.

"The DNA was a match. Leroux is wanted for at least five murders down here. I'm going to get a name and address in Canada for you; please keep me updated. Wish the hell I could come up there and help you bring him in."

After hanging up the phone, Chief Stevens shelved the evaluation forms. He'd conduct the appraisals tomorrow, as planned, and finish the paperwork later. He got up and grabbed his hat, "C'mon, Vickers, let's take a ride out to Drexel Furniture. Confidential or no, we're not leaving there without names and addresses. Bring copies of the bulletins."

The next day a man named Jim Morton was taking his two boys for a walk at Winding Stair Gap, on the A.T. The twins were playing with a boomerang. The curved, wooden missile veered to the low ridge and dove into scree before it. Both boys scrambled over rocks, which had tumbled from the ridge over the years. The boys found the boomerang, and Morton watched as they played about. Soon a German shepherd joined the twins.

"Dog's a police dog; he ran up when he saw the stick fly," Officer Wallace said, walking up to Morton.

"Oh. My kids have got a boomerang. Smart looking dog."

They watched as the dog sniffed the boys, sniffed the boomerang, and then bounded about rocks and scrub.

"Might as well let him play around a bit," Wallace said. "He's been working all morning out here."

The shepherd sniffed along the arête and Wallace walked up-trail while the dog meandered. The dog charged back to the rocks below and slowed down after thirty yards. Wallace watched his dog disappear into scrub, then heard him dig. After hearing the dog's insistent barks, Wallace worked his way over to take a look.

CHAPTER FORTY-NINE

Mᴏᴏɴᴡᴀʟᴋᴇʀ ᴀᴡᴏᴋᴇ ᴛʜᴇ ɴᴇxᴛ ᴍᴏʀɴɪɴɢ near the summit of Peru Peak. Storm clouds gathered to the north; a September wind gusted. The range was steeped in color—oranges, reds, purples. Autumn was everywhere, as he huddled over oatmeal and coffee, feeding himself with gloved hands. Sitting on his pack, with krummholz behind and in front of him, he witnessed it all, but none of the beauty registered. Two hawks circled above a tarn in the cirque, drifting in wind currents, round and round; Moonwalker was oblivious. He squinted to the northern horizon as he fired up a Marlboro. He only had two left. He looked on the distant shelter as if he hoped to see a lighted Food Mart sign hanging in front.

Can't hitch, can't take the chance of being seen. Got to hike day and night and get above the A.T./L.T. junction before they ever expect me to get that far, that fast.

He licked out the last of the oatmeal and took a swig of coffee, washing it about his mouth till it picked up every last morsel of nutrient, and swallowed. After two last drags of his cigarette he broke camp. Before leaving he scanned the area with binoculars and viewed no one, a temporary relief. Even so, Moonwalker dug out his shell, retrieved a black and white bandanna and tied it around his forehead—a different look, and got rid of the eyepatch, which messed with his depth perception anyway. He hooded up and pulled the drawstring, then put a garbage bag over his pack. He wondered what else he might do to make himself look different. As he poled off, the first droplets of rain blew in from the north. This served to calm him; his dress, his cover, should he meet anyone, was appropriate. He had already schemed what to do about provisions.

————————————

THAT SAME MORNING, AWOL AWOKE from another fitful night. His face hurt. He wanted to call Linda, but understood she wasn't ready for this news, plus he had trouble enunciating words. Awol worked his way to the bath sink. He gargled a saline solution the doctor had given him and spat it out. *No blood. At least something's going right.* He touched the bandage plastered over his reset nose. He was Jack Nicholson in *Chinatown. I can't wait to be there when we bring the fucker in.* He had wanted to go after Moonwalker himself, but when he talked the police into letting him assist, he figured Moonwalker would be caught quickly. A quick capture was needed, or another woman's life would be taken.

At half past seven, Awol bought a newspaper at the front office and waited for the others. They'd agreed to meet in the lobby at eight for the continental breakfast. Awol found a news item in the local section, reporting an A.T. hiker had been attacked at the Bromley Mountain Shelter. The last sentence read: "Authorities are trying to determine if this incident has any connection to the serial killer reputed to be loose on the trail."

"Your face looks like shit," Jersey said when they arrived.

"Could you sleep?" Malibu asked.

"Slept enough." Awol poured her some OJ as Bluebell, Turtle, and Yogi joined them. Awol grabbed a danish and sat at a table.

"You all headed back out?" Awol asked.

"Yeah," Yogi said, "we figure Moonwalker will want to keep away from us."

"I suspect so. But stay alert." Awol looked at Malibu and then to the other girls. "I'm sure he'll try to redisguise himself."

"What are you going to do?" Malibu asked. She slid the carafe of juice to Awol.

"I'm going to do everything in my power to bring him in. Aside from who he is and what he's done, it's personal now. I've had enough."

"Be careful, man," Jersey said, "guy's a stick of dynamite. Don't try to do it yourself."

"Thanks for the advice. I'm going back to the station; a detective is supposed to pick me up here at 8:30." Awol checked his watch.

They finished eating and drank last cups of coffee and juice in silence as the cruiser pulled up. Malibu went over to Awol, kissed him on the cheek, and gave him a tight hug as he stood. "Thank you, Awol," she whispered, tearing up. Awol patted her on the back, "Keep your eyes and ears open," he said to her. "Guys, make sure these ladies stay together. No one hikes alone, okay?"

Jersey extended his hand, "You got it, man."

Awol shook his hand and Yogi's and got hugs from Bluebell and Turtle. "Have a great hike all. Tell the big 'K' to hang tight. I'm still coming," Awol said, as he climbed into the cruiser.

AT THE MANCHESTER POLICE STATION, Awol was taken to a small conference room behind the chief's office. Chief Carlson entered with a cup of coffee and a manila folder. He walked with a gimp.

"We got a call from the North Carolina police," Carlson said, "the suspect has a cousin by the name of Raymond Ouilette who lives in Trois-Rivieres, Quebec. Ouilette is listed as a beneficiary on a life insurance policy. No other family member was listed. We think Mr. Ouilette is a person of interest the suspect will be or has been in contact with."

"And will meet up with," Bergman said, now seeing a purpose behind Moonwalker's trek.

"Right," Carlson said, glancing at his detective.

"Chief, have you alerted other towns in Vermont?"

"Taken care of. All towns have been alerted from here to the New Hampshire border. With the help of State, we're patrolling all the access roads from here to Rutland. Rutland's near where the A.T. splits from the L.T.?"

"Sounds right."

Carlson slurped from the cup, looking at Bergman, "Do you think he will switch off the A.T.?"

"Good question." Bergman pulled out a map of northern New England. "Can you get me a map of Quebec?"

Detective Chase returned a moment later and placed the Quebec portion of a Canadian map in front of Bergman. Carlson moved beside Bergman and fingered Trois-Rivieres which lay due north of Vermont. "Okay," said Bergman. "Here's the end of the Long Trail; it's right at the border. Look over here in Maine. The closest he can get to the border while walking the trail is Stratton, but then he has to hitch out of there to the border, or walk thirty more miles on road. He thinks we think he'll stay on the A.T. He doesn't know we've figured out his Trois-Rivieres connection. I'd guess he's gonna leave the A.T. and go straight up to Canada on the L.T."

Carlson scratched his nose and took another swig of coffee. He looked to Detective Chase, "What do you think?"

"It makes sense, Chief."

"I'm not saying we don't set up alerts on the Appalachian in New Hampshire and Maine," Awol said, "I'm saying we need to focus on the Long Trail, 'cause this is where he's headed." Awol poked his finger at Trois-Rivieres.

"Okay," Carlson said, "I agree. Smartest idea is to set our trap where the L.T. breaks away, up here in Rutland." The chief dropped his finger on the map again, "He'll have to make a choice when he gets right here and we'll nab him in the event he decides to go east on the A.T. Mr. Bergman will confirm the suspect, and we'll arrest him on assault charges."

"Perfect," Awol said.

"How long do you think it'll take him to hike from here to there?" Carlson asked.

"It's fifty miles. I've checked the terrain and it's not a cakewalk. Hikers can do it in four days, some will take longer."

"Okay, we're going to be there in three. Yesterday was his first day. You," he pointed to Awol, "Detective Chase, and two more of my best men are going to set up with me on Sunday morning right behind the junction."

CHAPTER FIFTY

MOONWALKER MADE IT TO THE split in just under three days. At 10:10 Saturday night he collapsed in front of a trail sign that, with the aid of his headlamp, read: Maine Junction. The left arrow pointed to the Long Trail, the right arrow to the Appalachian Trail. Moonwalker, on his knees and leaning on the front of the sign, turned off his lamp and fell asleep for fifteen minutes.

The dropping temperature shook him awake and with a start he forgot where he was. He felt what he imagined was a tree in front of him and turned on his lamp. He remembered now and read the rest of the sign: Tucker-Johnson Shelter, one-half mile. The arrow pointed left. At 11:00 p.m., Moonwalker crawled into his sleeping bag fifty yards behind the shelter. Moonwalker set his watch alarm for 4:00 a.m.

WHEN MOONWALKER HAD DESCENDED PERU Peak, after breaking camp Friday morning, his goal was to hike forty-two miles in two days. That Friday, yesterday, he had hiked twenty-one miles to a spot south of the Minerva Hinchey Shelter. He had arrived famished and exhausted in a light rain at quarter past eight in the evening. He could barely set up his tent for want of substantial food and sleep. He eyed the campfire at the shelter to his north and wished he could sit by the flames he could see flickering through trees a hundred yards away. After setting up he gulped water, finished the last half of his last Snickers bar, and crawled into his bag. He was dead asleep in seven minutes.

At 2:00 A.M., the wrist alarm beeped and Moonwalker gave the watch a slap. It felt as if he'd only taken a nap. He opened the flap and peered north into darkness as he scratched his crotch and reached for the headlamp. While emptying his bladder he smelled dying campfire embers at the shelter. The rain had stopped and a scattering of stars were out, but he didn't see a moon. Moonwalker dumped out a stuff sack of soggy clothes, hooded up his shell, and reentered the trail.

Several minutes later he neared the shelter. His sandals were quiet on the soft earth as he tip-toed. He had already removed his headlamp, but kept it cupped in his hand. By opening and closing his fingers he adjusted the light as needed. He saw no tents outside, but could make out the snores of at least four people in sleeping bags inside the shelter. Right away he spotted something he'd been looking for. He reached up and unhooked a ski cap from a nail inside the shelter and put it in his sack. He looked at food bags hung on nails and reached up to unhook the nearest one. He backed away from the shelter with the bag and crept toward the privy. Behind the privy, Moonwalker opened the bag. He shined his light into it, pulled out several packets of crackers and cheese, some granola bars, and all the oatmeal and hot chocolate packets he could find. He crept back to the shelter and laid the bag on the shelter floor as if it had been knocked down, then tiptoed away.

———————————

A SMALL BIRD WITH A ragged chirp woke Moonwalker much too early and filled him with dread. He craved a smoke as a damp morning sprinkle patted the tent. He ached but had to hike another twenty-one miles today. He ate a holdover breakfast of oatmeal, crackers, and cheese, and was on his second cup of hot chocolate.

He was waiting for the hikers in the shelter to leave, and scanned the camp with field glasses. Too tired to hike out before them, he hoped he hadn't made a mistake. He wanted to scrounge their camp after they left.

Moonwalker took the stolen black ski cap—a new look for him— and pulled it down over his ears, then hooded up. He took the bandanna and tied it to the side of his pack. Seeking further disguise, he pulled out his rubber flip-flops and tied them to the other side of his pack. Moonwalker did everything possible to look different.

At nine Moonwalker ambled to the shelter. Hikers would sometimes leave extra food or clothing they no longer needed or wanted to carry. He looked on bare nails, a deserted clothesline, empty corners. He scanned the register and discovered nothing of interest. He walked around back and checked underneath: one torn black sock, a busted hiking stick. He inspected the pit ashes ringed by stones and checked the privy—nothing usable. Moonwalker picked up his sticks and poled north.

The sun peeked out a short while later, and the day cleared. Moonwalker removed the hood, but kept his head covered with the cap, hoping not to run into its former owner. He had gone less than two miles. As he approached Vermont 103 he took out his binoculars to have a look; he'd have to angle across to reenter the trail up-road. He hardly had enough time to duck into thickets when he heard a vehicle approach. Crouching, he turned to see what he was certain was an unmarked cruiser. He discerned a uniformed man inside and noted an array of different antennas on the car's roof. *Lucky.* A mile later he drew near Clarendon Shelter and, being alone, refilled his water bottle and took a look around. Wrappers in the fire pit, a torn up rag, nothing. This place didn't even have a register.

Six miles later he neared Governor Clement Shelter and heard voices coming toward him. He snuck into pines to the east and observed a troop of Cub Scouts heading south. A young pack leader was in front and after eight scouts passed, a senior scout leader brought up the rear. He had a grim look on his face as he poked a lone wooden staff into the dirt on every other stride. Moonwalker smelled raisins and watched one of the boys reach into a small box as he walked along. But the shelter gave up nothing.

Nobody passed Moonwalker all day. Once, when he gained on two hikers in front of him, he hid off-trail, ate a snack, and napped. He didn't see them again. At twilight he was despondent as he stared at Killington Peak in front of him. The four-thousand-foot mountain looked forbidding, the temperature had dropped, rain threatened. Moonwalker didn't take time to boil water and cook a nourishing meal. He ate a granola bar and grabbed from a diminishing bag of gorp. He forded two streams before the ascent of Killington and at the second refilled his one bottle; yesterday, he'd lost one off a ledge.

Moonwalker moved out of sight around another shelter; at just past eight, any sane hiker had quit hours ago, and getting this close to his goal, he didn't want to be distracted by temptations in a campsite. He heard voices from the shelter and smelled food. His stomach ached for protein, yet he trudged on. At the shelter turnoff, he encountered two men coming toward him.

"You okay?" the taller one asked, glancing at his watch.

"Yeah, I'm fine. Being picked up at Route 4. Promised my daughter I'd make her birthday tomorrow." Moonwalker tapped his headlamp as though this explained everything. "You all have a good evening."

"Okay, my friend."

WITHOUT FURTHER INCIDENT, HALF ASLEEP on aching feet, Moonwalker managed to push on three more miles to get near the Tucker-Johnson Shelter on the Long Trail before he crashed for the night. His was a wild, contorted countenance. His mouth was open as he whistled air in-and-out. Every so often his legs quivered and his body shook, at which time he closed his mouth and stopped breathing. His temple furrowed and he struggled until, at last, he exhaled a gust and sang out a pale moan.

CHAPTER FIFTY-ONE

MOONWALKER PRESSED THE ALARM BUTTON and thumbed the illuminator: four o'clock. Dog-tired, but without a choice, he crept to the shelter twenty minutes later. As he was about to remove the biggest food bag, a hiker stirred. When the hiker snored again, Moonwalker unhooked the hanging bag and placed it on the ground. He'd been searching for something else and believed he might have found it; he lifted the black case next to a hiker and slid it in his pocket. On the ground he hoisted his pack and the stolen food bag and headed behind the shelter into a thicket. Here he jammed the food bag into his pack. He put on his pack and pulled out the black case in his pocket. He fumbled it open and winced when it turned out to be a camera.

Desperate, he ditched the pack and returned to the scene, looking over several packs hanging from nails. He patted the sides and when no one woke, fingered the pockets. At the side pocket of one pack he felt something solid and rectangular. He unzipped the pocket and fished with fingers. As he palmed the item, he felt the antenna of a cell phone. He stuck the baggie holding the phone in his other pocket and didn't move as he watched a hiker stir in front of him. Moonwalker waited a full minute and backed away.

He was exhausted, but had accomplished his objective. He'd push north until light and then find a place to sleep. A half mile later Moonwalker tripped on a root and fell down. He rubbed dirt from his left eye, the same one poked by Margie Santoro. While he was thankful his head hadn't bounced off rock, he trembled and shook; his nerves were shot. He stood and brushed himself off, as the first hint of light suggested itself in the east, then sat down on his pack; he was too tired to go any farther. He dozed for several minutes, then pulled out the cell phone. He was near Rutland and figured he might get a signal now, but not later. Three bars showed on the screen, and he checked his notepad for the number of Ray Ouilette.

"Allo."

"Ray. This is Paul. Did I wake you?"

"Yeah, you woke me."

Moonwalker chuckled.

"Someone called here about you two days ago."

"What? Who?"

"Some man, had a thick accent, asked if I knew a Paul Leroux. When I said yes, he hung up."

Moonwalker massaged his eye, felt the tenderness and, already, a swelling. "Is that all he said?"

"Are you in trouble, Paul?"

"I could be if you forget to tell me something."

"Okay. He said he worked for the United States Post Office and had a letter for a Raymond Ouilette in Trois-Rivieres. He asked, 'Do you know a Paul Leroux?' I said I did, then he hung up."

"One day, Ray, I will explain it to you. Meanwhile, keep this private."

"I owe you my life, Paul. I would have drowned. Tell me what you need and I will do it."

"Thank you, Cuz. You've always been my best friend. I'm getting close to Canada, but it'll be a while yet. Please don't let a soul know I'm coming. I'll call when I need you to pick me up. That's all I can tell you."

"I'll be here whenever you need me. You need money?"

"Not yet. Gotta go, I'll call you soon."

"You take care, Paul."

With a shaking hand Moonwalker put the phone back into his pocket. It was dawn, and he had a major decision to make.

CHAPTER FIFTY-TWO

AT SIX O'CLOCK IN THE morning Chief Carlson, with Awol beside him, pulled his Bronco into the "Inn at the Long Trail" parking lot. The Inn, popular with hikers, was within a mile of where they planned to set up, and Carlson wanted to sniff around inside and ask questions. Detective Chase, in a green Dodge Caravan, pulled in beside them, climbed out, and introduced two associates. All five were dressed as hikers; only Awol looked like one. The four policemen had radios inside their vests and were packing. Awol's white bandage had been changed to a skin-colored patch fixed over his nose.

Carlson looked inside but he was too early. No one was around and breakfast wasn't until seven. Awol checked the guest register and recognized several trail names of hikers ahead of him. Carlson suggested they drink coffee in Chase's van and plan it out; from the lot, they'd hike the short distance to the junction. They didn't have time to wait and question hikers.

"Okay," Carlson said, "me, Chase, and Bergman set up behind the junction." He took a sip of coffee, "We'll be able to see him approach and watch which way he goes. When Bergman IDs him, we arrest him and I radio both of you." He took a bite out of a chocolate cruller and spoke to the other detectives, "Conlon, you hike up the Appalachian about half a mile and hold up there in case he pulls a fast one. Harrington, you hike up the Long to the shelter. Same thing; I'll radio instructions."

Several minutes later they put on packs and poled by stands of birches up to the junction. The day was overcast and threatened rain.

MOONWALKER HAD COME TO A decision. He knew the police had figured out why he headed north, and would now expect him to take the L.T. to Canada. He hadn't sent any letter to Cousin Ray except the one Ray received months ago, and he'd gotten it without any call from a U.S. post office. *I need to get off this trail—now.* He would bushwhack east for a mile or so and set up camp far enough from the trail, far enough from people. He had food, and could wait them out. As he was about to push off, he thought about the new food bag. He pulled off his pack and inside, below the stolen food bag, retrieved his own. He dumped what was left into his pack and looked at the unmarked name tag at the end of the bag. He took his pen and, after hesitating, wrote "Moonwalker" on the tag. He took the bag up-trail and laid it down near a tree under some leaves, but left the end exposed. Moonwalker didn't meet a soul as he walked back to his pack and pushed his way east, through scrub and pine.

A SHORT WHILE LATER, OFFICER Conlon picked a spot on the Appalachian Trail by a stream he estimated to be one-half mile east of the junction. He radioed the chief he was in position. Chief Carlson, Detective Chase, and Awol had set up in bush fifty feet behind the junction. They could see any approach from the south. Awol was quiet. He thought it all looked too easy and doubted Moonwalker would be foolish enough to walk right into their trap. Carlson was buoyant. He sat with a camouflaged scope in front of him mounted on a tiny tripod. He swung the scope around and peeked at different spots.

"Chase, hand me the trail map." Carlson studied it and looked to his right. "C'mon Harrington, you should be there by now."

Awol sat by a birch and watched Detective Chase scribble on his operations pad. Chase checked his watch, wrote down the time, pushed a button on his watch, and recorded something else. Chase put his pad in his pack, took out a flashlight, and shined it in the thickets behind him.

OFFICER HARRINGTON REACHED TUCKER-JOHNSON SHELTER at ten minutes to seven. One person was rolling up his bag; two others slept. All looked too young and too small to be the suspect. Harrington asked the one packing up about the suspect, but the hiker hadn't seen anyone resembling him. Harrington went to the privy and while relieving himself, he radioed Chief Carlson that he was in position.

"No, Chief, only the usual campers; no one looks like our guy, and no one has seen him. Most of them are still asleep." He listened, while stifling a yawn, as the chief repeated previous instructions. "Roger. Over and out," Harrington said.

An hour later the last hiker stirred. The other had had no information and had left. A young man who looked as if he was sick stared at Officer Harrington from his sleeping bag. "What time is it?"

"Eight o'clock," Harrington said. "You okay?"

"I'm hoping it's just the flu."

"How long have you been sick?" Harrington asked.

"Four days. Do you have any giardia pills?"

"No. Sorry."

"Hey! Where's my food bag?" The kid lurched out of his sleeping bag; he looked anemic, his face contorted in shock. "I hung it right there." He pointed to a nail and looked at the empty floor.

Harrington watched him cradle his head; he looked as if he was going to cry. "I got my meds in there. I can't believe those bastards stole my meds."

Harrington proceeded to look under the shelter and around back. He walked all the way around and as he came to the front, met the first hiker he'd previously talked to, tramping in off the trail, his forehead crinkled.

"Tell me I left my cell phone here."

Officer Harrington radioed Chief Carlson about the sick hiker in need of medical attention. "Also," he added, "it appears someone has stolen this hiker's meds, food, and maybe a cell phone."

CHAPTER FIFTY-THREE

THREE WEEKS LATER, ON A bright September morning, bracing air tinged with wood smoke greeted Awol. Autumn had settled in and Awol was in New Hampshire taking a break at a giant cascade schussing from Webster Cliffs. Recent rains had engorged streams, and water burst from rocks with a roar. He faced the falls at an angle from the east and felt vibrations in the ground where he was back-seated to a boulder. A breeze feathered him from the west and now and then he felt a mist from the falls, blown to him from thirty yards away. Awol was thinking of Linda again. He missed her.

He thought back to the fiasco at the trail junction. When Carlson received word about the sick hiker, he had told Harrington, "Okay, Chase is on the way. When he arrives you go back to the lot with the sick one. Get a statement. As soon as he's picked up, hustle back up here. Got it?" Next, he radioed Conlon. "Hike up another half mile. Stay on the lookout."

They had waited in position until mid-afternoon. Carlson questioned all hikers going north, south, or east, but no one had seen a large, lone hiker with a blue pack who resembled Moonwalker. At 3:15, Chase radioed in from the shelter on the Long Trail.

"Chief, got a hiker here who found an empty food sack a half mile north of me. The inside tag on the bag reads 'Moonwalker.'"

"I'll be right up," Carlson said. "Harrington you stay; Bergman, you're coming with me."

Carlson had briskly gimped the half mile to the shelter, crunching over the yellow-red path of fallen leaves from maple and birch, arms swinging wildly about his sides.

"Well, no, Chief, I don't have the bag, he just said he found it by the trail and looked at it. Then he put it back where he found it."

Awol had wondered if the man they passed on the way up to the shelter was the hiker who discovered the bag, but Carlson was in too much of a hurry to stop, claiming Chase would have questioned him.

"Goddamnit!" Carlson said. "Okay. Bergman, let's go up and have a look."

They found the bag right away; sure enough, it was labeled "Moonwalker."

Carlson looked north and checked his watch: 4:30. "Shit. What do you think now, Mr. Bergman?"

AWOL WATCHED TWO HIKERS STANDING next to New Hampshire's Webster Cliff Falls. The girl's long hair lifted in a breeze that still shook down maple leaves, but the remaining leaves had a deadened-orange color. Green firs mixed with maples provided a backdrop as the guy pulled out a camera from his daypack and snapped a picture of his girl by the cascade. They sat down and he put his arm around her and pulled her close. She laid her head on his chest as they stared at the falls. Awol envied them and thought about his last attempt to phone Linda, back in Vermont. He'd had her brother Tom on the line because he'd given up trying to reach her.

"What do you mean she's gone?"

"She might have gone to our sister's. Jeff said she asked for two weeks off and mentioned something about going to see family."

Jeff was Linda's boss, and Tom's friend. "Figures, I guess. What's up with the answering machine?"

"Listen, where should I send that Connelly bid to?" Tom said.

FOR TWO DAYS, CONLON HAD stayed in the Appalachian Trail Shelter, during which time Harrington had switched out with Chase and stayed in the

Long Trail shelter. Chase and Awol had camped in separate tents behind the junction. On the third day, Carlson pulled Conlon. Carlson made visits, but worked out of his office and alerted towns near the Long Trail from Rutland to Canada. He had succeeded in getting the police in North Troy, Vermont, the last town before Canada, to assemble a hiking party that would proceed south on the Long Trail. The North Troy police had also alerted officials at the Canadian checkpoint. At the end of three days with nothing happening, Carlson had pulled everyone off the trail.

AWOL GOT UP AND SHIFTED into his pack. He took a last look at the cascade and at the mountains framing the ridge walk behind him, before poling north. Chief Carlson had been the one to bring him to the trailhead back in Vermont.

Bergman, we're going to get our Mr. Leroux eventually. Be good.

In the last three weeks, no one had seen or heard anything about Moonwalker. Awol had called Carlson twice, but there had been no break in the case.

"What about the North Troy hikers heading south?" Awol had asked, the last time he called.

"They gave up after thirty miles," Carlson said. "One of them took a fall and got hurt. Leroux must have hitched north and somehow got himself into Canada."

BACK ON THE A.T. AT the Nauman tent site in New Hampshire's Presidential range, Awol bolted upright out of a dead sleep. He felt his body, spiked with sweat, fight off a chill. As sure as he had ever known anything in his life, he realized Moonwalker hadn't taken the Long Trail at all. He was still on the Appalachian Trail, by now in Maine and approaching Canada. It's what he himself would have done. And Awol knew he was the only one who knew this.

CHAPTER FIFTY-FOUR

MOONWALKER REACHED IN A SIDE pocket for his compass. He took a bearing east-northeast. After he left the food bag, he didn't want to drift south to the A.T. The going was rough. Rocks, roots, and brambles slowed him with no sign of relief. He longed for his ax, but didn't dare risk leaving evidence of his bushwhack. Moonwalker snaked through dogwoods and thickets and took a compass reading every few minutes. After a half hour he took off his pack and sat, exhausted. His swollen eye hurt; he trembled from no cigarettes. He wanted to pitch his tent here, but got up and trudged on. *Need to go a couple of miles or more; they could bring in dogs.* He crossed several streams and in the middle of each splashed at least forty paces upstream or downstream. Each time he did this he checked his compass.

By mid-morning, Moonwalker selected a spot bordered by elderberry shrubs, ferns, and bush honeysuckle to the west; alee of a wooded chine to the east; and partially blocked by an enormous downed oak behind him to the south. The oak lay across smaller trees and stumps at a height of five feet, making a barrier. Ten paces to his north was a rill hidden by firs, pine striplings, hazel. He could see sky, but the overhang of oaks and firs prevented a view from above. Moonwalker couldn't imagine a more perfect hiding place. He set up camp and placed his socks and boots by the fallen oak to dry. Too tired to eat, he sucked down a slug of water and crawled inside his tent. He closed the flap, lay on top of his bag, and put a water-soaked bandana over his half-closed eye. He slept until midafternoon.

MOONWALKER WATCHED A DEER AND her fawn as he drew out the stolen food bag. They pranced across the rill and disappeared. He opened the food bag and noticed a ziplock of plastic bottles. Celebrex, Prednisolone, Motrin, Imodium. Another baggie contained a bottle of ear drops; then he fumbled with a baggie of cough drops; Q-tips came next. He laid them aside and after pulling out his shell, which he spread in front of him, dumped the contents of the bag. A cornucopia of food flopped out: ramen, Nestle's, a bag of dates and dried fruit, tin-foiled cheese with a heavenly aroma that made his stomach growl as he lifted the foil, a newly opened jar of peanut butter, a tin of Triscuits and Wheat Thins, a bag of gorp, which Moonwalker held up to the sunlight—Craisins, chocolate chips, almonds, cashews—the good stuff. Moonwalker sat there like an excited kid who had just opened the biggest present at his birthday party because now, legs aquiver, he snatched up a green and white carton half packed with Salem cigarettes. He stifled a roar and pumped the carton into the air. *Yes!* He boiled water while he smoked. With the food in front of him, plus what was left of his own, he could hide out for at least five days.

Twilight was mild as Moonwalker, in a tank-top, leaned back on bark of spruce, smoking and picking his nose. He reached down for the coffee beside him. Surrounded by wood fern on a thick carpet of fragrant evergreen needles, he discerned the faintest glow from the west as darkness passed in front of him. Two more deer scampered through the brook at the same spot as before, one a good sized buck. He'd heard the distinct call of the ring-necked pheasant and had seen grouse. Moonwalker was in good humor and was confident he'd reach Canada.

TWO DAYS LATER, HE WAS antsy. He paced about his hideout juiced up on sugar and nicotine. Feeling rested, strong, he was anxious to see how close he was to the Appalachian Trail, but decided not to make a move for two more days. The law would find the bag he had planted and hunt for him. If they had thought of trying to intercept him at the junction, they'd give up soon enough.

Another two days passed. Moonwalker began to ration food. On the fifth day, he broke camp and took a compass bearing east by southeast.

Moonwalker plugged through understory, roots, and rocks for fifty minutes and during a breather on top of a minor pinnacle, he saw a shimmer of light two hundred yards in front of him. He drew a hundred yards closer and by orienting himself with his map, confirmed he was west of Kent Pond, north of Vermont Route 100, and south of Stony Brook Shelter on the A.T.

Arriving at Stony Brook Shelter, he watched six people, all older and clearly not thru-hikers, having lunch inside. He decided to chance it.

"Hello." A smiling sixty-ish fellow touched his Red Sox cap in salute. "Ladies and gentlemen, meet a thru-hiker." He smiled and spoke for the group. "This man has walked a long way, am I right?"

Moonwalker faked a smile and shifted his eyes to the register lying on the floor. They looked as if they were out for the day and Moonwalker bet they carried extra food.

"Started in Pennsylvania."

"Well, a pretty darn long way," the woman next to the register warbled. "How far are you going?"

Moonwalker hoped they were headed south, perhaps for pickup on Route 100. He could cadge food. "Going to Maine. Would you hand me the register please?"

"Tell us about your adventures," squealed a woman from the back of the shelter. "Have you seen any bears?"

"Seen four." He found Yogi in the register who signed in a week ago. *That's about right.* He found no entry for Malibu, Awol, or the others, and put the register back. "Y'all finishing up a day hike?"

"God willing," their speaker said. "Can you use some extra victuals?"

Moonwalker thought he might be getting too lucky. He was grateful to fate, to the man upstairs, to whomever, but he didn't want to use up all his luck at once. Each one contributed goodies as Moonwalker held out his food bag; the last time he had felt like this was in Presque Isle, Maine, when he, dressed like a pirate, and Cousin Ray, dressed as Napoleon, opened a shared potato sack on Halloween.

After taking off to well wishes, Moonwalker hiked eight more miles and set up camp to the west of the trail near a spring, two miles south of Wintturi Shelter. After a delicious supper of chili and beans, groggy with food, he was too lazy to search for a high limb to secure his food and tied his bag to a nearby pine branch.

At two o'clock in the morning he wakened to thumping outside his tent. Moonwalker sniffed a putrid smell and as he dared a peek behind the flap, he viewed a gigantic creature, black in the moonlight, raise himself up on hind legs and, with huge paws, pull down and snap the branch holding his food bag. Back on all fours, the creature chewed the bag and shook his head, snapping the branch again. Moonwalker watched, helpless, as the bear, food bag hanging from his mouth, lumbered to the spring.

"Motherfucker!" he shouted into the blackness.

CHAPTER FIFTY-FIVE

AT THE RUTLAND, VERMONT POLICE station, Chief Ronald Carlson visited with Chief Paul Haag of the Rutland Police. Detective Chase sat to Carlson's right, across from Rutland's Officer O'Brien.

"You know, Ron, we were a bit miffed up here that we didn't seem to have a part in your plans for this arrest." Haag looked ancient with his full head of gray hair, mustache, and beard. He had announced his planned retirement for the end of the year. "Don't you guys in Manchester believe in teamwork? Telling us over the phone, 'we'll call if we need you,' seems a little cavalier don't you think?"

Carlson looked down on his file and peeked up at O'Brien who, from what he understood, would be the next Chief of Police in Rutland.

"Paul, you're right. I shouldn't have taken ownership on this one. I'm sorry, and I apologize. I'd like to see if we can do this together."

"Okay, Ron. Let's see what you've got."

Carlson opened his folder, took out sets of photos and passed them to each. "The first picture is the blow-up of Leroux taken from his license. The next is a sketch done from descriptions given by Bergman and his hiking friends."

"What a metamorphosis!" whistled O'Brien.

"The guy is big," Carlson said, "license says six-four, Bergman says he looks taller. The trail has whipped him into shape; he's very fit, very strong, and dangerous."

Chief Haag studied the sketch. "We should have had this posted at public campsites and sent to the other precincts. O'B, get this out to everybody right away. And don't forget New Hampshire." Haag looked to Carlson, "What about Maine?"

"Detective Chase and I already took care of that this morning—just in case—but we think he went straight up the Long Trail."

"Maybe he's hiding out in the woods," O'Brien said.

"We thought about it," Chase said, glancing at Carlson, "but the food bag we found was empty and it had his trail name on it. He wouldn't have been able to hide for long without food."

"But didn't you say earlier on the phone something about a bag being stolen?" O'Brien focused on Chase. "Along with a cell phone?"

The silence hung around the table. Carlson was the first to break it. "Well, we might assume Leroux was the thief. We don't know for sure."

MOONWALKER WOKE TO THE PATTER of rain. Not a rain that spit and thumped on his tent, but a steady rain, exact in beat, a rain that Moonwalker knew from experience over the last months, would last.

He searched for bag remnants beyond the brook, sliding around in the muck. He found nothing and rising waters gushed behind him as he scanned west into brush. Moonwalker gave up and as he recrossed, stepped on a rock midstream that shifted, and down he went. He felt his ankle twist and his boots fill with water. "You BASTARD!" he roared at the rock. Moonwalker hoisted himself out of the water and sloshed to the bank where he sat in muck massaging his foot. It wasn't a debilitating sprain, but Moonwalker was not thankful. He couldn't hike a full day on it. Even if he hiked half a day, the foot could turn into a major problem.

He changed his socks in the tent, scrounged up some duct tape, and taped around the sock, creating some support. He wiped out the slimy boots as best he could, packed everything and left. The rain hadn't lost a beat.

An hour-and-a half later Moonwalker hobbled into an empty Wintturi Shelter, which sat off the trail to the west. He had right-armed the two poles as a crutch the last half mile to keep as much weight as possible off his ankle. He examined every cranny of the shelter—not a crumb. He checked the register and read that Malibu, Jersey, Bluebell, and Turtle had overnighted five days ago. Even this didn't improve his spirits. They were where he wanted them to be, *but where was Awol?*

Moonwalker sat alongside the shelter, took off his boot, and massaged his foot. He brooded about the pills and food in the bag dragged off by the bear, including ankle tape. He wanted to smash something and looked around. Nothing. He reached for his guide; he would make a change in plans.

He was four miles from Vermont Route 12; five additional miles would take him into Woodstock. Hitching into a town was risky. But the weather allowed him to keep his head covered and he had grown hardy stubble since he pasted Awol. He had kept the ski cap down over his ears and his pack now appeared dark brown instead of blue, since he'd darkened it with mud and blackberry. Today was the kind of day where windows were rolled up and people tucked into themselves. He pushed off as the rain picked up a beat.

Four hours later, Moonwalker approached the junction of Route 12. His right foot throbbed. He slowed to scan the junction and forgetting about the ground right in front of him, his aching foot slipped on a root. The wet root couldn't have been slicker if it had been sprayed with WD-40, and he crashed as his sore foot slid out from beneath him. Now he'd aggravated his thigh. Moonwalker fought to keep his leg under him as he limped to the road.

After twenty minutes of Moonwalker vying for a ride, a beat-up, black pickup rolled to the side of the road. The passenger window cranked down and an older lady, hooded in a plastic, transparent scarf squinted at Moonwalker.

"If you want to hop in back, my husband says he can take you to Woodstock."

"Have him drop me at a convenience store in town. I'll find my way from there."

Moonwalker, unable to haul himself into the bed of the truck because of his bad leg, unhinged the tailgate. He threw his pack in, flopped onto the gate, and executed a complete roll. He sat up and banged the tailgate shut, whereupon the pickup jumped out into the highway. For the next five miles, as the rain picked up yet another beat, and as Moonwalker sat in a soup of muddy water and oil, the pickup jounced through every pothole, hit every bump, and swerved from every oncoming car. Moonwalker decided that the driver was deliberately tormenting him. *I could smash his rear window with my poles and grind my fingers into his fucking neck.* Moonwalker hunched and withstood the driver's game of punishing the hitchhiker. When the truck stopped in front of a food mart, he unlatched the tailgate and lowered himself. He seethed as he reached for his pack and winced as he hung it on his shoulder. Moonwalker, with an unadulterated hatred for the driver, slammed up the gate. He didn't look back as he hobbled into the store.

CHAPTER FIFTY-SIX

Mᴏᴏɴᴡᴀʟᴋᴇʀ ᴋᴇᴘᴛ ɢʟᴀɴᴄɪɴɢ ᴏᴜᴛꜱɪᴅᴇ ᴀꜱ he neared the cashier handling customers, and glanced again at a building with a flagpole two blocks away.

"The library open?" Moonwalker asked the cashier.

"Yes."

Moonwalker was relieved rainy weather allowed him to keep his hood up and keep some of his face covered. "When's it close?"

"Closes at four."

Moonwalker pulled a lighter from a display and a Vermont logo'd baseball cap and put them in his pile. He paid the cashier and jammed the bags into his pack. There was $188 in moist bills left in his wallet.

At the library, Moonwalker rested his gear in the vestibule and retrieved one of the bags he had put in his pack. Before entering the inside door, he peered through the pane and noted two women at a reference desk. Moonwalker opened the door and crept behind a wall of books, then edged around and entered the restroom.

Twenty-five minutes later, after washing up, applying liniment, and taping the ankle, Moonwalker returned to his pack. He took out a small notepad and after waiting for several children to climb the library steps, followed them in. He pulled the local paper from a rack, found the Yellow Pages phone book, and took a table at the rear of the library.

Authorities speculate Leroux is still heading north on one of the main trails. Although he might be off the trail, all hikers are urged to travel together and be vigilant. Chief Ronald Carlson of Manchester had this to say: "This man is extremely dangerous. Hikers need to practice the utmost vigilance and call local authorities if they see any sign of him or run into suspicious activity."

Moonwalker looked at the sketch accompanying the article—and froze. There he was. He turned the newspaper over and hid it under an Atlas. He took up the Yellow Pages and his pad. A minute later he limped to his pack, pulled out the stolen cell phone, and punched numbers. Low battery the screen read—but more than a charger, he needed to cop a new phone, before the owner of this one discontinued service, or had him traced. He noticed a pay phone at the corner and hiker-hobbled to it.

"North Country Livery, this is Harold."

"Howdy, Harold. I have a death in my family and need to get to Maine."

"We don't go to Maine; just Vermont and New Hampshire."

"I see. How close can you get me? My brother will have to come down and pick me up."

"I can take you to Gorham for $150. It's twelve miles from the border."

"Wow . . . jeez." Moonwalker remembered the $188 in cash. He was frightened, injured, and felt sick. He figured his picture was at every bus station.

"How soon can we leave?"

"Where are you?"

"At the library in Woodstock." He heard him talk to someone.

"One-hundred-fifty, cash, paid up front, and my son will be there inside of thirty minutes."

A half hour later a maroon Mercury Sable pulled up in front of the library. A wiry, acned teenager got out of the driver's side as Moonwalker exited the library and threw open a back door.

"You want this stuff in the trunk instead?" the teenager asked, pointing to the backpack and poles.

"Not a bad idea."

After slamming the trunk the kid, who sported a ring in his left ear, looked up at him. "I'm Junior."

Moonwalker extended his hand, "A pleasure, Junior. I'm Awol."

JUNIOR WAS ABOUT TO DRIVE off and glanced to Moonwalker. "Awol, I'm supposed to collect the money now, okay?"

"Sure." Moonwalker pulled out his wallet, counted out the fee, and handed it to the kid. Junior, with a look on his face that said, glad that's over, moved into the lane. At five minutes to four, Moonwalker glanced back at the library and saw a woman taking down the flag.

Moonwalker was relieved when he saw CDs beside him on the front seat.

"Junior, can we turn off the radio and listen to CDs?"

"Yeah, but these are my dad's. He's into old stuff."

"Yeah? Super. That's what I like," Moonwalker said, as he reached over and slipped in a disk. Moonwalker pulled out a cell phone from his pocket and turned it on. The battery indicated a full charge and he smiled as he clipped the phone to his belt. At the library, five minutes before Junior pulled up, a young girl had left her cell phone unattended when she'd gone to the restroom. As luck would have it, it looked like the same model as the one Moonwalker had. He swapped out the phones, then he'd hunkered down in the vestibule and busied himself by his pack until Junior came.

"WHERE 'BOUTS IN GORHAM ARE you going?"

They had gone twenty miles and Moonwalker was glad to see Junior obeyed speed limits. Moonwalker had turned up the stereo because he didn't want to make conversation.

"What's that? Oh, Gorham. You can drop me somewhere in town. Hey, one of my favorites, 'There Goes My Baby' by the Drifters." Moonwalker reached over and turned the volume up another click.

AFTER AN HOUR, JUNIOR SPIED a Burger King. "You hungry? I need something to eat; we can get it to go."

Moonwalker had been wondering how to get more money. He didn't want to blow the little he had left. "Go ahead. I'm going to get some rest in back while you drive. But please keep the Oldies on for me."

When Junior returned he saw his passenger stretched out on the back seat with his left knee up and his right leg extended up over the back seat almost to the rear window. He snored loudly beneath his hood.

MOONWALKER HAD BEEN OUT FOR over two hours when he felt the vehicle turn and stop. He opened his eyes on a Shell sign looking down at him through the rear window.

"Need to hit the bathroom," Junior said. "Want coffee?"

Moonwalker raised his torso and tested his sore ankle on the car floor. The elevation of the leg, plus the medication and pills, had combined to reduce the ache. He peeked at the all night truck stop. It looked safe, but he didn't want to chance it.

"Yeah, I'd love some."

When the kid came back, Moonwalker had moved to the front seat. "Thanks for the coffee."

The coffee had just cooled enough to drink, when a police car drew up behind them, gumball flashing. "Whoa, you got your license and registration handy?" Moonwalker asked Junior, in the steadiest voice he could muster. He was glad it still rained; he had his hood up and baseball cap on.

"I wonder what the problem is."

"Just relax and keep both hands on the wheel," Moonwalker said. He tried to sound fatherly, "That a boy, and do yourself a favor, if he asks, tell him I'm a friend of the family and there's been a death in Gorham, 'cause—well, I'll explain later."

After reviewing Junior's license and registration in his cruiser, the officer returned to the Sable. Looking at Moonwalker, who was gazing through the driver window at an angle to the officer, giving the impression he wanted to hear what he had to say, but had no need to look at him, the officer asked, "are you Mr. Caulkins?"

He glanced at the badge of Officer Salvi, "No, Officer, I'm just a friend of the family."

Officer Salvi looked back to Junior, "You got a brake light out on the left rear; here's a warning. You've got three days to get it fixed."

"Oh." Junior fingered the slip of paper in relief. "Thank you, sir, for telling me. I'll be sure to get it fixed."

AS THEY APPROACHED GORHAM TOWN limits, Moonwalker checked his map and located the trailhead in Shelburne, a short ways east. He gave directions. "Yeah, I can do that," Junior said.

Minutes later, in a light rain, Junior pulled in to a small graveled lot near the trailhead. "You sure you're okay here? I can swing you into town."

"Not a problem. Soon as I get on my cell phone, I'll be picked up. This is where we usually meet."

"So why did you want me to say you were a friend of the family?" Moonwalker ignored the question. "You know, back there with the policeman." Junior opened the trunk.

"Huh? Oh, sometimes if you give detailed explanations everything gets off-track. Less complicated, that's all."

After he watched the Mercury turn away, Moonwalker put on his headlamp. He took a cursory look around the empty lot, found a white blaze, and angled north.

Junior yanked out the CD and listened to the radio. Ten minutes later, Junior drove into a Dunkin' Donuts in Gorham. The news had come on his radio, and as he pulled up to the pretty blonde at the Drive-Thru window, the radio squawked: ". . . still no word on the alleged hiker-killer, Paul Leroux, last seen in Vermont. Authorities believe he is either still hiking north on the Long Trail or he has hitched a ride to New Hampshire or Maine." At the end of this last sentence, Junior had just finished giving the girl his order and was digging for pocket change. He hadn't heard a word of the radio announcement.

CHAPTER FIFTY-SEVEN

Awol drank from his water bottle and felt slivers of ice slide down his throat. He looked out at several other tents at the Nauman campsite and saw fog to the east, muting a rising sun. It was just after dawn, and he hadn't slept a wink since he'd bolted up out of a dead sleep last night. *Where was my head? How could I have been so stupid? Moonwalker's been on the A.T. the whole time. He's out here now. The clues are all there.* A couple of days ago, he overheard two *sobos*, "Pac-man, did you take all my noodles? And where's my cocoa? You owe me, man."

"You're hallucinating, Kiwi. I haven't taken your shit."

He remembered a couple of days before that, another south bounder had written in a register, "I'm missing my headlamp. If any sobos picked up an extra one, please save it for Zombie."

Awol knew this had to be more than coincidence. Someone was scrounging for food and supplies, probably in the middle of the night. He thought back on the sack Moonwalker dropped "accidentally" on the Long Trail. He had been eluding the police all along and didn't want anyone to know who he was; he would never have ID'd himself as "Moonwalker" on his equipment. Plus, his choice of name didn't make sense. The hikers Awol knew bought their equipment before they began their thru-hike, before they had taken trail names. Non thru-hikers didn't use trail names. So why would he have written his trail name? Hikers bought equipment and labeled it with their initials or their real names. In Moonwalker's case he would have left it blank. He wanted to fool us into thinking he'd taken the Long Trail north. Besides, Awol thought, hikers might leave a sock, or drop a bandanna, a glove, or some small item; to forget a larger food bag at a non-camping spot right on the trail was peculiar. *Stupid. Stupid. Stupid.*

Before leaving camp Awol stopped at the tents, "Hey everybody, listen up." He was going to reveal his suspicions about Moonwalker, but changed his mind at the last minute. He didn't want anyone writing anything in a register that might alert Moonwalker.

"Have any of you over the last weeks—north or south—had anything taken or stolen?"

"What about Zombie?" a girl said. "She had money stolen and her headlamp was missing."

"Right," a boy said, "she had sixty dollars stolen. Why?"

"I'm hearing stories about a thief who's ahead of us." Awol looked at the girl, "Can you tell me when and where the incident happened with Zombie?"

"A week ago; in New Hampshire, near Gorham. She's a sobo."

"How'd you find out?"

"She's keeping a journal on the internet; read all about it on the website, at Dartmouth Library in Hanover."

Hanover, New Hampshire. On the A.T.

"Okay, thanks. We need to stay alert; keep your eyes and ears open."

As Awol poled off, he heard the girl say, "I despise a thief, but I'd rather take my chances with a thief than with a sadistic killer."

AWOL APPROACHED LAKES OF THE Clouds hut on the shoulder of Mount Washington at noon. The mountain, at 6,288 feet, was considered to have some of the worst weather in the world. At the summit, an official recording of wind velocity at over two hundred miles per hour held the world's record. A bizarre geographical combination of peaks and valleys contributed to the treacherous weather zone, but on this day the elements held at a windy forty-four degrees. Awol eyed the cloud-covered peak after taking a break in the hut and began the one-and-a-half-mile final ascent. By the time he scrambled up the last of the talus-strewn slope and reached the metal-towered pinnacle, he had made a decision.

Hunched quietly ten yards from the official summit marker, Awol tugged the ski cap down over his ears, closed his eyes, and took his time. He was collected and resolved as he finished a prayer.

He picked up his poles and walked to the summit station where he bought a one-way train ticket down to the base of the mountain. Ten minutes later, after Awol strapped himself into a rear seat, the wood-fired boiler pulled the train out of the station. Awol smiled as he watched families aboard the train. Young kids shouted and banged on windows, and when the train whistle shrieked, they couldn't contain themselves. Awol had not felt so at ease in a long while.

He was the last to step off the train. He walked past the parking lot to the road, and within ten minutes he got a hitch up to Route 2. Twenty-five minutes later, he obtained another hitch all the way to Gorham. By nightfall he was in a motel room searching the local paper. Touching the motel room phone, he was tempted to try Linda again, but he knew he needed to avoid any distraction.

After listening to the local news, Awol gathered his handbook and maps and hoofed it to the red-roofed Pizza Hut. While waiting for his food, he scrutinized the maps. He had no proof Moonwalker was on the A.T. and had no evidence of his past whereabouts since the stuff sack found near Rutland, Vermont, but he was convinced Moonwalker was a couple of weeks ahead of him.

After finishing the entire pizza, Awol ordered another Coke. He was satisfied with his decision and confident with his plan. *There's no way I'm calling the police this time. They'll tip him off.*

THE FOLLOWING MORNING HE PICKED up the phone and dialed Linda. No answer. He tried five minutes later and again no one picked up. He tried once more ten minutes after that and still no luck. Twenty minutes later he got his first hitch to Maine. By nightfall, Awol had made it all the way to Stratton, where he figured he was one week ahead of Moonwalker.

PART FOUR

O, woe is me, to have seen what I have seen, see what I see!

—Hamlet

Moonwalker's headlamp blinked several times after Junior swerved out of the lot. Minutes later the light dimmed and went out. Moonwalker, not having a proper spare battery, gave up and grabbed his flashlight. He crossed the bridge spanning Androscoggin River under a dull quarter moon. He would have preferred to hike farther in, well away from the trailhead, but trying to hike, flashlight between his teeth, around root and stone was out of the question. The long car ride had numbed his sore leg and Moonwalker was afraid he might take another fall. He sought an opening and pushed in thirty yards to a suitable spot.

After setting up, he smoked in the inky tent, then applied another dose of joint cream to his ankle and left it unwrapped. He missed the headlamp because he wanted to study his handbook to learn about the terrain ahead. The flashlight was awkward and he couldn't take the chance of also using up those batteries. The continual creaking of tree limbs unnerved him, and he had a hard time going to sleep.

Barking dogs woke him too early. At first he thought they were after him as he heard the hounds woof from their throats. Moonwalker sat frozen in his tent and heard their master instruct, "Nyet! Nyet!" One hound sniffed the closed flap and Moonwalker heard approaching footsteps crunching leaves and twigs, and then what sounded like a riding crop strike the animal. "Nyet!" The dogs raced away.

Once he calmed down, he applied more joint cream and rewrapped his ankle. He flexed the sore ankle and popped three Aleve; after a smoke and a little bit of food, he packed up.

THAT AFTERNOON MOONWALKER CAME UPON Gentian Pond Shelter. He spied two backpacks on the shelter floor with two undersized containers of water purifier next to them and understood that the hikers went to fill their water bottles. Moonwalker closed his eyes and listened—silence. Working quickly he unzipped pockets and peeked inside. In seconds he'd removed a headlamp and slid it into his pocket. He looked under the top of one pack and noticed a bulge beneath a Velcro strap. He yanked loose the Velcro and palmed a ziplocked baggie wrapped with a rubber band. His senses keyed, Moonwalker heard nothing as he unwrapped the wallet and removed two twenties, a ten, and two fives. He returned the wallet and closed the pack. Hoping they planned to stay at the shelter for the night, Moonwalker hiked north to a bend in the trail and walked off the A.T. He crouched and focused the field glasses.

He spotted them once they returned to the shelter. The man and woman packed up and poled—south. Moonwalker hadn't noticed he was sweating. Fate had been kind to him; two problems had been solved, and he watched the hikers disappear forever.

Two miles later Moonwalker stopped for several minutes; he wanted to give the ankle a rest. He got his bearings on the map—Maine! Less than three miles. He'd had no idea he was this close and his heart leapt as he shuffled north again.

A short while later, he teared up at the border marker: "Maine, The Way Life Should Be." *Almost free.* Another marker pointed north to Carlo Col Shelter, one-half mile. Moonwalker set up a hundred yards or so from the campsite.

Moonwalker smelled a campfire. He lay inside his tent with the ankle raised on his pack. It was sore and still throbbed, even after he had taken two more pills with his dinner over an hour ago. More than any medication, the foot needed rest. He had no choice; his maps showed an unending series of altitude spikes.

He took the next two days off and remained by his tent. Late the second morning he gimped to the empty shelter. Finding nothing of use, he swiped the register and left. Again he checked listings for any sign of Awol, even though he certainly didn't expect him to be this far north. In his murky tent, he started to accept the notion that Awol was no longer a problem.

He pushed off at 9:00 a.m. the next day, thirty minutes after the shelter cleared. His ankle felt better. After five miles of hard hiking, he took a rest. Mahoosic Notch loomed before him, and that, according to all he had read, was a stretch of hiking anguish lasting for a mile. It was only a quarter of two in the afternoon; he had already cooked a meal and Moonwalker convinced himself he could do anything for one mile, even on a shaky foot. He rewrapped his ankle as tight as he could, took two Advil, and off he went.

He tackled the beginning of the notch gamely enough, but after fifteen minutes of ever-worsening rocky terrain, wondered if he had made a mistake. The poles were useless in this outcrop and after collapsing them, he tied them to the back of his pack. The boulders became the size of automobiles as Moonwalker scrambled in a play-land for giants. The temperature had dropped—the sun didn't penetrate around boulders, and he felt cold air misting up from depths below. Rocks were slick. He had to stretch his legs as he inched down over boulders, fingers pinching for purchase at cracks, and then, when he couldn't stretch any further nor feel footing any longer, had to close his eyes and pray, when he slid those last inches, that he'd reach something solid. After forty-five minutes of nerve-racking squiggles through openings of rock, dangerous jumps on one good foot over chasms, scrambles over and around ledges, Moonwalker encountered an impasse. He peeked at the white blaze painted on a boulder, but to get there he had to either crawl a narrow, slippery granite ledge which could drop him into a chasm or try to climb to the left and take his chances further up.

The sun was sinking as Moonwalker opted to climb. He was halfway when he began to slip and slide. Moonwalker panicked, hugged the boulder, and stabbed the bad foot into the rock to halt the slide. If he fell he would never be able to get out of the chasm. He pushed off on the bad foot and felt the ankle turn beyond its limit. Pain and adrenalin flooded Moonwalker, and with a roar, he pulled himself up the granite face another several inches where he had to repeat the same procedure again. Eyes shut, he pushed up again while the bad ankle arced into a new pain, but he was up another ten inches and with the help of his good knee managed to scrape up inch by inch the rest of the way.

On top of a facing, he dragged the bad foot over and cradled the ankle. He tried to massage it in his hands. It felt as if on fire, and he looked north to more of the same. Moonwalker didn't know he hadn't even reached the halfway point.

He swigged water and looked again on the white blaze, now down to his right. He found an opening through the rocks to the left and removed his pack. He crawled in for a look and calculated that he could make the drop on the other side if he could squeeze through. He turned around at the opening and backed in. Inching backward he snaked through and reached for his pack. He inched back, stopped, and then yanked the pack. He did this a dozen times—inch back, stop, yank—until he could feel his legs dangle over the edge. He strained for a foothold and sagged. Forgetting the pack, he reached up and grabbed it just in time. As he yanked it to him one of the poles caught on the rock slab above. He didn't realize this as he continued back and sagged over the side, dragging the pack as a counterweight. When he felt footing, he slid to it while the pole bent grotesquely above him. At the last moment he heard the pole snap and the pack slung through the rest of the opening down on top of Moonwalker. The other pole slipped out and Moonwalker watched it cascade below from rock to rock until it came to rest on an impassable ledge.

AN HOUR-AND-A-HALF LATER, A BATTERED man with a bloody bump on the side of his forehead limped through the end of the notch. His face looked like a lost battle. He appeared to be talking to himself as he hobbled off the trail—searching. Rock everywhere, but he leaned against pine. He put his face in his hands, became perfectly still, and listened. A crisp quarter moon peeked down on him; a breeze whispered from the west. A full minute, then two passed. He removed his pack, retrieved his headlamp and placed it above the swelling. He switched it on and shook himself into his pack. Without looking back, Moonwalker lumbered west to the promise of water.

For the next three days Moonwalker tented next to a brook seventy yards from the A.T., near the northern end of Mahoosic Notch. By the night of the third day he was out of Motrin and almost out of food. Unable to put weight on the doubly sprained ankle, even with a kind of crutch fashioned from a downed branch, he spent some of his days thinking about Canada, but most of his days and all of his nights fantasizing about women. It was all he had to fall back on as he waited for the foot to heal. He soaked the foot in the cold spring three times a day and elevated it to sunlight. Lying in sunlight Moonwalker shut his eyes and envisioned Nightwind or the buxom Malibu teasing his foot back to life with soft lips.

Kiss it again, sweetie. And do it nice. He felt Malibu's bare breasts slide down his leg and her nipples rest on his calf as she kissed the ankle. She worked her lips and tongue around his ankle joint as Moonwalker felt himself grow hard, right below her crotch. He cupped his hands over her naked buttocks and gripped the flesh.

Now, he rasped, *you come to Jesus, sweetie. You come on up and kiss Jesus.* She turned roughly and Moonwalker gave her a powerful swat on her ass. *Gently, baby. You do it nice and gentle. Y'hear?*

I'm sorry, she sobbed. *Please, I'm sorry.*

She went to work. *Much better . . . ah . . . that's good, sweetie.* And too soon, Moonwalker felt her warm tears slide down the side of his pipe.

After, he toweled off and napped.

Late at night, after taping his foot and before easing into his bag, he did it all over again, only this time in his fantasy, he choked her.

CHAPTER FIFTY-NINE

Mᴏᴏɴᴡᴀʟᴋᴇʀ sᴛᴜᴄᴋ ᴛʜᴇ ʙʀᴀɴᴄʜᴇᴅ-ᴄʀᴜᴛᴄʜ ᴜɴᴅᴇʀ his arm and trudged toward Speck Pond campsite, two miles north. It took him over two hours to near the campsite, where he picked a spot out of sight. Seven hikers came and left during the next three hours, but Moonwalker was patient. He couldn't sneak in during the night because of the crutch. Late that afternoon he watched two southbound hikers lay their packs in the shelter. He focused the binoculars and watched the young men remove shirts and put on flip-flops. One took from his pack what looked to be a small radio and the other grabbed a bag of what looked like gorp. Moonwalker observed them heading to the pond. At once Moonwalker left his pack and hobbled to the shelter. He filled empty pockets with packets of noodles and hot chocolate, switched out cell phones, and swiped two trekking poles. Moonwalker's previous stolen cell was nearly the same size as this newly swiped one, and he counted on the hiker not taking a close look at it for at least a few days.

Forty minutes later, Moonwalker had set up his tent east of the trail and north of Speck Pond Shelter. He wished he could have swiped Ibuprofen.

After a meal of spicy hot noodles and cocoa, Moonwalker got out his map. He knew now that he couldn't handle the rest of the Mahoosics. He had to make the jump to Canada. He would begin a new life in the land of his ancestors. As much as he wanted one last woman on the trail, it would have to wait. He scanned the map. All along he had planned to hike as far as Millinocket, and from there hike to the border. The map showed he didn't need to tramp so far north. The town of Stratton sat five miles west of the trail and thirty miles southeast of Canada. He could walk those last thirty miles in two nights. He wouldn't even need his headlamp—he'd hug the roadside and move only under darkness.

The immediate problem was the eighty-five miles of trail over unforgiving terrain before reaching Stratton. He examined elevation profiles on the side of his map and reflected on spikes that made the chart look like an electrocardiogram of a heart attack. He located the mountains that he'd have to climb: Old Speck, Baldplate, both west and east peaks; Wyman, Hall, Bemis—both peaks again; Saddleback, including the "Horn"; Spaulding, Sugarloaf, the Crocker peaks—north and south.

He threw down the map and brooded. A chipmunk darted by. The chipmunk peeked at Moonwalker from behind his boots and snatched an uncooked noodle with his paw. Moonwalker stared at the animal and seeing another noodle that had fallen near his leg, he picked it up and threw it near the chipmunk. The chipmunk stared at Moonwalker for the longest time and then darted to the noodle whereupon Moonwalker smashed down a trekking pole, barely missing the critter's head. The animal disappeared with the noodle for good while Moonwalker sat there flicking dirt with the pole.

Moonwalker stood up and tried to walk without limping. He couldn't do it and he didn't even have his pack on. He tried again, to no avail. He winced as he strapped the headlamp to his forehead. The swelling was reduced, but whenever Moonwalker touched his face above the lips, his whole head throbbed. He shook the last Marlboro from his pack. He hooded up his shell while he sat looking at the moon rising. Night came with chill and a breeze. No signs of rain. *Would I take rain for a better foot? Of course. What would I give for a way to the border right now? What would I give for . . . ?*

He crept into his tent and closed the flap, seeking refuge in his fantasy. After he was done, he crawled back out and once again took up the map, looking for the quickest way out. He'd take his chances on being identified.

AT DAWN THE NEXT MORNING, before anyone else was likely to be on the trail, Moonwalker shuffled north. He felt the icy shafts of the poles through his gloves. Rime ice had settled on rocks and vegetation bordering the path; red-flowered columbine looked frozen. Seeing his breath, he wished for a cigarette; he was out, but was at least moving and getting warmer. The ankle was stiff and he felt it burn. After a mile of rigorous climbing the ankle fixed into a pain and throb which remained consistent. *Just don't get any worse.*

He took a ten-minute rest every hour and seven hours later spotted the sign for Grafton Notch and Route 26. *Just as I thought; the gap is isolated. No way anybody will keep an eye out here.* Moonwalker began to think he could relax; he was a long way from Vermont, and North Carolina seemed an eternity ago. He hobbled to the macadam and laid the poles against his pack.

Moonwalker heard a rumble grow to a growl. A logging truck neared, but he knew enough to not even try for a hitch. It'd take the driver minutes to stop the double-bottom and as long to get it going again. Ten minutes later he heard a whine and viewed a pickup coming with two yellow canoes atop. Moonwalker hopped up and beseechingly folded his hands in prayer. The pickup stopped.

"Goin' to Bethel?" A blonde, stacked, in a cranberry jersey under an open fleece vest, moved a gym bag off the passenger seat. "You can throw your gear in back."

Moonwalker's body vibrated as he placed his pack and poles next to canoe paddles in the bed. He came around and sucked in air—twice—before climbing inside.

"I can take you into Bethel."

"Actually, was going to Newry and from there hoping to get a hitch to Farmington. You wouldn't be interested in going to Farmington would ya?" Moonwalker eyed her legs as she turned onto the road.

"No, 'fraid not. I'm picking up my boyfriend; we're canoeing with friends in Locke Mills, outside of Bethel. Sorry." She looked over to Moonwalker with a grin.

"I see. I'll get there somehow I guess. Would you happen to have a cigarette?"

"No. I don't smoke. Never have." She pulled out the ashtray without thinking.

"Then you're one of the lucky ones. Don't take it up."

She smiled and they rode in silence. "Are you thru-hiking?"

"No, finishing a section I've been meaning to do. Family's in Stratton, where I'm hoping to get tonight, somehow or other."

"You know, one of our friends we're meeting is from Farmington and his brother works in Bethel, but he won't get off for another two hours. He could maybe take you to Farmington. Don't know about Stratton; it's quite a ways."

Moonwalker half-wished the truck would break down so she'd have to pull off the road. He imagined a narrow path into timberland; night, moon, no one around.

"If your friend's brother wants to make some money, I'll pay him."

"I've got a cell phone; I could call him, but you can't get a signal up here. Hey, what happened to your head?"

Moonwalker had an uncontrollable urge to grab her thigh, but instead reached for a cigarette, winced when his hand came up empty, and concluded he had to cut loose from her or all would be lost. "Took a spill. You know, just drop me in Newry, okay? I know who I can call."

After the pickup pulled away from the one gas station in Newry, Moonwalker bought smokes inside and eyed the logging truck fueling at the diesel pump. While lighting up, he walked over to the driver who stood next to the pump.

"Chief, I know you guys aren't supposed to take hitchhikers, but you look like you might be headed to Farmington."

The driver was an old-timer with creases in his forehead. His shabby green cap read, "Fran's Snowmobiles—Farmington."

"Where'd you get that bump?"

"'Fraid I had one-too-many in Bethel the other night."

"Get in."

An hour later, Moonwalker was in Farmington. The log truck driver had a buddy in Farmington by the name of Palin, who sometimes fished Flagstaff Lake above Stratton. For twenty-five dollars, and two packs of Marlboros, Euclid Palin drove him to the trailhead near Stratton. Moonwalker was exuberant. In one day he'd made up the eighty-five miles of unforgiving terrain and saved his leg.

"Ray?" Moonwalker heard a voice, then static. He angled up the phone and tried turning around, but the connection was lost. He stood behind an Appalachian Trail marker in Stratton. The small, graveled parking lot was empty. He had a better chance of getting a signal here near the road as opposed to the forest he viewed in front of him, where he planned to tent. He tried the swiped cell again but got no signal at all.

AT DAWN MOONWALKER PUT HIS pack in his tent and walked back toward the road. He took out the cell phone again and had better luck.

"Allo."

"Ray?"

"Cousin Paul. Could you hear me last night? Paul, the police came here looking for you. Papa knows, I didn't tell him, but he knows the police looked for you."

"What happened? What did you tell them?"

"I told them—I had to—that you were my cousin. You see, they already knew we are related; it was on an insurance policy. But, and this is the truth, I told them I had not heard from you in years, and I thought you lived in Florida."

"I believe you, Cuz."

"Now look, you can't come here, they are on the lookout and Papa is nervous. They say you have killed people."

"I can explain."

"Okay, Paul. I owe you my life and haven't forgotten my promise. Where are you? You can trust me, Cuz."

"I'm on the Appalachian Trail, in Maine." Moonwalker heard his cousin shuffling papers.

"Es tu . . . ? Okay. Can you get to Millinocket, Maine? I have a friend who works at the Edmundston border checkpoint. He will come down Route 11 to Millinocket and bring you back up."

"I wish you could pick me up, Ray."

"I know, me too. But I'm probably being watched. He's a good friend; there won't be a problem."

TOO COLD TO GO OUTSIDE, Moonwalker lay smoking in his tent, hidden in a patch of red-stemmed dogwood. He was not sure what to do. He'd hardly slept for nerves and anticipation, being so close to Canada. His ankle was sore and he wished he had pills. He was out of noodles and hot chocolate; he'd made a mistake in not getting snacks from the vending machine at the gas station. He'd gotten excited and didn't think about it. *I've got to get to Millinocket. What choice is there? The stakes have changed, and I'm nowhere near Edmundston.*

He checked the map one more time. From where he was the most direct route to Millinocket was the A.T. The elevation spikes were muted; tough southern Maine and the Mahoosics were behind him. Moonwalker shook ashes off the map. To try to hitch from here to Millinocket looked involved. He'd have to backtrack and, because of the lakes, parklands, and isolation, would have to take a combination of routes totaling upward of two hundred miles. He'd be noticed. *No. My extra lives have run out. Besides, if I see another chick in a truck, I'll snap.*

After checking food and supplies, he concluded he would have to take one more chance in town. He packed up and headed to the road that would take him into Stratton.

CHAPTER SIXTY

STRATTON WAS A ONE-HORSE TOWN and everything Awol needed was on one corner. He bought a newspaper in the general store, then walked through a small parking lot to take a room at the motel, which sat across the street from the Stratton Diner. He wanted food, but while waiting for his room key, thought he would try to call Linda again. No luck.

Late that evening, he reached Tom. "Been trying like hell to reach you," Awol barked.

"Sorry. About that bid to—"

"First—how's Linda?"

Silence.

"Karl, I've got to tell you something. Linda's seeing someone else. I'm sorry, Karl."

AWOL LOOKED AT THE CLOCK radio—half past eight in the morning. He felt depleted. He'd had trouble getting to sleep brooding about Linda and had gotten up at 2:00 a.m. to try to write her a letter. He couldn't make it sound right and gave up at 2:45. Then he tried to focus on maps to choose where to set up for Moonwalker. He wasn't able to concentrate on that either and fifteen minutes later, stumbled back to bed. He bolted up from his Desert Storm nightmare at 4:10 a.m., and had been awake since. *Of course I needed someone with experience out in front—I was raw. Just for that Harrison would try to take me out? Then, fourteen hours later I . . .*

He rustled into clothes and lurched across the street to the diner. He wandered in and held the door for two hunters going out. A family occupied a booth; two freshly scrubbed little girls, twins, with different colored barrettes in their hair, were coloring with crayons across from their parents. The family was dressed as if going to church and Awol remembered today was Sunday. Three young girls and a boy shared another booth. Awol walked by an old man with a cane at the near end of the counter and spotted a big, hatted guy who reminded him of Moonwalker, looking straight at him from the opposite end. Awol walked down and spied the backpack leaning at the end of the counter.

"Howdy," Awol said, eyeing the orange Montero with ear flaps tied up, the yellow hunter's vest, and Moonwalker's stubble of beard.

"Well, well, look what the cat dragged in." Moonwalker stepped off the stool and, before Awol knew what was happening, sat in the empty booth between the booths of the family in Sunday best and the one with the teenagers. "Step into my office," he said to Awol, then louder to the waitress, "Cheryl, another paying customer. Set us up over here." Moonwalker stretched his arm across the back of the booth. His hand was inches from the twin with the blue barrette.

Reluctantly, Awol sat down across from him. "Going moose hunting, Moonwalker?"

"Heh, heh," Moonwalker chuckled, "I'm going fishing, Mr. Awol. Getting picked up in a few minutes. Now what's a fancy guy like you doing in a Podunk town like this?"

"What makes you think you'll ever get out of this restaurant?"

"Let me explain something to you, and you listen close; I've never killed anyone, my word against yours, but if I feel threatened in any way by you or the police, I'll snap that little girl's neck behind me. Then I'll reach for the other one," Moonwalker pulled his vest askew so Awol could see the hilt of a four inch Buck knife, "before I come for you."

"What'll it be, this morning?" Cheryl asked, coming up to the booth and pouring coffee for Awol. She set Moonwalker's half-eaten breakfast back in front of him.

"He's having what I had. Put it on his bill," Moonwalker said.

Awol blinked. "What makes you so confident? You're a wanted man." He noticed a swelling riding above Moonwalker's right ear which disappeared under the hat.

"Fact is, you have no evidence. And you need to face it. You've got the wrong man. My word against yours. You want to try to make something of it here? You'd make a huge mistake. What a tragedy. Would-be hero takes out wrong man. Three dead."

"I have the right man, Moonwalker. And I'm bringing you down."

"These two little girls don't think so."

"You are a sick fucking puppy."

"You can bait me all you want, Awol, but as soon as I finish my eggs, I'm getting up and going fishing."

"What if I said I had a gun pointing at you and I'm going to blow your dick off?" Awol shifted his hands in his lap.

"I'd say you're full of shit." Moonwalker poured ketchup on the remainder of his scrambled eggs. He took the salt and pepper from under Awol's nose and shook both at the same time over the eggs. "Go ahead, shoot!"

Awol glanced out the window and watched children walking toward the white steeple up on the hill. *Moonwalker's in front of me. But can I be 100 percent certain he's the killer? What if I'm wrong? Again.* He saw a dying Harrison. *I'm right on this one, but if I do anything that causes harm to anyone else in here, it's not worth it.*

Awol stared at Moonwalker's busted fingernails. "Why not turn yourself in, Moonwalker? You'll never make it to the border."

"I don't think you understand. Number one, I haven't done anything wrong. Number two, what's this border shit? I'm going fishing."

"There's a picture of you at every post office and in every—"

"Well, here comes my ride. So soon, too." Moonwalker put down his fork, took a last sip of coffee, and dabbed his lips with the napkin. He leaned in, "Make one move, someone gets sliced. There are plenty of kids outside as well." He stood up, "By the way, what happened to your nose? Looks nasty." Moonwalker flicked his bill over to Awol, hiker-hobbled over to the counter and hoisted his pack and sticks. He glanced once at the little girls and at Awol, and gimped out the door and into the van of Euclid Palin. Two fishing poles were fastened to a rack on top.

"Cheryl! Call the police!"

Awol couldn't make out the license plate number because people were standing in front of the van and then it had backed out and swerved away by the time Awol got to the door.

"Don't touch anything on the table where we sat."

The cook gave him a baggie and Awol sealed Moonwalker's cup, fork, both shakers, and used napkin.

"The police are on their way," Cheryl said.

Head up Route 27 toward Canada and the lake, he had told Euclid as he jumped in from the diner. *Do it quick! I'll explain later.*

Now, on an alternate route back to the trail, Euclid told Moonwalker, "You know there's another entrance to the trail farther up. You want to save yourself three miles of walking?"

"Shit yeah. Do it."

"Another pack of cigs."

"Figures. But I need one more favor. I'm low on cash. What'll you give me for this camera?"

Euclid glanced at the stolen camera Moonwalker had carried. "Does it work?"

"Course it does. Would I screw a fellow Frenchman?" Moonwalker had told him he was of the Babbineau clan outside of Toronto. "I paid seventy-five dollars for it and it's new."

"Well, Frenchman or no, I'm not paying those kinda bucks. Don't need no camera."

"Euclid, this camera is so new, you can gift it and no one would know. It's a Canon. How 'bout fifty dollars?"

"Thirty's the best I'm gonna do."

Moonwalker pushed his hat and vest into the pack. "Okay, but I keep my cigs." When the conversation stopped and Euclid was looking straight ahead, Moonwalker stuck his right hand in the door pouch beside him and copped a pair of shades.

Moonwalker, feeling stronger after hot food and victory, had already hiked two miles since being dropped off. The painkiller kicked in. He felt his sore foot on every step, but the discomfort was modulated and he convinced himself it wouldn't escalate. Moonwalker was relieved he'd gotten supplies, though he had used up all the money he'd had on him. But now he had thirty dollars, two to three days' worth of food, and Canada lay straight ahead.

CHAPTER SIXTY-ONE

OFFICER HOOVER FROM THE RANGELY, Maine police department pulled up to the Stratton Diner. For over an hour Awol had been nursing hot chocolate and pacing the sidewalk. He had thought of calling Chief Carlson in Manchester to try to get someone's ass in gear, but after a call to Rangely, where he explained to the dispatcher that he had DNA from the serial killer and said killer was on the way to Canada in a black van, he had been told someone was en-route and that if no one at the diner was under any immediate threat, it was not considered an emergency.

"So, what have we got here?" Officer Hoover looked at the plastic bag Awol held up.

"Officer Hoover, if you get the DNA checked on these items I'm certain it will match DNA of the serial killer everyone is looking for."

"The guy who's killed people on the Appalachian Trail?"

"Yes. We sat in that booth," Awol pointed behind him, "this morning."

Hoover squinted at Awol as he continued. "Two small girls sat inches away in the booth behind him and he threatened to take them out if I made a move. He made a point of showing me a knife under his vest."

"So, where is he now?"

"Got picked up where you're standing, a black van, but I couldn't get the plate number. The van headed up Route 27, toward Canada."

"Canadian plate?"

"Maine."

Hoover fumbled with the bag, placed it in the cruiser and drew out a clipboard with a white form attached. "I'll need more information. Let's sit down inside."

"Sir, as a former military officer, I respect procedure, but isn't there a way we can put a rush on this? The man is a killer, and he's heading for the border."

"Mr. Bergman, we do have an APB out for a black van and we've alerted border check points. So far we've turned up nothing. Without a plate number and without the mystery van, there isn't much we can do."

AT THE END OF THE interminable session, where Awol seemed to give more information about himself than about the killer, Awol asked, "Officer, when will you get results on the DNA?"

"Depends on how much they're backed up down there. We'll put the usual rush on it like everyone else does—figure a couple of weeks."

Awol watched the cruiser pull away and felt the blackest rage of his life building. He was near the end of his quest but instead of achieving peace, he'd lost Linda, let a killer escape—twice—and had not resolved his Desert Storm trauma. He walked in the direction that Moonwalker went, hands shaking and rage building, but after a mile, abruptly turned around and hoofed back to the general store. He bought a six-pack of Bud and headed straight to his motel.

Back at the motel, Awol came unhinged, and trashed his room. He threw a table lamp through the window pane, followed by empty beer bottles, up-ended the bed, shattered the bath mirror over the sink. He heard shouting and a bath-robed man burst through the door holding up a badge and shield while another man watched behind.

"You are under house arrest. Put your hands behind you."

Awol glared and slammed the door in his face. Twenty minutes later Officer Hoover walked into the room.

"Mr. Bergman, we can do this the easy way, or the hard way. Put your hands behind you and turn around."

Hoover cuffed Awol and led him outside. "Thanks, Charlie, I'll take it from here," he said to the off-duty fireman. Fifty minutes later, after background checks were completed, after his Massachusetts arrest was discussed, Awol, still handcuffed in the back seat of the cruiser, was informed that the owner, Oscar Peloquin, was pressing charges.

"Officer Hoover, please Sir, I want to apologize. Can you take me to Mr. Peloquin? I would like to speak with him."

Hoover led him by the arm to the side of the motel where Peloquin picked up pieces of glass at the busted window. Peloquin squinted at Awol in disgust.

"Mr. Peloquin, I'm so sorry I put you through this. I've got no excuse, but I offer you a proposition." Hoover stood with his hands on his hips. "I'm in the remodeling business. I'll repair that window, put in a new medicine cabinet for you; fix anything else I busted up. My cost, my labor, new products."

"If I don't press charges," Peloquin said, thinking. "But if I do press charges, you'll have to pay for this anyway. Peloquin glanced at Hoover, then back at Awol. "What else can you do? Can you shingle? Fix screens?"

THAT AFTERNOON AND FOR THE next two days Awol worked round the clock for Oscar Peloquin. He made the repairs to his room, reshingled a section of roof, rehung a door, and fixed three screens. He noted that Peloquin watched birds and had a couple of rickety bird feeders near his kitchen window. As a special thank you, late at night, he crafted a new feeder and hung it for Peloquin on his last day. Officer Hoover had torn up the arrest papers. The morning of the third day, Awol, packed and ready to hitch out of Stratton, walked to Peloquin's office to square up.

"You do nice work." Peloquin stuck out his hand for a shake. "You don't owe me for lodging these last two nights—it's on me. Charlie!"

Charlie, in his fireman's uniform, slid from the kitchen. He held up a bag of gorp and handed it to Awol.

"Charlie's my cousin—he's taking you to the trailhead."

Charlie put Awol's pack and poles into the bed of his pickup.

"Not much goes on in this town; what the hell happened?"

After Awol recounted his story about Moonwalker at the diner,

Charlie asked, "Did I hear you say he was going fishing?" He weaved his pickup around a logging truck and climbed the hill.

"So he said."

"Well, that has to be the direction they headed—Flagstaff Lake. People come from all over to fish Flagstaff. Hoover should have gone over and checked the lake for a black van."

Awol couldn't bring himself to tell the man he'd never passed on this information to Hoover. At the time, he'd had no reason to believe Moonwalker. But now, Awol remembered seeing fishing poles on top of the van. Moonwalker's driver no doubt came back to fish the lake after dropping him off in Canada. *He could have been questioned. Christ! Can't I do anything right?*

CHAPTER SIXTY-TWO

AWOL CLAMBERED DOWN THE SOUTH bank of Kennebec River, keeping a watchful eye. He had stepped by stinky moose scat all morning and upriver he spied two moose—a cow and her calf—foraging at a runoff. He was thirty-six trail miles north of Stratton and had to wait his turn to be canoed across the river. He had read that until several years ago, hikers took their chances and forded the river on their own—until a hiker drowned. The paper mill up north opened the dam for power generation at unpredictable times, and once the dam opened, the river surged rapidly and rose too high at the crossing. If a hiker was fording, it would be a race to get across in time. A person was now employed by the state to ferry hikers across, two at a time.

Although he was nearing Mount Katahdin, the end of his quest, Awol was distraught about the escape of Moonwalker, whom he figured was now in Canada. He tried to accept it and to focus on the main reason he came out here, but was mad at himself for what happened in Stratton. He climbed into the canoe with a hiker named Speedball who was the same size. They fit snugly. Awol crouched in the middle with his legs pulled up. If he swayed his body to either side, he felt the canoe shift.

"Do you ever have a problem ferrying big people?" Awol asked the girl who paddled the front while Speedball paddled the rear.

"Not often. Had a big guy a few days ago, but he was alone."

"Big as in tall? What'd he look like?"

"I didn't really take too much notice of him, other than he was big, and his fishing rods weren't tied on to his pack too well. I kept waiting for them to fall in."

"Do you recall what he was wearing?"

"Yeah, actually. He had on one of those Elmer Fudd hats, orange, with the ear flaps pulled down."

"Was he wearing a vest?"

"I don't remember."

They drew near the northern bank and she barked instructions to Speedball because she'd been distracted and was about to overshoot the landing spot. Awol waited until she secured the canoe and Speedball had climbed out.

"Miss," he handed her a five dollar tip, "tell me anything else you can about this guy? It may be important."

"He had a slight limp I think."

"Did he smoke?"

"Not near me. I didn't even want to take him because I was just off duty, but he popped out of nowhere and looked tired; I didn't have the heart to leave him."

"Did he have a bump on his head?"

"I don't think so, but his ear flaps were down, and he wore sunglasses."

<hr/>

AWOL HIKED INTO THE TOWN of Caratunk. He had thought Stratton was small; this place had only a post office. "Closed" the sign read, "Open Mon–Fri 9–12." No one was around, and Awol saw no sense in waiting, so he trudged north three miles, off-loaded his pack, and tented by Holly Brook. As part of his set up, he devised a tripwire around his tent composed of rope and brush. Before turning in, he zipped the tent flap and pulled out his Buck hunting knife. Under the headlamp, using a tiny emery stone, he brought the edge to a fiery keen. He used a section of his pack strapping as a strop and honed the edge and kept the knife within reach all night.

<hr/>

THE FIRST HINT OF MORNING light crept across Awol's tent. In fetal position, in his sleeping bag, he blinked. Ten minutes later he opened refreshed eyes. He turned onto his back. Awol was not sure what to make of the conversation with the ferry girl. He was sure some good-sized fishermen were out here, some of them might wear an orange hat, maybe one had a stiff knee. Yet—sunglasses. *But why would he back away from Canada? It doesn't make sense. Unless the girl described a different man, in which case Moonwalker has already escaped across the border.*

The ancient mossy rock facings were frosted and icy on this late September morning. Awol took extra care as he hiked up and over sections of rock with white trail blazes painted on them. He slipped, skidded, and skied in his boots. In the afternoon he hiked alongside crystal clear ponds, ponds so transparent that he watched small fish swimming above the stones that covered the bottom.

Late afternoon, after relieving himself, while cutting back to the trail, Awol was startled to see someone hunched by a blue Kelty backpack similar to Moonwalker's. Awol grabbed his knife and crouched, as the hiker turned to look. Awol saw the young man's face redden; he was holding a map and stood, all the while staring at Awol's knife, which had been hastily secured.

"Do you know how far it is to Holly Brook?"

TWO DAYS LATER AWOL ARRIVED in Monson, Maine, south of the famed "100-Mile Wilderness." Monson was the last town near the Appalachian Trail, as after surviving the trek through the 100-Mile Wilderness, you were nearing the base of Mount Katahdin, the holy grail for north bounders. Awol had hiked the thirty-four miles from Caratunk to here in two days and hoped he was closing in on Moonwalker.

He strode to the pay phone outside the Monson General Store to make another call to Rangely Police.

"Officer Hoover please . . . I see. Look, can I speak to the chief or anyone else in charge . . . It's about the DNA of the serial killer . . . It's Karl Bergman, I'm up here in Monson and I have reason to believe the killer is in the area . . . Well, when will we know there's a match? So when you know for sure, can you call the Monson police? There is no Monson Police? This area is handled out of Dover-Foxcroft . . . the county seat . . . shit!"

AN HOUR LATER, AWOL WAS talking with Officer Beauregard of the Dover-Foxcroft Police. Awol stood by the young officer's cruiser, which was parked at the Monson town offices. After Awol insisted, the Rangely Police had alerted Dover-Foxcroft, and they sent an officer.

"So, Mr. Bergman, you think you've seen the serial killer."

"Well, I sure as hell did in Stratton. And I'm quite certain he's on the trail in front of me."

"Quite certain?"

He began a recount of details to Officer Beauregard.

"Let's go inside, Mr. Bergman. We'll grab some coffee."

"Pierre," Beauregard said to a man inside, "I'm going to use Monique's office." Pierre peered up from the Monson fire chief's office and gave Beauregard a wave. Coke from the vending machine tempted Awol more than coffee. He took a wooden fold-up chair and faced Officer Beauregard who sat at a small desk. Awol sat to the back of the chair and rested his arms on top. A box of tissues beside a vase of zinnias looked peculiar in front of the hulking Beauregard. Awol heard a woman's voice through a side door, as Beauregard got up and told the woman, "Valerie, only if it's important," and shut the door.

"Okay, Mr. Bergman, tell me what you can."

For the next twenty minutes Awol presented as much detail as he could. "I'm telling myself he's got to be out here ahead of me, but I admit it doesn't make sense and he may well be in Trois-Rivieres right now, from out of Stratton."

Officer Beauregard reached for his coffee cup and stepped away to refill it. Awol noticed the well-shined shoes and the holstered-gun strapped to his trousers. When Beauregard stepped back to the desk, he picked up the phone and pushed at numbers.

"Keith, please. Officer Beauregard." While waiting he told Awol, "Keith Shaw's an institution up here; he hosts just about every hiker coming through. I don't think there's any hiker who wouldn't make some kind of contact over at his place."

"Keith, let me test your memory. I'm putting a man on my speaker phone who is going to describe a hiker who would have come through in the last two or three days. Need to know if you've seen him."

Awol listed the specifics.

"Doesn't sound familiar, but let me ask my cook and Henri." A minute later, "No, he didn't come in here."

Officer Beauregard next called the Monson General Store and conversed with Marcel, the owner.

"I haven't seen him," Marcel said, through the speaker phone.

Beauregard hung up and looked at Awol. "I want to help you, Mr. Bergman; I believe your story. But we don't have confirmed DNA. If we did, the state police, the sheriff's department, and the Maine Department of Inland Fisheries & Wildlife would also become involved. Without a smoking gun I can't waste anyone's time sending them into the 100-Mile Wilderness. And even then I'd be taking a big gamble, because he might not be in there."

Awol couldn't stomach the thought of four law enforcement departments tipping their hand to Moonwalker. *Why must it be this complicated? I'm on my own here.*

"What if he *is* in there?"

"Doesn't look like he's been around. I can't send men tramping through a hundred miles of roots and rocks. As you say, he may have already escaped over the border from Stratton."

"Can't you put pressure on Rangely to get the DNA results quicker?"

Beauregard pursed his lips, "Are you gonna hike in?"

"Absolutely."

"Tell you what I will do. Valerie?" Beauregard knocked on the wall and a gray haired woman opened the door, "Can we get Mr. Bergman a portable radio?"

"Sure."

"What I'm lending you is reliable in the Wilderness. You get in any type of trouble out there, or see any concrete proof, punch in and call me."

"Okay."

"When you get to Abol Bridge, after the Wilderness, you'll see the Ranger Station. Turn the radio in there."

AWOL OVERNIGHTED AT SHAW'S BOARDING House, joining a tradition with over a thousand hikers who had stayed there over the years. After the family-style evening meal, he chatted with several hikers and then made a trip to the Monson General Store. Something had been bothering him.

"Hi," Awol said to the man behind the counter. "We haven't met, but I'm the person Officer Beauregard had on his speaker phone."

"Oh, yes. You'd asked me if I had seen a hiker."

"Right."

"You know, I was thinking, ninety-nine percent of the time I'm right here. I live upstairs. Two days ago I had to have a wisdom tooth pulled and my daughter took over, but only for a couple of hours."

"This is why I came by, to see if there could have been any other person who might have seen him. Did you ask her?"

"Not yet. Let me call her down."

Awol looked around at food and supplies. As he fingered fishing line, a blonde girl swung around the corner aisle by the cooler. She looked seventeen or eighteen, stunning.

"Hi, I'm Renee. My father said you were looking for someone?"

"Hi, Renee. Thank you for coming down. The guy I'm looking for is big, strong-looking, at least 6'4"; he may have had a limp, and wore sunglasses—"

"Oh. There was a big guy with sun glasses and a hood who came in to buy food and cigarettes. And I remember a limp."

"Renee, do you remember what brand of cigarettes he bought?"

"A carton of Marlboros."

CHAPTER SIXTY-THREE

AWOL FINISHED WRITING THE LETTER to Linda that he'd been working on for weeks. He sealed the envelope and put two stamps on it. He addressed the front, stared at it for a moment, and touched her name to his lips.

He stared at his backpack. He had secured his food and replenished his water. Provisions were unattainable in the 100-Mile Wilderness, but Awol had to travel as light as possible if he was going to catch Moonwalker. He packed food for five days, instead of the ten days that were recommended. It would have to do—but he planned to make one more trip to the Monson General Store in the morning.

He shut out the lights and lay on his back on the cot. The boarding house was quiet. Rays from a street light peeked through a tear in the window shade and converged on the wall next to the cot. The branch of an elm swayed in front of the street light and made shadows on the wall. Awol replayed the day's events. After exiting the general store, he hadn't phoned the Dover-Foxcroft Police. After checking out how to use the portable radio, he didn't call Officer Beauregard. He thought back to the Gulf War—he thought about Harrison. *I ain't gonna fuck this up. I need to trust my instincts again.*

AWOL WAS THE FIRST HIKER to finish a breakfast of pancakes, scrambled eggs, and sausage the next morning. He drank extra orange juice and headed up to the store where he would be picked up by Keith's son for a ride to the trailhead. Awol deposited his letter to Linda into the mailbox and watched Marcel remove the "Closed" sign.

"You're an early one," Marcel said.

"That I am."

Awol grabbed a shopping basket and popped in a spool of twenty-five pound test fishing line. He bought two red flags, the kind truckers use to warn motorists of extended loads.

"Got any flares?" Awol asked.

"Should be one left."

"I see it. And I need more rope—here we go."

Marcel rang him up as Awol fingered the carabiners in the box on the counter. He picked one of them up and opened the spring clip and felt it snap shut. "Okay, two of these."

Outside, Awol packed in the new items. He had a few minutes before getting picked up and thought of making one last call to Officer Hoover in Rangely. He stood at the phone. *Nah—screw it.*

A short while later, under a windy overcast sky, Awol read from a posted sign:

CAUTION

It is over 100 miles to the nearest town. There are no places to obtain supplies or help for the next 100 miles. Do not attempt this section unless you have a minimum of 10 days supplies and are fully equipped. This is the longest wilderness section on the entire A.T. and its difficulty should not be underestimated. Good Hiking!

At about the same moment, Moonwalker crossed Long Pond Stream, a mile south of Long Pond Lean-to. His foot felt better, but remembering how easily he had twisted his ankle on a previous spill, he used the poles to stabilize himself as he hunched over, and took cautious old-lady steps. He tested each rock by poking it with his stick to see if it wobbled. He completed the crossing and after filling his water bottle, continued on and saw the sign for the lean-to, located two hundred feet to the west, but Moonwalker didn't need to scrounge. He was fifteen miles north of Monson into the Wilderness. He had supplies; he pressed on.

After eleven miles of moderate hiking, Moonwalker set up out of sight, near Chairback Gap Lean-to. Smoking into the night by his tent, he heard voices. The shouts and laughter grew louder, as if people were throwing a party, and he wondered if a bunch of hunters had taken over the shelter. Moonwalker mused about reaching Millinocket and calling Ray. He had seventy-five miles to go in the Wilderness and the extra-heavy pack of food and supplies—he estimated his pack weighed over sixty pounds—could tear up his foot. He'd been trying to compensate by putting more weight on the other leg, but now that leg was stiff, and it had cramped unmercifully the night before, waking him up in the tent at two in the morning. He pondered taking a recovery day to rest his legs, but then he would squander food and supplies needed to get out of this God-forsaken place. He had to keep a slower pace.

Later, in his tent, after remedicating the foot and taking more pain pills, Moonwalker reviewed his guidebook-map, looking to see if his cousin's friend could drive a few miles farther and meet him after The Wilderness. He learned that not only could this be done, it saved him another fifteen miles of hiking, eliminating the risk of hitching eighteen miles to Millinocket. Moonwalker was so elated with his discovery he snatched the cell phone hoping he might get a signal to call Ray. The area was flat; the night was clear. He crawled out of the tent and headed to a clearing. No signal, but he punched in Ray's number anyway. Nothing. He waited a minute, tried again, and gave up.

Moonwalker awoke with violent leg cramps at four in the morning. The cramp in his good leg was so bad he wanted to tear something apart. He straightened out the leg and massaged his calf; *Oh baby, easy baby.* He couldn't get back to sleep and at six boiled water for coffee and oatmeal. He had no need to check the shelter on the trail, but felt too tired to sneak out before the occupants woke. He heated up extra oatmeal and hot chocolate and smoked, waited, smoked. At 8:10 a.m., tired of sitting, he packed up. He entered the trail the same time as three men coming down from the shelter.

"Mornin'," the lead man said. The middle-aged men looked more like sportsmen than hikers.

"Howdy." Moonwalker noted their puzzled look. "Had to do my business back there."

"Could have used the privy," the second man said, pointing behind him, "right back here."

"Oh. I'll know better next time."

"Heading north?"

"Yes." Moonwalker glanced up the trail.

"You thru-hike all the way?"

"No. This is a section I haven't done yet." Noticing their half empty packs, Moonwalker asked, "Where you boys headed?"

"Monson. We've been exploring Gulf Hagas."

"Well, you all have a good one." Moonwalker turned north and took two steps.

"Hey, any chance you might do the Gulf Hagas Trail?" the lead man hollered. "I left my cell phone at the Hammond Pitch signpost on the Rim Trail." Moonwalker half turned, but didn't answer. "It was the one place I got a signal and I left it right at the sign post when I got up to leave. My address is inside the pouch; if you would mail it to me, I'd be much obliged."

"I'd be happy to if I go that way," Moonwalker said.

"I'd appreciate it. Too far back for us to go; we'd miss our pick up."

MOONWALKER APPROACHED THE WEST BANK of Pleasant River, about a mile before Gulf Hagas Trail according to his map, and saw he'd have to ford; there wasn't a bridge. At the bank he began to untie his boots; he needed to keep his footwear and socks dry for the miles ahead. But his feet were a mess and he had no idea what edges lay under the water. *Better ford in boots—fuck!* He felt his rage stir as he waddled the ninety yards across and felt the shoes take on water. At the other side he sat down and removed his boots and wrung out his socks. He was sore and wanted to sleep. He lingered as long as possible by the river, thinking he might nap and let his socks dry. But after a several long minutes, he tugged on the wet socks, knowing others would be coming to ford the river.

At one o'clock, he came to the sign indicating Gulf Hagas Trail, which broke to the left off the A.T. His ankle felt stronger, but he was fatigued. He rested for a snack, hoping sugar and carbs would revive him.

He stepped fifteen yards into Gulf Hagas and sat against a rock in front of a stream.

He remembered what the sportsman said about a cell phone forgotten on Gulf Hagas. He should try again to reach Cousin Ray and, moving to a clearing, his spirits rose when, this time, he got a signal. As he punched in the area code, he heard a beep and a voice from the phone; he held the cell to his ear and listened to a recording: "The cell phone is no longer active for this number." Moonwalker shut off the phone and a minute later tried calling Euclid Palin. Same recording. He peered at the phone and in a spasm of rage threw it into the trees. The phone arced into the afternoon, missing branches and after landing on a root, bounced back onto the Appalachian Trail.

Moonwalker had no intention of looking for another cell phone on a different trail. Nevertheless, he checked the map and noted if he crossed this stream and continued down this trail, Hammond Pitch, which the sportsman referred to, was less than a mile. *If I want Ray to pick me up right after the Wilderness, I no longer have a phone to tell him. I'd have to hike an extra fifteen miles. I need a phone.* Moonwalker gazed down the trail and stood up. He didn't even linger to finish his cigarette.

Twenty-five minutes later Moonwalker spotted the Hammond Pitch signpost and, sure enough, next to it, leaning on the post, was a cell phone in a leather pouch. He heard the rush of water from the gorge to his left, felt vibrations coming from bedrock under him, and saw the drop-off to an abyss. Moonwalker walked over near the edge and looked down. *Christ!* He pulled out the cell phone and turned it on. Weak signal, better wait. Moonwalker convinced himself that keeping to a short hiking day, giving extra rest to his ankle and legs, would do him good. He became further convinced when he noticed bosky patches thirty to forty yards behind the marker, which would isolate him. He bushwhacked through scrub, humming the Canadian national anthem.

CHAPTER SIXTY-FOUR

COBWEBS. GIANT WEBS STRETCHED COMPLETELY across the trail from bramble to bush, from bush to bramble. Every few yards Awol felt the pasty, dew-slicked webs plaster him about the face, arms, legs. He noticed them at the last second when their crosshairs lanced the available light. But that's the plan of the spider, Awol thought, to trap the unknowing by preparation and surprise. *That's how I'm gonna get you, Moon-mother-fucking-walker!*

On his first day into the 100 Mile Wilderness, Awol covered nineteen miles in ten hours. He had passed two thru-hikers and three section hikers. He described Moonwalker to them, but they hadn't seen him. At 6:30 p.m., he shook off his pack at Cloud Pond Shelter. He kept the sheath to his knife unclipped while he drew water from a runoff at the pond. He didn't want to sleep alone in a shelter and didn't unpack, choosing instead to eat out of sight of the shelter, but in a spot where he'd notice comings and goings.

After eating, Awol still hadn't seen anyone come by the trail or the shelter. Figuring the hikers he'd passed had settled in at the previous lean-to, he picked up his pack and, right before dark, tented in a hidden spot behind the shelter. Awol reasoned he had to be getting close—Moonwalker had a pronounced limp—but he'd seen no signs, no discarded butts, and nothing revealing him in any register. But Awol, too, had stopped posting in registers since his return to the A.T. in Massachusetts.

Inside the tent, Awol cut two six-foot lengths of rope. One he coiled and placed in a shell pocket. The other, he granny-knotted to a carabiner and coiled up into another pocket. The rest of the rope he looped around the old rope and tied the end to the bottom frame of his backpack. He crawled out of the tent and rechecked his trip wire of fishing line which encircled the tent from ten yards out. He crept back inside and zipped the flap. He slept with his knife unsheathed beside him.

AWOL WAS AWAKE AT 6:00 and on the A.T. not long after. He scanned the trail from side-to-side and turned around to look behind every few minutes. At around eleven, Awol stopped as three men came toward him. This was what he had been waiting for.

"'Morning, men." Awol held up a pole in greeting.

"'Mornin', yourself," the lanky man in the lead said.

"Maybe you can help me; I'm looking for someone. A guy about yay big. Tall."

Awol absorbed the news. Based on the time they said they'd met him, Moonwalker had to be just a few miles in front of him.

"Did he say where he was going?"

"Just said he was heading north, to do a section he hadn't done."

And according to them, Moonwalker was wearing a ski cap, sunglasses, no fishing pole, and no vest.

"Guys, can you tell me anything else?"

"You seem real concerned about this fella; is he wanted for armed robbery or something?" the lead man said.

"It's a bit of a story, but vital that I find him; I'd be grateful if you can tell me anything—where he might be headed."

"Last thing I told him was to mail me back my cell phone if he went on the Rim Trail in Gulf Hagas. Left the damn phone at the signpost for Hammond Pitch when we took a break. If you go to the pitch and find it, please mail it to the address inside the pouch."

Awol bid the men a hasty farewell and took off at a fast clip.

AT TWO O'CLOCK, AWOL NEARED the Gulf Hagas marker and spotted something black on the left side of the trail. He reached down and picked up a cell phone with a cracked screen. The phone puzzled him; the man mentioned a cell phone he left on the Rim Trail. *So what's this doing here?* Awol moved up and scanned the other side of Gulf Hagas brook as he turned on the phone. Despite the damage, the phone turned on and indicated a signal, but when he tried calling out, he got the cancelled service recording. He knelt down, trying to make himself invisible, and thought for a moment. He began to understand why the cell was discarded. It didn't make sense for the guy he'd just met to cancel his cell phone service this soon. He remembered the hiker in Vermont who had reported his cell phone stolen. *Could have been Moonwalker.*

Awol found faded footprints and as he followed them to the stream, he came across a cellophane wrapper holding a few crumbs. He sniffed the crumbs and smelled cheese. He fingered some bent weeds and noted a trail of ants carrying off more crumbs. Awol crossed the stream and on the other side followed fresh tracks. *Someone's been through here not long ago. But might be the hikers I just met.* He'd only gone a few steps further when he found a stubbed Marlboro in the middle of the trail. *Bingo.*

Awol crouched and slanted off the trail out of sight. He cocked his head one way, then another, as he absorbed every sound, but nothing resembled anything human. He took out his field glasses and scanned. Nothing. Awol checked the map. *Makes sense that Moonwalker wants a new cell phone if he discarded the other one. But did he already find the phone and come back out? Or is he in here now and coming back any second?* The tracks told the story; a set of larger boot prints that matched the ones near the cigarette butt headed west to the Rim Trail. Awol checked his watch. *The hikers said they'd seen him at about eight o'clock this morning, so he should be coming back out soon. But he can't be moving that fast—he's got a bad leg. Maybe he'll camp in here, because he's isolated.*

The trail guide showed Carl Newhall Shelter four miles north on the Appalachian Trail; Moonwalker might also camp up there. Awol opted to wait; if he didn't show by dark, he would hike in.

Hiding his pack behind a tree, Awol looked back to the other side of the brook and wished he could booby-trap Moonwalker as he emerged from the water, but Moonwalker might not be coming and another hiker could fall into the trap. *No, I'll have to spring on him from behind.* Awol selected the optimum spot for surprise—before a trail bend. He readied his knife and pulled out the two-way radio. A message waited for him: "Mr. Bergman, Officer Beauregard here, the DNA is a match. The man you met with in Stratton is the serial killer. Please identify your location."

Awol cradled the radio and hesitated before contacting Beauregard. He didn't want the police to foul things up. "Officer Beauregard . . . yes, it's Bergman. He's out here and was spotted this morning wearing a black ski cap and sunglasses."

Awol listened for a few minutes, and decided to keep the police at a distant enough proximity to ensure they wouldn't scare off Moonwalker, but have them close enough by if he needed them.

"I'm approaching the Carl Newhall Shelter . . . Okay. Good . . . Have the ATV get as close as it can to the trail north of the shelter, and hike south . . . right . . . okay, I'll keep the radio on . . . right."

Perfect. If the bastard by chance is back on the A.T., they'll get him. But, he's not on the Appalachian. He's in here, in Gulf Hagas. I can smell him. Screw Beauregard, I've got to go with what I know. Awol shut off the radio and pocketed it.

CHAPTER SIXTY-FIVE

MOONWALKER EMERGED FROM HIS TENT to a purpled sky as clouds covered a sinking sun. The temperature had dropped into the low fifties, he estimated, and his heart surged as he inhaled a breath of tangy, fall mountain air. *Canada weather!* He was hungry. After two servings of noodles, he took out the block of hard cheese. As he unrolled the tinfoil he remembered the smoking young blonde in Monson. *Could you wrap it in tinfoil, Hon?* Moonwalker imagined her struggling underneath him, and his crotch burned.

After eating, he drank a cup of cocoa and licked the cup and pot clean. He stretched and paced, spewing smoke at a bulging three-quarter moon. His ankle was coming back; he felt stronger. At seven o'clock, stars were already twinkling in the frosty night.

AWOL BROWNED AND GREASED HIS face with dirt and mud. He'd made the decision to go in after Moonwalker. No sense waiting and hoping he'd show. He had ample water as he had filled up at the stream. From his pack he pulled out the headlamp, all purpose plier tool, flags, flare, fishing line, old rope, and waterproof matches. He unlatched the day pack from the top of his main pack and put the items in along with a full water bottle, gloves, extra T-shirt, socks, fleece, gorp. He hesitated a moment, and transferred the first aid baggie, map, and two energy bars, one of which he pocketed, the other he opened and stuck in his mouth. Lastly he retrieved his sleeping bag sack and tied it to the bottom of the day pack.

He grabbed the hiking poles. While he sucked at the energy bar, he unsheathed his Buck knife, took out the fishing line, and drew up the poles. He adjusted both to the length of an M-16 rifle. He laid the poles side-by-side and coupled them together as one. He pushed the bottom hilt of the knife between the rubber cups of the poles and let the blade protrude beyond the pole tips. He wound fishing line around the poles' ends, which sandwiched the knife between them. The more Awol wound the more confident he became as he strengthened his weapon. He caught the glint from the honed edge and when satisfied the knife was secure, he lashed the sticks together throughout their length. Awol cut the line with his pocket knife and stood up. He jumped into the "ready" position—left arm extended with his double stick, left foot out in front, right arm tight by his ribs, body profiled to appear as an edge to his foe, tip of blade angled to the opponent's heart—and jabbed. Awol jabbed, parried, sidestepped; jabbed, parried, sidestepped; after each sidestep, he jumped back to the "ready" position.

Awol pulled the ski cap down to his ears, zipped his shell to the neck, and leaned into the Rim Trail like a hockey forward. While he was hiding he had read up on the location from the handbook: "Gulf Hagas is billed as the 'Grand Canyon of the East,' a five-hundred-foot-deep gorge like nothing else on the Trail, featuring five major waterfalls." The deepest part of the gorge was at Hammond Pitch, where he was headed. Outcrop dressed the trail as he crept along the southern edge. He heard the distant rush of water. At each bend, under darkening skies, he expected to meet Moonwalker.

Awol estimated he'd gone a quarter of a mile. He couldn't judge the distance because he'd forced himself to slow down. *Stealth.* But it was now so dark that if he wanted to keep going, he'd have to put on the headlamp. He clicked it on but angled the lamp toward the gorge where he knew no one would be. It provided just enough light for him to advance.

A half hour later, Awol made out a trail marker ten yards dead in front of him. He shut down the lamp. Awol adjusted to the moonlight, scanned, listened. He heard the rumble of water below him to his left. He felt vibrations beneath his feet and suspected one of the cataracts that squeezed water through "The Jaws," which he remembered from the map. He wasn't able to read the marker, but was certain he could smell a suggestion of food from behind it at two o'clock. And now he smelled smoke. Cigarette.

Awol backed up in a crouch without sound and turned the lamp on, pinpointing the light with his cupped hand, to recheck his map. He crawled back to the signpost, which read: Hammond Pitch, 300 ft. The arrow pointed south, straight to the gorge. Even at a crawl, the occasional twig snapped, and he couldn't see unless he used the lamp. Suddenly he heard a man talking and shut down the light for good. *Some hikers are camped? Maybe this isn't Moonwalker at all. Yet, the cigarette smoke; it all makes sense.* The voice stopped. Awol felt he had no choice but to wait for first light, and be certain who was up there. He crept back another forty yards and found a depression off-trail. Awol rechecked his pocket knife, positioned his lance, and backed in to his sleeping bag.

MOONWALKER WAS BUOYANT. HE HAD just finished talking with Ray and everything was set. Ray's friend Claude was going to meet him at Abol Bridge, after he emerged from The 100 Mile Wilderness. Moonwalker was to call him the morning of the day before he exited if he could get cell coverage. Worst case was he waited an extra day at the pickup spot. He was confident that this phone was safe for at least a week, more than enough time. He stuck the cell in his pocket, crawled into his tent, and into the bag. He was supine and bent his neck back to peek at the moon through the flap. He was relaxed enough to let his mind wander to women. *Tonight it will be Nightwind, the one who got away.*

AWOL HUDDLED UNDER THE MOON. His cap was pulled to his ears and the hood on his sleeping bag was tied at the tip of his nose. He napped and woke every twenty minutes. *Just like when I tried to sleep in the Gulf War; some things never change.* He was dreaming beneath the surface, and was drifting into nightmare. Awol stopped himself. Can't . . . not tonight.

AWOL JERKED UPRIGHT AND GRABBED his bayoneted stick as a monstrous crashing rumbled from left to right, twenty yards in front of him. He thought Moonwalker had found him as he heard a voice yell in the night. By the time he was out of his bag, he realized a moose had crossed between him and the other campsite. He could smell the animal and still heard him pound the earth. Awol listened to more rustling, and observed a shadow from light within a tent, not far away. Awol rubbed his hands for warmth and looked in his pocket for gloves. He noticed the light of his radio blinking which meant another message waited. He hesitated, crept back a way to crouch behind some scrub, and palmed the radio; maybe Beauregard had caught Moonwalker and he was stalking someone else. He turned the volume control down before turning the radio on and hunched his head down by his pocket, slowly increasing the volume, to hear the message: "Bergman! Beauregard here. You need to keep your radio on. No sign of him. We entered the trail three miles north of the shelter and hiked all the way down to it. We're here waiting for you. Where *are* you?" He crept back toward his spot until he realized he was looking at the silhouette of a large person not twenty yards in front of him. The silhouette was wielding a small ax. Moonwalker. Awol gingerly put the radio away. But in his distraction, he turned the radio around, and instead of turning the radio off, he'd turned the volume to the highest level.

Awol stayed frozen to his spot. After an eternity, Awol heard the man sniff and watched him turn, and head back up to the tent. Awol checked his watch: 5:30 a.m. *Getting light soon. I'm 100 percent certain it's Moonwalker, and he has a weapon.* Awol heard the snap of tent poles; the man was spooked.

Awol inched closer and using the general noise the man was making as a cover, got within twenty yards again. He could see some of the man's features now. *Moonwalker!* Awol waited for him to put on his pack. He watched him drop the ax through a loop on the side. At the moment when he looked down to belt up his pack, Awol, lying prone, lit a flare under cupped hands and threw it like a grenade—high and over—to land behind Moonwalker. As Awol prepared to rush, he watched Moonwalker, in an initial moment of bewilderment, look up at the arcing flare. But at this critical moment, the radio squawked into the morning air.

Moonwalker jumped, Awol aborted, and rolled to the left over jagged rocks. He shut off the hiss and static and squinted from a crouch in time to witness a running Moonwalker reach the Rim Trail and head deeper into the gulf.

Awol collected himself. He wasn't being attacked, but now Moonwalker knew he was hunted. He snatched the radio and stuffed it into his pack. *Shit!* He scrambled to Moonwalker's campsite and confiscated his poles. Moonwalker, in his panic, had also forgotten his water bottle. Awol put the bottle in his pack, collapsed Moonwalker's poles, and pushed them through the strap loops holding the sleeping bag. In the light of dawn, Awol crept back to scrub. He was bleeding from his fall behind the rocks. He drew out an adhesive bandage and covered a wrist puncture dangerously close to the vein. Awol got out the map, and in the emerging light, saw that Moonwalker had no escape in the direction he went. He had to come out of the gulf to get back on the A.T. If Awol set a trap west of here, Moonwalker couldn't escape at the shortcut to the other side of the rim loop. And without water, Moonwalker wouldn't risk hiking all the way to the head of the gulf and then backtracking the northern loop. *No, he'll come back to me and try to get his water.*

CHAPTER SIXTY-SIX

MOONWALKER THRASHED ABOUT FOR A place to hide and fell to his stomach behind a pile of rocks, out of breath. With shaking hands he tried to focus his field glasses in the morning light. *What the fuck was that? Police must have a walkie-talkie.* He couldn't see or hear anything, but still smelled the flare. His heart raced and sweat trickled down the bump on the side of his head. He looked to the right and crawled to a more secure hiding place. He peered through dawn with the glasses and didn't see anything suspicious. He heard nothing.

Moonwalker calmed himself as he came to understand that if the cops or feds were out here to get him, he would have been captured by now. Someone would have intercepted him when he ran, another would have been across the trail, there would have been back up. They knew who he was, and would not have done something half-assed. Only one person he could think of would play this game. The more Moonwalker waited and listened to the quiet, the more he became convinced Awol was behind this. He smiled knowing he could take Awol down. He looked beside him. In the rush, he'd left his hiking poles. Still perspiring, he quashed down a growing sense of dread and steeled himself. *Okay. Just take it easy. Thank God the leg is better.* He reached for his water bottle.

Moonwalker couldn't follow the path and remain hidden. He eased back out to the side of the Rim Trail with his ax in hand, and crept back toward Hammond Pitch. *If Awol had a gun, he would have used it.*

Moonwalker kept to the edge of the path and every so often swung the ax, as though to tell the world—don't fuck with me.

He'd been plodding without incident for over several minutes; he hadn't realized how far he'd run in his panic. He heard water churning from the gorge ahead and felt rumblings coming up from the ground into his feet. Moonwalker inched farther onto the trail as he neared the gorge, and wondered if what he was doing was a good idea. He stepped cautiously, but felt in command as long as he had his ax. He could also grab his knife in an instant. Without significant growth on the sides of the trail, he'd catch anyone who might leap out to ambush him.

Before a left turn on the trail and behind some rocks near the edge of the gorge on the right, Moonwalker spied two red flags, about three feet apart, stuck in the ground. He hadn't noticed them earlier when he ran off in the dark. Must be markers of some kind, he speculated. Probably warning of the drop-off into the gorge. He drew closer to the gorge and just as he recognized, behind the flags, his hiking poles and his water bottle, he heard a scraping noise behind him. Ax raised, he ran back from the gorge and tripped over fishing line. Moonwalker went down, hard.

CHAPTER SIXTY-SEVEN

AWOL LAY SQUINTING BETWEEN ROCKS, and watched Moonwalker advance. He'd spotted him on the edge of the trail. He had already planted the flags and laid down Moonwalker's poles and water, then had taken off his day pack and placed it out of sight behind him as he double tied the fishing line to a root about eight feet away. He'd had barely enough time to cover up the slack line with dirt and pebbles. Awol needed to spook Moonwalker at the exact moment.

Moonwalker broke away from the gorge and Awol, lying prone behind the rocks, yanked the line. As Moonwalker tripped, Awol rose with his bayonet in the ready position, and charged. Moonwalker sighted him just before he crashed to the ground. His head bounced off rock, but at the last instant he managed to swing out with his ax and bang the knife, deflecting Awol's lunge for the spleen. The bayonet pierced his buttock instead, and in a wail of rage Moonwalker reached behind and clamped his hand around the double poles. Awol yanked back, removing his lance, but Moonwalker held on and began to twist to his side. With his other hand Moonwalker swung the ax back over his head, grazing Awol's ear, the hammer end smashing down on Awol's wrist. Awol dropped his spear. Cradling his busted wrist, he jumped and measured his fall so that he landed flush on Moonwalker's head. He felt Moonwalker's nose crunch.

As Awol tried to reach the fallen ax, Moonwalker, from a prone position and with his pack still on, erupted and upended him. Moonwalker, his face bloodied and contorted, went for his knife with one hand and unsnapped his pack harness buckle with the other. Each was working on pure adrenaline now. Awol kicked the knife away just in time, then reared for a kick to the head as Moonwalker lunged from a crouch and pushed him down with one hand. Awol fell, but his last-second kick nailed Moonwalker's other hand as he snatched the ax, knocking it away. Moonwalker shook off his pack and threw it at Awol, knocking him down again.

Awol found himself underneath the powerful man and desperately tried to finger-stab his eye and bite his damaged nose, while Moonwalker angled for a death grip around the throat. As Awol stiff-armed Moonwalker's face, Moonwalker attempted to push his own face and neck downward so he could power through with maximum leverage and close Awol's windpipe. Moonwalker pushed harder trying to break through Awol's arms, but at the precise instant when Moonwalker started to break through, Awol intentionally slipped his hands away, and as Moonwalker's face came rushing down, Awol jammed the top of his own head right up into Moonwalker's nose. *Crack!* The death grip loosened. Awol grabbed a rock and smashed it into the bump on the side of Moonwalker's head. Moonwalker's hands fell away. Locking his foot over and under Moonwalker's bad leg, Awol smashed the bump again and managed to twist Moonwalker off of him before he realized what had happened. Like a piston Awol smashed the rock into Moonwalker's forehead, once, twice, until he was knocked out.

He wanted to pound him again, but stopped himself, arm in midair. The puffy eyes were closed on the battered face. Blood was everywhere. Moonwalker didn't move. Awol crawled back for the lance, and pulled the rope sections from his pockets. Not wasting any time and knowing this monster would rise again—he could hear air rasping through broken teeth—Awol heaved him over onto his belly and tied his hands behind him. Awol's busted wrist made it difficult and while tying Moonwalker's legs together, he had to stop for precious seconds and wait for the pain to subside. He finished tying the legs and reached the rope back up and over the tie at Moonwalker's hands. He pulled—stretching Moonwalker into a hog-tie—and tied the rope to the carabiner secured at Moonwalker's feet. He waited.

After only a few minutes, Moonwalker sputtered, and convulsed, coming to.

Awol picked up the ax and the other knife, and put them in his pack. He yanked out the portable radio.

"Bergman here—*Where the fuck are you?* . . . I have him," Awol panted, trying to catch his breath. "He's tied up, injured, here with—*I repeat my first question, where the fuck are you?* Go down to the main entrance to Gulf Hagas. I'm a mile in at the gorge—I know, I'll explain when I see you. It will take you about two hours if you're at the shelter. Yes . . . okay."

Awol, beginning to feel just how injured he was himself, shut down the radio and lurched back to Moonwalker.

"Water," Moonwalker rasped.

Awol dragged him a few feet and leaned him against rocks; he took his time getting water. He opened his own bottle and drank it in front of Moonwalker, studying his battered nemesis. Awol saw bruised eyes, one closed, the other looking back at him with calm fury. Moonwalker's face was covered in blood, his nose cut open and smashed against his face. He sucked air through cracked teeth. The pulsating, purple mass on the side of his head bled and expanded.

Finally, Awol leaned over with the water bottle. "I oughta pack kindling in your throat and light a fire. Open!" Awol dumped water into Moonwalker's mouth, and splashed his pulpy face. Moonwalker spit up blood and coughed. Awol let him take one more sip before capping the bottle.

Moonwalker grunted.

Five or ten minutes elapsed as they sat, facing each other in silence. Every so often Moonwalker spit up more blood, and coughed, wincing. He took a deep breath and focused his good eye on Awol.

"Got a favor to ask you, Awol."

Awol couldn't believe his ears. "You want a *favor*, from *me*?"

"Yes."

"And what would that be?"

"Finish me off."

Silence.

"Do it."

"No."

"Then let me do it."

"No."

Moonwalker rolled to his side, and by pushing his feet and flopping his chest, he started wiggling toward the pitch above the gorge.

"What in the fuck are you doing?" Awol watched the enormous effort it took Moonwalker to move several feet. He figured Moonwalker would quit or pass out again, but he kept going, and was on the path to Hammond Pitch. Awol got up and trudged over to stand in front of Moonwalker. He struggled to hoist him up with his good hand, and leaned him against rocks by the path. He wasn't sure he had the strength left to drag him back to where they'd been. He heard the gush of the water and noticed Moonwalker's goal: the sheer drop into the gulf not twenty yards ahead.

"Moonwalker, you can face your maker after you face a jury." Awol was bruised and ached all over. He needed to do something about his wrist and wobbled to his bag for tape. When he turned back around, Moonwalker had slithered farther down the path to the pitch.

"Hey!"

"Let me do it."

"Stop." Awol stood in front of him with the lance.

Moonwalker tried a different tactic. "So, Awol, what'd you think of Songbird. She was a cute one, wasn't she? You would've enjoyed a piece of that, am I right? She was scared, so fucking scared and helpless as I raped her, strangled her. I dumped her off the cliff, but only after I played with her for a while and beat her first. I enjoyed every sweet minute of it. She was so scared she—"

"You sick freak." Awol sat frozen, not sure what to do.

Moonwalker kept pushing. "Ever beat a woman, Awol? Ever watch the fear in their eyes? You got it in you, I know—"

"You sick fucking bastard." Awol raised the lance and held it over Moonwalker's head.

Moonwalker spit at him. "Do it!"

Awol, jolted back to his senses, lowered the lance. "Nah. Too easy on you."

"You got a woman, Awol?"

"What's it to you?"

Moonwalker smiled through busted teeth. "I'd love to beat the shit out of her and fuck her in front of you and then have you watch me—"

"Oh, so you want to keep playing games?" Awol looked toward the drop behind him.

"You don't have the guts to kill me." Moonwalker said.

"I do, but I'd rather make you suffer. Think you're hurting now?" Awol grabbed the remaining rope; it was the old rope he'd carried since Georgia, but it would do. "We've got over an hour to play, Moonwalker."

Awol took the rope and tied it around the rope that clamped Moonwalker's legs together. The other end he anchored around an outcrop of rock.

"Not sure if that will hold or not, Moonwalker. You'll have to crawl over head-first to test it."

"No guts, Awol. You're too scared to throw me—"

"No, Moonwalker. I want you to suffer." Awol smiled at him.

Moonwalker wasted no time and slithered and flopped in earnest. As he neared the edge, Awol understood Moonwalker didn't plan to crawl over, but intended to hurl himself, which might yank the rope out from the rock. So now when Moonwalker did dump himself over, Awol pulled on the rope. Awol gradually released tension and the rope held.

Awol crouched to the edge and looked over; Moonwalker dangled upside down along the face of the cliff fifteen feet below, but one of his arms had gotten free. It simply hung like the rest of his body.

"Now, here's what I want you to do, Moonwalker. You think of all those innocent women you killed. You feel that blood draining to your head? That'll help you think. And I won't have to hear any more of your crap."

Moonwalker said nothing, and Awol sat down away from the edge to rebandage his wrist. After a few moments he peeked over again. Moonwalker had drawn himself to the rocky face with his free arm, but that was all; he hung, unmoving, upside down.

"You've gotten quiet, Moonwalker. That must mean you're thinking. Good. You think about what a fucked up piece of shit you are. And don't worry; pretty soon the police and rangers will be here to haul your ass back up."

From where he sat, Awol could see two feet of rope that hung over the cliff. He watched the rope, just in case. Several minutes went by and

Awol noticed the rope quivering. He took up the lance and squinted over the edge. Moonwalker had managed with his free arm to grab the rope and raise himself up, and with the other hand loosened sufficiently, he was able to rub the slack portion of rope against a protruding rock. *Christ, how the hell does he have the strength?* With the hand jutted out from the tie, he kept rubbing the rope.

"You keep that up and I'll haul you back up myself."

"A man should have the right to end his own life. Cut the rope."

"You've lost your rights. Are you a coward, Moonwalker?"

"Aren't we all? But I'm a victim, too. I've only done what circumstance has made me. Like you, right? You a victim of circumstance too, Awol?"

Moonwalker was a contortionist hung upside down trying to get out of a straight-jacket. Awol watched him jounce and dangle but thought about his words.

Awol could see drops of blood fall from Moonwalker's face and head, from his wounds.

"For fuck's sake, Awol. Please. Cut the rope."

"A victim of what kind of circumstance?"

"I knew it. We're a lot alike, but still, different enough that you'd never understand. Women have fucked me over long before . . . come on, Awol. Fuck. We both know it's better to cut me loose. For everyone."

It looked to Awol as if Moonwalker was making progress, and now he could see the strands of rope that had been cut using the rock face. *Shit!*

Awol didn't know if he had the strength to haul him all the way back up, but he could certainly raise him away from that jagged rock. He dug into position behind the outcrop where the end of the rope was anchored, and using his feet against rocks and his one good hand, he pulled. He hoisted him two feet or more. Good; *he'll have to start rubbing all over again on a different section of rope,* he thought, *and I can play this game as long as he wants.*

Awol was about to secure a new tie when he felt a pull. The pull got stronger. *How in the fuck . . .* "It's no use, Moonwalker. Give it up."

"Cut the rope."

Awol dug in and pulled back. Like a tug of war, there was a brief time when neither side gained on the other. Awol worried that the rope was becoming too strained. *Okay, I caught the bastard, and I'm doing the best I can here, but if this rope snaps, that's the way it's meant to end. Sometimes it's up to circumstance.* Awol watched the portion of rope that hung over the cliff, but he still couldn't see Moonwalker. He saw the line quiver again and felt a strange vibration extend to his fingers; he felt the vibration again—just before the rope snapped. Awol was thrown back, and he stiffened as he listened to Moonwalker's magnificent roar. It seemed to last forever.

Awol sank on the cliff, right before the edge. He looked down into the gulf and let the water overwhelm and take over his senses. The gushing water into the Jaws still echoed Moonwalker's mighty yell, and as Awol buried his eyes into the whirlpool hundreds of feet below, he felt cleansed. That was where Beauregard and the others found Awol an hour later, still at the edge, staring down.

CHAPTER SIXTY-EIGHT

SEPTEMBER 29. BAXTER STATE PARK, Maine. Mount Katahdin.

Bundled against the cold and wind, on the summit of Maine's highest mountain, Karl Bergman sat alone. He'd been sitting for several minutes on a granite boulder, behind and thirty yards to the right of the summit marker sign. He didn't want to be disturbed; he didn't want to disturb the victory of other hikers who'd finished their quest. He pulled his hood further down over the ski cap and tightened the drawstring. He tucked gloved hands back under his shell. He was warm enough, but his healing wrist throbbed beneath the cold.

A kaleidoscope of thoughts and events from the last two weeks raced across his mind.

"*Bergman? He might be in shock. Bergman! It's me, Officer Beauregard.*"

"*Beauregard?*"

"*Where's the killer? Give him some water. Here. Drink. Why are you sitting in the rain?*"

"*Down there. He's down there. Got away from me and dropped into the gorge.*"

Beauregard and an EMT got him into dry clothes, gave him hot coffee from a thermos, and set his wrist. The next day, after a night in the shelter with the others, he was back in Monson, first in the regional hospital, then at Shaw's boarding house, where he recuperated for two days, wrist in a cast and a head full of pain meds. When Beauregard had unloaded Awol's pack and poles, back at the station, he took a closer look at the snapped rope, which he had also thrown into the cruiser. The frayed end of the rope was bloody. Beauregard picked off what looked like a piece of porcelain. As he did, something else from the rope-end dropped at his feet. Bergman reached down and picked it up. He stared at a bloodied incisor, that particular tooth of man adapted for cutting and gnawing.

"Linda?"

"Karl? Where are you? Are you okay?"

"Did you get my letter?"

"Yes. Did you mean what you said in the letter?"

"Absolutely."

"So was it . . . is this a proposal?"

"Yes—and it's about time. I'm sorry I've held back. I love you, Linda, and want to have a life together, as equals. Will you marry me, Linda?"

AWOL PANNED THE HORIZON FROM the summit. He removed a folded piece of stationery from his side pocket.

"You're crazy to go back out here. How you gonna hike with that?" Officer Beauregard pointed to the cast as they jounced in the ATV.

"I'll make it. Drop me off as close as you can to Newhall Shelter. When I finish Katahdin, I'm throwing the cast away."

Beauregard shook his head. Ten minutes later, when he could advance no farther he braked the ATV and shut off the engine. He handed Awol his main backpack, which had been retrieved earlier, and his poles.

"Off the record, what happened out there? At the end I mean."

Awol donned the pack. "Officer, it happened like I told you. He got away from me and fell into the gorge. I didn't have the strength, with just one hand, to pull him back over."

Beauregard looked long and hard into Awol's eyes, then extended his hand. "You take care."

ON THE SUMMIT OF MOUNT Katahdin, Awol unfolded the worn stationery and read a letter he'd written to Mrs. Virginia Harrison which had been returned, "Address unknown," over ten years ago. After finishing the letter, Awol reflected back on the night of the firefight and looked into his squad leader's eyes. For the first time in his memory, Awol didn't look away from Harrison's eyes. He watched them close, as he apologized and asked for forgiveness. Awol looked to the horizon. He turned with the wind and started tearing off tiny pieces of the letter. As he released them, one by one, they fluttered like snow, took off in the wind, and disappeared.

After releasing the final bits, he reached inside his vest and unzipped the pocket. He took out his bronze star medal, with combat V. He had carried it in his pack all the way from Georgia. He fingered the bronze star and held it up in front of him. *Harrison, I'm sorry,* he said again. *This is yours. Please forgive me.* He placed it between two rocks where it faced the afternoon sunlight.

For the first time in nearly twelve years, Awol felt peace flood his being. Moments later, Awol picked up his poles and began his descent toward home, toward life.

TWELVE YEARS AGO, I COMPLETED a thru-hike of the Appalachian Trail. It was a wonderful adventure. During the entire time I was out there, I did not encounter anyone who was a problem and I returned with a healthy new respect for our land and our people. For this reason I feel compelled to apologize to any hikers whom I may alarm or offend. Having said this, it is always wise to stay alert in the wild. Nothing in this world surprises me anymore. You just never know.

Marshall County Public Library
@ Hardin
Hardin, KY 42048

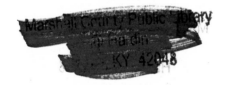

Marshall County Public Library
at Hardin
KY 42048

CPSIA information can be obtained at www.ICGtesting.com
Printed in the USA
BVOW08s1415220516

449090BV00005B/136/P